Kate suddenly realized that until Hank Mathison had set foot on her farm, she hadn't known she could feel like this. Alone. Lost. Alive. Blossoming.

She'd always known she was a woman, but until Hank Mathison she'd never known what it was like to *feel* like a woman. To want to *be* a woman, in every sense of the word.

Intensely.

To need to understand the physical subtleties of her body, to covet a knowledge she didn't possess.

Unconditionally.

To quite simply and emphatically crave Hank and everything he was, everything he would be.

Passionately, unequivocally, irrevocably.

To understand that for more than thirty-five years she'd been missing a piece of herself that she hadn't even realized existed, and that piece had a name—and its name was *Hank*....

Dear Reader,

I hope you've got a few days to yourself for this month's wonderful books. We start off with Terese Ramin's *An Unexpected Addition*. The "extra" in this Intimate Moments Extra title is the cast of characters—lots and *lots* of kids—and the heroine's point of view once she finds herself pregnant by the irresistible hero. The ending, as always, is a happy one—but the ride takes some unexpected twists and turns I think you'll enjoy.

Paula Detmer Riggs brings her MATERNITY ROW miniseries over from Desire in *Mommy By Surprise*. This reunion romance—featuring a pregnant heroine, of course—is going to warm your heart and leave you with a smile. Cathryn Clare is back with *A Marriage To Remember*. Hero and ex-cop Nick Ryder has amnesia and has forgotten everything—though how he could have forgotten his gorgeous wife is only part of the mystery he has to solve. In *Reckless*, Ruth Wind's THE LAST ROUNDUP trilogy continues. (Book one was a Special Edition.) Trust me, Colorado and the Forrest brothers will beckon you to return for book three. In *The Twelve-Month Marriage*, Kathryn Jensen puts her own emotional spin on that reader favorite, the marriage-of-convenience plot. And finally, welcome new author Bonnie Gardner with *Stranger in Her Bed*. Picture coming home to find out that everyone thinks you're dead—and a gorgeous *male* stranger is living in your house!

Enjoy them all, and don't forget to come back next month for more of the most exciting romantic reading around, right here in Silhouette Intimate Moments.

Yours,

Leslie Wainger

Leslie Wainger
Senior Editor and Editorial Coordinator

Please address questions and book requests to:
Silhouette Reader Service
U.S.: 3010 Walden Ave., P.O. Box 1325, Buffalo, NY 14269
Canadian: P.O. Box 609, Fort Erie, Ont. L2A 5X3

TERESE RAMIN

AN UNEXPECTED ADDITION

Silhouette®
INTIMATE™ MOMENTS®

Published by Silhouette Books
America's Publisher of Contemporary Romance

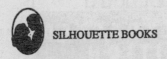 SILHOUETTE BOOKS

ISBN 0-373-07793-9

AN UNEXPECTED ADDITION

Copyright © 1997 by Terese daly Ramin

Books by Terese Ramin

Silhouette Intimate Moments

Water from the Moon #279
Winter Beach #477
A Certain Slant of Light #634
Five Kids, One Christmas #680
An Unexpected Addition #793

Silhouette Special Edition

Accompanying Alice #656

TERESE RAMIN

lives in Michigan with her husband, two children, two dogs, two cats and an assortment of strays. When not writing romance novels, she writes chancel dramas, sings alto in the church choir, plays the guitar, yells at her children to pick up their rooms (even though she keeps telling herself that she won't), and responds with silence when they ask her where they should put their rooms after they've picked them up.

A full-fledged believer in dreams, she says the only thing she's ever wanted to do is write. After years of dreaming without doing anything about it, she finally wrote her first romance novel, *Water from the Moon*, which won a Romance Writers of America Golden Heart Award in 1987 and was published by Silhouette in 1989. Her subsequent books have appeared on the Waldenbooks romance bestseller list. She is also the recipient of a 1991 *Romantic Times* Reviewer's Choice Award. She hasn't dreamed without acting for a long time.

For Sean, because he is.
And for Damaris, who said, "Write the book you want
to write." Thanks.
To Jeanne,
who took the pictures, made suggestions, worried and
always lets me take her for granted. Thanks for keeping
the Complaints Department open.

Acknowledgments

My thanks to Sheila Davis and Tom Pettipren, who
talked with me about their own and others' experiences
with foster children and foreign adoptions. You taught
me a great deal. Blessings on you and all of your
children. Thanks also to Kathleen Daly, med tech,
Denver V.A.M.C., for putting me in touch with live
llamas and their people, and with the V.A.M.C.
prosthetics service. Thanks and appreciation to
Bob Riley of Boulder Ridge Ranch, Boulder, Colorado,
for spending so much time answering my questions and
introducing me to his llamas, indulging my curiosity,
and for his patience and humor when I induced his
normally mellow friends to spit when they usually
don't—at people, that is—ever. Special thanks to
Dennis Luse, Certified Prosthetist, of the Denver
V.A.M.C. prosthetics lab, for his time and patience in
answering my questions about juvenile amputees,
prosthetic limbs and for showing me practical solutions
to impractical problems. I would also like to
acknowledge a research debt to the work
Motherless Daughters: The Legacy of Loss, by
Hope Edelman, Addison-Wesley Publishing, 1994.
Any mistakes, stretches of reality and leaps of faith
are entirely my own.

Prelude

Tuesday after Mother's Day

Evening sun slanted harsh and red through the low-slung windows, cutting a brilliant swath across the living room to catch in the miniature glass panes of the Victorian dollhouse that leaned half overturned against the couch toward the middle of the carpeted floor.

For an instant, when he saw the apparent chaos through the watery glass panels of the door in his vestibule, Hank Mathison's heart stopped. *Megan,* he thought. The voiceless mental whisper was filled with all the terror, panic and paranoia of a former undercover agent for the Drug Enforcement Administration who was also a parent and whose home didn't look the way he remembered leaving it this morning, *and* whose teenage daughter had failed to meet him when and where she was supposed to.

With an effort he forced himself to breathe slow and even, to remember that he hadn't worked deep cover in almost five years or done any undercover work at all in the past thirteen months. He was involved in nothing at the office that should cause his family to be the target of conspiracy. Panic, as he had firsthand reason to know, was a killer; composure was the only thing that would get you through a crisis. Especially if, as often happened, the crisis turned out to be imaginary.

On the other hand, no matter how foolish he might feel afterward, it never hurt to be careful. Especially where Megan was concerned.

Turning sideways to the door to make himself the narrowest target possible, Hank reached under his jacket for the weapon holstered at the small of his back, then stretched to turn the old glass doorknob. A gentle shove creaked the cantankerous portal open. He stepped into the house.

Silence lay about him, sharp and caustic, accusing. Dust motes, settled since the Molly Maids had been through the previous week, startled in the sudden soft swirl of air and fizzed against the sunlight. The stale scent of burned toast hung limp in the stillness, laced with the memory of this morning's loud generation-gap conflict and—

Muscles he'd long ago forgotten existed slumped gratefully. As quickly as panic had risen it stilled; the calm underside of his brain recognized "situation normal" as recall stirred. Megan, yesterday morning; him reminding her he'd leave work early to pick her up for their family counseling session after school; her cutting her last class and blowing him off, then not coming home until well after dinner last night.

She'd been much too giggly high to benefit from the where-the-hell-have-you-been, you-scared-me-to-death tongue hiding he'd needed to give her after an evening spent making frantic phone calls and calling in markers from his local law-enforcement buddies trying to find her. Worried as he'd been about her, and rebellious and hell-bent as she'd seemed the past couple of years, it was the first time he'd ever seen her come home high. And that had frightened him more than anything else she'd ever done.

Her behavior always peaked for the worst near and during the holidays. Mother's Day had never been meaner.

Disbelief, denial, anger—three of the five stages of grief. Even after five years, she had never bargained—with him or God— over her mother's life, and was nowhere near acceptance. Her anger seemed resolute. It was the world she lived in—at least at home with him—and dragged him into daily. As she reminded him often, *he* was the one with the sudden-death job, but Gen was the one who'd died suddenly. Damn him.

"Why couldn't it have been you?" She was passionate, filled with an anguish that refused to abate with time. *"Why wasn't it you?"*

He'd taken in her dilated pupils, the strained, pouchy softness beneath her eyes, the drugged lassitude of her movements and forced himself not to react to her bait, deliberately leaning over to smell her breath.

She'd shoved him away with a disgusted, "What do you think I am, Hank, stupid? I had to drive Zevo's car. I'm not drunk."

"You're high on something, Meg. What is it?"

"Oh, Daddy, you are such a narc." She'd rolled her eyes and given him "The Look," which proclaimed him stupid, naive and too damned old to get it. Her skin seemed unnaturally chalky against the artificial jet of her hair and the blackness of her clothes. The diamond stud piercing her left nostril flashed in the light when she moved her head. It was one of a pair Hank had given Gen on their tenth anniversary; he'd passed them on to Megan as Gen had intended to for her sixteenth birthday. He doubted that Gen had meant for Megan to wear one of them through her nose. "Lighten up and remember what it was like to be sixteen, would you?"

"Damn it, Megan, I remember perfectly well what it is to be your age, and this isn't it. Now what the hell are you on?"

She'd turned her back on him with a flutter of her fingers, pale against the dark leather of her fingerless gloves. The collection of earrings around the lobe of each ear bounced and clinked lightly against each other. "Don't get your boxers in a twist, Pop, it's nothing illegal." Then she'd added, airy, scornful, "It's not even prescription."

"Then what the hell is it and why are you high on it?"

"You call this high?" She'd laughed at him, shrill, delighted, and flounced off toward her bedroom, her calves a white flash between her short black socks and ankle boots and the hiked-to-the-knee wrinkles of her tight black spandex workout pants.

So far as he knew, she didn't work out.

"This isn't high, Dad, this is endorphins. This is just exercise trippin'."

He was shaking, angry, impotent, scared beyond belief for her.

She looked more fragile to him than usual, more...vulnerable. Her face looked pouchy and shadowed, almost mottled, beyond what she did to herself with cosmetics.

Too late to gain her trust, he wondered if she'd been crying. Her eyes were bright, shining with liquid and hidden pain, pupils swallowing irises, the whites around them lined with red. She was hiding stubborn secrets behind bravura, but he knew she was scared. He wanted to grab her and rattle her senseless and force her to trust him, to tell him what had happened, what was wrong—besides the obvious.

But he wouldn't touch her while either his anger or his fear could hurt her.

Disbelief, denial, anger.

"Tell me, damn it, in case I have to take you to the hospital in the middle of the night to get your stomach pumped."

Another mocking giggle, filled with the knowledge that there was nothing he could do—short of physical violence—to force her confidence. And the sword she wielded was the recognition that he loved her too much to come near her in anger.

"Megan—" he'd begun, softer and steadier this time, his ire, if not worry, controlled.

"Sorry, Dad." She'd yawned big and stretched. "Can't talk, gotta catch some *Z's*. School tomorrow."

Then she'd left him standing helpless and distraught, staring after her when she sashayed carelessly down the hall to her bedroom and shut him out of her life. Her Nirvana CDs played quietly deep into the night.

He'd gone to his own room and tried to sleep, but climbing the Matterhorn on his hands would have been easier. Hell was knowing that in her eyes his most grievous offense was that he wasn't Gen.

You're the one who should have died, damn you, not Mom.

Their conflict was old, charged with the moldering pain of them both still needing the woman who'd loved them and run interference between them; the wife and mother who'd died without warning and left them alone—strangers within their own skins— to cope with each other five years earlier.

Disbelief, denial, anger...bargaining...acceptance. God, he wished Megan could. That she *would*.

Instead, Megan told him constantly, one way or another, that the choices she made had to be her own for better or worse and he had no right to raise hell because of them. Of course, he knew all he really wanted was to prevent her making mistakes that would cost her more than her inexperience would allow her to imagine.

This morning he'd tried to talk with her—not *at* her, as she'd accused him; as he'd once accused his own parents—but sleeplessness and disquiet had taken their toll on calmness. Instead he wound up doing exactly what his parents had done: preaching and lecturing, while she grew more and more sullen and withdrawn.

He'd told her to be home tonight, that she was grounded for a week. She responded better to requests than commands; he tried to remember that, but didn't always—especially when she seemed to deliberately try to force his patience beyond bearing.

She'd told him to take his grounding and go to hell; he might be her keeper, but he couldn't force her to stay in his jail.

They'd had a rip-roaring argument about the previous night, other nights, other days that ended with Megan storming down to her room, grabbing up the dollhouse he'd made her for Christmas when she was five and storming back to dump it at his feet—a symbol, she'd said, of her returning all the love he'd attempted to buy and coerce out of her over the years instead of simply being there for her, the same as he'd never been there for Mom. She'd accused him, as she had often through the intervening years, of being the reason Gen was gone. She'd denied his right to censure her conduct, impugned his parental responsibility to monitor and teach—or attempt to—however badly he might do it, and rejected his right to be concerned for her.

Then she ran from him again, darting out the door to the car of a waiting friend in her omnipresent black uniform: Oversize T-shirt and too tight pants, black socks and scuffed half boots. Her punk-spiked, ebony-dyed hair and eyebrows, eyelashes, eyes and lips lined with obsidian kohl...only the almost vampire whiteness of her skin contrasted the unrelieved stygian mourning of her look. He hurt for her and for himself, but for all his years and experience with the world it seemed there was nothing he could do to relieve either of them.

How much do you love her? How badly do you want her back? Do you love her enough to...?

The questions wafted, too often asked, too often unanswered. Unanswerable.

To what? he wondered, not for the first time. To give her up, let her go, give in, get tough, request an intervention, walk away? To put a constant monitor on her behavior by quitting his job completely, living in her pocket twenty-four hours a day, seven days a week?

The last thought was neither realistic nor practical. He had to earn a living for them somehow, keep up with the mortgage, insurance and groceries, see to the needs of the living; she had to have some independence. Regardless of how irresponsibly she spent it, achieving some autonomy from her father was integral to Megan's growth, her future well-being and self-respect. Mistakes were part of the process. He just hoped neither she nor anyone else got hurt or worse while she went about sorting herself out.

Not to mention that short of nailing her into a barrel and feeding her through the bunghole until she was thirty, there wasn't a chance in hell he could make her do anything she didn't choose to do.

She was old enough to defy him, to demand his respect for her *right* to do what she chose with her own body. But she wasn't emotionally mature enough to understand that respect was a two-way street, that it must be given to be received. That she had to respect herself before she'd ever be able to comprehend respect accorded her by anyone else.

Especially her father.

Sighing, he clicked on the safety of his .38 and snapped it back into its holster, then righted the dollhouse. Spindled on a roof spire, a sheet of paper fluttered and crackled, catching his eye. He should be grateful, he supposed, that she'd at least left him a note this time.

He turned the bit of paper right side up, though he could read the cryptic message upside down. *At Li's.* Damn, he should have figured. She always ran to the Andens' house after they'd fought, took refuge with Li and her mother and siblings whenever she was frightened or unsure. Had ever since Gen died.

She wanted to move out there, live with Li and her family, leave him behind.

She'd first started asking if she could within a month of Gen's death. He'd tried to gently point out that they had a house, had a place to live together. She'd screamed at him that she didn't want to live with him; she wanted to live with Li and Tai and David and Bele and Kate-who-loved-and-understood-her and who had room for lots of kids and liked lots of kids and was always fostering some, and *not* with him, because he was never home anyway and she didn't know him because he was always working and never home the way Mom had always been home and she didn't want to live with a stranger.

Disbelief, denial, anger.

At the time he'd put it down to her being distraught over losing not only Gen but her unborn sister. Even five years ago, at eleven, Megan had understood enough of what the doctors at the hospital said to realize that if Gen hadn't been pregnant, she probably wouldn't have died when she did. Instinct let her blame Hank for killing her mother, let her run from him, refusing to hear anything further; it was safer than learning only Gen's own selfishness had caused the aneurysm that killed her. And Hank found he couldn't burden Megan with the truth so soon after. Later he hadn't had the heart to tell her that if Gen hadn't wanted another child so badly, if she hadn't been so opposed to adoption, if she hadn't lied to him about her doctor's warnings not to become pregnant, if she'd told him how likely it was she wouldn't survive to term, then he never would have...

Never would have slept with her again if he'd known, if she'd told him, if that was what it took.

But she hadn't and he had and that was what the present boiled down to: *if.*

If.

Disbelief, denial, anger.

Now he had a sixteen-year-old daughter in constant and escalating trouble, a child-woman who hated him on her best days and whom he couldn't reach even on his best; a career he'd gradually whittled back to nothing in order to be home with—and for—Megan as much as possible; and the desperate sense that he'd not only run out of ideas but options; that the next step he and Megan would take, no matter how badly he—and, who knew, maybe even she—wanted to avert it, would be juvenile detention, jail, drug rehab or worse.

And God help him, blind and naive as it might make him seem, he wanted to believe they needn't go that far, that she would come out of this...phase the better for having been through it. Trust that under all Megan's teenage angst, defiance and hell was a terrific, responsible kid he was too close to see.

His colleagues, most of whom had seen similar stories played out over and over again, called him an idiot; the psychiatric counselor who worked with him and Megan—or just him when Megan didn't show up for sessions—fed him the say-nothing pap that all parents wanted to believe the best of their children.

He'd laughed in the counselor's face, suggested their time was short and within it she'd better tell him something he freaking well didn't know. Only he hadn't been quite so polite.

He gave her credit for keeping her cool, for simply stiffening and asking him if he'd ever been a hostage negotiator.

"I know the drill," he'd said. *"Feed 'em lip service, but create trust. Stall for time, but don't lie. Request a show of faith, gain ground, find out what they want and use it to take 'em."*

She'd nodded. *"Exactly,"* she said, and waited for him to put it together with Megan, with discussions in past sessions, with the dawning knowledge of what he'd refused for far too long to see: he was his daughter's hostage, as she was his. Negotiating the path to their future as a family was the only hope they had.

Bargaining.

As the therapist suggested, in his fear of losing her—Judas H. Priest, what a laugh, huh? In his fear of losing her he'd lost her long ago—he'd flat out avoided giving Megan what she'd spent the past five years asking for: sanctuary with Li's family. It seemed wrong to him to involve anyone else in his travails, but God help him, he was at the point with Megan where if it would help get her back, he'd get down on his knees and beg the universe.

Acceptance.

She was his daughter. From the moment she'd been conceived, she'd owned his heart. But maybe she didn't know that anymore, couldn't know it. Maybe he'd forgotten how to tell her.

And maybe if he learned to stop isolating himself from her, to accept the terrible thing that had happened to them, she could, too.

In defeat he reached for the phone and tapped out the number for the most irritating and opinionated goody-two-shoes he'd ever met in his life: Li's mother, Kate Anden.

Acceptance.

Chapter 1

First of June

A pushmi-pullyu shoved at the screen window beside his bed, with both noses trying to get a better look at him.

Groggy and disoriented, Hank shook his head and blinked at the beast, wondering what a fictional creature from the pages of one of Megan's old Dr. Dolittle books was doing in his dream.

Nothing constructive apparently.

Shaped like a llama, but with a head at both ends—myth was a creative business, after all—Hank watched one delicate black nose find a weak spot at the side of the screen, then push hard enough for the lightweight mesh to tear. Immediately the nose on the head at the other end of the body enlarged the opening and shoved inside; the first head hummed inquisitively at the second head, which hummed conversationally back. As though reassured, the black head joined its red counterpart underneath the mesh. Two pairs of intelligent long-lashed liquid brown eyes studied him curiously; two sets of long banana-shaped ears twitched. Then the split reddish-brown lip below the blackish-roan-colored nose *lupped* up the cotton sheet covering his legs, pulling it off him.

"Hey," Hank muttered and yanked the sheet back over himself. Dream or not, no mythical creature—especially not one out of a child's book—was going to see him nude. He turned over and covered his head with his pillow, hoping that ignoring it would make the dream go away.

It didn't.

Instead the pushmi-pullyu's nearer nose flipped the pillow off his head and whuffled warmly in his ear.

"Hey!"

Startled, Hank jerked and rolled instinctively away, banging his hip hard on the bed frame before he hit the floor. So much for the hope that he was dreaming.

"Maizie, Clarence, get out of there," a sharp, youthful male voice called from somewhere just beyond Hank's window. "You're not supposed to be out here."

Guiltily, the pushmi-pullyu withdrew from the window, then apparently folded itself neatly in half and departed swiftly, both heads facing in the same direction. Which meant either he'd seriously gone round the bend imagining the two heads belonged to one animal, or there was one seriously double-jointed two-headed beast running around out there. In a moment the curious beast faces were replaced by the face and body of a slight-built Asian-American youth in his early twenties.

"Sorry for the intrusion, Mr. Mathison," this new apparition said, "but the *crias* didn't get to meet you last night when you and Megan moved in. They think they're supposed to meet everybody, so they decided to introduce themselves." Fine-boned hands reached through the torn screen to pull the levers that released the screen's frame from the window. "I'll fix this and have it back in a jiff."

Without another word he disappeared, leaving Hank almost more perplexed and unenlightened than he'd felt when the pushmi-pullyu heads first appeared in his window. Before he could gather himself back together sufficiently to either sort out his confusion over where he was or get off the floor, the youth who'd taken his screen reappeared as suddenly as he'd gone.

"I'm sorry. We didn't have a chance to meet yesterday, either, so you don't know who I am, do you?" He extended a friendly hand through the screenless window. "I'm Tai, Li's oldest brother."

Hank stared blankly at Tai's hand, desperately attempting to orient himself. He always knew where he was, *always*. He never got taken by surprise, never forgot himself, ever. It was too dangerous, one of an undercover agent's worst nightmares. But damned if he could figure out where he was or what was going on here. Tai? Li? Pushmi-pullyus and *crias*? Wasn't *cria* what llama babies were called?

He was pretty certain he hadn't been to Peru, Bolivia or anywhere else in South America where they used llamas for at least two years now. In which case, where the *hell* was he and how the devil had he gotten here?

As though reading Hank's mind, Tai turned his hand sideways and used it for punctuation when he prompted patiently, "Stone House Christmas Tree Farm, Stone House Originals? The Andens? Your daughter's my sister's best friend since kindergarten? You talked to my mother about some problems you were having with Megan, then rented our guesthouse and moved in last night—"

Light dawned—no mean feat in a cabin thickly surrounded by oaks, maples and towering pines.

"I remember." Wincing at the twinge in his bruised hip, Hank pushed himself back up onto the narrow bunk and extended his hand toward the window. "Tai, yeah. Hi. Heard a lot about you from Megan and Li. Nice to finally put a face on you. Excuse the, uh..." He gestured at the sheet. "I usually wear pants to meet Meg's friends."

Tai grinned. "No prob. We're not much for ceremony around here."

Hank grimaced. "I noticed. Meg didn't tell me you keep llamas."

"Llamas, alpacas, a couple of vicuñas we managed to find and import..." Tai shrugged. "They make a great security patrol, but mostly we raise them for the fiber, er, the wool. As to who keeps whom...that's a toss-up."

"Hmm," Hank commented, noncommittal, aware that some observation seemed necessary, but unsure what might be appropriate. "That's...interesting."

"No, it's not." Tai's frank grin widened, his dark eyes amused and wise to Hank's ploy. Almost automatically Hank filed away the knowledge that to underestimate this man on the basis of his youth and appearance of innocence would be a mistake he'd be well advised not to make—if he valued what remained of his ego, that is. "It's a fact you'd rather learn later when you're more awake, if at all."

"Mmm," Hank agreed before he caught himself, then shrugged, sheepish, and shoved unruly hair off his forehead. "You always do this to people you don't know?" he asked.

Tai nodded. "Pretty much. Ma says it saves time and establishes the ground rules without a lot of fuss."

Ma, Hank reflected darkly. The unsettling, wild-strawberry-haired, stubborn, tact-is-a-four-letter-word-so-I-leave-it-home Kate. He should have guessed. "Does *Ma* have a lot of ground rules?"

"One or two." Tai straightened away from the windowsill and collected the screen again. "Well, better get to work." He started to leave, then turned back, snapping his fingers. "Oh, yeah, I almost forgot. Ma said to tell you Megan snuck up to the house and spent the night in Li's room, and since you probably haven't had time to stock your pantry, if you want breakfast it's almost on the table, so you better come on up before everybody with hollow legs gets there and grabs the choice bits first—I'm quoting."

Hank yawned, at once covering unreasonable annoyance and sleepiness with the back of his hand. Of course Kate Anden had ground rules all the kids around here—including Megan, blast it—followed and repeated. He only need remember the list she'd handed him when he'd asked to rent this place: nice, neat and straightforward, positive, clear and concise, every "don't" preceded by a "please" and followed by a "thank you," and every "do" preceded by a warm "be our guest and..." Damned ornery woman would probably hand a list of ground rules to the Almighty on judgment day and expect them to be followed.

Damn it, what made Kate always appear to be so much more competent a single parent than he was?

She chose to be a single parent from the get-go, fool, that's what.

And Megan wanting to be here with Li, her siblings and Kate—Megan willing to follow Kate's rules *enthusiastically,* damn it!—

was the reason he'd shut up their house, *Gen's* house, and moved out here for the summer after all. It wouldn't accomplish anything if he didn't start out by making the best he could of a situation he didn't want to be in.

He knew it was fear that lay behind this unfamiliar sense of pettiness, fear of a future devoid of Megan. His daughter was old enough to make choices, and by her actions she found Kate the perfect antidote to life with him. But he couldn't lose her. Megan was his life, his last connection to the wife he'd loved to distraction but had never understood.

Quashing dissonance with effort, he nodded at Tai. "Yeah, okay, appreciate it. Let me get dressed and I'll be along. Thanks."

Maybe later he would mean it.

Kate Anden stuck out her lower lip and puffed air at her perspiring forehead. Glued into the sweat, strands of loose hair fluttered about her eyes, refusing to give ground.

Irritably she let go of her spade and swiped the back of her forearm across her face. Blasted stuff, always in the way. Where she'd ever gotten the idea it might be *fun* to grow her hair out she'd never know. An un-nunly vanity, no doubt, after years of wearing it tight cropped around her ears for the sake of practicality and health during the time she'd spent working in refugee camps in South America, Vietnam, Cambodia and Nigeria. But enough was enough already. She really was going to cut the blasted stuff this time, the very *instant* she had more than five minutes in a row and a pair of scissors.

Finding more than five minutes in a row and a pair of scissors in the same place at the same time was something of a family joke, however. Between Christmas-tree farming and llama ranching, custom handcrafting and parenting, 4-H sponsoring and a little of thising, a little of thating, the requisite items never did seem to quite get the hang of meeting.

'Course, it probably would help if she'd at least braided it this morning, like she usually did, instead of leaving it loose. What had possessed her to commit the rash act, she hadn't a clue—or rather, she *told* herself she didn't.

Believing herself was another matter entirely.

She'd *told* herself it was a cool morning and let it hang around her shoulders and back to her waist—she'd grown it out for a lot of years now—for the warmth it provided. But she didn't believe that, either. It was that *man* she'd rented the guesthouse to, Hank Mathison, who had her behaving like an irrational middle schooler or some female peacock spreading her feathers to show off for whichever male peacock happened to be in the area.

The fact that it was generally the male who preened for the female didn't help in the slightest. Heaven help her, she'd never behaved like this in her *life*. What the dickens was wrong with her now? Especially since she was pretty certain she and Hank Mathison didn't even *like* each other. At all.

Sighing, she spread gloved hands over the backs of her hips and stretched her back. In front of her lay an acre of freshly mulched and cultivated Douglas fir transplants; to her left and right, the fifteen acres of five- to ten-year-old spruce, firs, cedars and pines Tai and the boys would mow and cultivate over the next week for spraying in the following week; behind lay the house, llama sheds, toolsheds, workshop and recently-planted kitchen garden where she could see her two youngest sons playing with the hose. Mike and Bele, her eight-year-olds. From separate gene pools and different parts of the world entirely, but two of a kind nevertheless. She grinned and stretched forward, unkinking muscles from another direction.

A hawk screamed overhead, circling the empty field across from the house in search of prey. Around him the sky was clear and blue, sans even a wisp of cloud fluff. It had been on such a day nearly a decade and a half ago that she'd left the convent for the last time to take up life in an unsettling, unsheltering world. The clarity of a blue sky on a beautiful morning had not prevented it from being a scary day, however. Not because she'd been forced to desert the life she thought she'd been called to, but because she'd chosen to leave it, known in her heart she had to. Realized—with some regret—that her true place in life was outside the contentment and cloister a religious order had to offer.

But where she'd been headed, she hadn't a clue.

And now there was here, right now, this morning: three kids successfully adopted; one adoption in the works, nearing completion; two Ukrainian foster sons here indefinitely; one Finnish exchange student who would leave at the end of the summer; a dozen 4-H members here to work with the llamas and the trees;

and one bent-on-self-destruction teenage girl who happened to be her only daughter's best friend. And the teenager's widower father: a too-pretty-to-have-a-brain, arrogant, brutish—according to Megan—know-it-all, pain-in-the-butt sonofagun who'd been too busy risking his life cowboying after bad guys to be around his daughter much when she was still young enough to learn to trust him. A cretin with the sensitivity of a gnat when it came to women—and particularly adolescent women who were really still little girls in "hot babe" bodies; who was unable to appreciate good sense when Kate was willing to give it to him. And willing to give it to him *free* at that.

She glanced toward the narrow, dark tree-cluttered drive that veered off behind the equipment sheds en route to the guesthouse and grinned suddenly, laughing at herself. Well, maybe Hank Mathison was right after all when he called her a self-righteous goody-two-shoes. She wasn't certain how goody-two-shoes she was, but he *did* have a point when it came to her bouts of self-righteousness. It had never been any secret that she and the absolute conviction that she knew what was best for everybody—especially everybody *else*—were on excellent terms.

No wonder she'd done so badly in the convent.

But she still didn't have a great deal of use for Hank Mathison. No matter how belatedly concerned with his daughter's welfare he was.

No matter how unglued merely shaking hands with him over the rental contract had made her feel.

No matter how often she'd had to shove him out of her sleeping dreams since.

She'd never in her life met a man who'd ever made her feel unglued or even a tiny bit flustered, who'd ever had anything remotely to do with her dreams. She didn't think she'd ever in her life since she was a moony sixteen even experienced *that* kind of dream. And she could do very well without them now, thank you just the same.

Still, he had the softest, coolest, firmest right hand of any man she'd ever met.

A pair of young llamas bolted through Kate's patch of new transplants, interrupting her reverie, their soft-padded, two-toed feet neatly missing the unfledged trees. A pair of recently turned teenage boys followed close on their heels.

"Ma, hey, Mom!"

"Kate, Kate!"

Not nearly so graceful or surefooted as young llamas—size twelve feet on a fast growing thirteen-year-old body made grace a thing of the future, if it arrived at all—Ilya, the younger of Kate's foster sons, came to a halt in front of her. He wobbled precariously between transplants for a moment before unintentionally planting one oversize, unmanageable foot squarely on the fragile fir at her feet. She heaved an exaggerated sigh and made a face at him.

"Thanks," she said dryly. "That should firm the soil nicely. Where's the fire?"

"Excuse." Carefully he removed his foot, bent and straightened the squashed bit of green. It listed hard to port. He eyed Kate, guilty and hopeful at once, falling back on accented English and foreign ingenuousness in self-defense. The fact he hadn't possessed much of either since the start of his second school year here the previous fall didn't faze him in the slightest. "It will grow?" A question and a statement.

Kate leaned over to right the mashed seedling for him. "Is it broken?"

Ilya inspected the fir's twiggy shaft. "No?" Doubtful.

Kate swallowed a grin. Amazing how convenient his lapses of English were. "Yes, you mean?"

"Oh."

Crestfallen, the youth dragged a line in the dirt with the toe of his shoe. Beside him his best friend, Jamal, regarded Kate with a combination of fear and defiance—almost as though he expected her to strike Ilya for accidentally mushing a transplant.

That was ridiculous, of course. The baby trees were quite literally about a dime a dozen; she and Tai always overplanted, knowing they were bound to lose a few seedlings to any number of things: llamas, deer, rabbits, insects, kids' feet...

With an inward sigh Kate plucked the ruined tree from the earth and set it aside, then pulled a replacement from the bunch left to plant. This wasn't the first time she'd wondered about Jamal's home life. Unfortunately without either an invitation to butt in or Jamal trusting her enough to confide in her—*if* indeed there was anything to confide—her overly righteous nature and bad experience had taught her there were a few lines better left uncrossed.

Even though she would willingly, and had for other kids in the past. Wanna see the scars?

With a silent snort of *yeah, right,* she got to her feet, handed the new transplant to Ilya, collected her spade and made a slit in the dirt. "So," she said, "what are you two flying blind about?"

"Huh?" Caught off guard by the lack of dire consequences, Jamal watched her, puzzled, skittishly poised for flight. Waiting for retribution to sneak up and cuff him none too gently on the back of the head, Kate guessed.

Thoroughly unconcerned by contrast, Ilya knelt and fiddled the tree roots into the dirt gash. "We came to tell you the *crias* are loose." All but a trace of accent had disappeared.

"I noticed." Kate stamped the earth around the roots, stepped the square blade of the spade in a few inches away, then leaned it forward to pack the dirt tighter around the base of the tree. A few feet the other side of the transplant line Maizie and Clarence regarded her with interest, undoubtedly storing information for future use. The saw among llama owners and breeders was: "Llamas are the second most intelligent creature after dolphins, which probably makes them smarter than people. They will change your life." Absolutely true, all of it. Especially that last.

She made a face at them, then looked at Ilya. "Anything else?"

Ilya grinned. "Tai said to tell you they tore the screen out of Mr. Mathison's bedroom window and woke him up. He wasn't very happy about it and he didn't know we kept llamas. Tai thinks you'll hear about it at breakfast."

Another face, this one an exact replica of Ilya's older brother's *oh man, do I hafta?* She sighed, this time aloud. "Put Maizie and Clarence back with their mothers and get in to breakfast. I'll deal with Mr. Mathison."

Now if only she could figure out why she anticipated that prospect with such relish...

There was something decidedly...bewitching about the place.

He could feel it even through the fog in which he'd woken, could understand a little of what drew Megan here time and again, to hide in the shadows of Kate Anden's always green trees. Pagan beliefs, he'd told Megan a long time ago, explaining the origin of the Christmas tree to her, held that trees that stayed green all winter had magical powers. Maybe it was his own fault she ran here from him. It was the stories he'd told her when she was a child.

She was still his child.

The scent of dew-laden pine, balsam, cedar and spruce, of fusty earth and trampled ferns and wintergreen leaves, sifted into his nostrils when he stepped out of the cabin onto the front porch. The trill of red-winged blackbirds warning each other of his passing, the songs of finches, bluebirds and swallows, the constant chant of the spring peepers and the other frogs that filled the woods and marshy areas deeper in—the chaos of sound blended and caught at his ears, filtered through his nervous system to settle a soul jangled raw by too much civilization, paperwork, politics, news...by too much Megan in crisis.

The slur-sound of vegetation to his left made him start. Three deer shied and leaped away from the sough of his feet on the roadbed; he stared after them, lungs shuddering, heart pounding. It had been five years since he'd spent any time in the jungles of Colombia and Bolivia chasing cocaine farmers and their lords, and still his subconscious couldn't feel safe surrounded by trees.

With an effort, he stood still and breathed, letting scent and sound, the cool touch of shadow on exposed skin become an instant of peace he'd forgotten he'd been missing. Sweet solitude with no place he had to be, no responsibilities he had to face, no decisions he had to make that would affect anyone else's life. Two blessed minutes to himself—a lifetime it almost seemed.

If only he could figure out how to make it be enough.

He moved forward, walking the rutted quarter-mile trail from the cabin to the house that he and Megan and their luggage had jounced down the night before in the car, trying to take in everything around him at once. He wanted, he realized with a sudden disquieting start, he *needed* something from this place not only for Megan but for himself.

For *him*.

The kitchen was huge and warm, richly scented with sizzling meat, coffee and carbohydrates, a true farm kitchen.

Aromas dragging at his senses and making his insides gurgle in anticipation, Hank walked across the stone-floored mud room and rapped on the wooden screen door. When no one answered, he let himself in.

Immediately to his left, a long, dark green-painted wooden table with matching benches sat before a bank of open windows framed by filmy-looking lace curtains. Around the table a boisterous group of boys of varying sizes, colors and ages straddled the benches helping themselves to platters of pancakes, toast and sausages; plastic gallons of milk and juice passed hand to hand to fill mismatched plastic movie and superhero glasses from sundry local fast-food restaurants.

At the stove-top griddle on the far side of the kitchen stood two teenage girls in bright T-shirts and jeans with their hair ponytailed in vivid neon scrunchies. Without difficulty he recognized Li's long black hair and creamy Asian skin, her slim, graceful hands shoveling pepper-speckled scrambled eggs into a bowl. She looked the way she always looked to him: pretty, healthy, mature beyond her years, sure of herself and her place in the world, clear-eyed, knowing and...innocent as opposed to naive. Beside her, the girl with the laugh-curved mouth, soft brown hair and natural-glow skin wielding the pancake spatula also appeared fit and uncomplicated, young, and if not yet entirely certain of her direction, then at least convinced that she would eventually find one.

It took him a full thirty seconds and a startled heartbeat to realize the girl beside Li was Megan.

Talk, laughter and an astonishing variety of gross mouth sounds floated around Hank, yet he heard nothing. Stunned, he stared at his daughter, wondering who she was, how she'd gotten the black dye out of her hair so fast, what she'd done to liven up her skin tone from the ghastly paleness she normally sported and why she never looked like this at home.

Multiple personalities, his mind whispered, turning over possibilities in psychiatric jargon, searching for a pigeonhole. *Schizophrenia. Manic depression and this is the manic part.*

"Morning, Mr. Mathison."

Brisk and breezy, Kate Anden strolled in to Hank's astonishment, her flyaway, sun-kissed red-gold hair crossing his line of vision before the rest of her had a chance to. He looked at her.

"That's my daughter," he said, adequate response lagging well behind the event.

Kate nodded. "Different, isn't she?"

His mouth flattened, his wary gaze returned to his daughter. "I'm not sure that's the word I'd choose."

"No," Kate agreed without thinking. "It's probably not. You probably chose schizophrenic."

Attention arrested, Hank turned to her. Not a pretty woman by any stretch of the imagination; she was hardly what he could call plain, either. She had a quality, a beauty—honesty forced him to call it that—that was almost feral: big teeth in a slight overbite in a mouth that was overly generous, both literally and figuratively; eyes of a pale tourmaline blue with dark rings around the irises and in the left a rust-colored freckle next to the pupil; skin both freckled and flushed from a life spent largely outdoors; hair that was thick and riotous with a blend of autumn colors, fuzzy and unruly and playful—at present, an unbound rufous chaos that whirled about her waist; a body both slim and overly lavish, seductive but demure because she gave her attributes not one second of regard, didn't...play them up or take advantage of them or acknowledge them at all.

She also had a smile that could halt a hungry tiger in its tracks, a throaty, infectious laugh and a voice that would soothe the most cantankerous drug lord he'd ever met. Which was why he'd never been able to deny Megan permission to come here and get lost and found among the hordes of Kate's adopted children, foster children, exchange students and the multitudes of extras that drifted to her shores. When they'd shaken hands over the rental agreement on the guesthouse three days ago, he'd felt a shock from the center of his palm to the bottom of his toes—almost as if she'd hidden a practical joker's buzzer in her hand.

There'd been only skin between them, however. Hers hard and dry and impersonal, moisturized soft, but used to work. He shouldn't have felt anything, but she'd made his hormones snap, crackle and fizz awake.

Damn it.

He had a daughter to worry about; he didn't need to have his sleepy libido roused just now, and particularly not by a woman who couldn't have been further from his type—hell, who couldn't be further from any man's type, he'd guess—than the saintly and pushy Kate Anden.

He cast a glance at Megan, then back to Kate.

"Be nice if things were really this simple, wouldn't it?" Kate asked quietly.

Caught off guard, Hank nodded, his eyes once again on Megan, his thoughts focused on her and far away at once. "Yeah, it would. But nothin' ever is."

"You sound like you've got personal knowledge of that." Crisp and doubtful. Unexpectedly...gentle.

Drawn back from haunted places, Hank turned his head and stared at her. She viewed him, eyes frank and unwinking, blunt and psychic as she'd been four-and-a-half years earlier when she'd called him at his office to announce that he'd better stop on his way home and get some maxi-pads for Megan who'd started her monthlies a week after Gen's death and had been borrowing pads from Li regularly for the five months since. And to inform him that Li, then barely twelve, was the one who'd had to instruct Megan in the whys and wherefores of a woman's cycles and bodily functions and did Hank maybe want her, Kate, to pull Megan aside and correct any misinformation his daughter might have been given, since his daughter obviously needed someone to talk to and he, apparently, wasn't it?

He didn't like Kate any better now than he had then, despite the fact she seemed to hold the keys to his daughter's psyche—and probably because of it.

The center of his right palm itched with memory anyway.

He reminded himself that smoke didn't have to mean fire. That gentleness didn't necessarily equate with *like,* as in "I like you." That desire didn't have to be acted upon.

Still, in the interest of even footing he ignored the sensation of being singed and went on the attack instead.

"I knew you had a lot of kids, but these can't all be yours."

As though she'd expected the move, Kate grinned at him. There was something faintly mischievous in the curve of her mouth, imperceptibly mocking, subtly inviting. A sense of humor he'd been unaware she possessed. A you've-changed-the-subject-but-it-doesn't-matter-we-can-go-back-to-it-later.

A dare-ya.

He'd rented her guesthouse for how long?

"They're ours this morning," she said.

Chapter 2

She viewed him deadpan. Serenely serious.

It took him a minute to register the *ours*. Too late. Irritating and enigmatic as he'd ever found her, she sashayed across to the spitting coffee maker before he could call her back without alerting the mob at the table, collected a mug from the hooks underneath a cupboard and offered it to him.

"Coffee, Mr. Mathison?"

"Sure." Hank eyed her, out of his element, knots of ulceration forming in his stomach. A curious jigger of anticipation—not unlike the buzz of making a successful first connection on an undercover—doodled down his spine.

Up until Gen's death he'd been of the daredevil undercover DEA breed—necessary to the cause, but heavily monitored nonetheless—a risk taker, a cowboy who'd gotten juiced on bandying words, deeds and attitudes with the worst the world had to offer. A flea on the back of the drug-cartel elephant, he'd thought of himself: incessant and irritating; unable to stop the elephant, but occasionally causing an itch serious enough to bring it to its knees.

Still, none of that had prepared him for this.

Of course, he thought wryly, none of that had prepared him to be Megan's father alone on his own, either, and look how successful he was at that.

He saw Kate set down the coffeepot and crossed to her while watching the impostor Megan laughingly pass a platter of pancakes and sausages to the boys at the table.

She turned to him, clear-eyed and beautiful, the way he always wanted to see her. "Pancakes, Dad?"

"Who are you and what have you done with my daughter?" Kidding. Suspicious. Putting his foot in it.

She laughed, "Da-ad," and returned to help Li at the griddle.

Maybe he hadn't stepped in too deep. And if they'd made this much progress overnight, maybe they wouldn't have to even stay the whole summer.

"How do you take it?" Kate asked.

"An inch at a time," he said honestly.

She gave him a straight face. "Your coffee?"

"What?"

He looked at her; chagrin caught up with him at the same time the conversation did. He'd stepped into that one, all right. This woman had a mean sense of humor; he'd have to stand on his toes in order not to get caught in it again. "Oh. No, I mean milk, no sugar." He inhaled, consciously bringing himself back into the moment. It had been that conspiratorial *ours,* the intimation of *you-and-me,* when he was absolutely certain there wasn't.

Despite the return of the phantom fizz to the center of his right palm.

"Thanks." He accepted the mug she handed him and sipped, feeling awkward at the silence she didn't appear to notice. He broke it. Idly. "What exactly does *ours* mean?"

She grinned. "I wondered when that'd catch up with you."

"Not soon enough, apparently."

"You said you wanted this to be a working vacation." Silent laughter was bright in her eyes. She enjoyed poking and prodding him. Relished spooning the previous week's desperate pledges back at him with a shovel. "You said you wanted to get your hands dirty and be reintroduced to Megan and get to know her and forget about being a paper pusher with the DEA."

He gave her narrow-eyed scrutiny. "What, did you write our conversation down verbatim?"

She offered him glib. "Photographic memory."

"For everything, or only what it suits you to photograph?"

She looked at him, surprised by the question, the observation. She adjusted her view. Guarded.

Thoughtful.

"Touché," she said and saluted him with her mug.

He chalked a mental point in the air. Direct hit, score one. And he hadn't even intended to.

He also hadn't realized that bandying words with the enemy would return so naturally—or feel so good—any place outside a sting operation. It had been a long time since he'd worked a sting. Being an assistant director for the midwest DEA, Detroit office, meant spending half his time trying to halt the off-loaders of drugs within American borders. The other half was spent trying to train educators, families and the local police in ways to prevent drug dealers from permeating an area—often a depressing and thankless task. He'd had to develop skills for the job that were unlike any he'd used on the front lines, to learn to play office politics and budgetary tunes, to control his enthusiasm for any single operation by ever bearing in mind the big picture. To play party pooper—often not so different from parenting a teenager, he'd discovered—when *he'd* always hated the guy who put the damper on *his* party, when he'd been the one working the street.

But now, here he was again, lips working automatically to a tune somebody else had written, his sense of humor rusty with disuse but kicking in nonetheless, his brain improvising instantly in enemy territory. It felt *good.*

He hadn't even realized he'd missed it.

"Here you go, Dad, Kate."

Megan stepped into the middle of the eye duel he fought with Kate, plates at the ready. Knowledge and calculation glimmered almost perceptibly behind her eyes and inside the faint smugness of the smile settling her features, he noted. Whether deliberately or not, for the first time since Gen's death Megan had found one of the things she'd been looking for: a woman to play him against. A gender ally.

"Pancakes, eggs, sausage patties," she said. "Enjoy."

"Meg—" Hank began, but she evaded his voice and was back across the kitchen with Li, the table and the wall of vociferous boys placed neatly between them again.

Kate eyed Megan speculatively, recognizing the transparent ploy for what it was. And not liking it.

She'd been played against other adults by other kids in the past, but never more adroitly than it appeared she'd been played this time. It meant she might have to ally herself with Megan's father in the crunch, and she wasn't sure she'd want to.

Her jaw tugged tight, eyes puckered around the thought. "Cute trick," she said.

Hank nodded. "Yeah," he agreed, thoughtful himself. He looked at Kate, tracking the direction of her reflections by her expressions. "It is, isn't it?"

"She do this with you often?"

"Often as she can."

The corners of her mouth tucked a little. "Mom's a saint in heaven, but you're alive so you're the bad guy?"

He nodded. "That's the part of it I can figure out."

They viewed each other again, perspective canting. Communication on a wavelength only parents can hear—in a sort of parental shorthand instinctively improvised to maintain private communication in a world filled with big-eared kids—made him eye her hard, suspicious. This was not what he'd expected—*she* was not what he expected: a self-righteous goody-two-shoes, perhaps, but she wasn't blind. He might never be able to like her, but with a little judicious footwork he'd be able to work with her.

The same rapport made Kate look at him, too, a third time, and shake loose a fallacy she'd known better than to believe but had believed anyway: he was not who Megan—or even Li—said he was. There was something more to Hank Mathison than the self-involved DEA cowboy, hard-nosed pain-in-the-butt paper pusher she'd been told he was.

She consoled herself with the fact that she had no idea what "something more" was—and had no intention of finding out.

As often happens in a house filled with preteen and adolescent boys and two mid-teenage girls, a sudden shriek cut loose. As one, Kate and Hank turned toward the source of the cry, to find Li standing at the kitchen sink with one arm outstretched, a sealed Ziploc bag dangling from her fingers as far away from her as she could get it. Next to her, Megan hid her face in her hands and shuddered.

Hank started toward his daughter, all comforting, protective parent, then stopped short when he realized she wasn't upset by whatever it was in Li's hand. She was laughing so hard she could barely stand.

It had been years since he'd seen Megan laugh for pleasure instead of to cause pain.

"Who—left—the—stoat—in—the—sink?" Li asked, teeth locked hard together, every word glacially enunciated.

Grisha, Ilya's fourteen-year-old brother, started away from the table and grabbed the bag from Li. "It must thaw."

"Thaw?" she asked. "*Thaw?*"

"To make the..." he hesitated. "The taxidermy."

"Thaw?" Li said again, outraged. "This was in the *freezer?*"

Grisha nodded, eminently reasonable. "In the big meat freezer in the mud room. I found it last Thursday, freshly dead." He held up the bag so the tableful of boys could admire it. "I was most careful. I made sure it is very clean and the bag is closed very tight so you can see the green line like they show on TV to be certain, then I put the bag in Tupperware in the bottom bin where nothing was and washed my hands up to my elbows with that betadine scrub Dr. Chmiel says he uses between patients and before surgery. Bele and Mike have never seen a weasel. It is for science and education I brought it home. I told them we could skin it and stuff it like a taxidermist for their 4-H group. I could not leave it out to rot waiting for today."

Li stared at him, speechless. "That's...that's *gross.*"

Surprised, Grisha stared at her. "You have never dissected frogs or sheep's eyes or worms or anything for your biology class?"

"That's different."

"How?"

"Well, for one thing they aren't road kill—"

Hank glanced at Kate, looking for reaction cues.

She shrugged. "Don't listen," she advised. "It's the only way."

Lips pursing around a reluctant grin, Hank nodded. He'd had a feeling the way back to track would be drastic, but this...

He glanced once more at his daughter. On the other side of Li, Megan sagged against the counter and howled. Witnessing her enjoyment, deep inside him an ember stirred and began to glow. He swallowed, leery.

He'd been told that oftentimes grief ran in cycles, receding and returning in stages, that hope returned after the grieving process was complete, after you got through the denial and isolation, the bargaining and anger, the depression and finally the acceptance. As recently as yesterday it had still seemed that in five years he and Megan had hardly gotten through the initial round of anger, and were still a long way from hope. Today, within the space of twenty minutes and regardless of his wariness, hope kindled and a few skittish cinders took fragile flame.

Maybe, despite the table and the boys she'd put between them, the multitude of distractions, the woman Kate and her extensive brood, maybe out here surrounded by the magic of trees that stayed green even in the winter he and Megan could get to there from here yet.

After breakfast Kate showed Hank around.

It was a nervewracking job, but somebody had to do it.

"The sheds on this side—" she pointed left "—are for the mother llamas—we call them the 'girls'—and their *crias*. The 'boys' are on the other side of the workshop. Now over here—"

She was pretty sure she wasn't, but she *felt* as if she was babbling. She'd given this tour a thousand times to people who should have been far more daunting, but she'd never in her life felt so uncomfortable and awkward around anyone as she did around Hank Mathison.

"The workshop started out as a way for Tai and Li to earn extra pocket money, maybe pick up a little for college. They did dried flower and herb arrangements, some simple wood stuff—crèches, birdhouses, you know. We took 'em around to some of the local farm markets and things sort of escalated from there. By the time the other kids came along, we were running—"

It was a good thing she'd given this tour to other parents so many times before that she didn't have to think about what she was saying. Simply walking along beside him left her skin with the prickly, irritated sensation of an allergic rash and made her feel short of breath, restless, fevered and wishing to be elsewhere. Sort of. She also sort of didn't want to be elsewhere.

Mostly, and for no apparent reason, she wanted to scream. And giggle hysterically. And slap herself silly, so this obnoxious fluttery-prickly-stilted-feeling idiot would get out of her psyche now, at once, immediately.

Or sooner.

"And we sort of inherited the alpacas from a family who was moving to New York. My brother left me a llama with Mike when he died, and well, we found we liked 'em so much we took on a couple more and things sort of escalated from there. Now we work with a couple of the 4-H clubs, do parades, fairs, things like that, teach the kids how to train the llamas for packing or guarding sheep herds or whatever. We've just started taking a couple of the 'boys' around to the local nursing homes, doing a little, um, llama therapy. People who don't respond to anything else just sort of seem to take to the llamas. The llamas seem to have a kind of...empathy, sympathy, with people who are hurting. Li took Harvey in to one of the homes last week. There was a hundred-and-one-year-old lady who'd been basically catatonic since her husband died. Harvey sniffed her nose and she looked up at him and started crying, latched onto his chest wool and wouldn't let go. Harvey just took it." She grinned. "'Course Li paid for it later. Llamas remember things. When she took him out to put him in the van, he switched his hindquarters around, thunked her into the wheel well and gave her a look Li swears said, 'If you *ever* do that to me again—'"

She looked at Hank, watching his face—for what, she wasn't sure. She reminded herself of Li at thirteen, when her daughter had won backstage passes to a Bush concert: thoroughly and totally adolescent. And *why* she felt this way as thoroughly and totally escaped *her* now as it had Li then.

Fortunately, it didn't seem to show—much. Also, fortunately, becoming everybody's mother had taught Kate the value of laughing at herself and, for the most part, how to ignore adolescent side effects.

She concentrated on what she was saying, instead of on things over which she apparently had no control.

"And this is where we build the miniatures and do most of the other woodworking." She waved a hand at the long tables and tools set up in the heated pole barn behind the three-car garage.

Hank nodded, head on automatic pilot; he swept the room a restless glance. "Looks great." His impatience to move on was undisguised.

Kate shook her head and withheld a sigh.

It had been a long morning showing the distracted and therefore taciturn Hank around; wherever she pointed, his thoughts and gaze were elsewhere—looking, she presumed, for Megan, who'd disappeared with Li and Tai as soon as the breakfast dishes were cleared and loaded into the dishwasher. He had not, she was pretty certain, heard a word she'd said since breakfast. Or noticed anything "funny" or...or...*artificial* about her, either.

Or noticed her at all.

Darn it.

She rolled her eyes and shuddered at that inadvertent internal comment. How old was she, anyway?

Oh, just about *that* old. Or young. Or immature, as the case might be.

Grow up, she told herself rudely. *What on earth is the matter with you?*

She took a sideways peek at the almost too neatly trimmed honey-wheat hair, the time-chiseled features that flirted with a beauty not unlike that accorded the gods by sculptors, the unusual mead-colored eyes... Yep, she was right. Hank Mathison was simply too blessed pretty for her good.

He was the first man she'd ever found so, too. Which brought into the chaos of the moment a whole set of complications she'd never even considered possible, because she'd never thought them hers to contemplate. She had, after all and once upon a time, planned to spend her life in a convent where recognizing the existence of...of...cute guys, as Li would put it, and *libido,* as Tai had so succinctly phrased it when he'd discovered the existence of his, was frowned upon. And she'd never found cause to change that outlook since then simply because she was no longer, as it were, "married to God."

So why now? she asked heaven with some exasperation. *Why give me thirty-some-too-many years of no fireworks and no missin' 'em, then suddenly dump this into my life?*

Because there's no time like the present, heaven or her guardian angel whispered back.

Kate would have sworn there was laughter in the response.

She was glad at least someone found humor in the situation. She, herself, could see the potential for comedy, but it was the kind of comedy where tragedy lurked around the corner ready to pounce the minute it found an opening.

Megan Mathison was a cataclysm biding its moment. Never had that been more clear to Kate than this morning. Megan was also a child who'd lost her mother at one of the most crucial stages of her life, a young woman whose emotional psyche and ego were often still only eleven in a sixteen-year-old's body. She wanted all the things other children wanted—happiness, love, attention and a fairy-tale future—but her ability to achieve her ends by nondestructive means was seriously skewed.

Instinct had brought her to Stone House time and again; reflex made her behave like a kid with a split personality, acting to suit the moment and her own untempered perception of it, causing her to do whatever she had to in order to snow whoever she wanted on her side at the moment. In this instance, Kate. And if Kate managed to get to know and stop...discounting or disliking or something...Hank, if *she* started to act like a teenage girl with her first crush, who knew what Megan's unconsciously manipulative instincts would lead the real teen in this situation to try.

No, Kate sighed. This was definitely not the time to wind up infatuated, for the first time in her life, simply because her suddenly confused and unreliable hormones found Hank Mathison attractive.

"So what goes on in here?" Hank asked.

Kate snapped out of her reverie. She had no idea how long she'd kept Hank standing in the double-width workshop doorway, and it was clear from the look on his face that he had no idea they'd already toured the place.

She'd often thought from the way her late sister-in-law had handled her late brother—Mike's parents—that men as men and not as brothers or fathers or platonic friends must be exasperating beasts. Now she was sure of it.

Canting her head she looked up at him, shading her eyes against the sun haloing out behind him. The same irreverent imp that had been largely responsible for her getting asked to leave the convent reared its cockeyed sense of humor and made her gesture again at the tables, tools, the oversized supply locker along the back wall and say, "This is where we hide the bodies."

That brought him back from wherever he'd been. Fast. "What? What bodies?"

Kate grinned. "I wondered what it took to get your attention."

Hank viewed her irritably. "You've had my undivided attention all morning."

"Yeah, right." Kate snorted and shouldered by him, into the sunlight. "Your undivided attention. If this is an example of your 'undivided attention', it's no wonder Meg feels shorted."

"What the hell are you talking about?" Stung, Hank grabbed her arm, swung her about. A mistake. Especially since he'd already spent the too-long morning trying to curtail his body's awareness of this woman he wanted only to see as a rival for his daughter's affections, or as a means of getting Megan back and not as a *Woman*.

But *Woman* she was. And a hell of a lot of one, at that.

There was a spark in her he hadn't counted on seeing, an electricity in the tourmaline eyes that leaped and crackled, potent when it struck him like a physical blow square in the chest. His lungs grabbed for air as though he were suffocating; his pulse missed first one beat, then two, then caught and charged like the leader in an ice-skating game of crack-the-whip where he was the tail hanging on for dear life so he wouldn't fly off into a tree or a snowbank and come up full of bruises, disgracing himself.

He let go of her arm at the same moment her hand came up to pick his fingers off. Her hands were as strong as they looked, as magnetic as he remembered. Their physical link lasted an instant longer than necessary.

Too long.

He swallowed and put space between them, then completed his thought. "I don't short Meg any attention. My entire life revolves around her—"

"Your mistake," Kate interrupted flatly. It took everything she had in her to simply fold up the fingers that had touched his and not look to see if they were as blistered as they felt. "Not mine."

"So where the devil do you get off accusing me of ignoring my daughter, when you're the one making things so stinking easy for her here she'd rather not come home?"

"You think she comes here because life is *easy*? When she's here, I expect the same things from her that I expect from my own kids and every other kid that comes through here, and let me tell you, buster, that ain't *easy*."

"I mean," Hank continued as though she hadn't spoken, "the

least you could do—'' Damn, why couldn't he stop smelling her, tasting the sunshine emanating from her, let go of the sensation tingling through the nerves of his hand...of the imprint of steel strength and vitality encased in the silken skin of her arm sheathed in a clean cotton T-shirt ''—is make it less attractive for her to be here and—''

''Oh, and just how do you suggest I do that?'' Heat shifted and rose through her system: irritation and something else. Something sharp and clinging, tenacious and beguiling, dangerous. Sweet heaven, she wanted to get away from here, from him, from the sizzle and pop of a passion she couldn't understand and that had little to do with the disagreement they were having. That had everything to do with a *want* she'd never before experienced and didn't wish to experience now. Not for him. Not for anyone. She found scorn and let it filter into her voice. Anything to keep whatever this was at arm's length. ''You think I ought to start beating them or something—''

''Mom, Mom!''

''What?'' Kate snapped more sharply than she intended. Immediately guilty, she looked down at Mike and Bele who, oblivious to her tone, danced like excited puppies at her elbow. ''What's up?'' The grin her two ''babies'' almost always provoked was a shadow in her voice this time.

''You gotta come see what we found in the dig!'' Mike tugged at her arm, willing her attention with his enthusiasm.

''It's huge!'' Bele bounced, one-legged, at her other elbow, equally enthusiastic, his hands holding his crutches spread wide to demonstrate dimension. ''A bone this long at least. You have to call the University of Michigan—''

''Nuh-unh,'' Mike objected. ''Michigan State.''

''U of M,'' Bele repeated firmly, pale palms flashing wide for emphasis against the darkness of the rest of his skin, as remarkably single-minded in this as he was in all things. ''We found a really real dinosaur this time, not just some old cow bone and—''

''And Risto says,'' Mike interrupted, referring to the Finnish exchange student who'd spent the past ten months living with them while taking classes with Li at the high school, ''that if it's not a dinosaur, then it might be from a woolly mammoth or a saber-toothed tiger or maybe even an eohippus that migrated all the way up here from New Mexico, but Bele 'n' I think it's too big for that—''

"And even if it's not an eohippus or anything except something regular like a murder victim," Bele picked up the thread of the conversation from Mike, almost physically yanking it back to himself, "you still have to come see, cuz it's super important and we've never dug up anything like this before."

"Something regular like...?" Speechless, Hank stared at the youngsters, one fair and the other dark, too far removed from his own boyhood to remember the gruesomely delightful turns of a young boy's mind. The long-time cop in him keened instantly at the word murder; it took real effort to get him to back off this time and remember these were not his everyday bad guys he was dealing with here. But this *was* the second time in less than ten minutes he'd been caught by this family casually mentioning something about dead bodies. Hell of a good thing he didn't work homicide then. And thank *God* Megan's mind had never wandered down such macabre corridors when she was eight—so far as he knew.

But then he probably wouldn't know, gone as often and as long as he'd been, would he?

"Of course I'll come see," he heard Kate say. "But dead body or dinosaur bones, manners first." She turned to him. "Mr. Mathison, have you met my sons Mike and Bele? Boys—" She turned back to them. "This is Megan's father, Mr. Mathiso—" Arrested in mid-word, her focus sharpened on Bele's crutches, sank to his left leg, which Hank noted with shock ended a few inches below his knee. "Where's your leg, Bele? You haven't lost it again, have you?"

Bele made a face at her. "Mo-om. I only did that once and it wasn't my fault. Mike hid it."

"I did not," Mike said indignant. "It was right inside the window seat where I put it. And anyway, you wouldn't give me back my baseball glove and I needed it."

"I didn't take your old glove and it wasn't yours, it was Li's old one and they were going to play *me,* not *you* if you hadn't taken my foot and—''

"Boys." Exasperated, Kate stepped in and brought them back to the point she'd sidetracked them onto. Much as she loved them, there were moments when she wanted to squash them both like tomato slugs. *Insects by day, angels only in sleep,* she'd laughingly told one of the other nuns at the Red Cross hospital they'd set up in El Salvador, observing a pair of scruffy but angelic looking noninnocents con yet another journalist into the purchase of something the "angels" had undoubtedly just swiped from the reporter's pack. "We found the prosthesis, you both got your own baseball gloves, we're done with it, but it doesn't explain where your leg is now—"

"I have a sore on my stump," Bele said matter-of-factly. "I need a new leg."

"A new one?" Kate asked dismayed. "It hasn't even been four months yet, has it? Did you try a lighter stump sock?"

Bele nodded. "It's still too tight, and it's too short, too. I'm growing."

"And to think we once thought too much coffee would stunt your growth." Kate sighed.

"I don't drink coffee," Bele said, affronted.

"Maybe you should start."

"No way! It's disgusting."

"My tennis shoes are too small for me, too," Mike put in, not to be outdone—and because it was the truth. His feet had been triple-E width since birth. "And Bele's old ones are too skinny for my feet, even if his foot *is* longer than mine. I tried them on."

Arms akimbo, Kate eyed them with mock exasperation. "Weeds," she pronounced, then grinned and ruffled Mike's straight white-blond hair and brushed a hand over Bele's short-shaved wiry black curls. "Feed 'em, water 'em and ignore 'em and they grow like brush fire."

"Mom." Mike rolled his eyes and leaned away, after first reaching up to tap her face with annoyed affection.

"Mo-om." Bele looked up at her with *don't do that* in his voice and love in his eyes.

Back of her wrist to her forehead, Kate moaned with melodramatic sadness, "They don't need me anymore. Sigh, sob." They laughed and she grinned. "Okay. I'll call Dennis and make an appointment to get you fitted for a new socket and pylon, Bele, then while we're in Ann Arbor we'll do shoe shopping. Right, Mike?"

"And lunch at Arby's?" Both boys, in near unison, grinned at each other over this neatly laid trap.

"We'll see," Kate agreed dryly. She jerked a thumb toward the house. "C'mon, Bele, I want to take a look at your leg, make sure it's clean 'n' all. You'll have to use your crutches till it heals—"

Agile on his crutches as any other child on two legs, Bele danced out of reach, shaking his head. "Nuh-unh, you don't have to. Meg already washed it and put stuff on it. Come *on,* Ma," he said, impatient and imploring. "Before Grisha finds our bone—"

"And steals it to figure out how to test for *age* or something," Mike finished.

Unmatched sets of white teeth flashed first at each other, then at Kate, the grins of young boys filled with the possibilities of an entire summer stretched out before them. Eagerly they awaited Kate's laughing nod, then swooped away, looking back only once to make sure she followed.

It might have been his imagination, but Hank thought he discerned Bele moving a little faster to keep up with Mike, saw Mike unconsciously measuring his steps to match the sweep of his brother's leg; crutches and feet hit the ground in perfect time, matching the unbidden plummeting of Hank's heart to his stomach. What, how, who, when—questions he couldn't keep up with zipped past the back of his throat without touching his tongue; only one held any clarity amid the numbness in his brain: how could they...he was only a little boy and they were so...how could they just...

Accept?

Wait a minute. His mind did an unexpected double take. *Megan* took care of Bele's stump sore? *Megan? His* Megan? Willingly?

Four steps across the drive in front of him Kate turned and looked back, pale eyes clear as the sky, full of a knowledge and understanding he still didn't grasp and had never wanted to possess. But all she said was, "Coming, Mr. Mathison?"

Incredulous and...curious as he was, he couldn't bring himself to do anything less. Hank went.

Chapter 3

"It happened not long before he came to us," Kate said without preamble when Hank caught up with her. "He's from a tiny village in southwest Zaire. His family walked three hours to the river for water. He was very young, maybe four. A water skin got away from him. He walked into the river to catch it and a crocodile took his leg."

Hank's heart twisted, sinking in his gut. He'd seen worse things happen to children during his time in Colombia and Bolivia; the only way to deal with horrors he couldn't stop or control had been to look past them, harden himself, not get involved. Here, because of Megan, he was involved by default—even before he'd known there was a Bele. He couldn't—didn't want to—look away. He had to say something, but what? No matter how badly you wanted them to be, words were never adequate to tragedy. "That's terrible."

Kate shrugged, matter-of-fact. "At the time, yes. Now it's inconvenient sometimes, not terrible. Ask him. He's got the coolest left foot in the third grade and he can do anything on it the other kids can do on the ones they were born with and more things on one foot than they'll ever be able to do. The croc could have killed him. Instead it made him special."

"But—" Hank began and subsided. He was way out of his depth, his element and the range of his control here. "But Megan?" he asked finally, painfully, hating himself for needing to question his daughter's abilities. Hating himself for not knowing as well as he wanted to what her capabilities were. "She...took care of Bele's leg and you don't need to..." He hesitated, neither wanting to belittle his daughter nor indicate the depth of his inability to trust her to do the right thing on her own. "She's only a kid," he said lamely. "What if she... You don't need to...check on her work?"

Kate looked up at him, surprised. She didn't intend to sound sanctimonious; Lord knew, with all the mistakes she made with her kids—past and present—she had as little right to sanctimony as anyone. A trace of it crept into her voice anyway. "Every kid's got a story she wants somebody to listen to, Mr. Mathison."

"You think I don't know that, Ms. Anden?" Hank snapped. Nothing stung worse than truth. "I haven't exactly spent my life with my head in the sand when it comes to—"

"Mr. Mathison, please." Kate held up a hand and Hank chewed his anger into silence. "I didn't mean to imply..." She hesitated. No, that wasn't quite true. She probably *had* meant to imply exactly that. "I shouldn't have said..." Another pause. No, that wasn't true either. *Somebody* had to speak out of turn sometimes; if it had to be her, well... "I'm sorry. I can be rather, er..." She made a face. Confession might be good for the soul, but that didn't mean she enjoyed it. "I'm a little, um, self-righteous sometimes. It's not an attractive feature. I'm working on it, but I still have a tendency to react first and think later sometimes. I do apologize."

Astonished not only by her directness but by her willingness to recognize and accept her own flaws, Hank stared down at her. "That must have hurt."

Kate nodded and made another face. "You'll never know."

His anger faded abruptly. Caught off guard he grinned. "You might be surprised."

"Probably not as much as you'd like me to be," she returned.

Hank laughed. "Touché."

They stopped in the grass a hundred feet shy of the mound of earth Kate and Tai regularly salted with broken clay pots and sharks' teeth and had long ago christened the Stone House Burial

Mound and Archaeological Dig and exchanged wary grins. Common ground stood between them, ready to be claimed. Years of conflict peered over their shoulders, whispering caution in their ears. They looked at each other through curious eyes, and the fizz neither wanted to feel or recognize—that neither wanted reciprocated—tingled dully in the nerves of their right palms, hung like an itch out of reach between Kate's shoulder blades, sank like a hungry growl in Hank's belly without cause or reason.

Too busy gently brushing clay from the bone in the dig to be aware of adults in the midst of adult hankerings, no children appeared to rescue them from each other, nor from awareness and uncertainty.

A man who'd always had a knack for not wanting what he couldn't have and for taking what he wanted without regrets, it unnerved Hank to find himself desiring something—some*one*— he didn't plan to take. To find himself aching, drawn to step closer to Kate. To be near enough that loose strands of her long apricot hair reached out in the trace breeze to wrap around his fingers and cling to his hand seemingly to invite him nearer still. He threaded the web of coarse silk between his fingers and watched Kate's face through eyes hooded with self-loathing and desire.

Nervously Kate ran her suddenly dry tongue over her lips and watched him back. This sinking, quavering, butterflies-in-her-stomach, no-holds-barred, this-is-*it* thud of her pulse was beyond her ken, a sensation she'd never before experienced. She didn't *want* this, didn't know what to do with it, could read the *be careful* plainly printed on Hank's face and had no idea how. She also experienced a surge of heat and feminine power, a feline urge to stretch and taunt—a soul-deep fear that if she did, she'd suddenly find herself hip deep in a quagmire and sinking fast with no anchor rope to haul her back.

She flicked a skittish glance toward Mike and Bele, too far away and too up to their elbows in muck to be of any use, then returned her gaze to Hank. She shut her eyes and tried not to feel the primitive thing emanating from him. Felt his fist tighten in her hair.

A modern woman to the soles of her toes, Kate realized that if she wanted to be rescued before the unknown closed around her, she'd have to do what she always did and rescue herself.

She sucked in a deep breath and did so. "You don't like me,

do you, Mr. Mathison?'' she asked. It might do them both good to be reminded of where they'd always stood with each other.

Knocked unceremoniously out of the moment, Hank loosed her hair and blinked at her. The bile of self-disgust rose in his throat, mingled with the irritation and restlessness of an unwanted craving left unsatisfied. How did she do that? he wondered. Take a moment and twist it out of reach so easily. And why did he care that she had?

He swallowed and raised his guard, refusing to let the tightness in his shorts govern him. He'd come here to save his daughter, not to assuage his own loneliness with an ex-nun mother of seven. ''This isn't about *you*, Ms. Anden, it's about Megan. Period. For what it's worth, I don't feel I know you well enough to either like or dislike—''

''I didn't invite you to dance, Mr. Mathison,'' Kate interrupted with some asperity. ''I asked you a question. You came to me because of your daughter. The sooner you and I get things clear between us, the sooner we can get past them and help Megan.''

Hank's mouth thinned without humor, his eyes hardened. ''No, Ms. Anden,'' he agreed with contempt—whether for her or for himself, Kate couldn't tell. ''I don't like you. But I'll work with you. For Megan.''

''Why?'' Her mother had often rebuked her over how easily Kate's tongue raised blisters on other people's hides. Chided her about goading a person with her *why's* until she'd managed to rub the blisters raw.

But she had to go on, had to press until the other person gave her the answers she needed. Whether she wanted to hear them or not.

She repeated the question. ''Why, Mr. Mathison?''

Hank's mouth twisted at her stupidity. ''She's my daughter. I love her.''

''No.'' Kate shook her head, impatient. There was an answer here someplace, she could feel it. An answer about Megan. ''Don't get me wrong. You loving Megan is great, but it's not what I meant. What I meant was, why don't you like me? Is it just *me* the concept, *me* the blunt goody-two-shoes ex-missionary-ex-nun and you've got a thing about ex-missionary-ex-nuns, or is it because of something Megan said—maybe an idea she planted. A point of view she has that's maybe a little...'' She hesitated.

This was the man's daughter she was talking about, after all. "A little *skewed?*"

Light dawned slowly. This wasn't, as he'd assumed, about Kate, but about Megan. And about how Megan reported and interpreted things. About Megan doing her damnedest to...what? Play him against Kate since a long time before he'd had his first chance to witness her doing so at breakfast this morning.

His first reaction was anger at Kate, to choose not to believe ill of his daughter.

His second reaction was to understand that this was the sort of thing he'd suspected all along but chosen to ignore in the face of other drains on his energies where Megan was concerned. Another symptom of the dysfunction that existed between him and his daughter.

He sighed. "I don't know. Maybe. Probably. It's been so long the specifics escape me."

Kate nodded thoughtfully, and hands in the pockets of her jeans, turned and moved once more toward Mike and Bele's dig. "And a lot of the reason I've never particularly cared for you has to do with things Meg's told Li and Li's told me, with stray comments Meg's made when she's here—the fact that she's always sneaking over here. I mean, teenagers are pretty territorial, so why would a kid prefer to have somebody else's stuff around her instead of her own, if nothing's wrong at home? And you didn't know—she didn't tell you—about Bele and she's pretty much been his mother hen since the day he arrived."

"I see." He had nothing else to say. Nothing to feel but the same sense of deadness he'd felt the day Megan had called, hysterical, and he'd arrived home to find Gen lying near death in the shower with the hot water running cold around her. The two most important people in his life were also the two he'd always known least well.

"In all this time has Megan ever told you *anything* about what she does when she's here?" Delicacy wasn't her forte, but she could try.

Hank shook his head. Admission hurt. "No. She's always been a...private kid. And she's been coming here so long, maybe I forgot to ask, or she didn't answer or I didn't *want* to ask because I knew we were a long way apart, but never realized how far. I wish..." He shook his head. "No, it's too late for wishing on what's been. Here and now is where we start from. So...." Grimacing, he hunched into his shoulders, then straightened and puffed out an uncomfortable breath, grabbing the bull by the horns. "So," he said again, decisive this time. "What can you tell me about my daughter?"

They reached the boys before Kate could fill him in on more than Megan's history with Bele, beginning less than eighteen months after the death of her own mother. It was both too little and almost too much.

She told him how his daughter had been there when she'd taken the call from the nuns in Kinshasa, relaying the message that Bele's mother had died in childbirth the year before, that his father was dying and had requested the sisters contact Kate—who'd worked at the mission years before and knew the family well—and ask her to adopt Bele.

About Megan pleading to be allowed to go with her to collect the motherless boy—even though Kate was not taking Tai, Li or Mike with her. Megan pacing anxiously on the wide front porch the day Kate and Bele arrived home. Megan hiding in a corner where Bele wouldn't see her, weeping over the little boy's losing his parents, his probable fears about coming to a place so far from his home, her empathy over his injuries. Megan fierce and protective while the Anden family doctor tried to check Bele over and treat him; Megan coaxing and gentle, luring Bele into his first bath when he'd been too afraid of possible crocodiles in the open water to go in on his own.

Megan insisting on going with the rest of the family on Bele's first trip to the prosthetist who'd fitted his leg. Megan asking questions and demanding to be taught how to care for Bele's leg—then supervising to make sure Kate would do the job properly whenever Megan wasn't there to see to it personally.

Megan needy, giving, sheltering, loving.

Megan being all the things she refused to let Hank see.

It was a lot for a father who'd long been given only a view of the punk-haired-rebel side of his daughter to digest all at once.

It also made him even more afraid every time he wondered what must have happened the night she'd driven Zevo's car home and come into the house high. What his instincts told him had to be true: she'd been protecting someone, but he couldn't begin to imagine who or why.

When they arrived to admire Bele's and Mike's bone, he was reeling and ready for distraction.

After ascertaining that the bone was not from anything human, Hank surprised himself by letting his guard drop and getting into the spirit of the thing, delicately turning the bone over in his hands, brushing off the remaining dirt, using his brief stint in forensics to offer scientific speculation on what it was. It was almost certainly from a long dead cow or deer, but the boys were happier with other potential explanations: coyote, wolf, miniature horse or, of course, eohippus.

Ignored in the face of more learned counsel—pure bull, Hank assured her later—Kate watched him and the boys with interest. This was a side of Hank Mathison she'd doubted existed and could not have anticipated. The boys' reaction to him, their eagerness to drink up his attention, was something else for which she was not prepared.

She'd considered the necessity of an adult male example in the lives of her children, and especially her boys, only fleetingly. When she'd first adopted Tai and Li, her brother was still alive. Since he and his wife had died and left Mike to her when he was barely fifteen months old, she hadn't had time to doubt her abilities to be father as well as mother. The other boys had arrived in rapid succession and *voilà!* Here they all were.

Oh, there were men around Stone House during every tree-cutting and shipping season—hardworking and friendly, surly and sour, itinerants as well as family men—but she'd never noticed any of the children behaving then the way Mike and Bele hung onto Mathison's attention now. Curious. Maybe she'd simply been too busy with each harvesting season's madness to notice a difference in the kids. And maybe Megan's father was simply as different from other men where her kids were concerned as he seemed—*felt*—to Kate herself.

The vague flavor of jealousy on her tongue that Hank should so easily win their regard and the more powerful surge of pleasure she found in their excitement to hold his attention also took her off guard. Mr. Mathison was not the only one getting an education here. Her own private education hadn't even been *on* the list of things she'd imagined happening this summer, because *she*, unlike Hank, already knew everything she needed to know about raising kids.

Sort of.

She glanced at her boys, then to their intriguingly open and unforeseen teacher. But the unexpected was okay—within bounds.

Maybe.

Again she felt that curious flash of something she couldn't identify low in her belly, the fluttery, flirty tightening in her lungs. It was, she'd decided the moment he'd called, her job to unbalance Hank Mathison this summer, to be the one to make him sit up and take notice of his daughter. His unbalancing *her* was not part of the bargain she'd made either with Hank or herself.

And yet...the foreign sensations trickling through her bloodstream were not unpleasant. Anxious, yes, but not awful. Not even bad. Just restless. Like being a kid and waiting for something wonderful-dreadful to happen that might just be so good you'll get sick to your stomach if it doesn't turn out the way you're afraid to want it to. Similar to, but not quite the same as the way she'd felt waiting for the courts to decide she would be a suitable adoptive parent even without a husband.

She was pretty sure the anticipation of impending motherhood had made her feel as nauseated and expectant as any pregnant woman in her first trimester. But this, although she had no way of actually knowing *personally,* didn't feel like that at all. This felt a lot more like...

Well, probably a lot more like pregnant women might feel just *before* they got pregnant.

Oops.

Kate's jaw dropped; she stared at Hank, confirming the fizzle in her pulse, the constriction in her lungs, the sensation of...*quickening* that ran through her at the mere sight of him with Bele and Mike.

The mere sight of him anywhere.

Horrified at herself, she turned her back and covered her mouth. Jiminy Pete, of all the stupid, disgusting— Llamas were more civilized. Independent creatures that the girls were, *they* didn't get hot simply because some studly boy with the right length wool or the cutest little patch on his nose walked by unless they wanted to.

If her llamas could be adult about how they felt and when they felt it, it was ridiculous to think she couldn't.

But she couldn't.

Stunned by the suddenly duplicitous nature of a body that had never—as far as she recalled—betrayed her before, she turned to find some other distraction to think about. Instead she found Hank striding toward her, looking younger than she'd ever seen him, smiling back over his shoulder at something Bele was excitedly telling Mike.

Not that she'd seen him a lot before this morning, but still—

"Fly catching, Ms. Anden?" Hank asked, eyeing the mud on the end of her nose. So scrupulously clean as she always was around him, he found the mud both oddly comforting and mightily amusing.

Kate stared askance, too aware of him and the hamster running its squeaky wheel through her veins and arteries to comprehend his pointed glance.

A laughter he'd not experienced in years rumbled silently through him. A wicked grin tipped his mouth.

Hands on her hips, Kate glared at him. "Is something wrong, Mr. Mathison?"

"Not at all, Ms. Anden."

Hank's lips compressed; he glanced skyward trying not to laugh. He'd no idea what had happened to him in the few minutes he'd spent in the dig with Mike and Bele, but he hadn't felt so much himself in, well, an incredibly too long time.

A wayward sputter of humor escaped Hank. He took a deep breath and did his best to stifle it.

Kate's glare grew solicitous, mildly wary. "Are you certain you're all right, Mr. Mathison? You look like you're about to explode."

"Never felt better, Ms. Anden," he assured her, then bent double and howled when she rubbed her cheek and another streak of mud appeared.

"Mr. Mathison, what *is* the problem?"

There was an element of *schoolteacher getting pissed* in her voice that made Hank laugh harder. He couldn't help himself. He'd finally met someone on whom he'd have said there were truly no flies, a parent with seemingly perfect children to whom he'd often felt somewhat inferior. And the first time he spent longer than five minutes in her company, his competition wore mud on her face.

Competition. The word sobered him the instant it formed. Was that really what he felt? That this was a contest, a winner-take-all battle—and *all* was Megan?

He straightened. He'd never seen his attitude toward Kate in such sere light before. It wasn't a pretty picture.

"Hank?" Concerned. Not stilted with formality.

Real.

It was the first time she'd used the familiar form of his name. It sounded odd coming from her mouth. As if it didn't belong there.

Or as if it belonged there a lot. Breathy. Breathless. Against his mouth. Close to his ear.

His jaw tightened, his gaze slid over her face. Pale freckles and sun glow; laugh lines beside her eyes; small mouth, full lips.

Kissable.

Damn, he didn't want her. Couldn't.

Wouldn't.

Did.

The mud was no longer funny, a mar on the landscape. He moved a deceptively lazy hand, brushed her face suddenly and the smudge was gone.

He'd always had fast hands—except where he wanted to make them slow.

Shocked, Kate gaped at him. "Mr. Mathison!" The outraged schoolteacher was back in her voice full force.

Hank grinned, but there was flint in it this time. This was neither the time nor the place to resurrect his hormones. They were, after all, *his* hormones. He was their boss; he controlled them, not vice versa.

Yeah, right. Who was he kidding? "Relax, Ms. Anden." He shoved her chin up with the tip of one forefinger, closing her mouth, and showed her the mud in his other hand. "It's dirt, not an assault."

Then he dusted off his hands and stalked away.

Too dumbfounded for a moment to react, Kate stared after him, then at the muddy dust on her left boot, then once more at his receding back. Not a bad view, she decided without meaning to. He exuded power and grace in every loose-hipped movement, the impression of muscles bunching and smoothing even through the relaxed fit of his clothes. The phrase *nice tush* floated through her mind; her lips twitched. For a woman who'd felt totally furious less than two and a half minutes ago, it was not exactly the most outraged thought she'd ever had.

So, then, shut ma mouth, she told herself derisively. Laughter bubbled in her throat. He certainly had. Right after he'd taken the filth she'd never even realized was on her off her nose.

There'd been mud on her nose.

Because she'd been too busy staring at Hank Mathison's mead-amber eyes, tawny blond hair, pretty face and musculature to notice it.

And Tai's favorite sarcastic adolescent phrase—the one that was now the family's favorite complaint—had always been, *"Gee, Mom, no flies on you, are there?"*

The laughter in her throat broke free on a whoop. No wonder Mathison nearly rolled in mirth. She, who all too often thought—smugly, yes, be honest—of herself as far too smart to be caught unaware had been caught unaware. By the mud she was always telling her kids to wash off *their* faces.

She doubled over and laughed until her sides hurt and the tears ran. God always did find a way to give her a poke when she was being too smarty-pantsed for her own good.

"Mum, are you all right?"

Mike and Bele bounded up beside her, full of concern—and curiosity.

"Fine," she wheezed, trying to contain the chuckles, but failing.

"What's so funny?"

"Mr. Mathison—" She snorted laughter, swiped a hand across her face on a chuckling sigh. "Mr. Mathison told me a joke."

"Tell us," they begged. "Tell us."

"I can't—" A chortle got in the way. She cleared it out of her throat. "I can't." She shook her head, grinning. "It—you had to be there. It doesn't translate."

They were at an age where bad jokes and magic tricks were a major part of life. "Aw, Mom. Please?"

She shook her head again. Such a lot to have learned—mostly about herself, only some about Hank—in a morning and gee, wouldn't you know, the summer's dance had barely begun. "Sorry, guys, you know how bad I am with jokes."

Bele gave her a disgusted look. "Yeah, you always get the punch line in the wrong place."

"Sorry." She shrugged an unrepentant apology. "Nobody's perfect."

"Yeah, yeah, yeah," Bele agreed, still disgusted.

He was, Kate reflected with amusement, a long way from the frightened child she'd brought home from Zaire.

"Hey, I know!" Mike of the big ideas. "We can get Hank to tell us."

"Hank?" Kate asked, surprised. He hadn't invited *her* to call him Hank. 'Course now that she thought about it, she hadn't invited him to call her Kate, either. Probably ought to remedy that. Especially if she was going to have a crush on the man. And it appeared, she discovered with amusement and consternation, that she had one whether she wanted to or not. It'd make the daydreaming she didn't have time for so much easier, if they called each other by their first names.

"He said to call him that," Bele yelled, already starting away. "C'mon, Mike, let's go find him before he forgets the joke."

"Yeah, old guys, bad memories," Mike agreed, dashing after him.

Kate's lips compressed painfully on a snort, holding back guffaws. A thought occurred to her. "Hey, wait a minute. You guys know where Meg is? I need to talk to her." Needed to confront her—gently, of course—and ask her just what the dickens she thought this morning was about. Tell her to at least mention where she was going to her father before she snuck up to Li's room in the middle of the night, to make sure Li didn't mind the intrusion on her privacy and to quit yanking her and *Hank's* chains.

"Upstairs, cleaning out the shower."

"Thanks." Grinning she turned and headed for the house. If she couldn't straighten out the father without total distraction setting in, she'd go to the child. It was high time somebody quit walking on eggs and got a few things straight with Megan.

Bottle of glass cleaner in one hand, used paper towels in the other, Megan peered out the newly spotless octagonal window of the upstairs bathroom and watched Kate arrive.

Even if the windows hadn't been open and she hadn't over-heard Kate ask the little boys about her whereabouts, she'd been around long enough to recognize the look on her favorite mentor's face, to diagnose the purpose in her stride. Someone was in for what was known around the Anden household as a "chat."

Chats weren't necessarily *bad* things, but they were often a bit more revealing to the person on the receiving end than the chat-ee might prefer. In the eleven years she'd been hanging around with Li, Megan had been chatted with on more than one occasion. As uncomfortable as it might feel at the time, she didn't mind Kate's chats. Kate never chatted with anyone she didn't care about, rarely chatted without a reason and almost always expected and accepted back chat. She also always treated everybody the same, and unlike some of Megan's other friends' parents, and especially unlike Megan's own dad, neither Megan nor anyone else ever had to wonder where they stood with Kate. There was a certain comfort and security in that.

Still...

Quickly she gave the back of the toilet a final swipe, dumped the paper towels in the basket and put the glass cleaner under the sink. Now all she needed was someplace to hide. Because even if she hadn't heard Kate ask where she was, Megan knew with the dread of a guilty conscience that she was the one in for it. And security or no, it didn't mean she particularly *wanted* to be chatted with today. Particularly since she couldn't see where she'd really done anything to warrant one. And even if she had, she felt too mixed up inside to really want to discuss it now. Not until she figured out what exactly she'd done, why she'd done it and how to defend herself from it.

She'd hoped coming to live with Kate and Li and the llamas—sometimes especially the llamas, whose constant expression of stoicism and serenity, whose five-thousand-year connection with humans often made them appear wiser and more connected to people than their human partners could ever be—would just mag-ically make all this insanity running around inside her head come clear and go away. It scared her some that so far it wasn't, but it was early hours yet and she still hoped.

She was also still afraid.

Because, damn it, she couldn't even tell Li this, but it was really getting just so freaking hard some days to keep track of who she was.

Chapter 4

So she had a crush on Hank Mathison. After all these years of judging him...well, not one of God's greater creations, who woulda thunk it?

Not her, that was sure. She was way too old for this nonsense. She hadn't had a crush on a boy since...oh, probably Steve Heckerling in the tenth grade. And she'd gotten over that quick—crushed, yeah, but over it—the minute he'd told her to quit dreaming that the star of the track team would ever want to go out with a red-haired, bucktoothed, goody-two-shoes like her who wasn't going to put out.

Her braces had been off for six months at the time, her mouth not nearly as horsy as it had been. But the boys she'd gone to high school with were stupid about things like that. She'd called him a hormonal jerk who wasn't even strong enough to be in charge of his own mind. The insult had gone over his head and made her wonder how she could ever have been attracted to him in the first place. But the youthful heart made the eyes see what it wanted them to see: sensitivity, smarts and strength, where there wasn't any. Within the next year she'd felt the call to join the convent and that had been that for boys.

She hadn't missed feeling giddy and stupid and tongue-tied at all. Even if the mature part of her brain thought it *was* funny as all get out.

"*Phweet!* Hey-up! Come on, boys, granola time!"

Whistling and clapping, Kate leaned on a four-by-four fence post and called the studs and geldings in from the west pasture. Fanned out along the length of woven wire fencing designed to prevent stray dogs from bothering the herd rather than to keep the herd in, Ilya, Mike, Bele, Jamal and some of the 4-H-ers rattled Ziploc bags full of llama treats, adding encouragement. The three-legged rottweiler, Taz, ran up and down the fence line, slobbering and grinning. When the cloven footed got cookies, so did she. Part of her training, Ilya said.

Yeah, right. Kate rolled her eyes at the thought. Training, my left big toe. Spoiled-rotten dog.

It didn't take long for the llamas to respond. They enjoyed treat time. Humming and clacking they trotted over the rolling hills from their pasture, ears alert, noses twitching. Their leather-padded, two-toed feet made soft thuds on the bare earth as they approached.

Off to the north from the direction of the tree fields, came the rough roar of a tractor jouncing up a rutted track. Tai, Risto, Grisha and the 4-H tree team were on their way in.

Across the drive, Li, Megan and another group of 4-H-ers emerged from the catch yard—a pen small enough so the llamas couldn't run when you had to catch them for shearing, toenail trimming or other unwanted attention, but large enough so they could circle off their nervousness—near the females' corral and headed for the workshop. After an afternoon spent shearing the moms' bellies, sides and backs to ready them for the coming summer's heat, they were laden with bags full of llama, alpaca and vicuña wool. Tomorrow they'd shear the boys and begin to brush and card the fiber, cleaning it for spinning.

Hank strode behind them, carrying the sheep clippers and the granola-bribe bucket. Distance and the sun hid the expression on his tanned face, but from the way he walked Kate guessed he was not a happy camper. An afternoon spent listening to teenage and preteen girls could do that to any man, but particularly to a father. Kate would, no doubt, hear about it after dinner. They could trade insights and information just like real adults. And if he didn't volunteer the information, she'd ask—if she could keep herself from giggling like an eleven-year-old in his presence long enough to do so, that is.

Sheesh, what a horrible thing to contemplate. She didn't particularly remember wanting to be eleven when she was eleven. Twenty had seemed the perfect age to her then. Once she'd gotten there, twenty had been interesting, but now was better. Lots better. Mega, stupendously, infinitely better. It was also beside the point. Which being, that at least Hank had found his daughter today—and hopefully spoken with her—which was better than Kate had managed to do.

It was the first time in memory she'd suspected Megan of avoiding her. She'd have to quiz Li about that.

The first llama face hove into range, inquisitive nose thrust out to bump hers. Along the fence line llama necks stretched, noses reached for granola bags. 4-H-ers called to their favorites, offering goodies with one hand while they scratched hard, woolly necks with the other.

It was late afternoon after a hard working day. Time to feed the camelids, put the farm equipment to bed and send all non-Andens home to supper.

Except, of course, Kate allowed, for *him.*

Without invitation her gaze ran to Hank, who was emerging from the workshop. Dusty black jeans rode low on his hips, a stained gray T-shirt adorned with endangered rain-forest inhabitants clung to an irregular vee of sweat on his chest. Nice, very nice, one side of her brain murmured.

The other side wondered why sweat made him look even more appealing than clean had, then the two split into debate teams to analyze the issue. A free-for-all ensued over the topic of fairness—how unfair it was that men always seemed to come out looking better when they were filthy than women did—so Kate sighed and did the only thing she could think to do: told her brain to cut the comedy and concentrate on other things.

It would have been fine if her brain listened. But since she so rarely took her own advice, it didn't.

When he leaned into the fence next to her, she started, cheeks reddened. Either he didn't notice the blush or he ignored it. Point for him.

"They seem so serene," he said quietly.

"Mmm." Kate nodded. "They are, usually. Almost..." She

hesitated. People who didn't know llamas often misunderstood mention of the seemingly telepathic or sometimes spiritual connection between the animals and their humans. Hank looked at her, waiting. She shrugged. In for a penny and all that rot. "Almost mystical," she finished.

He rested his chin on a closed fist. "Mystical?" Curious, not disbelieving.

"It's hard to explain. Most of the time they just seem to...understand things that people don't." She pointed at a pure white male in the middle of the herd; head lifted, ears forward as if probing the air, he scanned the perimeter of the yard, obviously looking for something or someone in particular. "There. That's Harvey—I told you about him this morning."

"Llama therapy, the old woman at the nursing home." Hank nodded, grinning when Kate slanted him a sideways glance. "I heard. It only looked like I wasn't paying attention."

"Ah." She nodded wisely. "I see."

He snorted. "I bet."

She ignored him. "Anyway, as I attempted to tell you then, Harve...picks up on what people are feeling and...I don't know, *calms* them is the simplest way to put it. People in need gravitate to him, he finds them. He's particularly good with the kids we get out here. He's a...special friend of Meg's."

"He is." Flat and unemotional, tentative and...wistful.

Afraid to believe.

For a long moment Hank stared at her, then switched the intensity to the white llama leaning into his daughter's embrace. Was this where she came when she skipped their appointments with the department's psychologist? Had she instinctively sought and found her own treatment? Could he hope...no, he didn't even want to name the wish for fear of destroying it.

He'd never heard of llamas being used in this particular capacity, but he was familiar with the concept of pet therapy and its uses with Alzheimer's patients and the elderly, with chronic fatigue syndrome and psychiatric hospital patients, with dying children and adults. It had something to do, perhaps, with nonverbal communication, the psychic link between humans and animals and the will to live. Or, as with the Alzheimer's victims, psych patients and those with chronic fatigue, the will to remain within the moment. Maybe...

Naw. He swallowed, looked everywhere but at Megan and Harvey. He wouldn't think it. It was too easy to want to believe in what amounted to an experimental theory out of desperation. Sort of like believing in magic.

"So," he said with feigned lightness. "Is Harvey named after Jimmy Stewart's six-foot rabbit?"

Kate eyed him thoughtfully. Long experience with people who needed to doubt before they hoped made her scan his features in swift appraisal, let her see the almost masked fear, the desire to believe, the not quite hidden plea for time to digest, sort through. Empathy made it easy for her to give him what he sought.

"Very good, Mr. Mathison." Cheeky voice, exaggerated applause, she responded in turn to the flippancy of the question. "You're a classic-movie buff?"

"Hank. When I have a chance. You?"

"Kate." There, that took care of the Mr., Ms. nonsense. And about time, too. "I enjoy movies, period. Good, bad, classic, whatever, as long as it's escapism. We watched whatever we got hold of at the missions and in the camps. Funny how good even a bad movie seems after hours or weeks of trying to hold back other people's misery."

His expression was suddenly hooded and faraway. "I can imagine," he said quietly.

Kate studied him, drawn to something in his voice, behind his eyes—things he'd done because he had to, things he'd seen because of things he'd done. Almost an expectation of...judgment. "Can you?"

It was his turn to look at her. There was no presumption on her face or in her voice, only genuine interest, intense curiosity and...a quality of mercy he could almost touch. Odd. Mercy was hardly a commodity he equated with this day and age, with her, but there it was written in those iceberg-blue eyes. Not quite what he expected. But then, so little about her was. He nodded. "Yeah."

In the llama yard Harvey's ears pricked sideways, forward. The llama cast a glance toward Kate and Hank, then touched noses with the girl. She hugged him tighter, burying her face in the long wool. He stood quietly, allowing the invasion of his space without demur; after a moment he turned his head, his calm gaze settled once more on Hank, a speaking look. Uncomfortable as it made him, Hank stared back.

"What?" he asked Kate.

She shrugged. "He knows," she said simply.

"Knows what?"

"About you and Megan."

Hank turned sharply, but before the *"What?!"* could pass his lips, the first of the parent-collecting-kid vehicles pulled up behind the house and Kate was gone.

He turned back to the yard. Harvey stood a few feet from him, gaze calm and steady, studying him hard; the intelligence in the liquid brown eyes was palpable, undeniable.

Uneasy with the all too perceptive nonhuman scrutiny, Hank looked past the llama. Alone nearby, Megan waited, arms slack at her sides, watching them as if she hoped...what, he couldn't tell. Not sure what was expected, Hank looked to one, then the other. The whole thing felt absurd, but he'd witnessed too many unexplainable things—both bad and good—in his life to simply dismiss this one. Whatever this one was.

A sensation shuddered through him: warmth, comfort, compassion, understanding. A thought that wasn't his entered his mind unbidden: *Don't worry, Hank, we'll work it out. She wants to figure it out.*

Startled, he peered at Harvey; the llama blinked at him. Then its long throat made a regurgitating movement and Harvey turned away and resumed chewing his cud. Swallowing uncertainty, Hank let his gaze slide back to his daughter. For the first time in he didn't remember when, there naked on her face, Megan's vulnerabilities showed.

Evening crept in on shadowed feet, heavy with a symphony of tree frogs and crickets, the whisper of night birds taking wing. Light that would have seemed warm and inviting on a winter's eve showed through sheer curtains, an unreal electric yellow-pink that seemed almost garish against the soft pink-blue-violet shades of approaching night.

Voices hovered behind the light, youthful laughter stroked the shadows, mingled with the clatter of pans in the kitchen sink, the harsh, watery *shurr* of the elderly dishwasher. Normal life, alive and well in the countryside of mid-Michigan.

Caught by the instant, Hank leaned against the lumpy fieldstone side wall of Stone House, listening, half wishing this life belonged to him. That it *didn't* was and always had been his choice, he knew. To join the DEA, to be a part of some alternate reality was a decision he'd made long ago—Gen and Megan notwithstanding. But even they had never made him quite want to be part of *this*, the softness of daily moments, the slow and steady progress of a life that didn't chronically exist on the underbelly of violent death.

He understood with regret that even now a part of him resented being here, blamed Gen for leaving him here, forced to deal with day-to-day realities instead of living on extremes the way he'd done working the streets or undercover. Understood that another piece of his dissatisfaction lay in the fact that what he and Megan did could hardly be called *living* by any definition—often seemed hardly more than existing—was, in its own way, as extreme as any life he'd lived undercover, but without the adrenaline rush.

Without the momentary euphoria of a case closed, a job accomplished.

Living on the constant edge of a rush was easier, after a fashion, than living daily life. It was simpler—more black-and-white. You trusted yourself, your control of a situation, or that was all she wrote. You kept your eyes open, your ears sharp and slept ready for flight or whatever else might overtake you at a moment's notice.

Here was more complicated, less distinct, grayer, harder to control. Here there wasn't just himself to face, or be concerned about; here was Megan. He still trusted himself, his decisions, but too often that wasn't enough; *she* didn't trust him, his decisions; she made her own. And too much of the time they turned out bad.

For both of them.

He shut his eyes and again felt the strange weight of the llama's gaze on him, the bulk of Megan's unvoiced questions and vulnerabilities, the physical presence of compassion that flowed from Kate. The prayer inside his head remained the same as always: *Bless my daughter, Megan Genevieve, take care of her. Keep her safe, well, healthy, alive, breathing and happy. Help me to understand...*

"Dad. Hey, Dad, you out here?"

Hank started, as surprised by what she'd called him as he was by being hailed at all. *Whoopee!* zinged through his starved parent system. *Dad,* she'd called him Dad. Without sarcasm or ridicule, simply matter-of-fact, kid to parent, his name. It was ridiculous to revel so in the sound of a three-letter word.

He reveled all the same. Take what you can get, when you can get it, and enjoy it, he told himself. Rule number one for dealing with teenagers. "Here, Meg."

Megan's hair swung loose over her shoulder when she leaned over the side of the front porch to see him. "I'm going to the movies with Li and Risto, okay? We won't be late."

"That was a question?" Wary surprise and unintentional irony hovered in his voice. "You're asking me?"

Something fleeting flashed across her face: anger, rebellion, resentment, animosity...pieces of the Megan who'd lived with him the past five years. Reminders that however much her personality seemed to have flip-flopped since they'd arrived at the Andens', the problems that had brought them here were far from gone. Then her features smoothed and she was the Megan of this morning once again: disgusted teenager with the rolled-eye, let's-humor-the-poor-benighted-parent attitude.

"*Tcht,* Da-ad." Translation: say "fine" and don't embarrass me. "Okay?"

"Who's driving?" She let him parent her so infrequently he was almost out of practice. He had to keep his hand in while he could.

"Tai's gonna drop us off on his way to pick up his girlfriend and take Grisha and Ilya to the Comic Pit and the little guys for ice cream—"

"Hey, who you callin' little, shorty?" Mike asked, towering above her on the porch wall.

Megan didn't blink. "And he'll pick us up when the movie's over. Okay?" She grabbed Mike's legs and hoisted him down. "I'm callin' you little, wise guy, now get off there before you kill yourself." Then she turned back to her father, the epitome of an impatient, normal, well-adjusted kid living a normal, well-adjusted life. "Okay? Dad?"

"Okay."

"Thanks, Dad." She blew him a kiss. "See ya."

A kiss? A *kiss?* He hadn't gotten one of those from her, blown or otherwise, in longer than he wanted to recall. "Don't be late," he said, for the sake of saying something.

Again there was a flash of hostility quickly covered, another lurking reminder of her apparent ability to dissemble at will. But all she said was "Da-ad," in two syllables drawn out through tight teeth, annoyed. Then she was flying off the porch with the rest of the kids, piling into the van, and they were gone in a sputter of gravel and dust.

Thoughtful and more than a little unnerved by his daughter's mercurial moods, Hank jammed his hands in the pockets of his jeans and watched them go. Was this Megan a fluke, a mirage, or had he done something almost right for a change? Maybe? Possibly? Naw, probably didn't have anything to do with him. Right? Jeez, what was wrong with a guy holding out hope?

What was wrong with a guy pleading to see only the best for his child?

The aluminum screen door onto the porch whined open, soughed shut. Kate stepped onto the porch.

"Is it safe?" she asked warily. "Are they gone?"

"Is it *safe?*" Eyebrows cocked in mock astonishment, Hank stepped around the edge of the porch and looked up at her, the fuzzy apricot-gold halo of hair that framed her face caped out around her shoulders and arms. Sensation, recognition churned in his belly; he tamped it down. *Not the time, not the place, not the woman,* echoed hollowly through the halls of his psyche like some unfriendly specter on a rampage. He did his best to listen. "You, oh great queen of all mothers, slayer of dragons, font of all wisdom, are asking me, the devil dad from hell, if it's safe? As opposed to what?"

"Don't be sarcastic," Kate advised him. "I deal with sarcasm all day. It doesn't impress me and I'm too tired for it tonight."

"Sorry." Grinning, Hank mounted the steps to slouch against a support pillar. *Stupid to go closer,* his conscience whispered when scent coiled in his nostrils, slunk into the back of his throat; salt, musk and woman. *She'll bewitch you. Better to stay clear.* "You're the one with the endless patience, a gazillion kids and all the answers. I couldn't resist."

"Try," Kate suggested. "And it's strictly blind luck, you know." She slumped onto the porch swing on a sigh and pulled her feet up, trying to ignore the unfamiliar warmth that constricted her chest, curled into her toes when he smiled. "Man, that feels good. You know, I love that bunch of hooligans and I wouldn't trade them for anything, but they're exhausting and it's a relief to have them *gone* sometimes."

"You wouldn't say that if they were gone all the time." A statement flat and quiet, full of the conviction of experience.

"Nope." She shook her head, watching him while her pulse fizzed and jigged restlessly in her veins. Seemed she'd spent a lot of time watching him today. But what else did you do with an untamed, uncaged, exciting but potentially dangerous beast with which you were not familiar? She'd watched the communist soldiers who came through the refugee camps with a similar degree of wariness. 'Course, the only tattoo that had beaten in her chest when she'd seen *them* was fear, not this...nervy anticipation and...*crush*. "You're probably right. But they're not gone all the time, so I can say it and mean it."

"Lucky you."

She nodded complacently, choosing sincerity over irony. "You betcha."

Disbelieving laughter chuckled through him. "Jeez Louise, woman, you'd be easy to hate."

"Mmm." Kate stretched her neck and settled more comfortably into the swing, observing him. Enjoying the view. No harm in looking, right? "So I hear."

Hank grinned, then unslouched to move over and sit on the wall closer to the swing. *Dumb move,* his tightening gut assured him. *Dumb, dumber, dumbest.* "What, you mean I'm not the only parent who has a problem with you?"

She snorted. "Hardly. Most parents find out I'm an ex-nun, figure I must be perfect and use me as a measuring stick to decide what they will or won't let their kids do—"

"You mean like, 'Is Li's mother letting her go?'"

Kate nodded and finished the thought. "That or they remember the nuns they had in school and imagine me ten times worse."

Hank's turn to snort. "Yeah, I know that one. The neighborhood moms used to pull some of that with Gen, too. It's easier to point at someone else than have convictions of your own."

"What do they do with you?" she asked, idly curious.

"The single ones throw themselves at me, the married ones

bake macaroni-and-cheese and flirt." He heaved a regretful sigh. "Not one of them thinks of me as a role model."

Kate chuckled. "Poor baby."

"Yeah, right." He propped a foot on the wall and draped an arm over his raised knee. "So, what about the parents who don't think you're perfect?"

"They do like you," she said, squiggling her back to scratch it on the swing. "Call me *Ms.* Goody-Two-Shoes and take me in avid dislike."

Laughter shouted out of Hank, long and delighted, cleansing. "So," he said when he could speak, "I'm in good company, then."

Kate made a rude noise. "If you want to call it that."

"I do," Hank assured her, chuckling. "It happens so seldom."

"I'll bet."

"Ah-ah-ah. Don't be that way. Doesn't sound like Saint Mom to me."

"That's Ms. Goody-Two-Shoes to you."

"And that makes me who?" He grinned, his teeth a snowy gleam in the half-light, all wolfish charm. "The filthy beast?"

"If you like," Kate agreed equably, amazingly coherent for all that her pinging pulse kept shouting, *He's better looking than Cary Grant, hugely better, best!* "But I never said it. *Thought* it a thousand and a half times—"

"But never said it," Hank finished for her. "Right."

"You asked."

"My mistake." He settled back against the roof support beside him. "You ever see that movie?"

"The one with goody-two-shoes and the filthy beast?"

"*Father Goose,* yeah."

"Maybe fifteen, eighteen times." Kate dangled a leg off the swing and shoved her foot against the floor to set it rocking. "I think between that, *Life with Father, Cheaper by the Dozen, The Sound of Music, With Six You Get Egg Roll, Yours, Mine and Ours,* and all the rest of that insane-parents, fifty-zillion-kids genre I was pretty much brainwashed into this kid thing from the start. Looked like fun, you know?"

Hank studied her silhouette in the yard light, suddenly curious about her beyond the unwelcome call of his libido. "It's not?"

"Mmm, a lot of the time, sure. It's also nerve-racking, painful and never boring, and Lord—'' she sat up, sounding rueful ''—what I wouldn't give for a little boring sometimes.''

''Unh-huh, and I'll bet you were dragged into this nonboring life kicking and screaming.''

''No.'' She shook her head. ''I left the convent kicking and screaming—figuratively, that is. My choice, their suggestion—mutual decision—but it scared the bejeebers out of me. If I wasn't a nun, who was I? What was I going to do? All that rot. I mean, I could still be a missionary, work the food trains, volunteer with the International Red Cross, but that didn't answer the big question I thought I had the answer to when I took my vows. When I found Tai—or he found me—in that refugee camp it was like—'' Her hands popped wide in enthusiastic demonstration. *''Wow! Light bulb! Major revelation!* I didn't have a husband, so going forward wasn't a piece of cake, but the nun thing on my résumé has its uses. We didn't look back.''

''Yeah.'' Hank nodded, understanding. ''That's the way I felt when I first joined drug enforcement. Like a big sponge to be used to mop up the bad guys, make the streets clean for kids like Meg.''

''But it's not the way you feel now.'' It was a statement, not a question.

''No,'' he answered, an ounce of bitterness surrounded by contempt. ''It's the sort of work that no matter which side of the desk you're on, it uses you up. No matter how many battles you win, the war goes on. If you're not battling bad guys, you're fighting your own higher-ups to let you get at the bad guys. I moved up in the ranks hoping to change some of that, but it makes no difference. Now I'm a bureaucrat. That might be up some guys' alleys, but it's not up mine. At least,'' he amended wryly, appalled by his own vehemence, ''not with this attitude.''

''I'm glad you said that.'' Kate laughed gently. ''Saves me from having to point it out.''

''Gee thanks. I knew if nothing else, I could count on you to be tactless about my early mid-life crisis.''

She shrugged. ''Hey, what are ex-nuns for, if not a little verbal knuckle wrapping now and then?''

Hank chuckled, amusement edged in irony. ''I'll keep that in mind.''

They sat quietly for a bit, digesting evening songs and revelations, companionable.

Or as companionable as the intermittent flickerings of adult hungers allowed.

Hank recognized the difference immediately. Looking at her—the overly lush curves and summer hair, the wide open, innocent without innocence features; smelling her, remembering the touch of her hand in his brought the burn, without question. But it was no longer a burn without apparent reason, without liking. It was more. Harder, hotter, more insistent. More disturbing. More comfortable—God, when had it gotten comfortable to be with her?

More dangerous.

He couldn't get distracted from the reason he was here: Megan and only Megan.

Megan.

"She looked pretty tonight, didn't she?" he asked suddenly, wistful.

Kate nodded, without having to ask to whom he referred. "Megan's a beautiful girl, Hank." She slid down the swing, close to where he sat on the wall, and touched his jeaned ankle, then repeated with conviction, "Beautiful."

He stared at the spot where he could feel Kate's fingers on his leg, willing himself not to feel the spread of heat upward. An edge of tension ran down his spine. Undercover experience had taught him to ignore a potential problem at his own risk; to avoid the temptation to create one at all costs. If she kept touching him, they would have a problem of major proportions—instead of one that was just bigger than a bread box. He didn't move. "I wish she wasn't so..." He huffed a breath and hesitated, choosing his words. "So damned confused. So blasted confusing."

"Yes." She was silent a moment, then. "Did you talk with her about this morning?"

"No." He shook his head, shifting erect on the wall, sliding his ankle out from underneath her hand. Enough already. "She kept someone or something between us all day. I didn't have a chance."

"Me, either." Kate rose and moved to stand at the wall beside him, leaning into the top rail. Closer to him than she'd intended. Closer than she had a feeling she should be, than it was safe to be. But she didn't back up. Couldn't. It was a rule: go forward,

Always. No matter what. "She's avoiding me, too. She's never done that before."

Hank released the breath he'd held without realizing it. It seemed childish and petty to be glad, but he was. It meant he wasn't the only one. It meant he wasn't alone, as he often felt.

It meant she was too damn close.

He could feel her warmth adding to the heat of his own skin—near enough to touch, but far enough away so he shouldn't feel anything from her at all. Or as if he wanted to feel more.

He already felt too much.

It was a little like waiting to close a long prepared sting, or loitering around until the other shoe—one that was maybe a size ninety—dropped. Adrenaline in his veins, fever in his blood. Exciting, stimulating, challenging. Could he or couldn't he get out of the way in time? Did he want to? How close could he get to that icy fire before getting burned? How close did he want to get?

Real close, his pulse told him.

Soon.

He swallowed, tasting desire on the back of his tongue. Whoa, he thought. Not acceptable, not appropriate. Not here, now or ever.

But he wanted. Bad.

God help him.

He slid off the wall onto the porch, intending to put distance between them; decreasing it instead.

"Hank?"

A question he couldn't answer, so he didn't try, simply slipped a hand into the heavy cape of her hair and let it wash through his fingers. She backed away. He pursued her; he couldn't stop himself.

"Hank...please. I don't understand."

As though he did.

Her eyes were silver-white pools in the fading dusk and yellow glow of the yard light. Wary, not quite afraid. She looked at him the way she might if caught in a corner, as though he were, somehow, either predator or contagion. As though it would not be wise to turn her back even to run.

He viewed her as he might either human prey or something toxic: carefully, from all angles, with every sense open to danger. Knowing he was the taller, heavier, stronger, but that small size wouldn't necessarily make her less lethal. He backed her into a corner of the porch, trapped her between the pillar and his body. Surrounded her with his arms, hands cramped around the pillar to either side of her head.

"Kate."

Desire roughened her name in a way she'd never heard it, never imagined hearing it. Mesmerizing. The sound sent tongues of flame licking down her spine; heat made her shiver without understanding, wanting to hear him call her that way again. Instinct made her afraid of what she wanted.

"Please, Hank, I—"

He heard nothing but his name, the plea that lay underneath fear, the seductive whisper of invitation. His head lowered the nine inches separating his mouth from hers. "Kate..."

She made a soft sound of uncertainty, "No, I—" but the hand she placed on his chest to hold him away betrayed her, drew him closer. Before she could press her lips shut against him, he took her mouth.

Chapter 5

Soft.

Her mind registered the texture of his mouth with surprise. So very soft.

So very exotic.

It had been twenty years since the last boy kissed her. He'd been a friend, the kiss a shared moment sitting in the dark on theater steps waiting for the curtain to rise on the last play of their high-school career, more goodbye than hello. Nice, soft, yes.

Nothing like this.

For all its gentleness there was demand in Hank's kiss, a hunger and passion that claimed her response before she was aware of giving it. Before she was aware of her own need to give it and take his.

Drugging.

Breathless murmurs, the quiet whimper of a plea without words. Amazement slid through her when she felt the sounds coming from her own throat.

Her fingers were on his chest, kneading his chambray shirt, trying to bring him closer. Astonishment and fire laced through her when the length of his body accepted her invitation, and pressed hers hard into the pillar. Consternation made her gasp and stiffen when his hands moved to her face, thumbs pressed her jaw, urging her mouth wider; when his tongue caressed her lips, seduced its way by them to brush over the sharpness of her teeth, made an intoxicating sweep of her mouth. She didn't know how to kiss like this; that old friend on the theater steps had never taught her. Hank would find her lacking and stop and she didn't want him to and—

But he didn't. He anchored a fist in her hair, slid his other hand down her back, over her rump and deepened the kiss, coaxing her tongue to play. She melted and came to him because she couldn't resist him. Because she didn't want to.

Her hands, uncertain what to do with themselves, clung to his waist, slipped restlessly up his sides and chest, found his face and opened wide to touch him, to hold him.

So sweet.

She tasted like nothing he'd experienced before, like nothing he'd known existed. Innocence without naïveté. Passion without the darkness he was used to having accompany it. Power without corruption. Tender, hot, luscious, welcome...welcoming.

Rare.

He filled his hands with her softness, feasted on her rarity, gorged on her welcome. Shivered when her hands claimed his face, drew him into her. Went willingly where he knew he would drown.

Craven. Depraved.

He moved his tongue from her mouth to her jaw, her throat, her ear, back to her mouth. This was not how a man kissed a woman the first time; in some rational part of himself he knew the beast in him had crossed a line, but he couldn't care. Didn't want to. Wanted only to go on tasting and sampling until he'd fed on all of her, licked and suckled her head-to-toe and back again until she was boneless. Until he could make her part of him.

Like Gen, for all her loving him, had never been.

Shock bit him; panic, pain and horror—like ice water and acid fire in one—shriveled all his cravenness and passion in the stillness of a missed heartbeat. What was he doing, where was he going?

God, what had he done.

"No."

Hands clamped around her upper arms, he levered himself

away from Kate. Shuddered and caught her hands, backing out of reach when she moaned and would have drawn him back. He wanted to go back.

He wanted to go back into her arms and her kiss and more. More...

He shut his eyes and breathed great gulps of air while his lungs burned, his gut twisted and his body called him a dictionary full of unprintable names.

Kate's fingers curled in his, uncertain. "Hank?" Soft and bewildered. A plea to understand.

"No, Kate. God, don't." He let go of her and wheeled violently away, shoved his hands through his hair, bunched them into fists and jammed them into his back pockets where they couldn't get loose and reach for her again, do to her all the things he couldn't let them do. "I didn't want this. I *don't* want this. We can't do this, what are we doing?"

"I don't know." She was shaky and disoriented. Smoothing her hair behind her ears, she tried to regain order. "You kissed me first, so you tell me."

"You kissed me back."

"Yeah." She nodded, disbelieving. "I did." She touched her swollen mouth uneasily, made an inadequate gesture. It had never occurred to her to think she would ever kiss a man—*could* ever kiss a man, any man, but especially *this* man—like that. Feel compassion for him, yes, but this... "I guess...I don't know, maybe you took me by surprise." An understatement, if ever she'd made one. She'd taken herself without warning, too.

"I took you—? What...you mean you'd respond like that to anyone who surprised you that way?"

Kate swallowed. "I don't know," she told him truthfully. "You're the first person who's ever ambushed me successfully. I don't know how I'd respond to somebody else. If I would."

"You don't know how you'd...because nobody's ever...?" Incredulous, Hank rubbed a hand across his face and stared at her. Who the hell was she, anyway?

When it came right down to it, he knew nothing about Kate Anden except that she had a lot of kids and had once been a nun, yet somehow by default he'd trusted his daughter in her keeping for years. Assumption—as they'd already discussed—stated that because she'd been a nun, then a lay missionary, she must be the perfect saintly person, the holy, wholesome influence so many people—parents besides himself—thought her. Reality, as so often happened, was something else entirely. No matter how real the tapestry of kindness and generosity, the illusion of perfection that Megan and others verbally wove around Kate was merely that, illusion.

The real Kate, the woman behind that single, scorching kiss, was a thief who could steal him blind, a heart-and-soul looter with the potential to leave him wanting her to swipe him deaf and mute as well. Succumbing to the temptation of her lavish body, the compassion with which she treated his daughter would do neither him nor Megan any good. Could, instinct told him, damage his relationship with his daughter beyond repair—especially if things between him and Kate didn't go well.

Or went so well that the only thing he'd want to do for the rest of the summer was jump Kate Anden's bones. Went so well he wound up ignoring Megan, the way she'd accused him and Gen of forgetting her when they got wrapped up in each other every time he came home after an extended absence. And as drum tight as he felt right now, not to mention how many years he'd been celibate, forgetting why he was here in favor of a hot summer affair was a frightening possibility.

"Look," he told Kate evenly, emphatically, "This can't happen, I'm not here for this."

Something in his tone made Kate still and straighten. "Not here for *what?*" she asked carefully.

"This." He made a harsh gesture indicating the two of them. "Here. Now. A minute ago. Things are complicated enough without…" He hesitated.

"Without what, Hank?" She felt wooden, numb. Betrayed by a body she thought she'd known well—hers. It didn't matter. She'd functioned just fine feeling like a stick of wood in the refugee camp on the border between Burma and Thailand where she'd found Li, betrayed there by a calling she'd thought her own. She'd reevaluated and rebuilt who she was then; if necessary she would do the same now. "Us kissing?"

"Without us going where that particular kiss would have gone in another three minutes."

"I live with teenagers and eight-year-olds, Hank." She held control in a tight fist. Well, at least sort of. She lifted her chin, pretended he was the Burmese colonel who'd tried to intimidate her out of his way so he could get at a student protester, and kept her voice level. "We don't do subtlety here. There's too much opportunity for misunderstanding when things aren't spelled out."

Jaw taut, he stared at her. She knew nothing about him, but because he was Megan's father she'd offered him her guesthouse and in a backhanded way entrusted him with her children's lives. He had to make her understand—as bluntly as possible—that although he was hardly the beast his daughter's exaggerations had made him out to be, it still wouldn't be wise to get comfortable with him. The way he felt right now, he could easily turn into the wolf who'd destroy them all.

"Sex, Kate," he said, harshly, crudely. "I'm not here to get my rocks off with you."

She didn't flinch. Teenage foster kids often arrived bearing trunks full of emotional baggage and used their verbal skills to shock and rock, to keep her a good stiff arm's length away. She'd heard worse. None of it hurt like this, of course, but he didn't need to see that. "I didn't think you were," she told him calmly. "I know you're here because of Megan and only Megan. I know I agreed to rent the guesthouse to you because of Megan alone. I know we've never been particularly fond of each other. I'm not sure I understand why it happened, but that kiss had to be a momentary aberration. It'll never happen again."

Hank snorted. "Don't try to kid yourself or me about that, Kate," he said tersely. "You looked at me moon eyed most of the day and my shorts have been too tight thinkin' about you since we shook hands over the rental agreement, so don't pretend 'it'll never' because you say so. Even Mike and Bele could tell you different."

"Could they." Flat and careful, more challenge than question. A muscle ticked in her cheek.

"You bet." Hank nodded. "And if they couldn't, the older kids sure as hell can."

She eyed him oddly in the half-light, flabbergasted. Of all the arrogant, conceited, I-am-God's-gift baloney she'd ever heard, this had to be the biggest crock.

"Let me get this straight." She squared herself to him, arms akimbo, foot tapping. *Be afraid,* the stance warned him, *be very afraid.* "Because I've developed some sort of high-school crush on you and you're wearing too tight skivvies and we shared one boffo kiss, you're telling me I should run screaming any time you get within six feet of me unchaperoned because if I don't our hormones will turn into rampaging elephants we can't control, even though you think I'm a goody-two-shoes and I've often considered you a pain-in-the-butt sonofagun?"

Hank swallowed an unwilling grin. Put like that, his assessment of the situation did sound a smidgen melodramatic. Still... He shrugged and let the excruciating throb behind his zipper be his guide. "If the situation arises, it won't matter what we think of each other, Kate," he assured her quietly. "Moon eyes and tight shorts are a lethal combination any time, but right now...you need to know—I have to tell you—that kiss didn't do anything for me except make keeping my pants zipped around you a lot more painful."

Her lungs tightened, her heart pounded high in her throat. She couldn't catch her breath. "It does?"

"Yeah."

Something unidentifiable jittered up her spine. Nervousness, maybe excitement, probably fear...and something else. "Really? You've, um, been thinking about *me?*" She'd misheard him. Her ears were full of wax. That had to be it. She probably ought to make an appointment with Dr. Moody to get 'em washed out. Until then, maybe if she rephrased her original question she'd understand the answer better. "You lust after *me?*"

"Not by choice," he said ruefully, running his hands through his hair and wishing she'd shut up and quit doing whatever she was doing, which instead of relieving the itch in his pants, was steadily making it worse, "but yeah. I lust after you. You find that so hard to believe?"

"Yes...no...it's just, um...it's never, ah...*Me?*" she repeated, more to herself than him. She looked at him. "Are you *sure?*"

"Oh, absolutely." Hank nodded, amused by her astonishment in spite of the tension coiled inside him. You'd think she'd never heard it before. And the places she'd been, nun or not, body like hers, she had to have heard it plenty. Of course, maybe that was the problem. She'd heard it too often, under questionable circumstances with her hair tucked into a wimple. Maybe she'd never had to believe it in quite the same way before. "I'm sure. And I'm getting more sure by the minute."

"Oh," Kate murmured. Then, flustered again, she realized what he'd actually said. *"Oh!"* She viewed him wide-eyed and swallowed. "Well, then." She swallowed again and jammed a hand in a pocket, came out with something she used to whisk her hair back and tie it out of the way, the nun disappearing into her cowl. She took a deep breath, blew it out and repeated briskly, "Well, then. I guess we've spent enough time together for one day, then, haven't we?"

"Yeah," Hank agreed dryly, "I'd say we have."

"Oh. Okay." She edged a few steps toward the door. "I guess all that's left, then, is to say good-night."

"Mmm."

"Well, then." She nodded at him, then opened the door. "Good-night, Mr. Mathison."

"Good-night, Kate."

For a moment they stared at each other through the screen—Kate wary, Hank hungry—then she scooted into the interior of the hallway, out of the light, and Hank was alone with the fireflies and the unquiet knowledge that neither he nor Kate was as tame as they wanted the world to believe.

Nor as tame as they'd believed themselves.

With a grimace and a sigh he descended the porch steps. Such a lot to have learned in a day, and gee, wouldn't you know, the summer's dance had barely begun.

Chapter 6

July

Time passed, dragging one moment, like lightning the next.

Minutes, hours, days winked by, painful on two fronts: the one where Megan continued to do her best to be where Hank wasn't; and the one where he found it next to impossible to avoid Kate.

He didn't want to avoid her.

Being near her was torture.

She was a taste on the back of his tongue he couldn't get rid of, a drum in his veins, a curse calling to the beast within him the way wolves were drawn to howl at the moon. Within the civilized veneer he wore to make pretense look like reality at the office, he could almost feel himself unraveling.

There was infinitely more to her than he'd ever wanted to imagine.

She was wry, dry and sarcastic, funny, human and vulnerable. Like him she recognized and abhorred—and too often tried to ignore—her weaknesses, did not deny but reveled joyously in her strengths.

Something about her fed the part of him that used to get high on drug raids, fueled the adrenaline junkie in him: an element of danger, an undercurrent of risk, a genuine quality of mercy—a serenity and an innocence that underlay the knowing-but-refusing-to-be-cynical exterior; a threat and a promise of passion unexplored and therefore untapped, which beckoned even as it warned him away.

Unfortunately, he'd never been able to walk away from a puzzle until he solved it.

Living on a working tree farm and llama ranch meant, of course, exactly that: working. Dawn to dusk. What time the trees, garden, workshop and quadrupeds didn't require, the kids did.

They had music lessons, ball games, part-time jobs and early morning twice-weekly trips in to the local farmers' market to supplement their college funds. They had 4-H club, which meant local, county, then—with luck—the state-fair competitions to prepare projects for, parades to be in and costumes to create. They had dental appointments and doctors' appointments and prosthetist's appointments. Fortunately besides Kate, Tai, Hank and car pools, Li and Megan both drove—and did so willingly.

Before the day ended, Kate and Tai had office work to attend to: records to keep, wholesale tree buyers to line up for fall, calls to return and would-be llama owners to talk with. A city boy, despite his many treks to and through the jungles of drug-trafficking countries, the amount of work to be done between sunrise and sunset staggered Hank. And Megan's eagerness to participate in any and all aspects of Stone House's enterprises positively floored him.

For himself, he liked feeling physically bushed at the end of the day, liked the sense of accomplishment, the fact that he could literally see what progress the farm made day-to-day. Liked the grit under his fingernails and the appetite being outside gave him. And he got a kick out of seeing Megan, and sometimes Li, sometimes Bele and Mike, at least once or twice a day when they loaded lunch or a mid-afternoon snack onto a couple of the llamas and packed it out to the tree fields. Loved seeing so much less of the angry side of Megan, glimpsing so much more of the beautiful child she'd been at five—even though she continued to go out of her way to avoid him. He even enjoyed the calluses forming on his hands and the daily muscle aches of physical labor, because stripping down and showering it all away at the end of the day felt like heaven.

Liked very much not having to deal with kiss-ass office politics, agency jurisdictions, cowboy special agents and the constant barrage of walking-a-tightrope paranoia.

Instead of the daily office routine, the work he did varied by the day; when one job finished, the next began. One day he and Risto restrung electric fencing, the next he was pruning and shearing trees or whacking weeds or learning from Grisha how to use a hand lens to check Christmas tree needles for blight and insect infestation or getting Megan to—grudgingly—teach him to handle llamas. Spare time he spent in the woodshop reacquainting himself with his carpentry skills or sorting out the kids: getting Bele and Ilya to teach him to carve; talking insects and fungus with Grisha-the-budding-naturalist; learning how to train dogs from Mike; clandestinely salting the archaeological dig with Tai; learning that Ilya's friend Jamal spent almost as much time running away to Stone House as Megan used to; and keeping an eye on Risto.

He couldn't name why or how he knew—call it cop's instinct—but he knew something wasn't entirely right with the youth. There seemed to be something between the Andens' exchange student and Megan, an undercurrent of furtiveness and secrets known and kept—unwillingly. But exactly which of them kept whose secrets he couldn't tell. So he did what he'd learned at Quantico and managed, from experience, to be good at: he watched.

He also worried.

But none of what he did to occupy him elsewhere kept him from dreaming about and wanting Kate.

Tough age, he decided wryly. Both his and Megan's.

He knew without doubt that if he were simply here to play a role, was merely here to be Special Agent Mathison undercover, dealing with the escalating complexities of the situation would be easier. The man he became undercover was a straightforward two-dimensional individual who lived by simple rules.

Don't trust anyone; don't break cover for any reason.

You've only got yourself in there, so look out for number one.

Don't get close; don't get sentimental. Use people, but don't make friends.

Never consider the other guy; especially when he's probably the bad guy.

Tuxedo rules, he thought of them; basic black-and-white, custom designed to keep him sane and intact, return him home with the fewest scars possible when the job was done.

But this was not his job, this was his life, his daughter's life; no set of tuxedo rules, however frilled the shirt or fancy the studs, had ever been designed to guide him through that. And the hungrier being near Kate made him, the harder it was to concentrate on finding the path that would lead him to Megan.

Not that his losing sight of the path could ever really be Kate's fault—no matter how badly he might like to make her the scapegoat.

He thought of the picture of him and Megan in his wallet. Taken early the previous fall at a department barbecue, it showed him with his arm around his daughter's shoulders while she laughed at something off camera, her arm linked about his waist. Funny how much a liar a camera could be, how nothing ever looked wrong in snapshots from company picnics, but only seemed to go wrong when the camera was turned away.

No, *he* was the one who'd lost sight of the best ways to reach Megan. The simple ways that had brought them together easily when she was a child and he'd return from assignments had long ceased to apply: a quick hug and a toss in the air; a special because-you-had-to-stay-home-while-I-was-gone gift and a tickle contest; an hour or two spent examining and identifying the bugs on the sidewalk and in the sandbox that Mommy was too squeamish to look at. It was enough, Gen used to tell them both flatly, that she no longer killed spiders in the house because Megan had begged her not to after they'd read *Charlotte's Web*.

He remembered that family "discussion" with particular fondness. Megan had giggled over Gen's arachnid pronouncement and shot her father a conspiratorial glance; Hank had winked at her and congratulated Gen on her forbearance, since having spiders in the house was not only good luck but controlled the presence of less desirable insects as well and was, thereby, a boon to their environment. Then he and Megan had gone off and laughed themselves silly over "Mommy's little insect problem."

But Megan had been five then, Gen **was** still alive and "Father

Magic'' was a kiss that could equally mend a scraped knee or a broken heart.

By the time she was eight the hug, the gift and the tickling were still in, but the toss in the air was out and the insect hour had become a couple of hours spent at the roller rink, the batting cage or taking her and her friends to the movies or shopping at the mall while Hank felt guilty about leaving Gen to handle most of the things that required parent participation at school or about not being able to volunteer to coach Megan's T-ball team or even to make most of her gymnastics meets.

By the time she hit ten the gift was taken for granted, the hug was accepted if she had time, tickling was a Dad-I'm-not-in-the-mood thing and the one-on-one father-daughter moments were getting hard to come by. Friends and phone calls took precedence; school and extracurricular activities had increased. When he had time for her, her time for him was gone.

By the time Gen died he and Megan were nearly strangers, and lost time was a commodity Hank wished he'd invested in when the moments had been available and the price had been closer to his grasp. He missed her company, missed her innocence and cursed himself for the cynicism too often printed on a face that mirrored his—except that Megan had her mother's eyes. In all the years he'd known her, never once had he seen cynicism in Gen's eyes.

No, stubborn, constant optimism and never accepting *no* for an answer had been Gen's forte. It was also the sword by which she'd died.

He missed Gen and Megan most, avoided Kate most, in the evenings when his resistance was down and his druthers were closest to the surface.

"Morning, boys."

Kate's cheerful voice carried clearly through the open kitchen windows and Hank made a wry face. Kate, on the other hand, refused to avoid anything at all, regardless of what it was. If she had a problem she could identify—or one she couldn't, for that matter—she didn't hesitate to confront it. None of this if-we-ignore-it-it'll-go-away nonsense for her, no, sir. She went at a problem head on, pedal to the metal. He didn't think he'd ever met anyone as willing to face down what bothered her as Kate Anden. And since he was what currently bothered her...

"Appreciate the offer, but I've been handling this sort of thing by myself for a lot of years. Besides, it's not safe for you to be around me, remember," she'd told him yesterday when he'd come up on her in the middle of the driveway struggling to remove a stripped fitting from the mower and stopped to help. *"You get too close and I might lose my head because you just make me too crazy inside, Mr. Mathison. It's hard to think around you."*

The day before it had been something else in a long line of what he could only think of as confrontational flirting. Whatever she said, it was always exasperated—with herself more than him, she'd confessed two days ago—always honest and most often at her own expense rather than his. Unfortunately, instead of making her less desirable, her distracted comments only made her more so. There was nothing more attractive to a man—or at least nothing more enticing to *him*—than a woman with a sense of humor, who tartly told him to go away every time she saw him, because "you twiddle my buttons just by looking at me." He'd gone away wondering what she'd do if he reminded her it wasn't his buttons she twiddled with her glance.

He knew it was playing with fire, but in some perverse corner of his mind—if he couldn't spend the day with Megan—he was half tempted to spend the day with Kate just to see what she might verbally have in store for him today. He wouldn't, but he was tempted.

Sighing over lust's abominable timing, he stepped through the open mud-room door and walked into the kitchen.

It wasn't a 4-H morning, so only Kate, Bele, Mike and Jamal were in the room. Kate was at the stove humming something jazzy and making what appeared to be French toast, Jamal was setting the breakfast table and Mike and Bele poured milk and juice and played with the refrigerator door. Intensely curious to know what they were trying to do, Hank stood quietly in the outer kitchen doorway and watched. While one practically stuck his nose against the rubber seal and went cross-eyed, the other slowly shut the refrigerator door. They repeated the process, slow and fast, switching places until Kate finally rolled her eyes and looked at them.

"It goes out when you shut it," she said.

Two pairs of little-boy eyes—one pair brown, the other pair

black—and one pair of warm mead adult male eyes turned to her. The little-boy eyes were dubious and suspicious, the adult's curious to know what they might be talking about, but also amused underneath arched brows.

"How do you know the light in the fridge goes out when you shut the door?" Mike asked. "You can't see it."

"I know because I replace the light bulb if it's not on when I open the door."

"Yes, but," Bele argued, all reason, "maybe you have to replace the light bulb because it's on all the time and never *goes* out until it *burns* out."

"It goes out when the door is closed," Kate assured him firmly. "Trust me."

"Yes, but *how* do you *know?*"

"Yes," Mike echoed. "How?"

Kate eyed them thoughtfully for an instant, shrugged, and went to pull open the refrigerator door. She leaned over to point out the heavy round sliding peg on the door's inside frame. "See this button?"

They nodded.

"Watch." She pushed the button in and the light went out, then she looked at the boys' disappointed faces and sighed. Another piece of magic exposed for the charlatanism it was. "That's how I know."

"Oh."

Deflated, Mike and Bele each pushed the button several times, swung the door in and out to make sure that it would indeed push the peg in as it closed, then dragged off in search of more interesting mysteries to solve. Swallowing a grin, Hank crossed the kitchen to help himself to coffee; offered a cup to Kate. She declined.

"Do you always pop their balloons like that?" he asked.

"What?" Puzzlement cleared. "Oh, you mean the door?"

He nodded.

She shrugged. "Yeah. I hate to do it, but with two of 'em the same age with the same curiosities at the same time..." Another shrug accompanied by a grimace. "It's the two-puppy theory. What trouble one doesn't think of to get into on his own, the other will. Better I should puncture a few balloons than let them figure stuff like that out the other way."

Hank lifted a brow, an unspoken question.

"You know," Kate said, gesturing with the French-toast turner, "One of 'em gets inside the fridge, the other one shuts the door..."

A grateful fizzle of tragedy averted ran down Hank's spine. "Ah," he muttered, mentally shuddering at the unwelcome picture imagination painted. Thank God he hadn't had to think about that particular accident, trying to raise Meg by himself. "Preventive parenting."

Kate nodded wryly. "Only kind there is. Jamal—" She turned to the lanky youth who put down his last piece of flatware and looked at her—almost painfully eager, Hank thought. "You wanna call everybody in? Breakfast's about ready."

"Sure, Kate."

Jamal went out through the mud room and onto the porch to jangle the bell beside the door. Kate listened for a moment before going back to the stove, tapping her toes and humming the way she'd been before Hank came in. Sipping his coffee, Hank watched her, fascinated by her lack of inhibition, disturbed by how...simple...it had become in two short weeks to stand in the Anden kitchen every morning while Kate cooked or did whatever else came to hand and just...*be*.

It was hard to remember a time in his life when things hadn't been complicated, complex. And it wasn't as if they weren't now, but somehow...he couldn't define it even to himself. The hard stuff just seemed to feel like *less* here, the better stuff like *more*.

Quit trying to analyze it to death and enjoy it while you can, he cautioned himself.

He straightened and did his best to follow good advice. A sudden snatch of the lyrics Kate sang penetrated his consciousness, making him nearly choke on something between astonished laughter and an unexpected surge of heat when he realized what she was singing.

"*Oh, I wish that I could wiggle like my sister Kate,*" Kate sang, doing a two-step twirl with the spatula, over to get a box of eggs out of the refrigerator. She returned with an exaggerated set of shoulder-arm jiggle-shimmies that set her entire upper body asway accompanied by an ain't-misbehavin', throaty-voiced, "*shimmy, shimmy like jelly on a plate...*"

There was more, but all at once Hank found himself laughing

too hard to understand the verse. Personally, Kate's wriggles didn't so much remind him of a plate full of jelly as they did the gentler sway of a thick, rich pudding. Chocolate mousse with fine chocolate shavings was his personal favorite. Eaten slowly, flavor savored, spoon licked...

But it wasn't a spoon and chocolate mousse his wayward imagination put into his mouth, let alone made him envision.

Already warm, fever lit him without warning from the inside out. Unprepared for the quick, harsh wrench of desire, he inhaled too sharply and swallowed coffee wrong. Abruptly he found himself coughing and choking instead of laughing. Jamal left the bell clanging and was beside him in an instant, pounding on his back.

"Hank—Mr. Mathison—you okay?" he asked anxiously. "You need some water or somethin'? Bele—" He gestured to the child who'd returned to the kitchen in response to the meal bell. "Get him some water."

"Dad." The mud-room door banged and Megan came in, put a hand on his shoulder. "Are you all right, Dad?"

"Fine," Hank wheezed. "Just give me a min—"

Kate's hand was on his, pressing a glass into it. "Here's some water." The coolness of her fingers burned into his; he jerked away. The glass dropped to the floor in a clatter of plastic and splashing liquid.

Their eyes met; heat scorched between them, unbearable and provocative, seething and undeniable.

"No," Hank said hoarsely. Then he pushed by his daughter, through the herd of Andens coming in for breakfast and slammed out of the house.

Intent only on restraining physical urges that threatened to overwhelm him, Hank didn't feel the hand that reached for his shirtsleeve, nor see the wounded, little-girl-lost look Megan sent after him; didn't hear the soft, frightened, "Dad?"

Couldn't see, then, that for convoluted reasons she'd never been able—and wasn't able even now—to articulate, Megan thought he was running from her....

In a small pocket of quiet surrounded by chaos, Kate, Megan and Jamal stood trying to sort it out.

"Man, I'm starvin'," Ilya said in his exaggerated American accent. "What's for breakfast?"

"No apple juice?" Grisha asked, head in the refrigerator. "I think I would rather have apple juice this morning than orange juice."

"Mom, did you make bacon?" Mike rummaged in the meat keeper in front of Grisha. "Hey, Bele, look what I found."

Bele jammed himself into the open refrigerator beside his brother. "Huh, so that's where it's been. What's my baseball doing in the fridge?"

"Don't know," Mike said. "Maybe you forgot it was in your hand when you got an orange or somethin'—"

"Ilya, keep that blasted dog away from the girls. She's been teasing 'em again." Li, sounding disgusted, came in slapping a pair of goatskin gloves on her jeaned thighs. "She's covered in llama spit and now it's all over me, too."

"Phew." Ilya pinched his nose shut. "Get away from me. You stink."

"Oh, I do not. It's dry already, but if you don't teach that animal some manners I *will* make you stink—"

"What's up with Hank?" Tai removed his yellow-and-green John Deere tractor cap and stuffed it into his back pocket as he stepped into the kitchen. No hats at the table. It was a rule. "He looks like somebody's set the hounds of hell after him." He eyed Kate. "What'd you do to him, Ma?"

Too distracted to answer, Kate simply gave him a look. She couldn't be sure what was going on with Hank, but she could venture a guess—something similar to the toe-curling, jelly-for-knees shock she'd received when their fingers collided.

Jamal, deciding what he'd seen, said, "He inhaled his coffee. I think he went to be sick."

"You do?" Megan asked, painfully hopeful, agonizingly tentative. "Do you think maybe I should go see—"

"No, I'll go," Kate volunteered quickly. Yes, it might be good for both father and daughter if Hank really was sick and Megan went. On the other hand, if he wasn't, if it was something else...

A swift glance at Megan confirmed all Kate needed to know: insecure, bewildered child reliving some real or imagined parental slight from the past, mistakenly superimposing it on today.

Geez Lou-eeze, she thought. *Like there isn't something smarter*

I could do than go anywhere near Hank Mathison with jello knees and kiss-me-senseless soup for brains.

Still, since somebody had to do it, it was undoubtedly better if she went than Megan. And truth be known, she was more than a little curious about what had caused Hank's reaction.

"Didn't anyone ever tell you about curiosity and cats?" Sister Viveca had asked her once, reprimanding Kate over some mischief she'd caused while still a postulant.

"Sure." Kate had nodded intemperately, too wise, too young and too inexperienced for her own good. *"Curiosity killed it. But, Sister, it also teaches. When I was little I had to get singed before I really understood that fire burns."* And so it seemed she would have to go get singed to understand now.

Sighing, she offered Megan the pancake turner. "You do breakfast," she suggested. "I'll see about your dad."

"Would you?" Relief was evident in the way Megan snatched the spatula.

"Yeah." Kate headed for the door, tossing directions over her shoulder as she went. "Mike, get a rag and mop the floor, please. Bele, help Meg. Don't wait breakfast."

Then, leaving order behind, she went in pursuit of chaos and the discombobulating Hank Mathison.

She found him in the shadows behind the equipment barn, soaking his head under the cold spray from the hose they used to fill the llamas' water troughs.

Tongue tucked between her left molars, Kate watched Hank drench himself, torn between amusement and disbelief. There had been times when her brother was a teenager that their mother had told him to go soak his head and wash whatever immoral notions he was entertaining about his girlfriend—later his wife and Mike's mother—right out of his mind, but she'd never known Mike senior to actually do it. She'd never known anyone to do it.

"Does it help?" she asked.

"What?" Startled, Hank straightened and swung about; icy water splashed over his shoulders, down his bare back and chest, soaked his fly. He cursed. "Damn, woman. I should've known you'd never leave well enough alone."

"I *am* much better at interfering," Kate agreed modestly.

Hank snorted something impolite. Kate would have laughed, too, but for some reason her throat refused to produce the sound.

It seemed silly for a woman who couldn't understand why other women got so hot and bothered hunk watching at the beach to have to admit, but she couldn't quite seem to take her gaze off Hank's sculpted chest. Muscular without being overdone, his smooth pecs and abs held her attention to an indecent degree.

Made her wonder what they'd feel like to touch.

Air twisted, got fouled up in her throat at the mere thought. She couldn't seem to breathe right—no doubt the reason she couldn't find the breath to laugh. You'd think she'd never seen a half-naked man before, the way it felt as if her tongue was hanging out of her mouth, but of course she had. It was just that none of *them* looked like *him.* Had ever kissed her like he had.

Bad enough she couldn't sleep without dreaming about that kiss, him, without having to deal with how the memory of it, the sight of him, made her feel when she was awake—particularly when he was around. Hot and bothered didn't *begin* to cover it.

"So," she said, forcing her gaze and her thoughts away from the tiny furl of heat igniting deep inside her. Her eyes lit on the towel hanging from a ring screwed into the side of the barn and she whisked it out of the ring and tossed it to Hank. "I take it you didn't rush out because you're sick?"

He caught the towel, began to wipe himself off. "Oh, I'm sick all right," he assured her, "just not in the way you mean."

Kate swallowed against sudden dry mouth. "I'm sorry to hear that," she whispered.

He quit toweling himself, arrested by the sound in her voice. "Why?"

"Because..." She cleared her throat, moistened her mouth, suddenly uncertain how to proceed. Stunned by her unaccustomed hesitation, the desire to quibble.

She hated being at a loss for words, hated getting caught in inadequacy. Hated feeling that for Megan's sake as well as her own she should ignore rather than address this silent struggle going on between them. She'd never been very good at pretending something didn't exist when it did. In her experience ignoring a potential problem usually only made it bigger, instead of making it go away. Still, for perhaps the first time in her life, politeness won out over the desire to speak her mind.

"Jamal—" Another pause. Second-guessing herself. She hadn't wasted time on second guesses since the last time she'd blown a true-false multiple-choice test in high school. Didn't know why she was now. If this was what having a crush—or whatever it was adult women got—on a guy was like for a grown-up girl, no wonder so many teenage girls wound up in the kind of troubled relationships they did. "Maybe I should ask what you mean about how you're sick or not first." An uncomfortable two-breath lull. "For the, um, sake of, um...clarity. You know?"

He viewed her as if he didn't know who she was. "Clarity," he said carefully, making sure he'd heard her right.

She nodded, looking at the toe of her right shoe, ducking his gaze.

Hank studied her. The gently mocking, always serene sense of self-confidence that usually radiated from her irritated the hell out of him, but this was far worse. Timidity didn't become her. He didn't want her wearing it, not for him. Not because of him.

Odd.

He'd thought the only thing he wanted was her to quit messing with his hormones so he could concentrate on Megan. When had how Kate Anden felt become important to him?

Oh, probably about the night he'd kissed her and she'd sent him reeling by kissing him back.

Funny how that worked. Where the body wanted to go, the mind followed.

So where did that leave the heart?

Lagging to the rear, making sure nobody got left behind.

Waiting to see if it was safe to catch up...

Eyes thoughtful on Kate, Hank rubbed the towel through his hair, which was shaggier now than he'd worn it since he'd accepted the assistant directorship. He wondered briefly if Kate liked it better shorter or longer. "You sure you want me to *clarify* for you what happened?"

"No." She shook her head, didn't pretend to misunderstand him. Raised her chin and looked at him. Shrugged her mouth and grimaced. "Do it anyway. Because if it's me, we have to talk about it."

He couldn't resist. "And if it's not you?"

"It's not?" Relief and disappointment vied for position. She wanted to believe relief won, but it didn't. "Then you need to let Meg know you ran out so fast because you had to be sick, that you're all right now."

"What?"

"She's afraid she did something to make you leave."

His expletive was harsh and self-directed. "She didn't."

"I know that. You know that. Jamal told her he thought you were feeling sick. She believed him enough to want to come after you. I figured that might be a bad idea if..." Her voice trailed off uncertainly.

"If it was you and not something else," Hank finished.

Kate nodded. "But it wasn't, so—"

"Yes it was," he interrupted quietly. His eyes were dark, dangerously deep, his look as intense and intimate as a touch. "It is. You. I couldn't stay in the same room with you, I wanted you so badly. Want you still."

Stunned, Kate swallowed a ragged breath. No one had ever looked at her the way Hank Mathison saw her now, had ever told her...desired her...made her feel...

Like walking into him and drowning. Like turning forever into a moment. With him.

"Oh, spit," she whispered.

"Yeah." He nodded, troubled. "You could say that."

"But we can't— I don't— It wouldn't— It's not..." She pressed her lips together, staring up at him, lost. This wasn't her area of expertise. She knew everything she was supposed to say to the kids, to Tai, to Li, the limits she'd put on Risto for his stay with them. But that was them. This was her. This was her feeling things, both physical and emotional, she'd never felt before, that she'd never thought about feeling. That there had seemed no point to feel. Things that the wisdom of inexperience didn't cover.

One kiss more than a week ago... It was something that filled out night's restless dreams, that intimated a hundred things she understood only intellectually. Still, the roil of emotions, the sense of intimacy, produced by one kiss—even a kiss as hot as that one—should have subsided by now.

Shouldn't it?

She'd know how to handle this, know what to say, if it had to do with one of the kids. She'd managed a lot of situations doing relief work in military zones, dealt with threats of rape and worse things. But this was different. She didn't know what to say to herself, had no idea how to handle—or discourage—Hank's desire for her.

Or her desire for him.

"The thing about being an adult," her mother had once told her, *"is that it means not having to act on all your desires. It means being able to choose the way you want to go, not just the way that gratifies the moment."*

Kate had believed her. But she'd never before in her life been presented with a choice or an admission like this.

"I don't know what to say," she told him baldly. "I've been in a lot of situations, but this is the first..." She stopped, shook her head. No, don't tell him that. Keep it simple. He didn't need her to tell him this tension between them was getting to be as hard for her as for him. "Isn't there something you can do about..." A helpless pause. "Can't you... I mean isn't there some way for you to..." Another lapse while she hunted for evasive words. "*deal* with it...that doesn't involve me?"

An almost bruised amusement flickered across Hank's face; he nearly laughed. "I take it you weren't one of those nuns who rapped boys' knuckles then sent them to confession and told them they'd go blind if they *dealt* with it that way."

It took her a moment to decipher her unintentional double entendre and his response to it. When she did, embarrassment stained the pale skin of her neck, bled upward with its attendant heat into her cheeks. "I'm sorry," she mumbled, flustered. "I didn't mean to suggest..." She stopped, deliberating. Embarrassment drained slowly, replaced by perception. "On the other hand," she said thoughtfully, and Hank nearly choked, "That might be the practical solution, don't you think?"

Chapter 7

It was his turn to flush, to squirm, to chuckle with discomfort. He, who, because of his many years in drug enforcement, thought he'd seen and heard everything.

"Practical, maybe," he agreed, sounding somewhat strangled, "but hardly a solution." Of all the conversations he could ever imagine having with anyone—particularly with a woman who was an ex-nun—this wasn't one. So how had it gotten to this point, anyway? *Oh, just lucky, I guess.* "Certainly not satisfying. Definitely not long-term."

"Oh." She seemed wistful. Disappointed. Glad. Torn among emotions.

"Yes," he agreed gently. "Oh." He looked down at her, watching the pale eyes with the navy rings around the irises, seeking he wasn't sure what. Answers, strength, respite from the thing between the two of them that he knew was inevitable. And irreversible. "And not only that, but it wouldn't do anything for you."

"Oh, but I'm used to being celi—"

She broke off, biting her tongue on what she'd been about to say. It sounded too much like an accusation. He finished it for her.

"You're used to being celibate."

She nodded.

"So am I." He smiled thinly, draped the towel back through its ring to dry. "And it doesn't make a damn bit of difference."

"I wouldn't know."

"Wouldn't you?" A challenge. A dare to deny the truth.

Self-conscious in her desire to lie, she looked at the ground. "You must have dealt with this sort of thing before."

"No."

Surprised, she raised her head. "But you're a man."

The corner of his mouth lifted with scorn. He'd expected better of her. "And you're a sexist."

She laughed at that, a dry, humor-filled, self-deprecating sound. "Sometimes. But that's not what I meant here. I just meant you're a man, you've been married, you aren't a monk, you've been around, you must've had to...manage...desires you don't intend to act on."

"Yeah, I have. It's called not wanting what you can't have."

"I know that one," Kate said softly. "I use that one. It's not working this time."

Something in him leaped at her admission; he wasn't alone. In the next instant he quashed elation and regarded her steadily. "No. It's not."

Silence passed between them while they digested revelation, shied from it. Faced hunger, avarice, want. And discarded them as inappropriate to the moment.

"So what do we do?" she asked.

He shrugged. "Follow the rules. Remain focused on Meg, because I don't want to risk losing her. Don't wind up alone together. Never touch. And you've got to quit telling me how scrambled your brain gets when you look at me. For one thing, it's not dignified. For another, it's not dishonest to keep something like that to yourself. And third—" He grinned wryly. "Third, hearing how I make you feel makes me crazy. So far, it's only your timing and the number of kids who've been around that've kept me this side of the line we keep drawing in the dirt."

"Don't forget fourth," Kate said quietly. He looked at her. She hunched a shoulder and told Hank the same lie she told herself. "I don't know about you, but I think...I think I'd only be in it for the sex and that's not enough."

"Good point." But he looked almost as unconvinced as Kate felt. "So." He pulled his shirt off the shelf where he'd left it, next to the stiff brush they used to scrub out the llama troughs every day. Gathered it together in his hands and slid it over his head, aware in every fiber of Kate watching him. Of the fact that what he'd rather be doing was taking her shirt off her, putting his hands on her and feeling hers on him. Knowing damn well that, despite what Kate said, if she were to lay down with him the result would be far more than sex, but still less than either of them was entitled to. "We're agreed."

Kate sketched a line between them with the toe of her boot. "You stay on your side of the fence, I stay on mine."

He stuck out his hand. "Shake on it?"

Kate snorted. "After what we just talked about? Not likely."

Hank grinned. "You're learning."

"Yeah." She watched him finish pulling his shirt down over his chest and sighed regretfully. "And ain't education a bitch."

Then she picked up the hose he'd discarded, and to the sound of Hank's laughter, she turned it on herself.

Establishing the rules of their relationship didn't make it easier for Kate. If anything, seeing Hank on a daily basis—even from a distance—got harder.

She couldn't relieve her own tension simply by tossing some comment at him, because now she understood that as far as Hank was concerned such commentary was merely a tease that made self-control more difficult. Also, the more she saw him, the more she liked him.

He was hardly the pasteboard character his looks and his daughter had proclaimed him to be. He was as multidimensional as people come, as vulnerable as his daughter. And a man capable of emotions he could neither control nor let anyone else share.

She didn't know who he'd been when he'd worked undercover, but the man who sprayed and fertilized trees with her sons, who invited his daughter to help him raid their collections of South American souvenirs and Indian artifacts in order to keep Mike and Bele in "dig fossils," and who squeezed Li's shoulder when she was nervous before her audition for the county symphony, simply grinned and hugged her afterward when Li won her chair hands-down-going-away was a man Kate had never expected to meet. Never even considered might be out there.

Had never let herself dream of finding.

Besides being sexy as all get-out, the Hank she saw daily was decent, honorable, honest and able to laugh at himself—all things she'd recognized before but had half decided would diminish as the summer wore on. Instead of diminishing, however, Hank's talents only seemed to increase as time wore by until Kate uncovered the secret he hid deepest: he was a man capable of loving without reservation or restraint, without conditions.

No matter what game Megan played, he stayed within range, refused to walk away even in those moments when she treated him to her worst. That his daughter couldn't see past her own pain well enough to see how much her father loved her was something Kate recognized, as well. Understood that as much as Megan needed to hear the word, needed him to tell her rather than try to show her how he felt, Hank could hardly voice his love for her in any way Megan could hear. And it made Kate ache for them both.

Love them both.

It also made it harder for her to stay away from him. But she understood that he couldn't afford to let her near even to offer comfort—or perhaps that was especially to offer comfort—because she had a feeling she knew where *comfort* could easily lead. Passion was a sneak thief and a con artist that could gull and dupe its way through the noblest emotions, leave them stripped and tattered all over the floor. So instead of even allowing herself to do something as simple as offering to pour Hank coffee, she stayed on her side of the breakfast table and let him pour it for himself. Instead of enjoying a few minutes of purely adult conversation on the front porch after supper, she adhered to the rules and kept kids or llamas or bolted doors or an electric fence between them.

But she couldn't stop herself from seeking him out across a distance, meeting his eyes, reading the same sense of urgency, of need, in him as she felt in herself. Couldn't stop the want.

And July got older, bolder, hotter, greener, the sky stayed blue and streaked with jet streams and the sun burned....

* * *

The tenuous peace fell apart early on a brooding, muggy and torpid Michigan evening tasting of storms that refused to come.

It was the fifteenth of July, the thirty-eighth anniversary of Genevieve Mathison's birth. Hank never thought about the date. Megan did.

They were alone at the guesthouse—a rarity, what with Megan spending most nights in the extra bed in Li's room and with them both taking meals up at the main house with the family. As Kate put it when Hank had stiffly suggested he wouldn't want to intrude on the Andens more than he and Megan were already, since Hank was paying for his and Megan's beds but they were also putting in long days working for Stone House, the least the Andens could do was provide the board. Except that Hank was never quite sure what headway he and Megan were making as father and daughter, the arrangement worked well. But tonight when he came in to clean up before supper, Megan was there ahead of him, dressed to the nines and carelessly expectant.

Maybe he should have had a premonition or figured it out, then, but he had other things on his mind: Kate swimming in the pond with Mike and Bele, modestly attired in a skirted one-piece bathing suit that teased his imagination no end, for instance.

"Wow." He made a circling motion with his finger, whistled appreciatively when Megan turned slowly to give him the full effect. She was dressed in a slim-cut, sleeveless white button-front dress and white strappy sandals. There were small pearl studs in her ears, a pearl cocktail ring on her right hand and a slim gold watch on her left wrist. Her hair was soft, pulled gently away from her face by a comb in a style he'd always particularly liked on Gen. He didn't think he'd ever seen his daughter look more grown-up or more beautiful. "You're a knockout. Is that dress new?"

She shook her head shyly. "No. You've seen it before, but it's been a while."

"No-o-o," he said, light and teasing, drawn out with disbelief. "I'd remember if I'd seen you in that outfit before."

She flushed, suddenly all gawky teen. "Thanks. But you didn't see it on me. It's Mom's. She wore it to Aunt Sara's wedding. It finally fits me. I always wanted to wear it."

"Mom's." The foreboding that hadn't prickled through him earlier sifted along the edge of Hank's nerves. He'd thought he got rid of all Gen's clothes—or rather had asked her sister Sara to do it within months of her death. The jewelry he'd put aside for Meg himself, presented the pearls to her six months ago when she'd turned sixteen. Knowing what was inside it because he'd told her, she'd tossed the box aside without opening it. Apparently things had changed since then.

He took another long, hard look at his daughter. God, she did remind him of Gen. Not so much physically as something in her demeanor: hair, makeup, attitude...almost as if he was looking at a photograph. Almost as though Megan had taken a picture of Gen into the bathroom with her, set it up in front of her and copied the image onto herself.

Nope, he decided uneasily, this didn't feel right at all.

Things had been going misleadingly well of late, he knew, and he felt he should have been prepared for *something*. But dressing like Gen, to *be* Gen... Even given Meg's repertoire of creative ways to act out, this was a new one. He didn't like it.

But then, like many parents, he knew he was prone to not liking things he couldn't understand.

Still, this did seem awfully morbid and unhealthy. He also didn't know how to handle it. Or why it was manifesting now. It wasn't Christmas, Mother's Day, Thanksgiving, the anniversary of Gen's death or even the Fourth of July, so why...

Try to stay cool, he advised himself. *Keep it light. See where it goes. Maybe she's just got a...a special date.*

"Did Aunt Sara give the dress to you?" he asked idly.

"Un-unh." Megan smoothed tanned hands down the length of white. "She let me choose whatever I wanted to keep, when she was sorting through Mom's stuff. I kept most of it. We're the same size now."

Not *I'm the same size she was,* but *We're the same size now.*

He kept his voice neutral. "You mean you're the same size Mom was, don't you?"

"What?" Megan looked at him, distracted. Not sensitive to the comment the way Hank thought she'd be. Not actually seeming to notice it at all. "Oh, yeah, sure. Was."

Agreement, simple as that. So why couldn't he accept her concession without suspicion?

Without concern.

"So what are you up to tonight, all dressed up?" he asked.

Mistake. He knew that the moment the question left his mouth.

Her head came up, all of her attention captured; hurt crossed her face. "You know."

Oh, hell. Either she'd told him something he'd forgotten, left him a note he'd never read, or this was one of those read-her-mind-psychic-things, where no matter what he did or how carefully he proceeded he screwed up. He was already screwed.

"Uh, I don't think so, honey." Women who got hurt at the drop of a hat and who made him walk on eggshells so he wouldn't hurt them more were a pain in the butt. And yes, she was his daughter, she owned his heart, she'd inherited many of her emotions from her mother, but right now she was hurt, he was tiptoeing on eggs and, damn it, when she was like this she was still a pain in the butt. "I'm sorry if I've forgotten something, but maybe if you tell me what it is we can fix it—"

"Fix it?" She was offended, incensed; Hank knew he'd fix nothing tonight. "We shouldn't have to fix anything. I'm not your secretary, I shouldn't have to remind you, you should just know, you should be able to look at a calendar sometimes and remember on your own. Instead, you always have to ruin it—"

Sweet heaven. Hank stared at his daughter, pale and appalled. Memories tumbled backward five years to Gen's last birthday three months before she died, two months before she told him she was five months pregnant. Hindsight and hormones had explained the way Gen lashed out at him that night—in words and emotions Megan repeated, now, almost verbatim.

He hadn't known their daughter had been near enough to hear, let alone that she would remember.

She was ranting at him now, nearly shrieking. Had worked herself up well past the ability to hear anything, but especially reason. Stamping around, tearing off the ring, watch and earrings, pitching them onto a table, she was well beyond Gen's hormone-driven but justifiable—he *had* forgotten her birthday that year, many years, after all—anger.

Had forgotten many things important to his wife, in pursuit of his job.

But this wasn't Gen screaming at him now, it was Megan, and this anger was more like the temper tantrums she'd suffered from when she was three and four and didn't want to do something. Then he, when he was home, or Gen would literally have to lie on top of Megan while she screamed uncontrollably—often for nearly an hour—simply to prevent her from throwing herself into something or off of something in her rage and doing herself serious damage.

Small and young as she'd been, adrenaline had made her strong and frightening, able to nearly lift him off of her. And despite the time or two Gen had mentioned something about Megan giving in to moody rages since then—probably, now that he thought about it, about the time Megan might have been headed into puberty, like a pre-PMS sort of thing—Gen and Hank had both thought their daughter had pretty much outgrown her tantrums by the time she started kindergarten at five.

Now, however, it didn't appear as if Meg had outgrown anything. Her uncontrolled rage scared Hank more than anything he'd seen his daughter do since Gen died—including Mother's Day, when she'd come in high and thrown the dollhouse at him.

This was beyond his knowledge and ability to manage; beyond, he was very much afraid, even the department psychologist's expertise. For himself, Hank couldn't very well simply lie down on top of his sixteen-year-old daughter and let her scream and flail at him until she exhausted herself, the way he'd been able to cushion and protect her from herself at four. As for the department's psychologist...helpful as the woman wanted to be, her primary training was in test giving and dealing with adult agents who were as adept at disguising their anxieties and appearing normal in her presence as they were at dissolving in a crisis. She'd never been exposed to this side of Megan, felt that Hank was dealing only with adolescent rebellion complicated by the death of a same-sex parent. Clearly this was more than that.

Or maybe it wasn't. Maybe he was overreacting and this was normal sixteen-year-old behavior under this very specific set of circumstances. Sexist as it might sound, maybe this was merely a not-so-simple case of PMS and she'd be fine in a couple of days. Or maybe when this tantrum played itself out, everything would be fine. Maybe this was merely another form of release, like hysteria or crying.

And maybe he was a terrified parent grasping at straws of rationalization and hope.

Helpless, he reached out to touch Megan's shoulder, wondering how an expert would handle this; tried to gather her into his arms to quiet and reassure. She screamed and struck at him, scratching his arm with sharp polished nails and pushing him away, and he could only stand powerless, watching her remove herself to the bedroom she'd been assigned but rarely used. The door banged shut behind her, the lock snicked into place. Silence was abrupt and complete, as hard on his ears and psyche as Megan's rage had been.

Not sure what he intended, he walked to the door of her room, wanting to be near her, somehow. Inside the room he could hear her sobs—more like paroxysms of unintelligible wrath at first—and slumped to the floor beside her door, worn and alone, his back to the wall.

He didn't know how long he waited with his head leaned back, eyes shut, listening to her. Knew only that the time and voice of her pain, grief, rage, whatever, seemed interminable and costly. Gradually relaxed only when Megan's emotional frenzy took on the quieting tones of real tears. Then he wrapped an arm around one upraised knee, let his other leg slacken sideways and awaited Megan's return.

Kate wondered about Megan and Hank when they didn't appear for dinner, stopped when Li mentioned she thought father and daughter had some sort of special evening planned—dinner out or something, Meg had said. The announcement made Kate curious, but busy with supper preparations and mildly concerned about Risto's latest unannounced disappearance, she merely wished Hank a mental *godspeed* and hoped that the thaw between parent and child had finally begun.

It was a relatively mild evening—ninety degrees with a modest eighty-five percent humidity relative to the day's one-hundred-and-two degrees with its accompanying thick and cloying ninety-five percent humidity. They ate a cold meal outside in the shade of a spreading oak at the two long picnic tables set up for the purpose; citronella torches posted a perimeter around the tables to keep the flies and mosquitoes at bay.

With a lot of kids, the family's evening meal was lively and entertaining, occasionally informative and never boring. Outside on a hot July night, it was also a little raucous, prone to bad jokes, snickers and the sporadic flinging of macaroni or peas—

supposedly behind Kate's back. The dog, Taz, who was not allowed to beg from the table in the house, snuck underneath whichever table Kate was not at outside and cleaned up whatever Mike or Ilya didn't like. Born in a place where food was often scarce, Bele ate whatever was put in front of him—although he no longer had a tendency to gorge himself sick, not knowing when he'd have his next meal. Outside, Kate turned her back on minor infractions of the Dinner Table Rules and Manners unless the violations got out of hand.

After dinner the family's resident firebugs, Li and Grisha, tepeed the broken-up wood from old pallets—Tai brought them home regularly, free, from a local warehouse—in the nearby fire pit. Mike, Bele and Ilya cleared paper plates and cups from the table to add to the evening fire effort; Tai, his girlfriend, Carly, and Kate covered leftover perishables and removed them to the house, returning with roasting forks, bags of marshmallows, packages of Hershey bars and graham crackers.

Hot as it was, the younger boys urged swimming before dessert.

Kate eyed them, then her oldest son's girlfriend and asked, "Carly, will you lifeguard these hellions? I need to talk with Tai and Li a minute."

The younger woman cast her a curious glance, swiftly masked. She'd been with Tai four years now, considered his family hers, and there was very little Kate said to Tai but hesitated to share with her. Which meant she had a reason this time. "Sure."

"Thanks." Kate waited until Carly shepherded her appointed troops off to the pond before turning again to Tai and Li. Without preamble she asked, "Is Risto drinking again?"

They stared at her, surprised, then thoughtful.

There had been a problem with alcohol early in the exchange student's tenure with them, only partially excused by ignorance, cultural differences, and an ofttimes more lenient spirits policy in Risto's native country. He'd have been expelled and sent home by the exchange program on the spot had Kate not intervened on his behalf.

She knew from personal experience how difficult it was to be far from home, speaking a language you were familiar with but which was not your native tongue; understood the temptation to want to fit in whatever the cost. She also understood that Risto was the only child of a wealthy family and used to living by a different set of standards than she exercised. But after the first few turbulent months, he'd seemed to settle in nicely—primarily, Kate suspected, because he hadn't wanted to be sent home early. Or to return home to Finland at all.

Since school let out for the summer, though, and Risto had once more started disappearing without word, Kate wondered if she'd done the right thing in lobbying the exchange program to let him stay. Wondered if she shouldn't have let Risto be sent home, where he could return to being his parents' problem instead of hers.

Undoubtedly a selfish thought, but there it was.

Life's tough, get a helmet, she cautioned herself with an inward grimace, silently repeating Mike's and Bele's latest favorite cartoon advice.

And at least when she was worrying about what Risto might be up to—or *in* to—she wasn't thinking about Hank.

Now Kate looked at Li, who looked doubtfully back and said, "Drinking? I don't—I'm not sure, but I don't think..." She turned to Tai.

He shook his head. "He comes out pretty groggy some mornings, but I haven't smelled anything on him. He sleeps in with Grisha and Ilya and they haven't said anything—and Grisha's got the nose of a bloodhound."

"Do either of you have any idea where he is? Or when he left?"

Tai and Li eyed each other and shrugged.

"He left," Tai said, "probably around four, when he came in from the fields to do something and didn't come back. As for where he went..." He lifted a shoulder, let it drop. "Far as Risto's concerned, I'm an egghead plowboy, so how would I know?"

"Yeah," Li put in, "and I'm a nerd-geek-spook-egghead-goody-two-shoes-milkmaid-freaky-animal-lover, and guys like Risto don't tell girls like me squat because he knows if you ask me and I know and it's for his own good, I'll tell you."

Kate swallowed a smile at her daughter's offhandedness. In her day—gee, did that make her sound old, or what?—being called anything on Li's list was tantamount to being ostracized for life from all polite society. Li, on the other hand, considered such name-calling a compliment. *"Nerds are the world's billionaires,"* was her prosaic response—and had been since grade school.

"I see," she said, amused. Then she sighed. "Okay, so nobody thinks he's drinking or knows where he went, but he probably left around four. It's seven-thirty now. He didn't drive, he didn't take a bike, so—"

"I might know where he is."

Stuffed gym bag in hand, Jamal stood off to one side shifting from foot to foot, ill at ease. Kate regarded him, taking in both the picture and the implication behind it in a glance.

"Your mother out of town again?" she asked.

Jamal nodded once without looking up. "I think she be gone a while this time. She wondered, could I stay here like we been doin'." He lifted his head, face strained, not quite pleading. "It's time you need extra help an' all, an' I'll help out with everything—"

"I know you will, Jamal," Kate assured him quietly. "You always help, you work hard. We're lucky you can be here. That's why we keep Ilya's top bunk empty when you're not here. It's yours."

"Thanks." Jamal grinned shyly, giving Kate the impression that praise and simple acceptance were rare commodities in his life. She could change that. Other things she couldn't change.

She waved gratitude away and cautioned gently, "If this'll be an extended stay, you'll have to tell me what and why so we can make...temporary legal guardianship arrangements if they're necessary."

Jamal took a deep breath and swallowed hard. "Okay." He eyed her. "Y-you want we should do that now?"

Kate shook her head. "Later'll be soon enough. First tell me what you think about Risto...."

His legs and back were stiff, and he had to go to the bathroom.

Wrinkling his nose, Hank sniffed the air around him. He also needed a shower. Bad.

Stifling a groan, he shoved himself up the wall, stood a moment stretching. Behind Megan's door all was quiet; Hank wondered if she'd fallen asleep. He pressed an ear to the wood, listening, tapped gently and said, "Meg?"

No response.

Figured. Still, he hadn't really expected one. He knocked again, tried the knob. Again no response; the door was locked.

Sighing, he wiped a hand tiredly across his face and spoke to the door, hoping his daughter was listening. "I'm going to shower. You need anything before I do?"

Silence.

Defeated, he stared at the door, his shoulders drooping. The temptation to say *"Screw it,"* and leave Megan to whatever hell she chose to inhabit was strong tonight, as hard and bright as the light from the descending sun crowding into the living room through a minuscule break in the trees outside. The impulse was momentary and would pass, it always did; it was only the thought's guilty aftertaste that lingered.

His lips compressed; he puffed out his cheeks on a breath and let the air out slowly. Enough, for the moment, with letting his child rule both his every action and his psyche. He needed a shower, damn it, and he was going to take one.

Tramping firmly on doubt by telling himself he'd only be in the shower five minutes, that even parents with infants sometimes had to leave them alone in their cribs that long, Hank stalked through the kitchen, stripped off his clothes and stepped into the shower.

"You think he's where?" Kate asked incredulously—for the second time. *"Where?"* With all the legal bars that abounded, including some that served alcohol to minors, why would anyone need to run an *illegal* bar in this day and age?

"Blind pig couple miles up the road," Jamal repeated. "I heard him talking with Meg about it. I think they mighta been there before."

"A blind pig?" Kate mouthed the words as though they were foreign. "A blind *pig?* I thought they went out with prohibition."

Jamal shrugged. "Meanin' no disrespect, Kate, but if you think that, you don't know nothin'. There's a market, people gonna sell liquor without a license, you got prohibition or not. That's what my grandpa used to say."

"Yes, but a blind pig?" She felt like a broken record, but disbelief was like that. "And they serve *children* there?"

Jamal nodded. "Kids ten, eleven years old go if they want to drink, smoke, gamble. Parents even drop 'em off thinkin' maybe they just goin' to a battle of the bands at a teen club with their friends or whatever. Adults got no need for a blind pig anymore 'less they want to hold secret meetings or gamble or something.''

"Secret meetings?'' Kate stared at him. This just got worse and worse, and she felt stupider and stupider. Had she ever been a teenager? Had she ever known *anything* like the things her kids already knew? "What kind of secret meetings?''

"I dunno. Could be anything, I guess. Things like maybe—''

"Hate groups,'' Carly interjected quietly.

Hank swiped soap from his face and reached up to switch the shower head to "massage.'' He would take an extra minute, damn it, Megan or no, because he needed it.

Cool water chattered over the back of his neck, drowning tight muscles. Sighing, he let his head drop forward, forcing himself to relax. God, he'd needed this. There was nothing like washing crisis away with dirt in a cold shower—even when the reprieve was only temporary.

He enjoyed the peace as long as he dared, then shut off the water and toweled quickly, slid into a pair of running shorts and reluctantly let himself out of the bathroom. Time to rebeard the lioness in her den.

He was halfway across the kitchen when the receding sound of a car motor caught his attention. His head whipped around. He knew that motor. That was his car.

With a furious oath he glanced at the top of the refrigerator where he normally tossed his keys when he came in. Missing.

"Damn.''

Six long strides took him to Megan's open door. Gen's dress and the strappy sandals lay in a heap on the floor.

Megan was gone.

The boys had finished their swim and come rampaging back only moments before to burn their fingers and make s'mores; Carly had slipped over to stand beside Tai and join the discussion.

Torn between the desire to make himself some dessert and also to separate himself from the littler guys in favor of being included with the older guys—even Jamal was younger than him, after all—Grisha smashed a couple of cold marshmallows between a pair of chocolate bars and hung at the fringes of the group, listening. Ilya, on the other hand, quickly burned half a dozen marshmallows, built a handful of sticky treats and brought them with him—and generously handed half of them to Jamal, who made a distracted *oh, gross* face and passed them back.

For their part, Kate, Tai, Li and Jamal turned to Carly, appalled. "Hate groups?"

Clearly Carly's suggested reason for secrecy hadn't occurred to any of them—including the urbanwise Jamal. Or perhaps that was particularly the urbanwise Jamal.

The corners of Carly's mouth tucked wryly, her shoulders hunched an apology. "I'm a waitress, I hear things. I don't know how much I can believe most of the time, but that's something I heard in a way I couldn't *not* believe it."

Kate stared at her, not wanting to take it in. The fact that she had to sat poorly with her. "Risto might be at a blind pig run by a hate group?" Not only streetwise but worldwise, she'd thought there were few surprises any of the kids who came through her doors could throw at her. Apparently she was wrong.

Carly shook her head. "I don't know for sure, that's not what I meant. You were wondering, I heard about maybe one that exists like that where these...this *society* can print pamphlets and make plans and find recruits. It's not like I know where it is, so it's probably not the same one and that's not where he is, you hear what I'm saying? I mean, if some people can run one blind pig for one purpose, other people can run another one just to...just to...make easy money."

"I suppose," Kate agreed, hardly comforted. Risto was in her care, her responsibility—until he went home next month. Of course, if she found he'd been sneaking off to an illegal liquor joint—of any kind—she'd personally see to it he was shipped home under the exchange program's chaperonage by the end of this week. Risto's staying here was not a necessity but a privilege, and one he'd managed to abuse already, at that. She believed in giving a kid a second chance and even a third, but in this instance she had to think of her own kids and the effect Risto's activities would have—were already having—on them, too.

Especially if the police were involved.

And they would, of course, have to be. For the first time her mind turned to Hank—not as the subject of her errant daydreams, but as a cop who'd know how to handle the problem. Know who to call and how to bust the blind pig—if indeed there was one— and how to proceed with Risto afterward. Hank would probably even appreciate having the tables turned on her for a change, as in *her* needing his help to avert a crisis instead of vice versa. And this was one crisis she wanted to prevent *now*.

"Li—" She turned to her daughter. "Did you say Hank and Meg were going out to dinner tonight?"

"I thought that's what Meg told me. I didn't see their car leave—"

"It was parked at their house when we came back from the pond," Grisha volunteered.

"Good," Kate said. "Then I'll ask Hank to help—"

She turned at the sudden rumble of a car motor nearby. Behind her the Mathisons' dusty white Chevy four-door bounced up the back drive and out the front without slowing, Megan behind the wheel.

Chapter 8

The house was a big, dirty yellow clapboard thing with enclosed steps mounting the outside to the second floor.

Sprawling with additions appended at haphazard angles through the years, it had once been a legal combination of business and residence. Situated on a rural section of the main highway almost halfway between the affluent small town Hank and Megan called home and the slightly larger county seat, it was a perfect hide-in-plain-sight location for a teen-geared blind-pig gambling parlor. Run by a pair of twenty-something ex-cons, it was a lively place whose posted intent was to provide a venue for middle- and high-school-age garage bands to prove themselves.

In actuality, it provided what it advertised and more.

At the main-level entrance, it was strictly an unlicensed teen-to-twenty club that served nothing more stimulating than cherry cola. If a few ten-, eleven- and twelve-year-olds filtered through the cracks to mingle with a crowd that was primarily aged thirteen to eighteen, with a few immature twenty-year-olds thrown in, oh well. It was the bar that lay below the main level that provided much of the attraction, coupled with the poker, blackjack and roulette tables hidden in the attic above the second-floor living quarters. The first-floor club acted as a screening base for the other two.

Palms sweaty, Megan slid Hank's car into a spot hidden behind a pair of Dumpsters located at the rear of the gourmet deli-party shop about five hundred feet from her destination. Too many law-enforcement people in the area knew Hank's vehicle for her to risk parking any closer.

If he'd just remembered...

But no. She stiffened her jaw, felt the skin around her eyes tighten, her mouth harden with the movement. She was over that little parental screwup and on to better things.

Adrenaline, already pumping, spurted with renewed vigor through her veins as she alighted from the car and leaned the door shut. She breathed deep, savoring the rush. She'd been to the club plenty of times, but she'd never before stolen and driven her father's car, never come alone. And it was his own freaking fault that she did it tonight.

First time for everything, she thought, angling the side-view mirror and bending to check her appearance by the light of the setting sun. She fiddled a few stiffened spikes of heavily gelled bangs across her forehead, then tilted her head critically to eye the eight rings and studs in her left ear, the six danglies in her right ear; flicked the ring in her right nostril before glancing quickly about. Spotting no one, she slid a hand down the front of her tight-fitting bustier-style zippered leather vest to plump and adjust her sweating breasts. A humid ninety degrees and climbing was hardly the weather for leather anything, but Danny and Earl kept the air-conditioning up and the fans on, so she'd be comfortable enough inside. Also, the motorcycle-bad-girl look advertised exactly the wares she intended it to advertise and suited her mood down to the ground. Now all she needed was a dose of *ma huang* and a tequila shooter or two, and she'd be chilled just fine.

She slipped an arm through the thin strap of her tiny rivet-studded purse and carried the strap over her head. Then twitching her slim leather miniskirt into place and shining the metal toes of her boots on the backs of each other, she headed for the club.

Hank reached the house at the same time Kate was stepping into the van to go looking for Risto. She regarded him with surprise.

"I thought you went out with Meg."

"You saw her?" he asked grimly.

She nodded, taking in his disheveled appearance, the fury and fear that seethed beneath a facade of rigid control. "Fifteen, twenty minutes ago, maybe less. In your car." Her concern showed. "We assumed you were with her."

"No." Short and succinct, the single word stated volumes.

"She bolted?"

"That's one way to put it."

"What's another?" she asked softly.

Arrested by her tone, he looked at her, then away. "It's Gen's birthday. I guess she thought... No—" He shook his head, confused and angry. "I don't know what she thought. Anyway, she was all dressed up when I came in, made up to look like Gen. I said the wrong thing. She pitched a long tantrum, then waited until I got in the shower to steal my keys and the car."

His jaw worked. He gazed at Kate without seeing her, his eyes haunted. "She's never gone this far before, Kate. When she was little she had rages, but this...this one was worse than the one she had the morning before I called you. I don't know where she went, how much money she's got or if she's coming back. I hoped maybe she'd taken the car for spite and cooled off by the time she got up here. I guess not."

"You want to call the police?"

"I don't want to involve them unless it's necessary."

"It might be," she said.

Then she filled him in on Risto's disappearance and what the kids had told her about him, Megan and the alleged blind pig.

The basement was dark and hazy, raucous with laughter from voices that had yet to change, loud with music.

Just inside the doorway, Megan filled her lungs with the taste of secondhand tobacco and looked around, letting her eyes adjust. Kids milled everywhere: at the makeshift bar, the jukebox, congregated thickly around the two pool tables, piled together on vinyl makeout couches and chairs in the corners and along the walls. She scanned the crowd quickly, spotted her quarry slouched forward at the bar, one booted foot propped on the rail that ran its squared-off bottom length. Hand on hip, she put on a full-lipped pout and swayed over to drape a possessive wrist over his shoulder and blow in his ear.

"Hey, Zevo."

Zevo took a negligent pull on a squat-necked Pabst, threw back a shot of something cheap and vile-smelling before acknowledging her. "Hey, Megan." He shrugged out from underneath her wrist, deliberately turned to inspect the room, appearing to ignore her. "Long time."

"Been out of town." She ran an idle hand up his chest, playing the scene from old movies. She knew the difference; Zevo didn't. "I missed you, baby."

"Yeah," he said sarcastically, still refusing to look at her, "That's why you spending the summer hangin' with the brainiacs and llamas out at the Christmas-tree castle, cuz you miss me."

Megan's hand flexed on his chest, nails digging in sharply, suddenly, startling his attention her way. "Wrong," she said flatly. "I'm spending the summer with the geeks and the llamas because I want to, and you don't tell me what to do." Her voice changed timbre, softening to a purr. "But that doesn't mean I haven't missed you, too, babe."

"Yeah, okay, all right." Verbally backing off, Zevo rubbed his chest where the marks from her nails stung. "I missed you, too, Meg. A lot." He wrapped a diffident arm about her waist, no longer sure where they stood physically. Megan hung back for an instant, making sure he knew who held the power, then pressed into his embrace, caressing the line of his jaw with her cheek. He smirked out at the room at large and slid his hand possessively down her hip, turned his head to take her mouth in a boy's sloppy, greedy kiss. "Yeah, we back," he murmured. "Whataya want, doll?"

Megan's response was a sizzle of breath against his mouth. "Dose of herbal ecstasy and the usual."

Zevo grinned and hauled her more snugly against him. "Mmm," he muttered. "I like it when you get tight." He kissed her, with a lot of tongue, then tapped money on the bar. "Hey, Earl. Packet of *ma huang* 'n' a tequila shooter, lime, no salt."

Within moments a labeled plastic packet containing ten little blue editions of legal herbal speed, a shot of tequila and a piece of lime appeared beside Zevo's fist; the money disappeared. Zevo picked up the packet and handed it to Megan.

"Here ya go, doll."

"Thanks, Zevo."

Carefully she slit the packet open, collected five of the blue pills, and handed the rest to Zevo. He accepted them with a grin, offered her the tequila, watched her wash her dose down. She shut her eyes and shivered slightly when the liquor hit her throat, then quickly bit the lime, chasing tart squirts of juice after the tequila. A sigh of anticipated artificial well-being escaped; hazy eyed and calm she leaned out of Zevo's arms and peered through the atmospheric murk at him.

"You seen Risto?" she asked.

The feel of Kate's fingers in his hair in the fading daylight might have been immensely gratifying—if not for the circumstances and the number of other people watching her fluff and consider the strands. Unfortunately Hank's rebellious body didn't see it that way and he was having great difficulty paying attention to particulars, namely the unmarked sheriffs' and state policemen's cars sitting in the shadows off Kate's front drive and the reason her fingers were playing with his hair in the first place.

"So buzz it and carve your initials in it," he snapped, feeling the heaviness of Kate's breasts against his upper arm, much too near his face. All he had to do was turn his head to find that damp, inviting cleavage at mouth level. What his body wanted was nothing more than to drop her on her back and bed her on the spot. What he was getting instead was flak. He was tired of the ongoing argument over whether or not he'd be of any assistance setting up the blind pig for a raid—and delivering Megan and Risto from it, assuming they were inside, before it occurred. "I don't give a—" He bit back an obscenity, controlling his temper with an effort. "I don't care what it looks like in the polite world, as long as it does what it's supposed to for the moment. If there's a chance Meg's inside, I'm goin' in."

"I could give you a mohawk and paint the number of the beast on your face and you'd still look like somebody's narc-enforcement parent in jeans and a T-shirt," Kate snapped back. She was finding Hank's proximity equally distracting.

She'd never before found the scent of hot male particularly alluring, never had so much trouble giving an adult a haircut. No matter what she did to stay out of the way, every time he moved some part of his arm came in contact with her nipples, irritating, teasing and stimulating. She could barely think under the influence of that unintentional friction, let alone skin his head to resemble something—oh, for cryin' out loud, who knew what he needed to resemble. Something extremely neat and military probably, but with him distracting her by living, she couldn't guarantee the result without worrying about lopping off his ears in the bargain. And she rather liked his ears exactly where they were. Lord, maybe she should have gone parking with Steve Heckerling the single time he'd invited her back in tenth grade. Then at least maybe she'd have a little experience to fall back on in dealing with whatever this was she was feeling and Hank wasn't doing to her here.

She yanked his head firmly in the direction she wanted it and tightened her hand on his chin to hold him in place, the same way she had to with Bele and Mike. Perhaps she'd have better luck ignoring her body's importune announcements if she thought of Hank as just another one of the boys. *Yeah, right,* her mind snorted. *As if.* "And if you don't sit still, I'll be carving scalp with these clippers in a minute instead of hair."

"If you want my opinion," Tai said, not for the first time, "Hair or no hair, if this joint's teen geared you're gonna be too old to get in."

"Yeah, but," Carly argued, repeating her own theme for the evening, "if it's a recruiting point, buzz him, dress him right, give him the language and he'll fit right in."

"I don't give a fig what you do to him," the local sheriff muttered peevishly to the commander in charge of the local state-police post standing beside him. "I don't want a civilian screwin' up my operation—"

"I'm not a civilian," Hank pointed out for the hundred and fifteenth time. "I'm a—"

"Even if," the sheriff continued emphatically, glaring at Hank, "he is some sort of glorified used-to-be-undercover desk-jockey fed. Civilians and any kind of feds always confuse the issue and muck things up, cuz they don't understand local sensitivities."

"Not to mention the amounta paperwork ya gotta file and the

Infernal Repairs malarkey ya gotta deal with if anything happens to 'em,'' the statie concurred mournfully, deliberately referring to the department's IAD team by one of its more repeatable aliases. "And they're so outta touch with the bottom line that somethin' always happens to 'em.''

The sheriff scratched his thinning pate and chuckled morbidly. "You got that right,'' he agreed. "And the worst of it is, they always find a way to put themselves in charge and drag you down with 'em.''

Hank eyed them without rising to the bait. He wasn't dragging anybody anywhere. He was going after his daughter and leaving them the rest, that was all. Then they could be up to their eyeballs in jurisdictional squabbles over disposition of seized booty with the ATF—Alcohol, Tobacco and Firearms—and the FBI to their hearts' content and leave him out of it.

His own opinion of the state, city and county cops represented here—unvoiced from necessity since Kate still had his mouth and chin squinched between her fingers, holding his head in place while the hair clippers buzzed beside his ear—was that the locals were the ones who had a tendency to drop the ball in joint operations, which was why he was a fed in the first place. Feds, or at least the DEA anyway, simply did it—

Kate's fingers brushed the sensitive skin at the side of his throat, interrupting the completion of his thought; reaction was quick, a straight fizzle of heat to points south, all senses wrenching awake and alive with the adrenaline rush preparing an undercover brought. Hank shut his eyes and his jaw clenched against bad timing; his mind wryly rejoined the thought in progress. As far as he was concerned, the DEA simply did *everything* better. Period.

And some things even better than others. He caught Kate's eye. Reaction and recognition were physical, mutual, immediately denied. But that was an assertion best pursued some other time, if at all.

If.

He shut himself off from the sudden tang of wistfulness on the back of his tongue, forced himself to feel only the itchy drift of hair down his cheeks and neck. Megan liked Kate. Maybe that would make it okay, someday when he and Megan got done with this insanity, to entertain the unchaste thoughts and daydreams of this autumn-haired former nun that he could no longer avoid.

Never depend on someday, his father's voice whispered at his mother's funeral. *All you can ever be sure of is now.*

But *now* was impossible, and both he and Kate knew it.

The clipper's drone ceased; his shorn head felt almost cool in the heat.

Kate released his chin and stepped back, cocking her head to regard him critically. "I dunno." She handed him a mirror, picked up a second and angled it so he could see the back of his head. "I can take more off the top if you want, but that's about all I can do with the back and sides."

Tai shook his head. "I don't know," he told Hank dubiously. "Seems like a heck of a lot of hair to leave to the birds for five minutes' work, *if* you can even get into the pig."

"Oh, I don't think it looks so bad." Carly leaned her chin on Tai's shoulder and combed her fingers playfully through his straight, collar-length black hair. "Looks cool and comfortable." She grinned into Tai's neck. "Maybe you should try it, Tai. Be cute on you."

Tai's response was an impolite snort.

The waiting cops' observations were both ribald and largely unprintable. Kate glanced back at the house, but if any preteens or adolescents with big pitchers had escaped Li's watchful eyes to eavesdrop on adult conversations, they weren't visible. *Good,* she thought. Ilya's and Grisha's American vocabularies were quite unprintably large enough as it was.

For his part, Hank didn't bother with the mirrors, disregarded the comments. Instead he ran a hand over his head, closed his eyes and *felt.*

Yes, there it was, the soft bristly sensation of a military buzz cut with enough left over on top to satisfy vanity. He dug a little deeper, getting into character. And there, hiding in the corners of his psyche, was the clean-shaven military washout with the off-kilter smile and the axe to grind against the world. He was a not-quite-scary sort of guy who never wholly fit in anywhere. He'd been different from his classmates in grade school and the two years of high school he'd managed. Not terribly intelligent, but narrowly read and lately liking to think himself an intellectual. He was a loner who gravitated to the edge of trouble without quite participating in it. He wanted to, though. That was why the marines had appealed to him. Tough guys, ready for trouble, willing to take it to the limit. But they'd rejected him. Psychologically unfit. The reasons were nonspecific. He knew he was marine material—special-forces quality—even if they didn't. One day he would prove it. Maybe soon. But not tonight. Tonight he just needed a few beers in an out-of-the-way place. Maybe lay out a few feelers because he'd heard maybe somebody with a special project in mind was recruiting guys like him.

Guys who were ready to do anything.

The corners of Hank's mouth lifted slightly, part of the rough contours of the character he was creating and becoming. The keen edge of a familiar rush, more potent than any drug, teased at his system, promising more to come. He opened his eyes and looked at Kate.

The change was subtle but distinct, a trifle frightening. Her eyes widened; she stepped back.

"Hank?" she asked uncertainly.

He nodded, looked at the cops. Ready to chuckle some more, their laughter died aborning.

"Judas-stinking-Priest," the statie muttered—respectfully. His hand swept in the direction of his weapon, paused, suspended like his laughter somewhere between incredulity at what he was seeing and what he knew to be true.

The sheriff merely shook his head, disbelieving, a testament to Hank's "talent."

Tai's comment was succinct and to the point, a word he rarely used. "I guess this is why you worked undercover, huh?"

"Guess that means I don't remind anybody of somebody's narc-enforcement dad anymore," Hank responded quietly.

Kate shook her head. "If this was how I first saw you, I'd warn the neighbors and not let my kids anywhere near you."

"Good," Hank said. He turned to the locals. "So, we ready to do it?" he asked.

Risto was playing poker at a rickety round trestle table in the center of the attic casino. His normally ruddy-complexioned Scandinavian features were pale; the pile of chips in front of him was sparse. He acknowledged Megan's approach by pulling his handful of blue-backed cards tighter to his chest and ignoring her. She laid a hand on his shoulder.

"Time to go, Speedy," she said, calling him by the nickname he preferred.

He shook his head, impatient. "Not yet."

"Risto—"

"Do you have money?" he asked without looking up.

"Not for you," she said, short and irritated. They'd had this conversation before and she understood compulsion too well. She wouldn't give him away to Kate or Tai, but she also had worries enough of her own without feeding Risto's addictions, too.

"Meg—"

"How much you down?" Brutal and direct was the only way she knew how to deal with a friend who'd lost control of his limits. It was the way Li dealt with her, the way she'd learned from Kate.

"It does not matter." Risto smiled crookedly up at her. "I will win it back this hand."

Megan peeled his cards away from his chest, viewed them scornfully and let them slap back into place. "Not with these cards."

The other poker players grinned; the one to Risto's left made a big show of tossing a pile of chips into the pot, which the exchange student couldn't match. Risto threw his cards face down on the table, swearing vehemently at Megan in Finnish.

"I'm out," he said, shoving back his chair to rise.

One of the other players, older than the rest, stayed him, holding out his hand, rubbing thumb over fingers in the universal symbol for money.

Risto shook his head. "You know I don't have the money with me."

"Make sure we get it—with interest—within seventy-two hours." The man's voice and face were avid with threat and anticipation, a reminder that an opportunity for violence would be almost as welcome as cash.

Risto nodded, looking only at the fist around his arm. "You hold my..." He hesitated, searching nervously for the term momentarily lost from his English. "You have my IOU."

"Let him go, Danny." Megan stepped forward to take Risto's

arm. "You've got his marker and his word, you hear what I'm saying? He's never welshed before, so give it a rest."

"He's never been down over a grand before." Danny's voice was lazy, his features were anything but. "That's serious green, so you hear what I'm sayin', little girl. Speedy comes through, or we work out a payment plan that could include you."

Megan's lip curled with contempt. "You'd like to be tough, wouldn't you, Danny?" she asked. "But bein' tough's hard when you keep wearin' a little boy's name."

She turned to go, but Danny released Risto and grabbed her wrist, jerking her back. "You better watch your mouth, babe, 'fore it winds you in a world of trouble."

Megan smiled, eyes hard and amused at once—the look, if she'd but known it, a carbon copy of Hank's scary don't-corner-me-or-we'll-find-out-who's-tough challenge. A bead of sweat appeared on Danny's upper lip, his eyes skittered over her face. Megan didn't congratulate herself; she'd inherited a certain reputation as Zevo's on-again, off-again girlfriend, but it didn't take a whole lot of chutzpah to weird Danny out. Without visible effort, she twisted her wrist out of his grasp.

"Go bite yourself, Danny," she advised him evenly. Then she took Risto's hand, turned on her heel and walked away.

The sun was below the horizon, but the sky was still rippled with color: orange-gold-pink along the lip of the world, going up to almost white, fading into mauve and indigo above that; below, the earth burned with faintly retained daylight, fading quickly to dusk's hard-to-see-through gray and black.

Watching the sky, Hank pulled the scuffed S-10 pickup he'd borrowed from Tai into the small lot beside the yellow clapboard house and shut it off. The engine knocked with post-ignition noise, hiccupped, sputtered, then whirred to silence. An almost nauseating eagerness thrummed his veins, sent cocaine-like clarity rushing to his brain while his heart picked up speed and the bottom fell out of his stomach with the electric pulse of adrenaline. For the first time in five years he felt wired, alive, hyperfocused, fearless; wondered how the hell he could ever have given up this sensation, this arrogant, all-consuming knowledge that tonight he'd once again found his zone and could do no wrong. That tonight, every shot he took at the basket would swish through unencumbered and unquestioned.

Then he remembered Megan and the electricity turned up a notch, took on subtly different overtones: fear, worry, doubt, anger.

He wrapped his hands around the steering wheel and squeezed, channeling all his energy into a simple isometric reach for unfettered awareness and calm. He was a DEA agent in an assistant director's suit, but he was not an agent tonight, he reminded himself. He was a parent. This was not a branch of a South American drug cartel he was after here, but his daughter, his child—and other people's children. He was not a rodeo rider charged up to take on a killer brahma tonight; he had to gear down, keep it low-key, remember that he had an entire tricounty area's narcotics-enforcement team waiting on his signal to do cleanup. He was not out here alone, and though he would enter the house by himself, he didn't think he'd come out alone. He was here to collect Megan—he hoped to hell she wasn't inside—period.

He was also here because of Kate—to protect Risto.

At the mere thought of her, a dull, thick ache centered low in his loins, brought pain with the tightening of his jeans. He could almost feel the rub of her nipples through her loose T-shirt and modest brassiere when she stood behind him clipping his hair; sense the swell of her breasts much too close to his cheek—the memory and sensation enhanced, he knew, because like any addict, he was high right now on his own drug of choice, one created by his own body. Nothing like a good rush to bring the noblest intentions to their knees.

Megan, he reminded himself grimly, *you're in this for Megan. Sex with Kate is not part of the program. Wanting to have sex with Kate is not part of the program. And even imagining making love and not just having sex with Kate is way too complicated and absolutely stupid. Idiotic. Out of the question.*

Torture.

And not only that, but he wanted, with all his heart, to make love with Kate Anden and to hell with the consequences.

Needed to make love with Kate, explore every facet of her body and her person, without worrying—or even thinking—about Megan.

The timing of his needs, wants, desires had never been more inconvenient.

Damn. He released the steering wheel and stepped out of the truck, easing his pants away from the uncomfortable stiffness in his crotch. He didn't need this.

He did *not* need this.

So he slammed the truck door, reminded himself of the names he'd been given to get himself inside the blind pig and strode purposefully toward the entrance, concentrating only on the task of the moment.

And not thinking about Kate.

"I don't believe you did that," Risto exploded when he and Megan reached the steps down to the main floor. "You are *crazy.*"

Megan grinned, exhilarated. "Yeah, but it worked, didn't it? C'mon, let's go downstairs, I'll buy ya a drink."

"*Ei kiitos.*" Risto shook his head. "No, thanks. I don't drink anymore in America. I promised Kate."

Megan peered at him. "You won't drink, but you'll gamble?"

Risto looked away, guilty as questioned. "I didn't promise about gambling."

"That's splitting hairs, Speedy." Thoroughly righteous, thoroughly hypocritical. "This is illegal, too. And you're addicted to gambling, even if you aren't to alcohol."

To his credit the youth didn't deny the truth. "Oh, I'm a black pot, but you are a clean kettle, right?"

Megan straightened, deliberately offended. "I don't know what you mean."

"Yes you do." His lip curled disdainfully. "You cannot have it two ways, Megan-*terttu.*" His nickname for her, the word meant "cluster," referred, in his use, to the number of different people she seemed to pack into her singular personality. "You do *not* ask me to confess about me what you..." He paused, locating the word. "What you...*nix* about you."

"Nix?" she asked, mocking him and his command of her language. Avoiding a truth she recognized but refused to admit. "Don't you mean *deny?*"

Risto's jaw tightened under her derision. "You are a bitch."

She grinned, accepting complaint as compliment. Moistening the tip of her index finger, she made a mark in the air.

He flushed but continued, "I like the rush winning cards gives me, but you like danger. You didn't stand up to Danny for me, you did it because making dangerous men look ridiculous in front of their friends gets you high."

She sniffed. "Danny's not dangerous, he's a coward."

"*Ja*," Risto agreed seriously. "He is a coward. Being a coward is what makes him dangerous. He would stab you between the shoulders and you would never see it coming."

"He'd stab me between the shoulders, if I turned my back on him—if we were alone," Megan corrected. "But I won't turn my back and we'll never be alone, so he can't. Anyway, it's not me he's after right now, it's you. How the hell did you lose a thousand dollars to him and how you going to get back your marker?"

"I don't know." Worried, he shrugged his entire body. "And I think the cards are marked."

Megan tapped her upper lip thoughtfully. "Are they," she said. Her eyes gleamed.

Risto eyed her warily. "No," he said emphatically. "Don't help."

"But I want to." She smiled. "It'll be fun."

"No."

"Sure it will." She caught his arm, tugged him down the steps. "C'mon, you can buy *me* a drink and we'll talk about it."

"*Nej*, no, *nyet, non, ei*, absotively not." Vigorously Risto shook his head, dragging away from Megan's hold. "You will *not* help. You will—"

He stopped short, eyes wide. A single Finnish expletive hit the air. Loosely translated, the word meant "pig manure."

"What're you bitchin' about hogs for—" Megan began, turning back to him, then saw what he'd seen: Hank crossing the main floor toward the basement steps in company with Earl. She swallowed. "Oh, damn," she whispered. Then anger hit. "Well isn't that just kick-you-in-the-crotch-and-spit-down-your-neck fantastic. The bastard doesn't trust me."

"I could guess why," Risto offered helpfully.

Megan quelled him with a glance, then hesitated, suddenly unsure which direction to go.

Risto caught her hand. "You have a car?"

She nodded.

"Out the side," he suggested.

They went.

She wasn't there.

Neither was Risto.

Hank didn't know whether to be glad or concerned; the rush in his system dropped off briefly, then returned at a more intense level as the pure cop in him took over from the cop-parent. Not having to think about Megan being here, it was a high he could savor and fiercely enjoy. It wasn't quite the same as kicking down doors and facing possible death on a supercharged DEA raid, but it was far superior to desk work. He wandered through the hazy rooms with one of the men whom the police were outside awaiting his say-so to arrest, noting the apparent ages of the participants, counting heads, taking it all in.

The air was of one big party; the party goers of all ages and not, as Jamal thought, strictly teens to twenties. The youngest kid in the place appeared to be about thirteen, the oldest about forty-two. High-school students—many of them with beers in hand, not a few of them blitzed beyond the ability to know what they were doing or that they were doing it in public—did, indeed, appear to make up the bulk of the underground nightclub's patronage to the tune of about one hundred seventy-five partiers in all.

Pulse rat-a-tatting to the beat of a variety of emotions, Hank observed several liquor and drug-paraphernalia sales, bought a beer out of a pop machine and a bag of marijuana and some cigarette papers from Earl before making one last sweep of the interior on his own. When it became indisputably apparent that Megan and Risto were nowhere on the premises, Hank went outside and turned his purchases over to the officer in charge who gave the signal to commence the strike.

Among other items confiscated, the raid netted twenty-three thousand dollars in cash, controlled substances, narcotics paraphernalia, the pop machine filled with beer, twenty-seven bags of marijuana, pagers, gaming tables, a roulette wheel, computers and computer files pertaining to controlled-substance trafficking, alcohol sales and gambling activities.

Of the 183 persons present, over a hundred were minors under the age of twenty-one. Forty-three under seventeen were ticketed for drinking under the zero-tolerance law; twenty were released to their parents and the remainder were eighteen or older.

The bust gave Hank a grim buzz of satisfaction, the knowledge that, because the area was rural instead of urban and consequently less populated, he'd helped to put a real crimp—however brief— in the local narcotics pipeline. He felt for the unsuspecting parents called to collect youngsters from the scene, but at least they now knew where their children were. Which was a helluva lot more than he could say for himself.

Damn.

Megan dropped Risto off half a mile from Stone House so he could pick and choose his own route home while she went in another direction.

She was flying high after their unwitnessed escape, talkative and jittery, buzzed on the *ma huang*—also known as ephedra, a major source of ephedrine—and faintly intoxicated from the tequila she'd had with Zevo. In other words, in no shape to encounter Kate, her father, Tai or even Li.

It was too bad, really, because the way she felt at the moment she could deal with anything. Sometimes the inside of her head was like a bad neighborhood she shouldn't go into by herself, an isolated village with no way out—unless she…medicated herself. And then she all too often paid for the indulgence in so-called sanity…later.

At the moment, however, all the little pieces of herself that had earlier seemed as if they were going to fly off every which way and get lost so she'd never be able to gather them together again were now firmly cemented in place. The trouble, as always, was that she didn't know how long the pieces would *stay* together. They had a bad habit of ripping to bits every time she turned her back on them. Right now she didn't trust them farther than she could throw them—which wasn't far. Nope, someplace else would be better than going back to Kate's just yet.

Mind elsewhere, she gripped the steering wheel and casually veered her father's car out of the path of oncoming headlights. The wail of a horn followed the other vehicle's retreat. Megan shrugged, waggled a hand at the back window and giggled, giddy.

"Don't get your jockeys in a twist, buddy," she yelled out the open window. "All's well and all that rot, you know."

God, it felt *good* driving tonight. She threw back her head and whooped loud and long. Yeah, *damn* good. Probably didn't have anything to do with driving a car she'd stolen from her father, either. Or leaving Hank hanging back at Danny's and Earl's with his thumb up his butt wondering where she was.

"Whoo-hoo!" Laughing, she whooped again, enjoying the crudity, wishing Zevo were here to share it with. Adolescent male that he was, he appreciated a good laugh at her narco dad's expense. And, God, the look on Hank's face when he stood there lookin' around and didn't spot her—*priceless!* Totally stellar.

She sobered for half a second, recalling how her father had looked with his head shaved, in his seen-better-days clothing...the expression on his face standing beside Earl. There had been a slow moment where she almost hadn't recognized him. If she hadn't seen him dressed to go undercover once when she was a little girl and supposedly in bed long asleep, she might not have. He "didn't bring his work home with him," he'd always told her when she'd asked. Home was for family, not what he did to maintain the family.

In fact, she wasn't supposed to know he'd ever been a cop undercover—and might not have if her mother hadn't told her once when Gen had been in one of her "moods." It was after this revelation she'd started spying on Hank whenever she could, trying to learn why he left them, what "undercover" looked like.

Why he'd left her alone with a mother who often hadn't been quite able to...maintain her balance in the world...when he wasn't around. And how he could possibly not have known what his own wife was like.

No. She shook her head. She wasn't supposed to think about that. Her mother had been beautiful, perfect, exciting. Her mother had loved her to distraction when Hank wasn't around, had told her secrets bigger than herself. And she'd been good to her promise and her mother's memory and kept those secrets from her father, because who could talk to a man whose first wife was his work? Nope, Hank was the fly in the ointment, then as now.

Now...

Already wide, her eyes suddenly widened further as realization struck. Ohmigod, *undercover.* Security at Danny's and Earl's was slim to nonexistent, limited to keeping parents and other questionables on the main floor near the outer doors where there was little to see, but Hank had come in *undercover* to start the raid—and find her. Laughter perked and bubbled, burst in near hysterical giggles and guffaws that made her feel as if she had to wet her pants. Undercover, God. The big hotshot narc who'd gotten a busload of commendations for plying his talents and she'd beaten him at his own game! Damn, whoa, *yes!* She'd beaten him, yeah! What a picture. She was better at his game than he was. Not bad for a kid who felt as if she was flying apart inside her head half the time.

Not bad at all.

High from the punch of achievement as well as the liquor and herbs, she pushed the accelerator to the floor. She swerved the steering wheel again, this time around a deer leaping over a ditch and onto the edge of the road. Smooth. Damn, this felt righteous. She could drive like this all night, pushing the car to the limit, playing chicken with herself. Maybe that was what she'd do—at least until she sobered up enough to go back to Kate's, and until enough time had passed that nobody would guess she and Risto had been out together. Had to keep them guessing...

Of course—

A little of the wind went out of her sails when the qualifier slipped into her mind. Of course, there was always the chance her father would get the police to issue an all-points for his car. And for her. It wouldn't be cool to get caught by the cops in her current state. That might be worse than simply trying to duck Kate and company back at Stone House. She thought about it a moment. Yeah, that could be tons worse. She could lose her license and her freedom and...

And any respect Kate might have for her, any of the trust she'd come to value at the Andens', any time with Bele or the llamas, her friendship with Li...

"Damn."

Swearing, Megan pulled the car to the side of the road and rested her forehead on the plastic wheel. Intermittent traffic whooshed and rushed past her, kicking bits of sand and gravel through her window to sting her arm and cheek. She was seriously screwed up right now, beyond anything she wanted anyone to see, but the possible consequences of just driving on were more

than she wanted to face. She didn't care what Hank thought—
She hesitated. At least she didn't *think* she cared what her father
thought about what she was doing tonight. But Kate's and Tai's
and Li's and Mike's and Bele's and Grisha's and Ilya's opinions
meant something to her. More than something. A lot.

"Okay." She shrugged her mouth and swallowed. "Think,
girlfriend. Use your brain. Get it in gear." She thought for a bit,
alternately folding her lips around her teeth and gnawing on a
fingernail. "Okay, all right, here's what you'll do. Drive in to
Speedway, put gas in the car, buy a toothbrush and toothpaste,
use 'em, get a large espresso with ice, drink it and go home."

Hell. She grinned suddenly, enjoying the conjured picture. If
Hank and the cops were as busy bustin' Danny and Earl and
roundin' up everybody at the club as it looked like they'd be, it
might even be she could get back to Kate's before he did with a
full tank of gas. And that oughta really keep him guessing.

"All right." Even white teeth flashed back at her when she
eyed herself conspiratorially in the rearview mirror. "Let's do
it."

In a spitting shower of gravel and dust, Megan wheeled the car
back onto the highway and headed for Speedway.

Chapter 9

Twilight was hot and restless, coated with clouds whipped around by hot breezes.

Kate sat on a stool inside the female llamas' night enclosure, eyes closed, meditating, while the hot and humid wind prickled her skin, drying sweat and replacing it almost simultaneously. The taste of brewing storms teased her mouth, sent unease skittering like ants underneath the sweetness of the silence she drew around herself, troubled her silent vespers.

Behind her the house was dark, all the chicks in residence and tucked up beneath the quiet roar of the attic fan pulling cool dehumidified air out of the basement.

Risto had returned before dark and apologized, shamefaced, for not letting someone know he was taking off to see friends. There had been a quality of evasion to the admission. The fact that he'd assumed mistrust and offered to let her smell his breath, give him whatever drunk test she wanted, made her feel oddly uncomfortable and not the least bit reassured.

Megan had spun into the driveway and parked behind the house about forty-five minutes after Risto's arrival. She'd alighted from the car dressed like a suburbanite's idea of a biker chick, and without explaining her absence hesitantly asked if her father was around. Informed that he was out looking for her, her face had taken on a strange tightness; when she kissed Kate good-night her breath was mouthwash sweet, her eyes were iris-less and wild.

Unable to judge simply from Megan's behavior, Kate couldn't be sure if the all-pupil look had to do with something the teen had ingested or with the diminishing light level. When Megan had asked if it was okay to spend the night with Li, then asked Kate to tell Hank where she was when he came in, Kate had assented out of uncertainty rather than kindness.

Uncertainty was why she was out in the llama pen communing with the girls and her thoughts.

Sitting with the llamas was calming, somehow gave clarity to fuzzy situations, made thought easier and enhanced meditation. She didn't do uncertainty well, had been confronted with indecision only rarely in her life. Not even Tai's adolescence had thrown her—and he'd been her first. Li, too, was more mature than her age. Dubiously Kate supposed—having heard it suggested by other families who'd adopted children of Asian descent with a similar lack of problems—that ethnic and genetic heritage might be the difference. But it didn't explain Grisha, Ilya and Jamal, with their entirely different backgrounds.

Of course, Grisha and Ilya weren't sixteen yet, and Jamal, while he'd spent an awful lot of time with Kate's family, had just started living with them tonight. For all Kate knew, things would be different once Jamal got used to being here all the time. She hoped they wouldn't—and even went so far as to doubt they would—but anything was possible.

No, although Tai, Li, Grisha, Ilya, Jamal, Bele and Mike all had their little quirks, Kate had only rarely experienced disquiet over anything to do with them. And even then the disquiet hadn't lasted more than a moment or two. Nope, it was merely Risto and Megan who left her feeling she didn't know what to do, or how to handle their...uniquenesses.

Of course, maybe she just didn't know as much about her kids as she thought she did. For instance, did Tai sleep with Carly? He and Carly were both twenty-one and she supposed whether they did or didn't was no longer any of her business. But she'd also never wondered before, either. As complete in and of themselves as the couple seemed, Kate imagined the two of them sleeping together was likely, but...yes, thinking about it was awkward for her, made her squirm.

Probably the same reason she'd never wondered...uncomfortable parent things...about Li—other than the fact that Kate always knew where Li was and couldn't imagine when Li would find the time to do sex, drugs or other harmful things.

She sighed. A parent had to let go of a child sometime, and if Tai hadn't learned where care and caution were needed, where love was necessary before now, Kate could no longer teach him. And anyway, now besides being her son, he was the senior half of their Christmas-tree partnership and her friend. She trusted him.

Perhaps, she consoled herself—grasping at straws, yes, but every parent was entitled to a little straw grasping now and then, weren't they?—her lack of conviction in dealing with Risto and Megan lay in the fact that they weren't really *hers* to deal with.

So then how, she asked herself dryly, do you account for how uninhibited you are if Jamal needs to be corrected when he's here, hmm?

That was different, she assured herself—earnestly. He came with Ilya, they were a pair. If one got in trouble, the other was usually there with him. Same as Bele and Mike.

But, the devil's advocate in her brain argued, Megan came with Li. You've never had a problem dealing with her before, so why now?

The answer rose unwillingly. *Hank.* It wasn't Megan who made her unsure; it was having Hank here with his daughter. It was a sudden caution about stepping on parental toes that were not her own. It was...

Hank himself.

It was standing behind him clipping his hair and brushing up against him and not being sure if she was brushing up against him on purpose because she liked the way he felt, craved the physical sensations that ignited with any unexpected touch. It was the memory of a kiss and a conversation. It was the powerful knowledge he'd given her when he'd told her how much he wanted her. She didn't remember any man ever wanting her because she was herself and not because she was healthy and buxom and had big breasts.

Not that she had a lot of experience to fall back on there.

It was also because she liked him, Hank the father, Hank the man. Hank, who made her blood boil. Hank, whom she'd discovered it was easy to love on the friendship level and whom she didn't think she'd mind loving on whatever other levels were left.

Emotionally.

Physically.

Head and heart, soul and body, all the facets that made up her person. And his.

The truth of the matter was that until Hank Mathison had set foot on the farm, she hadn't known she could feel...

Like this.

Craven. Alone. Lost. Alive. Blossoming.

True, she also hadn't known until she'd left the convent that she could be anything besides a nun and a missionary; hadn't known until she'd found Tai and Li that she could be a mother or a tree farmer or raise llamas or run a miniatures business. From experience, she'd always assumed that need begot ability. But ability had nothing to do with Hank.

She'd found Stone House because when she left the convent she'd needed someplace to go; the crafts had started as something to do with her hands and as a way to help make ends meet. The tree farm had happened as a means to put college money aside for the kids, when she'd adopted Tai and Li. The llamas had arrived accidentally with Mike, inherited from her brother with his son. She'd meant to sell them and never gotten round to it— and now they were a major part of her family's life as well as income. For better or worse, her life was a series of accidental discoveries that grew out of each other and taught her things she'd never known before. And that was Hank: an accident with unforeseen consequences; an education she'd never expected to have.

She'd always known she was a woman, always appreciated the uniqueness of her gender, but until Hank Mathison she'd never known what it was like to feel...

Like a woman.

To want to be a woman in every sense of the word.

Intensely.

To need to understand the physical subtleties of her body, to covet a knowledge she didn't possess.

Unconditionally.

To quite simply and emphatically crave Hank and everything he was, everything he would be.

Passionately, unequivocally, irrevocably.

To understand that for more than thirty-five years she'd been missing a piece of herself that she hadn't even realized existed, and that piece had a name, and its name was Hank.

When in doubt, she thought moodily, take 'em by surprise. Including yourself. It was the motto she lived by.

Lord, why did she have to pick the very moment Megan was in crisis to figure this out and admit it to herself, and who on earth had put Murphy's law in charge of timing?

Probably some masochist, the imp in her head said.

It was one of those rare occasions Kate agreed with the imp.

A llama's sudden warning *clack* brought her alert from reverie. The whinnying, crowing call echoed from the females' pen to the males' loafing shed. The twenty males and geldings lined their fence, the twenty-five females and their young bunched together, curious and watchful, ears alert. Their attention seemed concentrated toward the front of the house. Sure enough, within moments Kate heard Tai's truck rattle down the drive. Mind full of cautions, heart full of care, she let herself out of the pen and went to greet Hank.

He was out of the truck by the time she reached it, leaning over his car with his hands flat on the hood. Trying to feel how long it had been there, Kate guessed, whether it was just arrived or had sat a while.

"She came back about an hour after you left," she volunteered. "Risto got here before she did."

Hank started, jerked around looking for her. She moved around the truck into his line of vision, and stood against the car's driver-side door. He relaxed slightly, took his hands off the hood, then hooked them into his back pockets.

"She all right?" The question was tight, controlled. Worried.

"She's fine. Dressed like a biker babe and lookin' for you—sort of. A little...spooked looking, but none the worse for wear, I guess."

"Was she—" He swallowed, chasing a dry mouth, hating the question. "Was she...high?"

"I don't know, Hank." Kate gave him an unhappy one-shoulder shrug. "Her eyes were all pupil, but the light was bright. She was lucid, she wasn't wobbly. A little wound up maybe, but not high the way I remember seeing kids hopped up when I was in school—or even when I was working the missions."

He ran a hand across his face and through what was left of his hair, then nodded tiredly. Gentleness ran through Kate.

"You okay?" she asked.

"I dunno, Kate. She's here, she wasn't picked up in the raid, but the kid she dates when she wants to make me crazy was. He said he hasn't seen her for weeks, but I dunno. I just don't know."

"Anything I can do?"

"Nah." He shrugged, lost. "I don't think so. Where is she?"

"Upstairs in bed. Asked me if I'd invite you to have breakfast with her. So I am."

"I should go up, tell her I will." He looked like he didn't want to.

"And quiz her?" she queried softly.

"Yeah." Hank laughed without humor. "How'd you guess?"

"Predictable Parent Response number five seventy-four," Kate intoned pompously. "When a kid flies off the handle and takes off, question her about it no matter what time it is."

Hank's jaw tightened, his mouth forming a hard line. He took a step toward her. "You think I should wait?" There was a hint of challenge and ugliness in his voice, a note of *back off, babe, you're crossing a line.*

Kate heard the unspoken message and ignored it. "For what it's worth."

"Not much."

The snap of anger surfaced, aggressive, threatening. His eyes were an occasional glitter in stray moments of light.

A frisson of anticipation ran through Kate, fierce and almost joyous, consolidating the murk of her uncertainties over Risto and Megan, focusing thought, word and action on Hank. On the immediate pleasures of offered battle.

Never formally a soldier, she was nonetheless all warrior at heart.

She inhaled, drawing herself up, taking her own step closer to him, planting her feet. Ready.

"You don't want to do this," she warned.

He shifted, wary, but not backing off. "Why not?"

"Because I'm not the person you're angry with. And I'm on your side. And you're too smart to alienate an ally."

His stance relaxed without losing any of the tension. "You sure?"

"I'm sure."

He regarded her for a long moment, his jaw working. Something in the shadows of his expression altered; intensity and tension proceeded from anger to some other, rawer, less controllable emotion.

He moved another pace toward her and raised a hand...then stopped, his fingers closing tight around a handful of humid night as though to grip something sliding through the sweat of his grasp.

Excitement fingered Kate's skin, trickled with perspiration through the fine sensory hairs standing alert on her arms. With an effort Hank drew a harsh breath, then sighed it away.

"Okay," he agreed abruptly, pivoted and left.

Almost before Kate realized he was going, he was gone, long strides taking him past the llama yards, the workshop and equipment barn, and out beyond the wolf oak that dominated the grassy knoll separating house grounds from the male llamas' knobby day fields. When surprise abated, resolve firmed and she followed him without thinking.

Caution told her to let him go.

Neither instinct nor her heart was familiar with caution.

"Hank," she called softly. "Hank."

"For the love of God, woman, stay away from me." His voice was rough with strain, ragged with invisible exertion. "I can't let you near me right now. Do you understand that? I can't."

"And I can't let you go off alone like this."

He lengthened his stride, outdistancing her again. "Go away, Kate." It was both plea and demand. "It'd be better for both of us if you did."

"Why is it only better for both of us when you decide it is, not when I do?" she wondered aloud, hustling to stay in easy earshot.

"Because I'm bigger'n you and the mood I'm in I could hurt you and I doubt you could do me any real damage."

"Wanna bet? I've been around a lot more dangerous people than you, Hank Mathison, and nobody's managed to maim me yet. I may have been a nun, but that doesn't mean I'm a pacifist or that I don't know how to take care of myself."

"Oh, man." Hank stopped short among the trees at the west edge of the llamas' meadow and spun to face her. "Lady, that is such a crock. You don't know jack about takin' care of yourself in a situation like this. If you did, you'd be on the other side of a door with a deadbolt right now, not out here challenging me, away from anyone who could help you."

"I'm not here to challenge you, Hank." She came to a stop in front of him, put out a hand. "I'm here to help, if I can."

"You can't—" Her fingers touched his arm; he jerked violently away. *"Don't."*

Her hand stayed where it was, poised where he'd left it in the air. She moved toward him again. He watched her come, his breathing unsteady.

"Don't what?" she asked.

"Don't touch…" Air hissed savagely between his teeth, sucked hard into his lungs when she laid her hand on his. His muscles were hard and knotted with restraint; he twitched backward a step, but didn't pull away. "Judas, woman." Each word was an explosion, contained only by force of will. "I'm hanging onto sanity by my fingernails here. Do you know what you're doin'?"

She shook her head and worked her fingers into the fist he made. She didn't know for sure what she was doing, but she wanted to.

Real bad.

Eyes intent on the shadows that were his face, she stepped forward, reclaiming the space he'd put between them. "What am I doing?"

His fingers clenched around hers, drew her hand toward him. "Making it hard to breathe." He swallowed. She was too close; he could almost taste the texture of her skin on his breath. He couldn't think. Couldn't do anything but want. Her. Need her. "Making it hard, period." He exhaled, a rough sound. "Everything." He looked down at her, drew a fast breath of courage and opened her hand, flattened it against the bulge in his fly. Fought himself to simply hold her fingers there when she flinched in surprise and tried to draw away. *"Every*thing," he repeated.

Gulping air, Kate stared down at where she could see the outline of her hand, pancaked under his like a child's game of hand-on-hand, light against the darkness of his jeans. Sensation was intense, detail clear and mesmerizing.

The denim was soft and worn from a thousand washings, the ridge beneath it fascinatingly bone-like. Of their own volition her fingers flexed along that stiff outcropping, causing it to pulse tauter, eliciting a painful hiss from Hank. His fist clamped with crushing force around the contours of her hand and it was as though a savage had replaced what was left of this civilized man. She raised her face to see him, understanding with sudden clarity how important it was to take advantage of time rather than letting time take more advantage of her than it already had.

"You follow me now?" he asked tightly.

"I think so."

She spoke so softly, he couldn't tell if there was loathing or something else in her voice. She didn't try to take back her hand and he didn't think he could let her go to save his life. It had been so long.

So *long...* and nobody else he wanted to share this with.

Only Kate.

The wind chose this moment to shove aside the clouds and loose the moon. Light slanted in to join them beneath the trees, revealing what shadows concealed. Hank saw not loathing on Kate's face but curiosity and gentleness, passion and empathy in almost equal measures. Her free hand lifted; the side of her forefinger defined the shape of his cheek and jaw, chin and throat. He stood very still, feeling the pulse in her fingertips, the willingness and longing in her touch, and forgot everything he was, including his name, in the fullness of her.

"Kate." A single breath, that was all he could catch.

Looking at him, *seeing* him in a way she hadn't before, Kate felt something inside her clutch and give way. Lungs tight, she touched the side of his face with the flat of her palm. He shuddered. Power flowed through her, innately feminine; knowledge uniquely female made her smile. Her palm relaxed against his face, traced down to cup his jaw, drew him within reach. She leaned forward and his breath murmured roughly across her lips.

"Kate." He was floundering. Fumbling to hold onto the boundaries he'd set around them for reasons he could no longer remember.

Trembling.

Her mouth grazed his briefly and withdrew, blew a soft sigh across his dampened lips and nuzzled them again. Boundaries ignited and crumbled, burned to cinders and blew away. When her mouth opened on his, he was there ahead of her, taking as he gave, sucking her breath into himself, feeding his back to her, sharing life.

The kiss consumed like rage, but infinitely sweeter, relentlessly hotter. His hands were everywhere, touching, kneading, holding. In her hair and sliding low down the small of her back, anchoring her to him twice; she wrapped her arms underneath his and held onto his shoulders, pulling him to her with all her strength.

They didn't kiss so much as feed like starving people who'd had food set before them, then been forced to see, to smell, to imagine, but not eat. Finally released, they had no time for amenities, to ask permission, to be polite. There was only time to touch, to feel—to frame each other's faces between their hands, to slide fingers down chests or tunnel them through hair. To pull at clothing that was in the way and discard it as quickly as possible without losing contact the way they'd already lost control.

Tongues dueled and clashed, laved and suckled salty skin; already feverish, their bodies slickened with sweat and would not cool even in the gathering wind. Their hands were as desperate and needy as their mouths, sliding through perspiration to places heavy and aching for relief. When Hank's fingers tangled in the red curls at the apex of her thighs, teasingly low but not low enough, Kate gasped and squirmed, finally brought her own hand down to place his where she wanted it. Hank's laughter at her impatience was rich and touchable, brushed her eager skin like a thousand extra fingertips.

His fingers made her body burn and weep, drew sobbing pleas from her throat. She clutched his shoulders and ground herself against him, bringing her belly tight to his loins and rocking. He gasped, but continued to let his fingers stroke and torture until Kate slipped a hand between them. When she cupped him and rubbed the pad of her thumb over the head of his moistening sex he jerked and went rigid. Then before she knew what was happening, he kicked her heels out from under her and laid her back on the pile of clothes they'd shed.

He didn't need to part her thighs, she did it for him. When the tip of his sex breached the flesh guarding hers, nudged the damp bud just above her opening, she whimpered and arched, pursuing him, luring him. When he leaned forward and brushed his length heavily against her a second time, she unraveled a little and cried out; her pleasure flamed with her ragged breath in his ears, so he held himself above her and pushed against her a third time. Her hips bucked hard upward, rubbing his length, begging for him. Her throat called him, her body wept harder, pleading.

He thrust at her entrance; tiny tremors surrounded him, clasping and milking his flesh as though in welcome for the missing prodigal. His ears filled with Kate's *oh-oh-oohs* of culminating pleasure.

Exerting what little control he had left, he pressed into the small shocks that coursed through her, withdrew slowly, slid forward again a little further. The gasping *oh*s became inarticulate murmurs, then shocked, breathless pants of intensifying rapture that called to him to join her even as they urged him to drive her higher still. Her body felt like heaven, tight and wet and lushly extravagant. He pushed deeper, thrusting with each contraction, his own looming ecstasy increasing with hers. So tight, so slick.

Too tight.

In the moment of lucidity before madness he felt it: no barrier, but the path had never been used, was wild and precarious, a passage he forged for himself. With the last of his strength he braced himself to look down at her, her face abandoned, her hair a wild carpet spread around them. He didn't know if he could stop if she asked him to, but the gift she presented him was too precious to accept without trying.

"Kate."

Her throat arched, breasts plumped against his chest, engorged nipples pouted with invitation. He tried not to look at them. To remember how they tasted.

"Kate, listen to me."

"Hank," she said breathlessly, her back bowed, belly undulating against his, hips pumping and rotating frantically, raveling his resolve. "Please, Hank, please."

"Kate." He was desperate. Every time she moved, a bit of the ledge he was poised on crumbled, drew him toward frenzied completion. He couldn't keep her still.

He didn't want to keep her still.

"Kate, look at me."

Her head moved back and forth, arms tried to draw him down into her. He wanted to slam into her and into her until they were both screaming. Instead he caught a fistful of her hair, forcing her attention. Eyes dark with desire stared up at him. It was a hell of a time for an attack of conscience, he knew, understanding the pleasures her body was only beginning to experience for the first time, understanding that rational thought—under the circumstances—would probably be even more difficult for her than him, but he had to make the offer. Hell, it was already too late to go back in one sense. He hadn't climaxed, but his body had begun to leak for her the moment she'd touched him. Still, he had to be willing to stop if she came to her senses and told him to.

Even if it killed him.

"Kate." Judas, he didn't even know what to say. *Please don't say no, please don't say no.* "Are you sure you want this—want me? Are you sure—" He hesitated. She lay almost still looking up at him, eyes heavy lidded, mouth curved in a come-hither smile. The muscles around her pelvis clasped at him, shuddering a little. His mouth went dry and he shifted slightly, realizing the mistake even as he made it. Fought himself for control when she shut her eyes, tipped back her head and moaned, letting the shimmy of current take her, bring him further inside. "Kate, damn it. Please—" He swore when she moved to pull him deeper still. Grimly tightened his grip in her hair.

The grin she gave him was impudent and knowing, fully female. He swore again. She laughed, husky and seductive, and that ripple of movement nearly undid him. He struggled physically to hold himself back.

"I want you, Hank," she assured him. "I choose you. I give you what's left of my..." The grin became a low, thick, tempting chuckle; languid hands caressed his chest, trailed dilatorily down between them to touch the beginnings of their joining. Her heart filled her voice, even as he felt himself growing thicker and more rigid, stretching to fill her, to touch the deepest part of her and himself. "What's left of my virginity...because you're the only man I've ever wanted to have it and could ever imagine wanting to give it to. Now would you please shut up, and like the songs say, rock my cradle, because I'm damn close to something that feels like it might be spectacular and I want to know what it is and you're the only man I intend to let show me."

"I am." A groan that was almost a question.

She nodded. "Yes. You are. Now tell me, teach..." She dug her heels into his back and undulated her hips, causing him to rock forward off balance. To slip in their shared sweat and lunge deeper into her slick sheath. "Does it do anything for you if I move like this? Does it help—"

She wasn't able to complete the question around the tongue that suddenly stopped her mouth, could as abruptly form no more words even in her head when he stole them with her breath by pulling back and thrusting hard to embed himself fully inside her. Could only gasp when each succeeding thrust drove a little deeper, pulled a little more from her. Could only cry out when the contractions took her, scream her pleasure when he sucked the crest of one breast into his mouth and pumped hard into each small earthquake to create a monumental one.

Stabbed harder and faster until there was nothing left of her alone and she was a shouting, sobbing, sighing part of him.

And in the humid earth of her body, Hank spilled potent seed into her unprotected womb.

Chapter 10

All in all, it was quite a night.

Once found, they were loathe to leave each other—though they tried often enough. More than once, one last kiss turned into more; clothing, reclaimed, was discarded before they had a chance to put it on.

Out of sight of the house, they played like reckless children set free of the watchful eye of parents after dark for the first time, laughing and chasing, splashing and wrestling in the pond to cool off—children, that is, until wrestling gentled and intensified, leading to adult pursuits.

They took and gave and shared, exploring each other until Hank would have thought they were so familiar with each other's bodies that there was nothing more to discover. But there always was. There was this mole or that scar, this spot touched just so that turned her body into a molten flow of lava shuddering beneath him, that spot caressed, which made him stiffen and bow and scrabble to hold onto the earth while he begged her to stop-don't-stop-oh-God-Kate-*please*.

Even when they finally forced themselves to remember who they were and headed back toward the house barely three hours before dawn, they were still too new with each other to stop kissing and touching.

When Kate's enthusiasm knocked him on his butt on the bench around the old wolf oak at the juncture of yard, field and driveway, Hank was already hard again, had one hand up her shirt, the other down her shorts. Somewhere at the back of his mind, he'd no doubt they'd both be sore in the morning, but just now couldn't bring himself to care.

She was his only avocation at present, his preoccupation, and this was the time they had, with no future guarantees. He didn't want it to end. Hands on her hips, he leaned back against the tree when she straddled his lap and watched her face while she rode him, close enough in the shadows so he could read her expression, intoxicated with concentration and desire and euphoria. When she opened hot eyes and looked at him as she reached her peak, he shattered.

The contractions of release pulsed through them long after she slumped forward in his arms and wrapped him up in hers.

It shouldn't have been possible, he knew even if she didn't. He should have been...drained dry...long before now. But so should she. Should have been raw and at least uncomfortable if not in actual pain. Should have been exhausted and temporarily sated. But they weren't. And no celibacy, however long lasting, nor blind-pig-raid-adrenaline-high could explain why, not more than twenty minutes later, Hank found himself once more in such desperate need that he backed Kate up against the rear of the equipment barn and took her where they stood—twice...although the second time he was too wobbly kneed to stand for the entire experience and wound up on his back in the dirt with his hands fisted in Kate's hair and her mouth sealed tight to his while they both bucked and cried out in release.

And he knew damned well that *that* time should have definitely been enough to last him...for however long it had to last him. And it *was*—sort of, at least for the moment—but it also wasn't. Because now that they really were finally both panting and tired and relaxed and giddy and full of each other, they still held onto each other, shared a single space, walking as close together as two people could without falling.

He didn't want to let her go, however briefly, to spend what was left of the night alone in his narrow bed. He wanted to be in hers, have her in his—it didn't matter which—as long as they slept together. As long as they were together.

For her part, Kate was well beyond the ability or the desire to think. What thinking she chose to do had been done early in the evening while she'd waited for news, for Risto and Megan, for Hank.

When he'd arrived she'd simply followed instinct and gone to surrender her body where her heart already lay. She could not give one without the other—at least not this piece of her heart or this part of her body. Her heart was an easy captive, ensnared without reservation—particularly by children—elastic and more durable than anything else created by God or man. But the piece she gave to Hank was different, had been cached forever, forgotten like the smallest jewel at the bottom of a dragon's hoard until the very moment she'd snatched it up and handed it to him. And it didn't matter whether or not he realized how dear the gift was to her. It was his now to cherish or lose, keep, return, put away or give away as he chose. A true gift was given and forgotten, did not have conditions placed upon it, should not have to be worn or displayed simply because the giver came to call.

She recognized, too, the gift Hank gave her in return. Whether his heart was fully involved or not, he'd given her his body, too, shared his passion, rendered to her all he had to give anyone at the moment. The knowledge that he did not waste fleshly desires anywhere and anytime the urge struck him was a powerful aphrodisiac, a priceless treasure. She could no more have withheld from him whatever he asked than she could have held back a comet by its tail.

When they reached the back porch where she'd earlier—forever ago, it seemed—clipped his hair, they stood in the semidarkness before sunrise, holding each other with gentle, reverent hands, and kissed softly. Laughed painfully, conspiratorially at the discovery of swollen mouths and bitten lips; kissed again, anyway, in spite of the bruises.

Hank buried his face in her neck. "You smell like me," he whispered.

"Funny," she murmured into the hollow of his, "I was just thinking the same thing about you."

He shoved her hair aside and pressed a kiss below her ear. "Yeah, I know, I stink. Ain't it grand?"

Kate chuckled, rubbed the backs of her fingers over his stubbled cheek. "Don't think I've ever smelled anything sweeter in my life than you right now."

"Mmmh." He ran his hands the length of her back, over her rump and back up again. "Me neither, you."

Quiet closed around them, thick with humidity and the singing of frogs. Hank roused himself to lean back and look down at Kate.

"You should go in and get some sleep while you can."

She brushed a smile across his throat. "So should you."

"I'm not ready to go in yet."

"Mmm." Kate folded herself back into his arms, snuggled her cheek against his chest. "Neither am I."

"Good," Hank murmured into her hair, gathering her close. "Good."

Down the road at the neighboring melon farm a rooster crowed; Harvey pricked his ears and ran the perimeter of the boys' pen humming and calling. Daylight, rife with heavy clouds pierced by searing sun, touched the horizon: nearly time to rise. Reluctantly Kate pulled away from Hank.

"I should go in and put the coffee on, get breakfast started."

He shook his head. "I'll do coffee and breakfast. You go in and take a hot bath before your muscles stiffen up. You're going to be sore."

She didn't, he noted with amusement, argue. "What about you?"

Gentle fingers traced her cheek. Hank smiled. "I have never," he said truthfully, "felt better in my life." He dipped his head to place a light, lingering kiss on her mouth, then repeated for emphasis, "ever." Then he turned her and guided her firmly up the steps, through the mud room and into the kitchen. "Now, go soak and clean up," he commanded, "before we both find out how depraved I really am and I attack you again."

"Not if I ambush you first," Kate muttered agreeably.

Hank grinned. "We'll experiment with ambushing later," he promised. "Now, go."

Tai passed Kate on her way through the living room to the back bedroom hallway and the first-floor bathroom.

"You're up early," she said, surprised—and guilty. He could have walked in on her and Hank in the kitchen—not that they were doing anything much, just sort of wrapped up in each other, but...

But, she admonished herself practically, it would have been a little embarrassing for all of us, yes. Still, Tai was a big boy, old enough to handle his mother "gettin' some" without the very idea damaging his psyche. Not to mention that—given his rather droll sense of humor—he probably would have found Kate mooning over Hank in the kitchen pretty funny.

"So what's up?" she asked.

Tai shook his head. "Not much. Gotta meet Gus Krahn out at his farm in Cohoctah in an hour. Got the ag agent comin' out to look at some sort of blight in his trees he's never seen before. I want to hear what Shiner's got to say about Gus's trees and get back before it storms, but other than that it's B-A-U."

Kate raised her eyebrows. She'd just figured out what the phrase *24-7* which Li and Megan tossed around, meant—twenty-four hours a day, seven days a week—and now here was another one. "B-A-U?" she asked.

Tai grinned. "Business as usual," he told her.

She rolled her eyes. Of course. "I should have guessed."

"You're gettin' slow in your old age, Ma." Tai bussed her cheek and headed for the kitchen. "There coffee?"

Kate sniffed the air, rich with the aroma of the Jamaican Blue Mountain roast. Her mother had brought the beans back from her latest jaunt with Habitat for Humanity to rebuild homes near Kingston destroyed during a hurricane. "You can't smell it?"

Tai shook his head. "Hay fever's got my nose in a snit."

"So take your medication and breathe deep," Kate admonished and shut the bathroom door behind her.

For a moment Tai stared thoughtfully at the closed white six-panel door. Just a second there, he would have sworn his mother glowed...not unlike the way Carly did after they'd spent a long *hot* evening at her apartment. But no, he dismissed the idea as ludicrous. That couldn't be. Kate was his mother, for God's sake.

He shook his head. Nope, not possible. Mothers did not, at any time, act like some horn dog's girlfriend. Although he'd often thought she should, his mother didn't even date, so how and when could she...

Still, her mouth *had* looked a bit swollen, also like Carly's last night after...

No. No, nope, hun-unh. He shuddered, slapped himself on the forehead and told himself to get his brain out of the Dumpster. She was his mother, and unlike Tai where Carly was concerned, his mother had self-control. He was out of his mind to even consider anything else.

Spurning the notion for good, Tai hiked up his jeans, stepped into the kitchen and startled Hank.

She hated his haircut and he looked like sex.

Eying her father with calculation, Megan set a tray of coffee, juice, bagels and strawberry cream cheese on the large electrical spool Tai had found and Li had cleaned up and painted for use as a table on the front porch.

Peering guardedly back, Hank poured himself his sixth cup of coffee of the morning and wordlessly offered to pour Megan a cup. She shook her head and poured herself some juice instead, offered Hank the plate of bagels and cream cheese. He selected a pair of bagel halves, glopped cream cheese onto each and withdrew. Megan made her own selection, smeared a dainty layer of the pinkish cheese over it and sat in the bamboo chair near her father, the spool table between them.

The air was still and sticky, the sky gray-green with the possibility of tornadoes. Already south-central Michigan was under a six-hour watch with a severe thunderstorm warning in effect. So far this summer, however, the weather had been full of threats without follow-through. Oh, some medium to heavy squalls, but nothing as destructive as the meteorologists predicted. The weather was more like building tension, layer on layer, that petered out just when you thought it would either explode and have done or blow over altogether.

A lot like his relationship with Megan.

"This is nice," Hank said, although he wasn't sure whether it was or not. He wanted to ask Megan where she'd been the previous night, but she typically did not respond well to questioning, preferring to volunteer information—if she was going to inform at all, that is.

Watching him, Megan nibbled at her bagel and nodded. She

couldn't, for the life of her, remember why she'd invited him to breakfast-for-just-the-two-of-them this morning. Spending time alone with him was always so awkward since her mother had died. She suspected that a large part of the problem was that she and Hank didn't particularly like each other, although she was aware he loved her. She wasn't real sure sometimes how she felt about him, but he was what she had.

And damn it to hell and back, this morning when he should have been fit to be tied over her disappearance and the raid from the night before, he looked like freaking *sex,* sorta the way Zevo did when they'd been doin' some heavy makin' out and he'd been tryin' to get inside her pants and got carried away. Like Zevo's, her father's lips were swollen and there was a love-bite bruise at the right corner of his mouth and *damned* if he didn't have a *hickey* on his throat. And for a man who seemed like he wanted to either question his daughter or throttle her for scaring him half to death he looked too pretty stinking *satisfied* with himself for belief.

He was too *old* to look so...so...like he'd gotten *plenty* last night, when common knowledge was that men hit their sexual peak when they were still boys of eighteen and it only went downhill for them from there.

God, it was just entirely too gross to contemplate.

Not to mention that, if he'd really loved her mother he shouldn't be gettin' any *anything* from anywhere but his wife. And dead didn't matter, loyalty did, and he was her *parent* for spit's sake and his betrayal set a bad example for *her,* didn't he realize that? He was her father, and fathers—even widowed ones—weren't supposed to need or want or act dishonorably and they weren't supposed to...

What they "weren't supposed to" got a little muddled in Megan's head from there, but she was pretty certain it made sense—if only she could straighten it out enough to bang that sense into Hank's head.

Or even her own.

Instead, because confusion, disappointment and pique made her forget anything she might have said that was remotely civilized, she swallowed the bite of bagel she was chewing, swigged a mouthful of juice and said conversationally, "Gee, Dad, you look like you've been in a whorehouse, and maybe you shoulda showered before breakfast. Who'd you screw last night, anyway?''

The bite of bagel Hank was about to take fell out of his mouth and into his hand. His eyes narrowed, his mouth thinned. ''Pardon?'' he asked softly.

Megan shrugged, enjoying the shock on his face—life would hardly be worth living if she couldn't knock Hank on his heels at least several times a week—and simplified the already coarse language for him. ''Was it anyone I know, and did you at least wear a fun bag to the party so I don't wind up an orphan in a few years?''

She'd made love with Hank Mathison.

And not just once, but several times.

Kate tried to hold it back, but the grin came anyway, uninvited, wide and naughty and joyous. Wow. Double and triple *wow*. So *that* was what the fuss was about. No wonder. It was *amazing*, incredible.

And Hank, himself, was more than she had words to describe.

She'd realized that long before she'd known she would lay with him, but now...she understood more, knew everything she'd already known about him in some deeper part of herself—inside her heart, inside her soul and inside her body as well as inside her mind. He was decent and honorable, funny and wry, possessed of an able-to-laugh-at-himself sense of humor. He was passionate and uninhibited, unrestrained and capable of giving wholly, unconditionally of himself. He was a man of strength, as capable of violence as he was of love, but a man who knew himself well enough to hold violence in check...even as he could not say love.

And that was the thing she knew about him now that she hadn't realized before. That he had seen and heard important words used too lightly to convey things they didn't mean. He meant what he said when he said it, but he preferred to ''show, not tell,'' because the fewer words used, the fewer lies that could be told. He'd seen and done enough lying in his career to know.

She climbed out of the bathtub—tepid to cool water in the morning's already stifling heat, instead of the hot water Hank had prescribed—and sloughed condensation off the mirror, wondering if the imprint he'd made on her heart showed as plainly on her face as it felt like it did. There was her mouth, plumped out from kisses as though she'd had collagen injections; below her left ear, the sucking print bestowed by teeth and tongue, and there, in the fleshy mound above her right breast a similar but darker brand that named her as his.

Looking down at herself, Kate fingered the symbol of Hank's claim, noted the softened but still distended pout of her breasts and nipples. Even now they ached as much for his touch as they did from it—and that ache was as sweet as the sting between her legs, the awareness that if he asked she would gladly welcome him there again, this instant.

Whether he knew it yet or not, he was hers.

And that was the difference she saw in the mirror when she looked this time: a softening around her mouth, the glow in her eyes that proclaimed her not only a woman who'd taken a lover, but a woman who'd chosen a mate, a woman who loved.

"Was it anyone I know, and did you at least wear a fun bag to the party so I don't wind up an orphan in a few years?"

Two hours later, still reeling from his daughter's verbal punch in the face, Hank sat in the shade near the equipment shed and stared at the bits of llama halter in his fingers. It hadn't occurred to him until Megan's...ill mannered, to say the least...question that he and Kate hadn't been the least bit careful.

Startled he might be, but Hank couldn't regret not using protection when he did realize it—well, he *could* but it wouldn't do any good now—because, well...regret wasn't his way. Not to mention that it wasn't possible for him to regret anything he'd shared with Kate the previous night. Not no way, no how, as Gen's granddad used to say.

Blood tests wouldn't be out of the question, of course, but he'd been clean as of his last physical, and sitting behind a desk for the past five years rarely, if ever, put him at risk of accidental exposure to anything except whatever flu was going around the office at any given time. And as for Kate, well...he'd gone with her when she took Bele into the prosthetics unit at University of Michigan Medical for his fitting. While Bele and the prosthetist had gone about deciding whether the boy needed only a new pylon or both pylon and suspension, Kate had gone off to the lab to donate a pint of blood—a regular routine, according to what Dennis had told him. From the health standpoint, Hank figured they were as safe as conservative, nonrisk behavior could make them.

Which didn't make Megan's question any easier to answer.

It wasn't her crudity that bothered him so much as her attitude. Crudity he understood, had on occasion used himself as a cover for emotions he needed to hold at bay, or to disguise realities that were too vulgar to deal with in any given moment. Crudity buried insecurity, fear, forced attention away from an instant, substituted for boldness, acted as an anchor to peers in the rough seas of adolescence—and, as often as not, adulthood.

No, although it was hardly attractive and certainly didn't make his daughter more likable, and while he hated both hearing it come out of her mouth too easily and finding himself shocked when it did, the gritty-to-obscene language she used to voice her observations wasn't the problem. It was the whole way she seemed to look at sex, love and everything else.

He *could* say, "You won't be an orphan because of my carelessness." Or he could go on the offensive and ask her—God, what a thought—what *she* used.

Or he could sit where he was and feel as if she'd ripped out his heart with her callousness, then jammed her thumb in his eye for good measure.

None of those responses were acceptable when what he had before him was a prime opportunity to talk with his daughter about the differences between love and sex, peer pressure and choice, reckless behavior and commitment.

Still, it was difficult for a father to describe the difference between having sex and making love to his hard-as-nails sixteen-year-old daughter when he wasn't ready to admit the possibility of *love* to himself. Harder, yet, to explain the differences between the willingness to make a commitment and a casual fling, emotional experience and inexperience, choice and the acceptance of accountability, whatever the outcome, to someone who was still going out of her way to avoid certain responsibilities and who, because of her lack of years, thought she knew it all. So he didn't try.

Besides, at this juncture, it was none of Megan's damned business anyway, and Kate hadn't said, "Hey, go ahead, spread the news, tell the kids we made love last night and that we're probably going to again and see how they deal with it.''

He also wasn't ready to share his new...relationship—for want of a better word—with Kate with anyone else yet, and especially not with Megan.

Despite how...permanent...being with Kate had felt the previous night, they were still way too new to be sure of each other. Whatever he'd felt, she'd felt, might all have been an accident of time, place and circumstance, rather than something lasting. He didn't think that was the case, but it had been a long time since he'd shared intimacies with a woman and it had been a "never before" for Kate with a man, so what did he know?

Not much sometimes, judging by Megan, that was sure.

Which brought him down to the thing that troubled him, sitting alone in the doorway of the equipment barn repairing a llama halter and watching the ominous sky: what he'd actually said in response to Megan's provoking question.

"Honey—" He'd risen to lay his palms flat on the table, then leaned forward until he was nose to nose with her; his tone had been scalding. "If I even considered doing anything like you suggest last night or ever, you don't have the language to describe it. I do not now, did not last night, nor will I ever screw anyone. The only time or way to have sex is when it's more than sex, when you're ready to make a commitment to another person and make love, with love. Until you've got that figured out you're not anywhere near old enough to even consider it for yourself, let alone question me about my alleged activities. You got that?''

Then he'd left and Megan had been the one with the fallen bite of bagel in her hand and the shock on her face.

Shocking her for a change felt good, but Hank wasn't certain he'd handled...the details...as well as he might have. Wasn't sure he'd said all there was to say and was pretty convinced he should have stayed where he was instead of leaving.

Was sure he could have put things in a little more positive light, left room for further discussion instead of closing off potential dialogue quite so...effectively.

Still, whether he let her know it or not, she'd had quite an effect on him. Within thirty minutes of leaving Megan, he'd showered, dressed and taken a run into a pharmacy for condoms. It might be a bit like closing the barn door after the llamas got loose, but the flip view was: better late than never.

Or so he hoped.

Chapter 11

The day progressed in dregs and bits, cranky with humidity and crowded with emotional portent.

With the sky as threatening as the weather report, everyone stayed out of the fields and near the house. As the heat rose, Kate had the older kids rig awnings to extend the cooler areas around the loafing sheds and the surrounding trees. Bele and Mike also helped Li run hoses and set up sprinklers and wading pools in the open pens to keep the llamas cool.

The bandanna Kate wore to hide the hickey on her neck did double duty when she wrapped a tube of crushed ice in it and once again tied it under her hair. The chill was heaven amid the temperatures of hell. Hank made sure no one was around to see, then dropped a kiss on her temple when she brought a similar ice-filled bandanna to him. She smiled up at him and drew her finger along his jaw in a gesture of intimacy and familiarity that spoke volumes.

He had trouble letting her go after that, but anything further was inappropriate to the moment so he did—reluctantly. Time was a commodity they both needed and neither could afford, stretched as it was to accommodate more than possible already.

Maybe he thought, watching Kate stride across to the house, they could squeeze in dinner together one night, a movie or something.

It was the "or something" that lay closest to the surface of his heart.

Troubled eyes following her father whenever he was in sight, Megan stood in the shade with Harvey and, hardly aware that she was doing it, brushed the patient llama in the same spot until he trod gently on her toe in an attempt to get her to quit or move on. When that failed, he switched his hindquarters around and bumped her into the maple they stood beneath. When she rocked sideways into the tree and eyed him with surprise, Harvey stretched out his neck to sniff noses with her before swinging his head and butting the brush out of her hand. The message was as plain as the body language, "Enough already, knock it off." Then he touched his nose to hers again, looked around at where her father helped Bele reposition a wading pool, and turned back to her. Harvey's communication this time was equally—if disconcertingly—clear inside Megan's head. *"It's been a long time, little one, and he's not like llamas. All life cycles forward, it doesn't stop for death. Your father is a lonely man, and a lonely man needs a life mate. Time to grow up, little friend, and get over it. Time to respect your father's humanness the way you want him to respect yours."*

Having experienced this inexplicable sort of...telepathic communication with Harvey before, Megan was hardly surprised by the gentle rebuke. Kate had long ago matter-of-factly told her that five thousand years of interaction with humans made some sort of communication between their two species probable. She'd suggested Megan consider the contact she shared with Harvey as a bridge to understanding, a far more advanced and enhanced version of the type of communication that existed between humans and house pets such as dogs or cats.

Accepting whatever kind of special rapport existed between herself and the llama, however, didn't mean Megan was also willing to buy Harvey's...*observations* as gospel.

No matter how right he might be.

Hank jumping down her throat this morning when she'd accused him of having indiscriminate sex had been both eye-opening and disturbing. It had never even occurred to her he might fall in love again—nor that, being a man and a seemingly rather obtuse man at that, he would have such romantic notions of what sex should be. If he wasn't her father, she might find his attitude cute, but archaic.

Nearby Harvey tossed his head and made hawking and spitting sounds in her general direction. Megan ignored him, refusing to believe the camelid might actually be commenting on her thoughts.

Tai arrived back from his discussion with the extension agent at Krahn's tree farm, thoughtful and determined. Although the new strain of blight that was attacking Gus's trees and turning them brown before killing them seemed to be confined to the specific genus of firs he grew and apparently wasn't spreading to his pines and spruces, Tai knew better than to be complacent simply because Stone House didn't grow the firs.

Against Kate's admonishings and in spite of the storm warnings and rising winds, he collected his hand magnifier and headed for the fields on the tractor. He would, he assured his partner—and he stressed the word, separating Kate from her maternal instincts as effectively as possible—take Risto with him and do a fast check of the trees and come back in and, oh, by the way, her bandanna was slipping and she had a bruise on her neck that looked like a hickey and she might just want to cover that up before Ilya and his rampant imagination concocted a story about it....

Tai wasn't the only one who had comments to make Kate think twice about...well, *things.* Li also had a few things to say—although none of them was directed at Kate per se. But they did strike home.

Hard.

It was early afternoon in a quiet kitchen. Kate was boiling macaroni and preparing raw vegetables for a macaroni-salad supper; Li and Megan were at the table separating the day's mail. Amid the pile of envelopes were two that were identical, one addressed to each of them. Li quickly slit hers open, while Megan paused first to read the return address.

"Baby shower," she pronounced scornfully before Li could pull her card loose and tossed the envelope aside unopened.

Li nodded, regarding Megan thoughtfully. "Lynn Deering's. She must have decided to keep the baby after all."

"Or she let her parents decide she was going to keep it."

Trying to appear as if she wasn't, Kate moved quietly about the kitchen, ears hard pricked, listening.

"You don't think she should?" Li asked.

"I told her I thought she was a fool for screwin' around with Barry at all, let alone without protection. She said they were in love—" Megan exaggerated the word "—and Barry doesn't like condoms cuz they 'don't feel natural,' and it didn't matter if she got pregnant, anyway, because creating a baby would show their *love* to the world. I tried to tell her to open her eyes, that Barry's puttin' it to Kiki Sorensen and Ellie Dane and God only knows who else, too, and everybody *knows* they're not exactly *discreet* about where they spread their legs, so she better get down to the clinic and find out if she's got anything ugly and she tells me to stuff it in my bra and pretend I've got boobs. But she goes to the clinic anyway, and everything but her pregnancy test comes back negative, so they give her a bunch of literature on her options.

"So then she goes and tells Barry and he smacks her in the eye and calls her a liar and a bunch of other things—like slut— and dumps her and goes off and knocks up Marcia Glass and does the whole routine again because 'they're wrong,' and Lynn figures she's been an idiot and decides it'd be better for her and the baby if she gives it up and finishes school so much the wiser. But now she's not because her parents think that 'doing the right thing' means she should keep a baby she's not ready for because 'she made her bed and now she's got to lie in it,' an' it just cheeses me that when there are so many people out there who can't have kids the natural way and are dying to adopt babies that her parents can't see that 'doing the right thing' could mean so much more than keeping a baby nobody wants because it's your flesh and blood. So no." Megan shook her head, all self-righteous I-told-her-so. "I'm *not* goin' to her baby shower and look like I approve of what she's doin', when I think she's just a damned weak-bellied idiot."

The stamped foot and *so there* were absent, but loudly implied.

"Megan!" Shocked, Kate—who wasn't supposed to be eavesdropping, even though the girls were sitting not ten feet from her and hadn't lowered their voices so she couldn't—swung about to say something suitably appalled and hopefully wise, but Li waved her mother aside and beat her to it.

"She's your *friend*," Kate's daughter said tightly.

"Friendship has limits," Megan observed, unperturbed, rising to stack the mail in piles at the end of the table.

Li stiffened, then worked her neck and made herself relax. "Does it," she said mildly. It was hardly a question. Her eyes sparked, but instead of clenching, her hands spread open before her, almost in offering. "And what limits do you put on our friendship?"

Megan viewed her, surprised. "None, of course."

"Why not?"

"Because I don't."

Li's jaw jutted. "Wrong answer," she said softly.

For the first time since Kate had known her, she saw Megan squirm uncomfortably. "Li..."

"Why not?" Li repeated. A thread of strong emotion ran like tensioned wire between the two words.

"Because..." Unease settled in Megan's features. "Because...I can count on you no matter what."

"And you've never been able to count on Lynn?"

"Lynn's always in my face about stuff," she said defiantly. "You're not."

"I get in your face all the time," Li pointed out. "Especially when you're hangin' out with Zevo and that bunch of scags."

"Yeah, well, I've known you forever," Megan said with asperity, "and you don't screw around or date guys like Barry."

"And I always let you in, no matter what you've done lately, and Lynn's mother won't let her."

"Yeah, well..."

"So what do *I* get out of this relationship? I mean, do I have to worry about you deciding you don't like who I'm seeing or something and dumping me because it's too hard to cart the friendship around anymore, even though I lend you my mother anytime you need one?"

Megan's lips pinched and her eyes clouded, vulnerable. "Li, I know how it seems sometimes, but you know that's not the only reason I come here. You're like my sister. We fight, but it doesn't change anything."

"Yet," Li supplied.

"Ever," Megan shouted.

"Yeah, well, that's the way Lynn thought you were with her, too. She's as much there for you as she can be, when some guy isn't messin' with her head. You've known her since diapers. That's longer'n you've known me. Now she needs you to buy her some."

Megan's mouth opened, then closed for lack of retort. Her shoulders slumped; she looked at Li. "Sometimes I hate you."

"Yeah, well, get over it," Li responded dryly. Then, prodding Megan with her elbow, "You want to go shopping?"

Megan rolled her eyes and grimaced. "Do I have a choice?" she asked.

Grinning, Li shook her head. "No."

"Oh, fine, then," Megan agreed—ungraciously. "But I'm not buying diapers."

Li bent to drag her purse out of the pot cupboard. "You don't find the symbolism appropriate?"

"What?"

Li eyed her, all innocence. "You don't think she should have stuck rubber pants on Barry before—"

Laughter hiccuped out of Megan, cutting Li off. "Geez, Li. And we all thought you were the nice one."

"I am," Li said firmly and turned to Kate. "Okay if we take the van and run into town?"

"How does the sky look?" Kate countered.

Li shrugged. "Not worse. Don't worry, we'll keep the radio on and hit a ditch if we have to—and we won't be gone long."

Kate looked from her daughter to Megan and back. "Okay." She nodded, then added, "Take the grocery list?"

Li eyed Megan who shrugged. "Sure," they agreed.

Kate went into the office and came back with an envelope containing the grocery list and money, handed them to her daughter with a couple extra bills and a quick hug. "Get Lynnie a baby bathtub from me, okay?"

"I will, Mum." Li returned the hug with a swift peck on Kate's cheek. "Thanks."

They left.

Lips pressed tight together against the foreboding she'd hidden in front of the girls, Kate collapsed on one of the long benches and rested her elbows on the table. She gnawed her thumbnail and swallowed hard. Rubber pants. Oh, crumb.

She hadn't even thought about condoms the night before. Or anything much else, for that matter, except having Hank as deeply inside her as possible, as often as possible. And she couldn't even claim being a teenager for an excuse since she hadn't been one for close to twenty years. And it wasn't as if she'd never considered birth control. She had been on the pill during her years in refugee camps set up at the edge of border or civil wars. Her decision had come in the wake of the rape and murder of mission nuns in Central America and Africa. It was, she felt, better under the circumstances to prevent the possibility of pregnancy by rape than to bear a child condemned by the violence of its conception.

But she wasn't on the pill anymore, and the rest was neither here nor there at the moment.

Worrying the inside of her cheek between her teeth, she rose and went to pull the appointment calendar out of the kitchen's telephone drawer. Counted backward to the date of her last period. Bit her lip at the number: fifteen days today. Mid-cycle.

Possible.

Hand clutching her stomach, she shut the drawer and breathed. Stared thoughtfully into the middle distance trying to think. Possible. Having had an irregular monthly before she went on the pill and an extremely regular one ever since, Kate knew too much about the rhythms of her own body, had participated in too much emergency midwifery and family counseling to deny likelihood when it stared her in the face.

She sucked air, blew it out. Pregnant. Maybe. And Bele's adoption wouldn't be final for another two months. If she was, and family services found out, would it mess things up? But maybe she wasn't. Better not to obsess over it then, and maybe appear guilty and nervous, in case the adoption rep picked up on something that wasn't even there to worry about. And what about Megan...and Hank?

She felt herself pale. Oh, Lord. What had she done? She didn't really know Hank all that well. She'd let emotion get away from her because, well, he just...

Felt *right*.

Bad excuse, she knew, but there it was. Wars and marriages had both been started over less. And if it was just himself, he'd probably be all right with...whatever. But Megan... Oh, Lord, *Megan.* She barely accepted her father as he was, let alone...

Oh, gosh. Oh, blast. Oh, stupid, bloody *hell.*

But maybe she wasn't. Maybe...

She huffed another breath and straightened. Maybe she ought to go find Hank right now and apprise him of the possibility so he'd—no, *they'd*—have plenty of time to figure out how to handle all the potential situations if a consequence of thoughtless loving came to call.

The sky was black with clouds when Kate crossed the drive in search of Hank.

In the southwest thunder growled; heavy wind from the same direction spit dirt and light gravel at her, pushed her hair into her mouth and eyes. In the llama yards, the shade awnings alternately snapped taut in the wind and sagged toward collapse on keeling poles. Around the yard and fields, trees swayed and bent, branches swung like wild arms tangling and parting.

Kate gathered her hair together, and with a quick glance to gauge the storm's nearness and a worried one down the track to see if Tai, Risto and the tractor were on their way in, changed course for the pens to drop the awnings before the wind took them down atop the milling llamas.

On the other side of the drive, Hank emerged from the wood-shop with the five younger kids and their constant canine companion. When he saw Kate struggling with the canvas, he jerked a thumb, sending the boys toward the house, then ducked his head and ran to help her.

"Where're the kids?" she yelled over the wind when she saw him.

"House, basement," he shouted back. "Girls?"

"Shopping. Hopefully they'll stay put till this blows past."

Dragging canvas into a quick, transportable bundle, Hank nodded. It was ten miles to the department store-strip mall complex, far enough in Michigan for a completely different set of weather to exist. "What about Tai and Risto?"

Kate collapsed the last of the awning poles and cast a worried look toward the tree fields. Overhead the wind grew wilder and the sky roiled black with clouds. The first fat drops of rain splatted her face and hair. "Still out. I hate it when Tai does this."

"You want me to run out and drag 'em in?"

"No." She shook her head. "Either he's on his way in or—"

The sudden crack of lightning and a prolonged crash of thunder cut her off. The wind gathered breath and roared, severing a branch from one of the trees above the picnic tables and pelting them with hail. Hank grabbed Kate's arm.

"Come on!" he shouted.

Together they ran for the nearest shelter: the barn.

"Where's Mum, isn't she coming in?" Bele asked, frightened.

Standing on a chair so he could see out one of the tiny basement windows, Jamal shook his head. "She's okay. She 'n' Hank got to the barn. They'll go down in the pit."

"Is there a tornado here yet?" Mike asked, interested. "The radio says one's coming."

"I can't see anything," Grisha announced from his post at the west side window. "Too much rain an' stuff. But I hear a train."

Ilya shoved his brother off the wooden box he was standing on. "We don't have a train here."

They looked at each other, then at the rest of the boys.

"Tornado!" they all shouted at once—or perhaps crowed would be a more accurate description, and *Adventure!* a more accurate shout. Grinning at each other in half-delighted terror, they dashed to a corner farthest from the windows, huddled around the radio and held onto the dog's collar, clutched their flashlights and waited.

Whatever the new blight that was decimating Gus Krahn's Fraser firs, it hadn't come near Stone House's Douglas firs.

With a sigh of relief, Tai allowed the wind to tear the last branch he'd chosen to examine out of his hand and let the hand magnifier he wore on a strap around his neck swing free against his chest. It swayed lazily with the ripple of his T-shirt; he faced southwest, gauging the sky, letting the strengthening wind whip his hair out of his face. Thunder sounded close overhead, green-black clouds raced toward him, leaving a muted gray swath peppered by lightning gashes at the horizon. Behind him he heard a fizzle and *crack,* turned in time to see the storm fold and break one of the birch trees clumped at the north edge of the field.

He ran for the tractor, tagging Risto on his way. It was way past time to head in. Instead of following, the Finn grabbed Tai's arm and gestured wildly at the dark funnel forming in the western sky. Without a word the two turned and dashed to throw themselves facedown with their arms covering their heads in the shallow gully on the opposite edge of the field.

Loitering under the shopping-center overhang, smoking and waiting out the weather so he could continue skateboarding illegally with his buds, Zevo spotted Megan and Li when they parked outside of the mall.

"How 'bout I go to Hallmark and get the wrapping paper and cards for Lynn and you get the groceries," Megan suggested.

Eyeing the sky, Li nodded. "Good idea, save time." She checked the number of items on Kate's shopping list. "Meet you at the car in, um, half an hour?"

"You got it."

They parted. Mood as black as his jacket, Zevo waited until Li was inside the grocery store before taking a last long drag then pitching the stub of his cigarette into a puddle near the curb. Hands tucked into the pockets of his sagging baggies, he sauntered forward and barred Megan's path.

"Hey, babe," he said. There was nothing friendly in the greeting.

Megan attempted to step around him. "I don't have time right now, Zevo. I'll talk to you later, okay?"

"No." Zevo shook his head. Faster than Megan would have thought possible a hand came out of a pocket and fisted around her wrist, pulled her roughly forward. "Now."

"Zevo, stop it," Megan said sharply, twisting her arm, trying to free it. Without success. She looked up at him, saw the something in his eyes that told her this was not "business as usual" between them, that he'd unwrapped himself from around her little finger and figuratively taken the ring she'd always led him around by out of his nose.

That he and only he, not she, would be in charge of this conversation's beginning, middle and end.

For the first time in their relationship, she tasted fear. "You're hurting me," she told him in the cool, scathing tone that had so easily kept him in his place in the past.

He smiled. "How 'bout that?" Once again Megan tried to wrest her arm from him. His grip tightened, he wrenched her back. "You know how tight handcuffs get, Meg?" he asked softly, shaking her wrist. "Just like this."

"I don't know what you're talking about and I have to go, Zevo," she said. Alarm showed. She swallowed it. "Really."

"Your cop pop put me in handcuffs last night, Meg." He spun her around and caught her other wrist, fit it into his hand with the first. She struggled to no avail; he shoved her face first into the wide expanse of brick between store windows and held her there with his free hand between her shoulders. "Like this. Then he dragged me out to a car and locked me to the seat and made me sit like that. It wasn't comfortable."

"I don't know what you're talking about, Zevo." The brick beneath her cheek was damp and rough, scraping whenever Zevo pulled up on her wrists to make sure he retained her attention. Beyond the overhang, rain poured down in sheets. Zevo's smoking buddies grouped around him, hiding him and Megan from chance gazes. "I wasn't there. I told you I came in last night to find Risto. I had to take him home."

"Who tipped the cops to the club?"

Puzzled, she tried to look at him. Yeah, so Hank was the law, big deal. It had never made a difference before, what of it now? "What?"

"Your pop, Meg. There's a raid and he's the first cop in, but you're gone. Him and me, we meet once, but first guy he picks up is me. Who told him about the party, Meg?"

"Not me—ow! Damn it, Zevo. I didn't know he'd come lookin' for me. Ease off."

"Not till you tell me—*Geez*—" He broke off swearing when a van skidded up to the curb behind him and sent a wave of rain splashing up his back. "What the—" He turned and the splash of rain flung by fast-moving windshield wipers hit him in the face. His friends scattered.

Li slid half out of the van and yelled over the downpour. "Hey, Meg, quit screwin' around, would ya? We gotta go."

Zevo stabbed an angry finger at her. "Back off, Anden. Meg an' me got business to finish."

"Yeah, yeah." Li nodded. "I see *you* got business, but I don't think Meg does, and if you don't let her go before the sheriff gets here—" A dull wail rose over the thunder. Li cocked her head. "Oh, great, listen, there they are. I think I hear sirens."

Zevo's head snapped around, his grip loosened. Megan yanked free and scooted into the van at the same time Li ducked back inside, put it in gear and backed up. Then she shifted into drive, roared forward and splashed Zevo once again.

Megan viewed her rescuer with astonishment. The deliberateness with which the even-tempered-to-a-fault-Li had gone about drenching Zevo was a side of her friend she'd never seen. Usually Li simply scorned him. "Li?" she asked, not sure if it was.

Li ran a hand down her wet hair and snapped the cool water into Megan's face like a wake-up message. "Yeah?"

Euuw, Megan thought. *P.O.'d for sure.* "Nothing," she said carefully. "Just checking."

They were silent for a moment.

"I thought you were done with that jerk," Li said—although "exploded" might be more accurate.

"He's not that bad."

Li veered right out of the parking lot. "He jams you into a wall and you defend him? What have you got, Meg, rocks for brains?"

"Back off, Li, it's my business, not yours."

"You mess with him on my time and you make it my business," Li shot back. "What would he have done if I hadn't come up then?"

"Nothin'. Somebody would've seen him and called the cops, same way you did."

"I didn't call the cops, you dolt, I bluffed. The phones are down and the electricity's out. That's the civil-defense siren blowing. They've spotted tornadoes west of town. I was comin' to get you to get inside somewhere, but I think we're better off out of Zevo's reach. What was he threatening you about anyway?"

Threatening her? Megan glanced sharply at Li, recognized the truth and paled. God, he had, hadn't he? Because of her nosy, Dudley Do Right father. Threatened and tried to intimidate and...

Physically hurt her. Or at least might have. In broad daylight—well, murky rain light, anyway—with people around and everything. And she couldn't have done anything to stop him. For all her would-be toughness, she didn't know how. Oh, damn. She was stupider than Lynn by a long shot. At least Lynnie never let Whatshisjerk get violent—or anything that came close. At least Lynnie knew where to call a halt and when to make a choice. But she didn't. She only knew the choices all seemed to get made for her, or by accident or default or something. That she didn't really have anything to do with them.

Except, somehow, to precipitate them.

No. She shook the thought away. It wasn't her fault, it wasn't. None of it. She wasn't to blame. Her mother didn't get pregnant and die because Megan wasn't the perfect child; she got pregnant because Hank couldn't keep his hands to himself, then wouldn't let her have the abortion the doctor thought she should have. And she died alone because Hank was too busy to be there, got there too late to be of any use, even though Megan called begging him to come, to hurry, to fly.

At least that was what Megan thought she remembered. But suddenly it all seemed awfully fuzzy and she wasn't sure...her memory didn't seem quite...accurate.

In fact, it seemed dead wrong. She was scrambling events, mixing things her mother said with things Gen had done, and they didn't make sense. But they were supposed to. They had to. Otherwise, what did she have left?

Nothing.

Oh, God. Barricading her face behind her hands, she swallowed the taste of bile. No, she was right the first time. She had to be. It was Hank's fault, this problem with Zevo, her mother, all of it.

Hank's fault.

Without warning her stomach churned and rolled, as muddled as her thoughts. Clutching her middle to hold her insides in place, she grasped at Li's arm.

"Pull in somewhere," she said tersely. "I think I gotta be sick."

The pit was a narrow cement rectangle cut into the floor of the equipment barn, which the tractor or other vehicles could be driven over so that someone could stand underneath and work on them. When not in use it had a heavy plywood cover that rolled into place to prevent accidents. Kate and Hank sat inside the pit, backs to the concrete, with the cover pulled partially over them to protect their heads.

Between the storm and the clouds, the pit was lightless and cooler than the surrounding barn, clean but faintly redolent of gas and oil coupled with the scent of a man and woman who were attracted to each other in close proximity. It was a short step from nearness to the age-old means of seeing by touch in the darkness; from touch to the wordless communication and comfort of fingertips and lips on each other's skin.

Exploration went no farther than a few gentle kisses and enough touching to reassure themselves that they were each the same people they'd been the night before. *Want* was a companion here, but not ruler. Rather they held each other close while their minds strayed to other concerns... The children—all of them— and whether or not they were safe; each other—and what to do about this thing that groped for footing between them; last night and how to approach each other about their recklessness.

Outside the wind howled, the rain pounded, thunder deafened, lightning flashed.

Hank's hand drifted idly over Kate's hair while his arm held her pillowed against his chest. One leg thrown across his lap, she listened to his heart beat, his lungs fill and empty. Conversation and courage had never seemed so evasive. Finally, though, Kate lifted her face to confront issues, at the same time that Hank's free hand cupped her chin and raised it.

"It's the middle of my cycle and—" she began at the same time he said, "We were pretty damned careless last night and—"

"What?" they chorused together, then chuckled, self-conscious.

"You first," Hank offered.

"No, it's okay. You go ahead."

"Sure?"

Kate kissed his wrist and nodded, uncertain. "Yeah."

"Okay." He drew a breath, touched the pad of his thumb to her lips wishing he could see her. "I wasn't too careful with you last night. I should have protected you. I'm sorry. I bought condoms this morning, but if..." Damn, how did he say "if you're pregnant, I'll do whatever you want, but I don't know what *I* want?

"But if...whatever..."

She stopped his mouth with her hand. "I understand, I think," she said. "You need to know, it's the middle of my month and the condoms might be too late, but I wasn't thinking either, and maybe I should have protected you." She felt amusement stretch his mouth beneath her fingers. "I'm sorry, but I'm not, you know? And if I'm pregnant...well, it never occurred to me before that I ever might be, and I certainly never planned on it, but if I am..." She hesitated searching for words.

"I'll be here no matter what you decide," Hank said firmly, then repeated sadly, "No matter what."

Another woman might have taken offense. Kate grinned. "Will you," she said dryly. "That'll be handy since all I planned to do was say, 'Thank you.'"

He caught her face between his hands, "What?" Now he really wished he could see her. It might help his hearing if he could, because he didn't think she could possibly have said what it sounded like she'd said.

Kate raised herself to brush a kiss across his lips. "Thank you," she whispered against his mouth and he felt drugged, all powerful, joyously male. "Thank you, thank you, thank you." Her fingers played about his waist and a smug grin plastered itself to his face. "And I mean that. Thank you for the possibility, for the...the...unexpected maybe. I just never thought...I mean, *me* having a baby of my own. Wow. That's...that's..."

"Intimidating," Hank supplied.

"Incredible," she corrected. Then she added honestly, "And scary. And maybe not as well timed as it could be, what with Megan and Risto, and Bele's adoption not being final and—"

"And maybe not anything at all," he reminded her. He'd spent the past five years with the serenity prayer as his dearest and most oft ignored companion, but not today.

Kate touched his face, a gentle benediction, almost as if she'd heard his thoughts. "And maybe not," she agreed softly. "But it was a pretty exciting minute wondering, wasn't it?"

Hank laughed. It was a pretty exciting everything with Kate around. "Your middle name wouldn't be Pollyanna, would it?"

"Nope, sorry, it's Mary. Same idea, though. Find the best part of a situation and make the most of it."

He huffed something that was more irony than amusement. "Not every situation has a best part," he said.

"No," she agreed quietly. "But we can worry about the bad parts later. If there is a *later* to worry about. *Lord, grant me the serenity* and all, you know? Right now I'd rather make the most of the time we've got right here."

"How should we do that?" he asked—warily.

"I don't suppose," she mused, running her fingers lazily up the center of his chest, "that you happen to have those condoms with you?"

He shut his eyes and felt *want* constrict his lungs, pool with the blood in his loins, distracting him from the moment's worries. In less time than it took to expel a breath she became the fever in his pulse, his only need, his all. It might be a little soon to discuss it, but if she was pregnant, he would do more than merely be here for her. He would be here, there and everywhere for her as long as she would have him. As permanently as possible. Rings, licenses, witnesses and everything.

And if she wasn't pregnant he still wanted the permanence, the commitment—her days and nights and forevers—as soon as possible.

And Megan would just have to accept it.

His fingers stole across Kate's breast unhindered by restraint. "As it happens, I'm sitting on a couple of rubbers right now. Why? You interested in a lesson in their use?"

She shrugged, grinning. "As long as we're stuck here and it's for the sake of my education... If you feel up to it, it might help keep our minds off the kids."

"If I feel up to it?" In an instant Hank had her flat on her back, and loomed over her in mock outrage. Laughing, she held her arms open to him.

When the sound of wind traveling by freight train passed overhead, he was deep into demonstrating exactly how very up to furthering her education he felt.

The outer barn door slid open and gray light intruded, almost blinding despite its dimness.

"Mom?"

Engaged in disarranging clothing they'd each just finished *re*-arranging, Kate and Hank came guiltily apart, gulping air.

"I'm here, Mike."

Kate pushed herself to her knees in the pit, hastily reaching to hook her bra. Naturally, inanimate object though it was, because she was in a hurry it had no intention of cooperating. Getting behind her, Hank brushed her impatient fingers aside and smoothed the hooks into place. His hands lingered underneath her T-shirt for a moment, smoothed the contours of her breasts in farewell; he dipped his head to nudge the wealth of her hair aside, his lips brushing a gentle brand at the back of her neck. Leaning into him, she reached back and touched gentle fingers to his face. Then he released her and reached up to push back the pit cover, boosted her out, hoisted himself out after her.

She got to her feet and dusted herself off, carefully not turning to offer Hank a hand up even though she wanted to. Wishing, briefly, that she had enough experience to know how to make reaching for him a natural part of her life instead of the stolen moments it had so suddenly become—and, in a family this size, could not remain. But she'd never particularly cared for dating the few times she'd gone out in high school—too awkward—and she'd never had a lover, so there was an awful lot she had to learn. Besides how to make condoms a pleasurable part of love-making. She smiled to herself.

Like how to go about having a...a...more than a friendship with a man in front of the kids.

Full of their basement adventure, Mike and Bele rushed forward to greet her and Hank; Ilya, Jamal and Grisha followed more...nonchalantly, as if the storm hadn't bothered them at all. As eager as the younger boys, the dog mooned anxiously around Kate's knees, licking at her hands.

"Is the storm over?" she asked, hugging rain-damp sons and patting Taz.

"Yeah." There were excited nods. "The radio says so. It's only raining a little now."

"Yeah, an' the house is okay," Bele said, "cuz we looked, but there's branches down and trees and—"

"We don't have 'lectricity or phones—"

"I, um...started the...*generator*," Grisha volunteered.

"An' one of the loafing sheds is sorta sagging," Mike continued as though there'd been no interruption, "but the llamas are okay."

Hank came up behind Kate. Without thinking, she stepped closer and settled into place half a step in front of him. Sharing space. Of its own volition, his hand strayed to the small of Kate's back, slid up to her shoulder. He pulled it away, tucked it safely into a pocket. It just felt so much more natural to have her in the crook of his arm. He had to watch that.

Had to figure out how to make being with her an acceptable part of their kids' lives.

"Are the girls back?" he asked.

Jamal eyed him oddly but didn't comment, merely shook his head. "Not yet. But the radio said only one tornado touched down and it wasn't in town, so—"

The sound of motors and gravel under tires cut him off and took them all to the barn doors. From behind the barn, the tractor bearing Tai and Risto—wet, but apparently none the worse for wear—jounced up the track and into the yard. At the same time, Li pulled the van up behind the house, a county sheriff's car close behind. The deputy drove straight back to the barn, parked and got out, putting on her hat.

Recognizing the young woman as one of the officers involved in the previous night's raid, Hank moved forward to meet her. They shook hands.

"Director Mathison," the deputy greeted him formally.

Official, Hank thought. *Bad news for somebody.*

He nodded at the law-enforcement officer, becoming in the instant the formidable shirt-and-tie DEA AD he was at the office. That he was more than a little grimy and wore jeans and a T-shirt didn't matter. The deputy sheriff squirmed almost visibly and straightened.

"Deputy Schulhauser," Hank acknowledged coolly. The tone commanded respect; Schulhauser's demeanor gave it. "What news?"

Deputy Schulhauser glanced at Tai, who moved up to join the group in the shelter of the barn door, and Risto who swallowed and hung back, then over her shoulder at the scuff of sandals on gravel that signaled Megan and Li's approach. She looked at Hank, then apologetically at Kate.

"Are you Kate Anden?" she asked.

Kate nodded. "Yes."

Schulhauser eyed the number of children regarding her with interest and gritted her teeth. "Perhaps you'd like to send the kids in the house out of the rain, ma'am?"

Kate glanced at the boys and Li, took in Megan's defiant stance and cocked an eyebrow at Hank. He lifted a shoulder, then let it drop. *Your call,* his expression said. Kate turned back to the sheriff. "Is this about last night?"

Schulhauser nodded.

"Then I think," Kate said judiciously, "we'll go ahead and just consider this today's classroom and you the visiting speaker." She eyed her crew. "Pay attention, guys."

Yeah, right. As if they wouldn't.

Schulhauser pulled a notebook out of her hip pocket and glanced at it. "We understand you have a Risto Pal—" She struggled with the pronunciation a moment, then gave it a creditable go. "Palmunen staying with you?"

Kate nodded, looked over her shoulder to catch Risto edging away and crooked a no-nonsense finger at him. "Yes, I do." She moved to stand beside the pale exchange student. "This is Risto."

Schulhauser snapped her notebook closed and viewed the youth and his American family. "I'm afraid, ma'am, that we found his name next to quite a substantial sum in the gambling files we collected last night." Her stance changed subtly, squared as if in readiness for either fight or flight. "I have to take him in for questioning."

Chapter 12

Late August

The stick had a plus.

Swallowing, Kate stared at the pink cross on the end of the third home pregnancy test she'd taken that morning.

Correction. The third *positive* home pregnancy test she'd taken this morning. And since they were all different brands, really the only thing left now was for her doctor to confirm it.

And, of course, telling Hank and the kids.

Sightless, she stared at the bathroom mirror. Physically she'd never felt better in her life, had the feeling that pregnancy as a condition would thoroughly agree with her. She had no morning sickness, wasn't tired, nothing. Her breasts were maybe a little tender and her emotions seemed closer to the surface than usual, but she could live with that. Still, the moment five weeks ago when she'd told Hank that all she could say about the possibility of being pregnant was *Thank you!* seemed a long time gone. A lot had happened since the day of the storm.

A lot.

She and Hank had, for one thing, started dating—much to Tai's amusement, Li's shy pleasure, Megan's consternation and the younger boys' enthusiastic encouragement—and she'd gotten to know him a lot better. Enough to know that loving him would be both the easiest thing she'd ever do in her life and the hardest. It would be for keeps. He was a man with whom she could not only share a child but a life, if a few intrinsic pieces of their previous lives—like their personalities and Megan—didn't keep getting in the way.

Megan had been moody and strange ever since the day of the storm and kept more and more to herself, avoiding even Li. Perhaps part of her behavior had to do with Risto being returned to Finland as soon as the police were through questioning him after the raid. Certainly some of it had to do with her father allying himself romantically with Kate and therefore establishing a place for himself within a family Megan had always considered her own private haven. And no doubt some of it was related to the tree that had split in the tornado and gone through the roof of the guesthouse, bringing Hank to live in the main house.

Although he, himself, was the one doing the primary repairs, Megan had been rather vocal in suggesting that her father would do better moving back to their own house for the rest of the summer. *She*, of course, would stay with the Andens as planned. She didn't, she said, like the idea of putting Kate and Tai out of their office by moving a bed in there for her father. The fact that Hank was up as early as or earlier than everyone else and didn't need the office during the day was of little import, as far as his daughter was concerned.

She'd also said that what with him and Kate *dating*—the very word was twisted with a wealth of emotion and confusion—and all, him sleeping in the house hardly seemed appropriate.

Kate warmed a little with the thought. Megan might have a point there. It *was* awfully difficult to simply say good-night and watch Hank go off to bed by himself. The fact that Kate and Hank had both done some careful after-hours sneaking around and had gotten very little sleep—whether together or apart—in the weeks since Hank had moved into the house seemed only to confirm his daughter's concerns. No matter what she told herself, Kate couldn't seem to stay put where Hank was concerned. He was equally bad when it came to her.

And it wasn't just the physical stuff—although that was pretty *Wow!* to say the least. It was being together rather than separate. It was having a best friend for the first time in heaven knew when, learning that sharing anything with Hank was infinitely more intoxicating than keeping it to herself. It was having him *there,* close enough to reach for, to laugh with.

It was also watching him with the boys, watching them blossom because of him—even Tai, grown, graduated and his own man though he was—and seeing Li turn to him as she'd never had a chance to turn to a father for seemingly inconsequential things that Kate hadn't realized Li cared about. Like how her daughter looked before she went out on a date. When Hank told her she was beautiful, Li glowed. When Kate said the same thing, Li accepted the compliment, but it was a compliment that carried less weight for being expected.

As for Megan...

Certainly there was jealousy on Megan's part when Hank paid compliments to Li, or gave his attention to the boys, but there was more to Hank's daughter's moodiness than the green-eyed monster accounted for. Kate could feel it. Megan wanted Kate to be there for her, the same as always, but she didn't seem to want Kate near her father. Or her father near Kate. But whether that was a divide-and-conquer sort of tactic or more jealousy, it was impossible to know.

The girl also seemed to have developed a rather... *eclectic*...sense of reality.

To say the least.

Megan's perceptions of what was going on around her were skewed—often in the extreme—frequently paranoid and more than a little unpredictable, even where Bele was concerned. Where seven other people—Anden kids, in this instance—saw a thing happen one way, Megan was certain to interpret it another, and most often in terms of how it affected her personally. Kate didn't even want to *think* about what might have gone on in Megan's mind the one time Megan had caught Hank kissing Kate. His daughter's verbal reaction had been quite astonishingly loud—and incoherent. And the kiss hadn't even been one of the mind-numbing kind Hank excelled at, but a gentle buss of the kind Kate found melted her heart and soul into a quivery puddle at his feet.

It was that almost chaste intimacy between Kate and her father that seemed to incense Megan most.

She'd also begun to disappear at odd hours, pretty much stopped working with Harvey and dumped what she referred to as her "goody-two-shoes clothes" into the trash. She still spoke to Bele, appeared to want to do things with him, but even where he was concerned she was reserved and...not exactly tense, but something close to it. She was frequently up, then very down, sometimes almost giddy, sometimes afraid. She was also disruptive and all too often angry enough that even the boys—besides Ilya and Jamal—who were usually oblivious to the moods of the people around them, walked carefully.

In short, living with Megan was a stunning illustration of how easily one person could affect both the tone and quality of the lives of those around her.

Drugs were, of course, the first thing they considered, but neither snooping nor a watchful eye nor a—on the face of it—routine back-to-school physical complete with urinalysis and bloodwork turned up anything untoward. She refused, even at Kate's, then Li's request, to participate in a psychiatric evaluation, making that course impossible to pursue.

Li's response, when asked about her friend, had been a firm albeit unhappy and guilty apology and an anxious, "I couldn't say."

Wouldn't say was more like it, Kate guessed, but since she'd never had reason to distrust her daughter before, she wasn't entirely certain how to go about doing so now.

That Kate *wanted* to trust Li no doubt played a big part in it, too.

And now Kate was pregnant. Not doctor-officially yet, but as officially as a missed period, three positive home pregnancy tests and the absolute knowledge of a woman who knew her own body extremely well could make it.

She tapped a fingernail against her front teeth, considering. How was she going to break this to the kids? Especially after all the lectures she'd given them on the dangers of unsafe sex and the value of abstinence until marriage. And now here she was, twenty-some-odd years older than any of them, and she'd managed to, well, bluntly put, screw up once and get caught. Some example she set, huh?

For almost thirty seconds she considered attempting to sell them on the idea of another immaculate conception. Unfortunately, llama breeders that they were, they were far too well versed in the how's, where's and why's of procreation to believe even briefly. Even Bele and Mike had seen Mike's maternal aunt's birthing-room video and could quote chapters from *The First Nine Months of Life* at her, so...

She wasn't terribly concerned about her own kids—oh, they'd have questions and certainly comments, but in the end a good time would be had by all—in particular the doted-on-by-its-siblings and soon-to-be-spoiled-rotten baby. Especially given that it was Mom who'd messed up, not one of them. But there was no telling how Megan would handle this news. She seemed to be having a difficult enough time being Hank's only child, and now that he and Kate had managed to complicate the situation with a very unplanned number two...

Kate grimaced. Maybe she should make a doctor's appointment, confirm her condition and get a prescription for prenatal vitamins, but then wait until Hank and Megan moved back to their own house to make the announcement. Why that would necessarily make a difference Kate didn't know, but it was an option. Still, they'd be here only another ten days or so, and what was another week and a half out of nine months?

Better than one third of her first trimester, that was what.

On the other hand, it didn't seem particularly fair to keep Hank hanging for even another day, let alone another week. It might be *her* body, but he'd made it perfectly clear her body could contain *his* child and that meant he had as many decisions and choices to make, as many parental rights, privileges and responsibilities, as Kate did.

Which might, now that she thought of it, actually be a good reason to keep the news from him a while longer. He was already plenty darned arrogant as it was. Add a baby on top of it and...

She sighed. And nothing. And he was also restless.

He didn't talk about it, but she'd felt his mood more and more clearly since the night of the raid. It affected everything he did. He missed the action of undercover, she was certain, craved the kick, was balking at the mere thought of returning to his desk in less than three weeks. She didn't want to be one more chain binding him to a life he didn't want but couldn't, out of his own sense of duty, commitment and obligation leave.

Not that she wasn't considering this a little late in the game. If she didn't want to...tie Hank down, what had possessed her to make love with him in the first place?

Thoughtlessness, that was what. And greed. And lust. And need and desire and liking him and....

And a sense of caring that easily translated to love.

In short, although it was certainly no excuse, he was the right man—even if it was the wrong time—and she couldn't help herself.

She didn't want to.

So, where did that leave her? Tell him now or tell him later, she was still going to tell him.

Sighing, she drummed her fingers on her neck. Decisions, decisions...

He couldn't sleep.

Restless, Hank prowled the house, checking doors and windows, peeking into rooms, looking at the kids. It was easy to move silently. After only five weeks, he knew every squeaky board in every floor, had done what he could to shim or lubricate or reattach most of them. The simple labor, the ability to seek out the problem, give it some thought and fiddle with it until he'd corrected—or at least improved—it was probably one of the most satisfying things he'd ever done. Brains and brawn working in cooperation at *his* command, not someone else's.

He liked that, enjoyed being his own man for the first time in who knew how long, owning his principles instead of having to...manipulate and rationalize them to accommodate someone else's bidding. Here at Stone House no one was second-guessing him, changing the rules, rewriting the script, straining his resolve. Or at least, when they did, there were reasons for the second-guessing, changing, rewriting that he not only understood but could applaud—life reasons, not political nuances.

At the office, even as assistant director, he had his higher-ups to answer to; they wanted results from him now as badly as they had when he'd been merely an agent, but they also expected him to *get* results from his agents and underlings without telling them everything they might need to know to resolve their cases, let alone what they sometimes needed to know to stay alive. He hated it, but it was a job he knew and could do while he tried to let Megan grow up. And like it or not, that was bureaucracy; everything was "need to know." He was told no more than someone in the upper echelons deemed needful, was allowed to pass on even less.

Until this summer he hadn't fully realized how poorly he'd slept since becoming AD, but Megan had always been his bottom line, his reason enough. Now he knew that sleep either hadn't come out of constant fear for someone else, or when it had it was like the restless sleep of the haunted dead, without repose. He wouldn't trade Megan for the world, but he half thought he'd sell his soul not to have to go back to office politics and the uncertainties of life in a suit. He didn't want to go back to deep cover or anything close to it, either.

The truth was he finally accepted what he'd been seeking for the past five years—and maybe longer. Life with Kate and the kids and the farm was plenty complicated, but it was also simple, basic. He worked hard not simply to make a buck, to feed some nebulous adrenaline addiction, but because he wanted to, because here he was part of a whole, something infinitely larger than himself and Megan. Here, he made a difference.

Here also made a difference in him. And for the first time in more years than he wanted to remember, it was a difference he could like.

If only he could somehow make it permanent.

He cat footed across the open second-floor landing to an open doorway. There were the boys, Bele and Mike, asleep in their bunks on the north side of the upstairs. Their floor was coated with debris: fallen Lego pirates and knights, a stormed castle to be repaired before the next invasion, Bele's prosthesis—still wearing its shoe—the peg leg Hank had made for Mike and a tumble of shared clothing both clean and dirty. They were a constant ad for the concept of "what's his is ours," no matter which *his* was whose at the time. And that included Bele's leg. Occasionally pirate kings needed a peg leg, so why not use the ready-made one?

No amount of pleading, commanding or reasoning on Kate's part could convince them that Mike shoving his folded knee into the socket of Bele's prosthesis was hard on both it and him. It was a problem easily solved in the woodshop, though. Kate had called him a show-off for thinking of making Mike a peg leg, but Hank had been plenty pleased with himself for doing so.

Grinning at the memory, he left Bele and Mike's room and poked his head into the one next door. In variously contorted stages of deep slumber, Grisha, Ilya and Jamal snored, their personalities evident even in their sleep. At the foot of Ilya's bunk, clothes lay where and how they'd fallen; at the head of Jamal's, everything was neat and precise, draped or folded right side out. On the other side of the room, Grisha's makeshift desk—two sawhorses with a solid-core security door stretched across them—was cluttered with his microscope and slides, notebooks and specimens. The star theater Kate's mother had given him for his birthday stood beside his bed, turned on and forgotten, casting the print of constellations over walls and ceilings. Smiling, Hank stepped carefully over and pulled the plug to turn it off, then paused with his hand on the foot rail of the lower bunk. Something like regret slid against his conscience when he looked at the bed Risto used to occupy.

Though she'd dealt with it openly, Kate had been devastated by the questioning the youth had undergone, the spate of scrutiny and questioning she'd been forced to undergo because of Risto's activities, and his eventual removal from Stone House. And during it all, there had been the other kids to deal with, their questions, their hurt and the youngest boys' inability to understand why one of their favorite people had to be summarily withdrawn from their lives before he was supposed to be. Then they'd recovered relatively quickly and left Kate with her own demons to deal with, the sense of failure that she hadn't prevented what she knew she really couldn't have prevented.

The feeling that she should have known, should have seen what was happening. He could hold her, make love to her, try to tell her passionately that there was nothing she could have done because that was what he believed, but he couldn't make what she felt change overnight. And he couldn't change his part in the revelations.

He moved on to Li's room.

The moonlight revealed both girls asleep, lightly snoring. It pained him to know that if he didn't actually see Megan's head, or her arm and one leg trailing outside the sheet, he'd have gone in to make sure she hadn't stuffed her bed with pillows and snuck out. Being unable to trust his child hurt more than anything he could remember—except Gen's suicidal betrayal of his trust.

He moved on, not pausing when he passed the third-floor staircase on his way back downstairs. Tai hadn't yet returned from Carly's. With amusement and empathy, Hank wondered how long Tai would be able to live with the nightly trips to and from his lady's apartment, how soon it would get too difficult to leave Carly before morning—and how Kate would deal with the situation when it arose. It was one show he definitely wanted to be around to see.

The thought of Kate brought him to her door, his ultimate destination when he'd begun this restive prowl.

Hank smiled softly to himself. He didn't think he'd ever seen anyone more beautiful in sleep. Nor more beautiful awake, either, for that matter. It was just harder to enjoy when she was awake. Kate rarely stayed in one place long enough for him to savor simply looking at her.

He'd made the complaint one evening, wishing she'd be still so he could gaze at her. When he'd called her beautiful, she'd been insulted, reacting as though he'd accused her of something odious. She was, she'd snapped, much too busy to stand still like some mannequin and be beautiful for his benefit. In almost the same breath she'd accused him of being obnoxiously handsome and requested he "do something" about his appearance so she could quit staring at him and get something done. Like what? he'd asked, laughing at her. Like clean up, she'd responded tartly, since it was when he was filthy that she had the hardest time keeping her hands to herself.

He'd made a quick check for prying eyes at that and hauled her into an empty closet in the woodshop and urged her to demonstrate what she wanted to do with her hands instead. The result had been immensely rewarding for them both.

The memory of that half hour made him hard and aching. Her willingness to drop everything for a momentary exploration, her ability to pull from him more than he'd ever thought possible in every capacity, the way she could become part of him, share intimacy with a glance no matter who was around, never ceased to amaze him. To sleep without her was to lie awake wanting her, or to fall into the hottest dreams he'd ever had. In either instance, thoroughly dissatisfying. He wouldn't wake her, but it was better to stand in her doorway and watch her a while, let the sough of her repose lull him than to fall into a slumber her spirit or his latest falling out with Megan would interrupt.

When long enough had passed, he turned to go. The light shifting of her mattress stopped him.

She jacked herself up on an arm. "Hank?" Her voice was soft and drowsy, a sound he didn't get to hear often.

"It's me." He padded noiselessly to her bedside, touched gentle fingers to her cheek. "I didn't mean to wake you. Go back to sleep."

She drew his hand under her cheek like a pillow and snuggled into it. "I will as soon as you lock the door and come to bed."

God, exactly what he wanted, needed. Had for weeks. Exactly what he didn't dare do. "Tai's not in yet."

"I know. He's at Carly's. He'll be home before the kids get up." She yawned and shifted, reaching to pull him closer onto the bed. "You can get up then, too."

An invitation, a temptation and an insight all in one. Amazing. Even half asleep she could cover the bases without missing a beat.

"I shouldn't," he whispered. "What if Megan...the kids—"

"Lock the door," she murmured, a suggestion, a command. "If they knock, you can go out the window and come in through the back."

"Sneak around?" he asked, chuckling. "I'm not seventeen anymore."

"Neither am I," she said softly. "I'm an adult and that means I get to choose where I sleep and with whom. If I was seventeen I wouldn't need the sleep, but I'm not and I do and so do you, so shut up, lock the door and come to sleep before I wake all the way up and keep you awake for the rest of the night, too."

It was difficult to argue with illogic when he didn't want to, so he did as he was told. She butted contentedly up against his erection and went back to sleep while he lay awake in exquisite pain wryly cursing himself.

The dream was a pleasure so intense he didn't want to wake. He was in Kate's bed, his hands filled with her hair. Her mouth was on him everywhere, her tongue running in long, slow torture over his chest, his nipples, down his stomach, tickling his belly. Gliding wetly through the furl of hair on his abdomen, into the nest of his thighs. She flicked the tip of her tongue up his jutting length, then took a slower, heavier taste, finally taking him into her mouth.

He didn't know if he made a sound, but he couldn't lie still. His heels and shoulders dug into the mattress, bowing his body taut. His lungs sobbed for air.

He tried to pull her off, to tell her he couldn't hold on, but didn't know if he succeeded. Then he felt the rub of her nipples up his chest, tasted himself on her tongue when she kissed him and straddled him. He thought he held her away, pleaded with her to wait until he could protect her. Thought he heard her gentle his protests with the promise that she didn't need or want protection from him, that caution of that nature wasn't necessary any longer, so please, Hank, let me love you.

Then, because neither his body nor his heart could say no to that, he found himself suddenly taking charge, turning her so he could touch and taste and taste and touch...driving her as she'd driven him until he couldn't hold back anymore, until all he could do was enter her, fill her. Slide and pump, strain and gasp and meet her until they were no longer two hearts beating in syncopation but one pulsing to a single rhythm. Until they were a stormy jumble in the center of her bed, mouths fused to catch and hold each other's cries, bodies joined so tightly, so smoothly it was impossible to tell where his ended and hers began.

Shaking in the aftermath, he thought he heard her say it, words he badly wanted to hear but couldn't say for fear of cheapening them, "I love you."

But it was only a dream and dreams often lied, so he couldn't be sure and didn't ask the dream Kate to repeat it. Then the dream faded and he slept the sleep of the dead with Kate wrapped around him.

It was late dawn before the whine of the back screen door opening and closing woke him. Groggy and disoriented, he rolled out of bed and stood swaying in the morning light, trying to get his bearings.

He was on the east side of the house, not the west as he should be. He blinked and looked at the filmy half curtains and valances, the short, wide rocking chair with its green flowered cushions, the mirrored dresser and small antique writing desk. Kate's room. And he was naked, alone.

Confusion and a kind of startled amusement pulsed through him in equal measures. What the hell had he done? And wasn't not knowing where he was or how he'd gotten here exactly where he'd come into this thing with Megan and Stone House and Kate two months ago?

He had a vague memory of falling asleep with Kate, but the rest of it...he had no memory of shedding his clothes, even in his dream, no memory of anything except the incredible intensity of passion and the most profound sense of completion and peace he'd ever felt in his life.

Except judging from his current state of undress, it probably hadn't been a dream.

He shut his eyes and breathed. Memory woke. God, no, not a dream. Certainly not the fact that he'd crossed a line and slept the night in her bed. Certainly not the physical part. As for the rest... He couldn't be sure about the rest, but he had to find Kate. They had a lot to discuss.

His gym shorts were on the floor beside the bed; he picked them up and slid into them, stepped to the door and slipped into the hall.

And ran into Tai.

Shoes in hand, Kate's eldest son stopped dead at the foot of the stairs and gaped at Hank. Hank stared back. Between them flared an awkward silence. Hank broke it first.

"Morning, Tai."

"You slept with my mother last night," Tai responded. Straight to the point, every bit his mother's son.

Hank grimaced. So much for the assumption of innocence until proven guilty.

"Yep." He nodded, surprised by how easy the admission proved. "I did." He crossed his arms and propped his shoulder comfortably against the wall, a man on a mission that had yet to be revealed. "You just getting in from Carly's?"

Tai's turn to look uncomfortable—briefly. "Not that it's your business."

A smile ghosted Hank's features and retreated. "Nor this yours," he agreed.

"She's my mother," Tai pointed out. "I got a sister and younger brothers to look out for."

Hank nodded, not the least offended. "Yes, you do, you're right. But your mother's a grown-up and my intentions are...honorable."

Tai flattened an unruly grin. "I kinda thought so, but I had to check."

Flabbergasted, Hank stared at him.

Tai shrugged, didn't bother hiding the smile this time. "You guys were on the porch swing when I got home one night a couple weeks ago. You were too...busy...to hear me when I hit the porch. I turned around and came in the back way."

For the first time in twenty years, embarrassment climbed Hank's neck. Great, just great. He was farther gone on Kate than even he had realized if he couldn't even hear one of her kids approaching when he was kissing her. Or whatevering her. Especially whatevering her.

Mortification climbed higher, into his cheeks. Geez Louise. Caught necking and petting—and he hadn't even known he'd been caught—by a twenty-one-year-old with a sense of humor. Exactly what he needed. Who else had seen them that he didn't know about?

The question must have been written on his face because Tai's grin broadened. "Li saw the two of you come back from the pond one night pretty late, too. Frankly, I'm surprised you didn't try the bed sooner. The ground must be pretty tough on older bones and—"

"Tai!" Kate exclaimed, dumbfounded, coming out of the living room behind him. Tai reddened at the sight of her. "I can't believe—what do you think you—you're talking about me—who—" At a loss for words, she closed her mouth and looked at Hank. This was her bed they were talking—*laughing*—about here. When she wanted Tai to know Hank was sharing it, she'd tell him herself. "And you! I can't believe you're standing here encouraging him to speculate about—"

"It's a guy thing," Hank assured her—and recognized the mistake too late to call it back. She'd been a little more sensitive than usual of late. A symptom of guilt over last night or...

"A what?" Kate asked carefully, calling him back from speculation before any further ideas had a chance to form. He viewed her, guilty but unrepentant. She was pretty sure he wasn't smirking—quite—but he might as well be.

The flush started in her belly and crept upward, flashing heat through her chest, sent fire climbing up her throat and neck, into her cheeks. Anger, sweet and pure and clarifying. Egotistical, provincial, sexist *pig*.

Oops, Hank thought, noting her rising color with interest and anticipation. He grinned. It had been a long time since he'd been within range of good old-fashioned female fireworks. Kate's reaction bore all the markings of the killer queen of female fireworks. He could hardly wait.

Just as well, since he didn't wait long.

Her eyes flicked from him to Tai and back, then to the top of the steps where the grunts and groans of rising boys filtered down the stairwell.

She set her jaw, jabbed a finger at Tai. "We'll talk about you, Carly and the guesthouse later. You—" she turned and grabbed Hank's wrist, yanking him away from the wall "—come with me. I want to talk to you."

"My sentiments precisely," he agreed and yanked her back, startling her.

Tai gave him a *What do you have, a death wish?* face and headed up the stairs two at a time, getting out of the line of fire. Hank stopped him with a word, silenced the fuming Kate with a glance and a gentle finger to her lips.

"Tai."

Tai turned.

"We okay with this?"

Kate's son inclined his head, shrugged his mouth. "I got questions and concerns, but adult to adult, you're right. It's not my business. Just don't let it hurt the kids." He glanced at Kate. "Or Ma, either."

"*Ma* can take care of herself," Kate snapped.

Hank nodded at Tai. "Do my best."

Tai ascended the stairs. Hank looked down at Kate who stuck her nose in the air, turned her back and crossed her arms. He sighed, turned her forcibly around and rested his hands on her shoulders.

"Kate..."

She glared at him, ducked out from under his hands. Men could be such high-handed idiots sometimes. "Not here," she said firmly and, head high, back stiff, stalked off through the kitchen and into the office.

Hank followed to the percussion thump of boys barging half-way down the stairs, then grabbing the railings like parallel bars and swinging the rest of the way. The thud at the foot of the steps shook the house. Given the force of their landing and how many of them there were, no wonder it felt as if there was a slight dip in the floorboards at the foot of the staircase or that there were constant black handprints on the wall beside the front door from when they flew too hard and had to catch themselves.

"Knock it off," he automatically called over his shoulder—just like any real parent. "You'll break the banister." *You'll hurt yourself* was a mother's admonition, not a dad's.

If they heard they ignored him. Just like real kids.

Mentally reminding himself to check for a loose newel post or rails, Hank stopped in the kitchen long enough to collect a cup of coffee and say a strangled "Good morning" to Li, whom he hadn't expected to see. Then he stepped into the office, shut the door and faced Kate.

She sat cross-legged in the middle of the desk waiting for him, face set, pale eyes darkened with intensity. Her hair was pinned here and there about her head in a futile attempt to control it.

He wanted to step forward and abet its escape, but a glance from her stopped him.

Irritably she collected an unruly bunch off the back of her neck, twisted it up and plucked a plastic pin from the nest atop her head and skewered it into place. More rebellious wisps fell into her eyes and she glared at them, stuck out her lower lip and puffed them aside. Hank did his best to keep his smile to himself. The situation before them seemed to call for decorum—or at least restraint—but she did make him want to laugh more than anyone he'd ever known.

It wasn't merely that she was often funny—though she was. It was the sheer sensation of release and relief he found in her company, a quality of joy, an effortlessness of being. The welcome that greeted him no matter what or where, no matter when.

The same qualities that made control impossible when he touched her.

The same reasons he wanted to touch her now.

He kept his hands to himself.

"About last night," he said quietly, and let it hang, watching for her reaction.

Her eyes lit, her mouth softened. "Last night was lovely," she said.

"I shouldn't have stayed. I'm sorry if I...embarrassed or..." He hesitated over the old-fashioned word, but couldn't find another that seemed to fit as well. "Compromised you in front of Tai—"

"Tai and Carly are getting married," Kate interrupted.

Hank stopped. Grinned. "That's great," he said. "Carly's terrific. She'll be good for him."

Kate shrugged, troubled. "They're young," she said, surprising him.

He cocked his head, watching her. He'd never been able to guess what went on in Gen's head—besides frequent contradictions—but Kate was different. Not predictable, different. He'd have thought she'd be excited by the prospect of having Carly as a daughter-in-law.

"They're young," he offered slowly, feeling his way, "but they're mature. They know who they are, what they want and where they're going. They've known each other ten years and they've been dating for five. I wasn't even twenty-one when I married Gen. Tai's got a whole year on where I was. Young marriages can work, Kate."

"I know."

"Then what?"

She wrinkled her nose and shrugged, chagrined. "Well," she hedged. Very unlike herself, she knew. But with Tai suddenly engaged and planning his wedding, things had grown far more complicated in the past half hour than she'd anticipated. From where she was standing, thinking about Megan and Bele and last night and any number of other things, they didn't look to get less tangled any time soon. She looked at Hank, then quickly away. "Well..."

"A very deep subject," he agreed, "but I don't think your well is the reason—"

An excited clamor of whoops and yells rose in the kitchen, cutting him off before Kate had a chance to.

Exasperated, she swiveled and scooted off the desk, headed for the door to find out what was going on. "I'm not *punning*."

"I know you're not." Hank caught her before she'd gotten six steps and made her face him, ran his hands up her arms.

She tried to ease away. "I should go see what's up before they—"

"Kate." He hushed her with her name and a look. "Tell me," he urged.

"Well..." She made a wry face, eyed him sideways when he groaned and grimaced. "Sorry. It's just that, well—I mean *um*— I don't know, ah, Tai and Carly want to get married in March and I don't know. I mean her parents...hmm." She puffed out a breath, glanced up at Hank and gathered air back into her lungs, then let it out on a *whoosh*. "I don't know how well they'll handle the groom's single, ex-nun mother showing up eight months pregnant for the wedding, especially since they can't hide me because Tai's asked me to walk him in and give him away, too, and I said sure, why not? Now, he might change his mind after I tell him—"

The tumult in the kitchen now pounded on the office door. "Mom, Ma!"

Hank swallowed a wealth of emotions he could neither name nor separate. Delight, chagrin, worry, doubt, Megan—who had an entire battlefield of emotions of her own. Disappointment when he decided that was what last night must have been about. Kate was pregnant, they were both healthy, love could be as careless and spontaneous as they wanted to make it. Somehow, he'd figured there would be more to the moment, if it arose, than that.

Disbelief because somehow, despite the odds, he'd probably figured that maybe this moment wouldn't arise at all.

"You're preg—"

The door burst inward in the middle of the word, spilling Mike, Bele and an attempting-to-hold-them-back Ilya into the office. "Ma, Ma! Tai and Carly are—"

"nant?"

The three boys stared at Hank and Kate in utter fascination, their excitement over Tai's announcement lost in the possibility of more intriguing news. Kate closed her eyes and let her face thump forward into her hand. Geez-oh-pete-oh-man. This wasn't how she'd planned to tell any of them, Hank included, but well, that was the reason you had to be fast on your feet, wasn't it, because how often did life adhere to plans?

With a sigh and a glance of apology at Hank she eyed Mike and waited, knowing what was coming.

But she was wrong. Oh, Mike's mouth was open, the words were formed, but it wasn't he who stepped into the room and put the question to Hank like an accusation. It was Megan.

"Who'd you knock up?" she asked.

Chapter 13

Pandemonium reigned.

"What is 'knock up?'" Grisha and Ilya wanted to know, their English lacking a certain amount of slang.

Quick on the draw, Jamal looked at Kate. "Who's knocked up? And why does Meg think Hank did it?"

"Is one of the llamas pregnant and we didn't plan it?" Bele asked.

"I thought Hank said somebody was going to be an aunt," Mike said, puzzled.

"Tai, is Carly pregnant? Is that why you're getting married?" Li poked her older brother.

"What?" Tai, whose head was elsewhere, eyed Li as if she'd not only lost her marbles but had deliberately buried them somewhere, then forgotten where "somewhere" was. "No, Carly's not pregnant. What are you talking about?"

"Hank said someone was pregnant."

"Oh, and you just assumed—"

"Hank didn't *say* someone was pregnant," Megan interrupted tightly, "he *asked* if someone was."

Li eyed her, amazed. "Who did he ask, you?"

Megan looked at her. Li misinterpreted the look.

"Oh, Meg, you're not, are you? I mean, not Zevo—"

"God, Li, as if! Would I do that to a kid? Besides, I know how to use a condom and anyway, what I asked was who *he* knocked up. He didn't ask *me* anything."

"Who *he* knocked up? But I thought you said he was the one asking somebody—"

Mike tugged at Kate's arm. "Is 'pregnant' like when we let Harvey in with one of the girls an' she lets him mount her an' we call it breeding her, then if it takes, in eleven months there's a *cria?*"

"Michael Anthony Anden, you know darn well what pregnant is."

"I know," Mike agreed. "But everybody's talking 'bout different things at once, so I thought I'd just check an' make sure we're all on the same page."

"Make sure we're all on the same page?" Kate pulled in her chin and looked down at him. "Who've you been talking to lately?"

"Nobody. Jus' Bele."

"Yeah." Bele nodded. "But we been listenin' to lotsa people an' that's what they say."

"So," Grisha said to Hank, "'Knock up' means make pregnant?"

"That doesn't sound very good," Ilya observed. "Knocking on somebody sounds like it would hurt and I don't think getting pregnant is supposed to hurt until the baby is born. Now if you said—"

What Ilya might consider more plainly descriptive than the term "knock up" was something Hank had no desire to contemplate, let alone hear. "Enough!" he roared, unable to stand the lunatic speculation any longer.

Surprised, everybody looked at him—even Megan. He looked only at Kate. She hadn't yet answered his question, and while the answer might embarrass him briefly in front of all these ears, he did rather want to know he'd heard her right, that he was about to become a father for the second time. And since it appeared he didn't have a choice, he'd worry about how Megan would accept or reject the idea later. Himself, he didn't plan on rejecting anything, especially not a baby or Kate.

"Kate?" he asked quietly.

She glanced at the kids, shrugged her face, turned to him and nodded. "Yes, I'm expecting a baby."

The silence went from surprised to stunned. The kids looked bug-eyed at each other, at Hank, at her. Their mouths opened, closed; questions formed visibly on their faces, got lost before they could be voiced. The translation process from disbelief to reality hit them each differently.

Mike viewed her with abstract interest; if there were undercurrents of impropriety in her announcement, it didn't occur to him to recognize it. Babies, schmabies. Lots of kids had come to live with them in his short life, what was one more? A big family was fun, and besides he always got to give and get some sort of present when they came, so hurrah for them.

That none of them had been infants delivered from Kate when they'd arrived was neither here nor there, as far as he was concerned.

Bele, who knew his adoption was not yet complete and whose eight-year-old misperceptions understood only that part of the reason he'd come to live with Kate was because his birth mother had died while delivering a baby sister who'd also died, looked apprehensive. He neither wanted anything to happen to Kate, nor did he want to have to leave this home and family, too.

Grisha appeared ready to discuss the event as it related to his naturalist's mind and his somewhat vague memories of when his mother had been pregnant with Ilya. He also shot a look at Jamal and Ilya that said something to the effect of *All right, it's not us in trouble this time.*

Ilya missed the significance of the event altogether, because it didn't apply to him specifically and didn't look as if it would in the immediate future. Long-term affect was not yet up his alley. On the other hand he did eye Hank with speculation, as though forming an opinion.

Jamal's face took on a look of pinched concern; unwed pregnancy was not new to his life; he'd seen it happen a multitude of times, but didn't know how to react in this specific instance. He was looking to Kate for his cues on whether or not to congratulate or console or protect. He also shot her a somewhat judgmental look that stated louder than words that she was no better than anyone else he knew if she couldn't follow the very rules she'd blathered on about regularly to every kid in earshot.

Staring at his mother, Tai sat down in the nearest chair looking as if someone had punched the air out of his gut and stolen the one sacred relic of his existence.

Li darted shocked glances from Kate to Hank to Megan and back; her mouth worked, forming expressions and discarding them, settling finally into an ambivalent but hopeful half smile. As in, maybe she wasn't really here at all and had heard Kate wrong, to boot.

Megan's jaw clenched and relaxed in concert with her fists; a single word slid out with the softness of expelled breath, hung in the air unheard. Her expression remained hooded, her gaze focused at a point near her left toe. Fury, terror, revulsion and excitement quarreled among themselves, supersized emotions competing for position. He just couldn't leave well enough alone, couldn't let her be happy, could he? He always had to get in her way, no matter what it was she wanted, he always had to ruin things. How could he do it, how could he?

It wasn't enough he'd always been able to take her mother away from her by walking through the door, now he had to do the same thing with Kate. Why did he have to come here with her for the summer? Why couldn't he have just let her come to Stone House by herself? If she'd just run away and complained to somebody he was...oh, hell, she didn't know, abusive and neglectful and oh, God, *anything,* maybe he'd never be here at all, never have been able to pull his damned Mr. Charm act, walk through the Andens' door and steal Kate away when *she'd* found her first.

And it wouldn't even be so bad if he'd only taken Kate away from her by dating Li's mother and turning her into one more adult on his side against her, but he had to go and do what he'd done to her mother, too. He'd taken Gen away forever by getting her pregnant and leaving her to die, now he had to make a baby with Kate and maybe kill her, too.

She couldn't let him do this to Li and Bele and everybody, take away the only constant any of them had ever had in their lives, but preventing the act was beyond her control. It was already done.

Oh, God, she'd wanted the baby sister the doctors had said Gen would have borne if she'd survived; she *wanted* the sibling inside Kate, wanted the family she only had here with the Andens, but in her head the pain and commotion were too much, memory flaunting her ability to contain it. All the why's she didn't know; the wherefores no one had ever explained to her about Gen and Gen's death—and she knew there had to be some excuse for some of her mother's behaviors, her mother's...*ways,* for everything her father had done then, did now...

Damn, oh damn, oh damn. She couldn't hold on to the rush of thoughts, the worry, the fear that somehow it wasn't all Hank's fault, it was hers for not being good enough, for being too troublesome, too erratic the way her mother had sometimes been erratic—for making her mother want another baby badly enough to die to try to get one. *Please, God, please, don't let anything bad happen to Kate, God, please.* Oh, *God,* she couldn't be here, she couldn't do this. She had to drown the agony, numb it, kill it for once and all. Her mother was gone and she couldn't just stand here and watch it happen because of *him* again, not to Kate, she couldn't. She had to get out of here *now* because if anything happened to Kate before the baby was born it wouldn't only be Hank's fault for not being able to keep his hands to himself like grown-ups were supposed to be able to, it'd be hers for letting her father get anywhere near Kate at all. And, God help her, she would do her damnedest to punish him for that.

Watching her father, she sidestepped an inch, then a pace, then another toward the door. Hank didn't take his gaze off Kate.

Eyes full of Hank, Kate, too, missed Megan's move.

Hand unconsciously guarding her belly, Kate searched his face, soaking up expression and nuance, both uncomfortable under his scrutiny and hoping their baby would get Hank's honey-mead eyes, wheat-brown hair and beautiful, tempestuous mouth.

Well, maybe not the tempestuous part, at least not right away.

She couldn't be sure how he felt, but she thought he might be...pleased. Also a wee bit apprehensive. She saw his glance flicker over Megan and Tai, alight briefly on Li, then Jamal, flit over Grisha and Ilya, linger on Bele then Mike, to return, furrow browed, to Bele.

She took her own quick tour of the kids' reactions, found a multitude of expressions that would have to be sorted and dealt with individually. The apprehension on Bele's face, however, was her most immediate concern. She opened her mouth to ask him about it, but Li broke the silence first.

"When is the baby due?"

Releasing a sigh she hadn't known she was holding, Kate turned to Li. "The middle of April."

"*April?*" Tai repeated, indignant. "As in a month after Carly's planning the wedding, so you'll be built like a house at it?"

Half laughing, Kate shrugged apologetically and nodded. "Timing's lousy for you, I know."

"April. Geez-oh-*man*." Tai rolled his eyes and slumped in his chair, resigned. "Great, just great. Thanks, Ma. What, you couldn't listen when you explained to us where babies come from and why we *plan* when the llamas will have theirs, so it's best for the *crias* and the girls, as well as convenient for us? I mean, for pete's sake, you never heard of condoms?"

"Yes," Kate responded tartly, "I have. And I believe I also suggested to you that condoms—a man-made item, if you'll remember—can leak and are therefore not foolproof, in which case, the only sure prevention is abstinence."

"Abstinence?" Tai eyed her pointedly. "Since you're the one telling us you're pregnant, I don't get your point."

"Tai—" Hank started, anger rising, but Kate held up a hand stopping him.

"Gee," she said levelly, viewing her son pointedly back, "I guess now you'll understand that if you don't practice what I preach it *can* happen to you."

Tai's grin was instinctive, reluctant and appreciative. "That's good, Ma, I didn't see that one coming. And, yeah, I guess it does prove what you preach—in a backward sort of way."

Grisha nodded. "Examples are much easier to remember," he agreed seriously and Hank choked. "Like when they show you a picture of what a word in English means, instead of only telling you in Russian." He cocked his head and studied Kate innocently, speculatively, the nosy mind of the naturalist-philosopher who read everything that crossed his path ready to ask embarrassing questions simply because he truly wanted to understand the answers. Hank saw the fact they'd be mortifying coming but, totally miscalculating the direction they'd take, failed to step forward in time to prevent them. "For example," Grisha wondered, his accent thickening with thought, "are you get...*knock up* on purpose from a...sperm bank? Or are you get—"

"Grisha!" Li gasped.

Tai slid out of his chair onto the floor from laughing too hard. Li kicked her brother. He rolled out of range but couldn't stop snickering.

Hank could only stare at all three of them in amazement, laughter startled out of him. What the hell had he gotten himself into?

As indignant and huffy as Hank had ever seen her, Li turned her back on Tai, poked Grisha in the chest. "That's not the kind of thing you say," she told her foster brother flatly.

"Why?" Grisha asked, genuinely puzzled. "You don't want to know who the...sire...are—*is* so you know what comes in the baby? You know, like we only keep a few of the boy llamas...*intact* because they're the only ones who will make good fathers and breed the right long fiber or something?"

Incensed, Li sputtered, "Llamas are *not* people. You don't *breed* people for the right kind of baby—"

"Hitler did," Jamal began, eyes alight.

"I'm the father," Hank said firmly before that discussion could get started.

"Well, of course you are," Grisha, Ilya and Jamal agreed, surprised he felt the need to announce a paternity they'd assumed by his presence.

Tai stopped laughing and rolled to his feet. Li stood beside him, accusations softer and torn printed on her face.

"I thought," Tai said somberly to Hank, "you told me you wouldn't hurt her."

Hank looked at Kate, then back at her eldest son, who held his gaze steadily; a muscle ticked in Hank's cheek. What to say, when so much needed to be said and he hadn't enough words to say anything? How could he explain without appearing to make excuses, reassure without seeming to patronize or sugar coat?

"What do you want me to say?" he asked, holding out his hands. "That I didn't intend—"

Mike tugged at Kate's arm, pulling her attention away from her elder children and Hank.

"Bele's scared," he said, concern showing. "He thinks you could die from having a baby like—"

Kate dropped to her knees and reached for Bele before Mike could finish. "Oh, Bele, your mama—"

"I'm *not* afraid of anything." Unhearing, frantic to shut Mike up and not be seen as a scaredy-cat, Bele socked him in the arm.

"An' anyway I said don't tell, everybody always worries when you tell."

Mike socked him back. "You always tell for me and besides, Ma says we don't hafta face everything we're scared of alone until we're older'n Tai at least, and you are *too* afraid she'll die and never finish adopting you an' you'll hafta leave, you just tol' me you were."

"Bele." Gently Kate took his chin in her hand. "Is that true?"

Bele looked at the floor. "Sorta."

"Which part of 'sorta'?"

Bele's mouth twisted as he viewed Kate sideways. "Sorta all."

"Oh, sweetheart!" Kate pulled him into her arms. "Your birth mother was sick from the ebola virus when she died. Your father was afraid you'd get sick, too, and asked me to take you home with me and adopt you when he found out he was dying, too. I'm not sick from anything and I'm not going to die from being pregnant."

"Are you sure?" Mike asked, checking the facts for his too-anxious-to-ask-himself brother.

Kate swallowed a smile. "Very sure."

"And Bele won't have to leave, ever?"

"Why would he have to leave?"

"If you don't finish adopting him cuz of the baby."

"The baby?" Kate asked, astonished. "What does the baby have to do with anything? Of course I'm finishing adopting Bele, what are you twits talking about?" She hugged both boys fiercely. "Nothing could make me not adopt you, Bele. I love you, you're my son just like Mike. You're ours. We see the judge the day after Labor Day and take the day off school and have a cake to celebrate, the same as we did for this guy—" she grinned at Bele and squeezed Mike "—and he's a lot more trouble than you'll ever be."

Bele sucked air, tremulous but relieved, and slouched against Kate. "He is a lot of trouble, isn't he?"

"Not more'n you," Mike told him indignantly. "You get in the same trouble *I* get in." He relaxed, tapped Kate on the head. "But it's still good he doesn't hafta go away like Risto, cuz I didn't want to hafta leave like I told Bele I would if he couldn't stay."

Kate groaned in mock exasperation, covering stronger and

more maternal emotion. "What did I tell you about Risto? He was never staying in the first place, he was only visiting for a year. And second..." She tickled both boys, who squirmed but not hard enough to leave the circle of her embrace. "What would I do for entertainment if you guys left, huh? I'd be bored to *death* and you wouldn't want that on your consciences, would you?"

"Well, we *are* pretty interesting," Mike agreed.

"And we'll never bore you," Bele promised. "We'll always find something to keep you busy."

Kate cringed. "Don't work too hard at that, okay? For a mother, a little boredom sometimes can be a wonderful thing. But I will need you to entertain the baby. She or he will worship the ground you walk on and feel so lucky to have two such terrific big brothers."

The boys looked at each other, pleased. Something passed between them, an unspoken, apparently telepathic understanding that Kate had long since learned to be wary of.

"What?" she asked with misgiving.

Mike looked at Bele who looked at Kate. "Could we have a girl?" her dark-haired son asked.

"Yeah, a sister," the blond agreed.

She eyed them strangely. So far as she knew, they both thought girls one of God's less useful inventions, especially when they were your sister. "You don't want a little brother?"

"No." They shook their heads and shuddered.

"Nathan Leung has a new baby brother," Mike informed her, "and he said it pees straight up in the air on him when anybody has to change its diaper."

"Yeah." Bele nodded. "And we're not changing poopy diapers, either."

"I see." Kate choked back a laugh. "Not that you've ever changed poopy diapers before, but I suppose that's beside the point. Anything else?"

Before they could put together a list and get back to her, she was distracted by voices raised on the other side of the room. She caught the tail end of Tai's vehement tirade, something about Hank's responsibilities to his mother and the baby, interrupted by an exasperated, frustrated Hank who sounded as if he'd had enough of being verbally castigated and had already attempted to tell Tai the same thing he told him now in six other ways.

"Damn it, Tai, shut up and listen and quit being your mother. I am not, *N-O-T*, going anywhere, I don't want to go anywhere, this baby is *mine* as well as your mother's and I damn well intend to be as much a part of its life as she is and more, if necessary, because I want this baby as much as I wanted Megan. Can you get that through that pigheaded skull of yours? *I'm staying*. Period, no arguments, got it?"

"Oh, I hear that part," Tai said evenly. "It's the rest of it I wonder about."

"What rest of it?" Kate got to her feet and came to stand protectively beside Hank. "There is no 'rest' of it."

"Yeah, there is," Tai responded flatly, eyes on Hank. "There's a *lot* more."

"Like?"

"Like..." Li hesitated, looked from Hank to Kate to her own feet, then squared her shoulders and faced them both. "Like is he going to do the right thing and marry you?"

"What?" Kate asked, dumbfounded. The idea of marriage had never occurred to her once while she'd been holding her breath wondering if she was pregnant, nor when she and Hank had continued to be lovers.

Li swallowed and repeated herself. "Is he going to do the right thing—"

"Yes," Hank interrupted quietly, firmly, "I am going to marry your mother," while at the same instant Kate asked flatly, "Right for whom?"

Astonished by their opposing reactions, Kate and Hank stared at each other.

Houston, Tai thought with resignation, *we have a problem.*

Chapter 14

"Out!"

Kate cast one infuriated look at Hank and waggled a thumb between the kids and the door, ushering them quickly out. She spun on Hank the moment the door closed behind them.

"What do you mean, 'of course' you'll marry me? Did you even intend to ask or were you just going to tie me up and haul me off to the nearest Vows-R-Us wedding chapel or whatever it's called and file my 'I do' at gunpoint?"

Hank winced. He'd known the moment the words started to leave his mouth he'd made a mess of his intentions. "I spoke out of turn, I'm sorry, and yes I intended to ask you—"

"I mean," she interrupted, too incensed to acknowledge the apology, "it's not like we've ever even talked about marriage or anything, or like I ever planned on it in my life, or like I haven't done just swell raising God knows how many kids on my own and Risto doesn't count, I didn't have him long enough or young enough to do anything with him and—"

"And what the hell did *you* mean, 'right for whom?'" Hank's voice rode over hers, completing his diverted thought. "For the love of Mike, right for the baby, of course, right for the kids, right for me, right for you—"

"Right for the baby, the kids, for me *and* for you?" Interrupting her own tirade, Kate stalked the room, eying him as she might any other lunatic who confronted her. "That's a pretty darned arrogant assumption, don't you think? Who the dickens died and put you in charge of knowing what's right for everybody, anyway? 'Cause I don't see six feet of dirt over *my* face and I *am* legally responsible for seven of the eight kids we're talking about here, and that doesn't include the one inside me—"

"Which I put there," Hank pointed out.

"And very nicely, I might add," Kate agreed, not missing a beat, "and that's another thing—"

On the other side of the office door the kitchen buzzed with whispers and silence.

"D'you think she'll marry him?" Li asked, stirring waffle batter for breakfast.

Tai snorted. "Because she's pregnant? Sister Kate? You're joking, right?"

Li shook her head wistfully. She might always have had the mother Megan envied, but Megan was the one with the dad. "I didn't think so," she said.

"What is?" Hank asked, diverted by Kate's *and very nicely*.

Suddenly distracted, she paused, mouth open, and looked at him. "What is what?"

"What is the other thing *that* is?"

Was he laughing at her? Kate viewed him suspiciously. His eyes gleamed, more amber than mead, but his face was merely curious. "What other thing?"

"*That* other thing?"

"Hank." Kate controlled her temper with effort. "If you don't speak plainly I am going to rattle you senseless."

"You've already rattled me senseless by letting me wake up in your bed this morning and announcing you're pregnant," he pointed out. "I can't imagine what more you plan to do."

Kate raised her brows and looked at him.

He grinned, waved her away. "I know, I know, give you six seconds, you'll think of something."

She snorted, and turned to shuffle something on her desk. "You're cute, but I'm still not marrying you."

"Why not?" Hank caught her arm, pulled her around and forced her to look at him. "I want my child, Kate."

"I know you do, Hank." She offered him a sad smile, touched his face. "I won't keep the baby from you. We don't have to marry, just so you can be its dad as well as its father."

"Damn it, Kate." He slammed away from her in frustration. "I'm not going to do a weekend-hobby thing with another kid. It didn't work for Megan and I was married to Gen. I also don't want a six-months split. Or even joint custody. Joint custody doesn't give me the first year of 2:00 a.m. feedings and silly baby or crabby baby and colic and teething. Even if Meg and I keep living in the cottage after the repairs are finished, I don't get that because I'd be in a separate residence." He tossed a hand in a gesture of helplessness. "I want to be *here,* Kate. Not just for the baby or for myself but for you, too. To take up the slack when you need to sleep. To be part of all of it. Your kids' lives, the farm, all of it."

"You said it yourself, Hank." It was her turn to pursue him, make him look at her. "You were married to Gen and it didn't work for Megan because you were married to your job, too. I'm not going to be your wife so you can go back to deep cover knowing you've got a safe place to leave Meg."

"Go back?" He stared at her, appalled. "I'm not going back. I don't want to go back, I want to go forward. You think me going back to undercover is what this is about? Job convenience? Adrenaline highs?" He ran a hand through his lengthening hair. "Damn, I don't even want to go back to the office next week. I mean, hell, Kate, think about it—"

"Can you hear anything?" Bele asked, ear smashed tight against the keyhole.

Beside him, antenna ears angling for best advantage against the door, Mike shook his head. "Nope, nuthin'. We need Grisha's stethoscope."

"Or a microphone to slide under the door," Bele suggested.

They eyed each other, consideringly.

Li crossed the room to pull milk glasses out of the cupboard near them. Sun flashed in the glass and figurative light bulbs lit simultaneously over Bele and Mike's heads. Glasses! They could use glasses to magnify the sound.

Or they might have if Li hadn't noticed them and said, "Get away from the door, you guys. If Ma wanted you to hear what they're saying in there, she'd've invited us all to stay."

Rats. They looked at each other. So close and yet foiled again. Sighing they moved toward the mud room, feet dragging. But not for long.

Mike brightened first. He grabbed Bele's arm, dragged him out of the kitchen. "Window!" he whispered excitedly.

His brother's eyes lit. "It's open," he agreed.

Casting a quick glance behind them to make sure their goody-two-shoes sister hadn't overheard, they slipped out the mud-room door and dashed around the side of the house to stand underneath the office window.

"Hell, Kate, think about it..." Hank laughed without humor. "If I wanted to go back undercover that badly I could have dumped Meg in foster care or on Gen's sister a long time ago. Cripe, I probably could have found some woman willing to marry me and mother Meg for the price of an absentee husband and a signed-over paycheck, not to mention my insurance policy. So if that's what you think, if that's the holdup, just tell me what I gotta do to convince you I want to be here, nowhere else, and I'll do it."

"You know there's more to it, Hank."

"Then don't dance with me, Kate, spell it out."

"There's Megan, Hank, there's love."

"Love." Face carefully blank, he skipped the issue of his daughter as too much to deal with in a word and moved on to bolder things. "You need a word, you want a declaration?"

"Don't you?" she asked gently.

He shook his head. "Words don't cut it for me, Kate, they never have. I need pictures. It takes more to hold a family together than words."

"Yes, you're right," Kate agreed. "But I thought you were talking marriage here, too, not just family. And that's meant to last longer than the kids, so it's got to start someplace besides great sex and an accidental baby.''

"It's more than sex, damn it—''

She held up a hand to halt his automatic protest. "I'm glad.'' She smiled briefly. "Very glad. But you have to remember, I don't have a frame of reference for that the way you do, and marriage has never been on my agenda, not even once in my life, Hank. And now you want me to consider not only having...'' she laughed, uncomfortable with the inadequate concept "...a boy-friend for the first time ever, but to think about two weddings, our baby, Bele's adoption and what's best for *all* the kids, all on the same day at the same moment.'' She raised an open hand, let it drop closed at her side, asking for understanding. "I can't. I shouldn't. Neither should you. Not all at once. Geez Louise, I mean—'' She shrugged, looked at him. "Don't you at least want to get used to the concept first? Let the kids get used to it? Let Megan...I don't know...I just can't think it's wise or even fair to...'' She hesitated.

"Dump a baby, a wife, seven siblings and a whole new life-style on her all at the same time?'' Hank supplied bitterly.

Kate nodded. "Yes,'' she said softly.

"She's always wanted to be part of your family, Kate. She's begged me for years to leave her here and go away. When she runs away from me, I've always known where to find her. She's always here.''

"She's run here because it's safe and to get your attention.'' She hated pointing it out, reminding him. "She's run here be-cause—'' she snapped her fingers "—my doors are open and it only takes me that long to decide to take on a kid. But since you and I started...dating...she's run from here, too.''

The pain was deep, an ache with a sting beneath it. "She al-ways comes back.''

"So far,'' Kate agreed. "But who's to say what she'd do or where she'd go if she couldn't get your attention because you were too busy giving it to me or the baby or one of the other kids. She used to tell Li how much she hated you for the way you'd come home from work and she felt like she'd stop having a mother because Gen paid all her attention to you.''

"Yeah,'' Hank said tightly, "and I used to get it from Gen for how much time I spent paying attention to Megan. God.'' He pinched the bridge of his nose between two fingers, smeared unexpected emotion away. "I didn't even know I remembered that."

He hunched his shoulders, turned to look out the window. "I used to feel like a toy they fought over, like it wasn't up to me how to divide my attention, but them. It didn't happen all the time, just sometimes, family junk, you know? Like I'd walk into some battle I didn't know they were having because I was out of the loop so much. Meg'd tell me one thing, Gen'd tell me another. She was my wife—who was I supposed to believe? That's why I want to be here for this one, because I don't want to be out of the loop again."

"I'm not arguing that, Hank. I only want to do what's best for the kids. And I don't know how best for any of them it'd be to bring Megan, you, a baby and an uncertain marriage into their lives full-time all at once. I mean, Li's already started covering up something for Meg, I can feel it. She's never done that before. The way Megan behaves affects them, affects you and me—and all she has to do is walk into a room. If she's happy, great. If she's in a mood..." She grimaced, let Hank draw his own conclusions.

"There's a lot of lives we've got to consider here, Hank, and if you and I can't start out—" She grinned lopsidedly, using Mike's phrase. "If we can't start out on the same page, where're we going to end up? I mean, I didn't go into being a nun to quit, or because I thought I was making a mistake, I thought I was pursuing my life's vocation. I was wrong. Being a mom, that's right. Being a wife...I don't know if I could do that, Hank. And marrying for the sake of convenience... What would that say to the kids? Life's a throwaway as long as it's convenient? That's not fair to any of us, and how good is it going to be for Meg, when we're not even sure about it?"

"I'm sure," Hank said quietly. "I lie awake nights thinking how sure I am. I want you in my bed, in my life, in Meg's life. I want to be in yours and the baby's and your kids'. I never make promises lightly. I will be here because absentee parenting is a crock."

Bele looked at Mike. "A father," he breathed.

"He could really be our dad." Mike fairly trembled with excitement. "And he *wants* to!"

"An' if they got married *today*," Bele suggested, "he could 'dopt me 'fficially with Ma next Tuesday. Then I'd be a Mathison like Meg and the baby, not an Anden."

"No," Mike objected. "You can't be a Mathison if I'm an Anden, then we wouldn't be brothers."

"Yes we would, you dork." Bele punched him. "Cuz we'd make him 'dopt you, too, as part of the deal."

"Ooh," Mike said, drawing it out clownishly, making a show of light dawning. He pursed his lips. "What about Li?"

"I dunno." Bele shrugged. "Maybe we should ask her."

They dashed back around the house in pursuit of Li and the dream they'd just begun to have.

"But again you're talking about *parenting*, Hank," Kate said flatly. "Not marriage."

"Damn it, Kate." Tired of arguing, Hank swiped a hand across his face and through his hair. "Parenting is what this is about right now."

"Like hell it is," Kate shot back. "Be honest. Is that what you're going to tell Meg? Tell her it's okay to walk into marriage, whether you love someone or not, because there's a baby on the way? Then will you also tell her why Gen really died?"

He regarded her mutely, an answer without voice. "What's Gen got to do with this?"

"Maybe a lot. Did you see Meg's face when I told everybody about the baby? You have to tell her, Hank. It might not make—"

"Tell her what, Kate? That the mother she idolized wanted another child so badly she lied to me about how it would affect her, then told me not to worry about it she was on the pill, anyway, then she went ahead and let me get her pregnant? That I trusted Gen, but she was so stubborn and so selfish that the only thing she could see or hear was what she wanted, and that she didn't think twice about what she might do to Megan or me? I can't trash her mother's memory. Even if I wanted to, why would she believe me now?"

"She needs to know so she can make her own decisions about it, Hank. Whether she believes you at first or not, you have to treat her like a grown-up and tell her, now that she's old enough to understand it. She needs to know you got hurt, too, and she needs to mourn the real reasons her mother died so maybe she can move forward to something new. She needs to learn to trust you and yourself, but mostly she needs to see you trust *her* emotionally with a truth you've hogged to yourself since you found out Gen was pregnant.''

He studied her, torn between humorless laughter and disbelief. God, what pap. How had she ever survived the life she'd led, being so naive? The way he'd been raised, a man did *not* dump his personal pain, his marital problems on his child, no matter what the provocation. He didn't ask his *child* to shore him up, when what he was supposed to be doing was taking care of her.

Ruthlessly he ignored the little voice inside his head reminding him that not so long ago, the staff psychologist had told him much the same thing. Of course, five years ago, she'd told him the opposite. But that was then. Five years, for him, in terms of growth and maturation was very little time. Five years for Megan had taken her from childhood to adolescence to being a sometimes mature, sometimes immature, young adult. Kate and the psychologist were probably right about what he should tell her. Trouble was the how and when.

God, it was hard trying to grow up with your children. Trying to know when to treat them like adults and how to do it...

"Life's not as simple as telling anybody anything, if they can't or don't want to see it for themselves, Kate.''

"Maybe not,'' Kate agreed softly. "But people—especially kids—need to be told things anyway and—''

Tai stepped into the kitchen wiping his hands on a towel from the mud room, where he'd washed up after turning the llamas into their fields for the day. "They still at it?''

Li placed a pitcher of juice on the table. "You mean you weren't outside listening under the window like Bele and Mike?''

"Fat chance,'' Tai returned. "I'm older'n that.'' He waited half a beat, then couldn't help himself. "They hear anything interesting?''

Li grinned. "I thought you were too old.''

"Spill it, small fry, or I'll give you a noogie.''

"Real mature, Tai. Carly's going to marry you?"

He made a gesture of mock threat.

She laughed. "Okay. All they heard was Hank say he wants to be out here with *all* of us, which they translated to mean him adopting them and being their dad, too."

Tai's brows raised. "Wow. I never thought of that."

"Me neither. I'm still trying to get used to her actually dating. You think Hank has? Or Megan?"

"You got me." Tai shrugged. "But you can bet Ma's thought of it. Talk about your blended families."

They were silent a moment. Then Li said cautiously, "I wouldn't mind if he wanted to adopt us. He's not at all like Meg said. I think he'd be a good dad."

"Yeah." Tai nodded. "But it's not up to us." He shook away his own vague wistfulness. "Anyway, speaking of dads, you seen Meg? I need her to help me with Harvey. He looks a little lame this morning."

"No, and she was supposed to help me with breakfast."

They looked at each other. This wasn't the first time in the past several weeks that Megan hadn't been where she'd told them she'd be.

"You think we should worry?" Li asked.

Tai puffed up his cheeks, blew out a shrugging breath. "Got me. You know her better than I do. Maybe she's just off someplace trying to...I don't know, put it all together or something. It's sorta a lot to take in at once."

"I dunno," Li said doubtfully. "She usually takes Harvey for a walk when she's tryin' to figure something out."

"Maybe she's helping Ilya and Jamal in the woodshop?"

"You didn't look?"

"Why would I do that?" Tai asked, and went, chuckling, when Li picked a spoon off the table and threw it at him.

"Turkey," she muttered, disgusted. Then she ran to the door to yell after her brother. "Tell 'em all to come in. Breakfast's ready."

Hank cut off Kate's lecture on the merits of people telling other people things. "Why did you invite me into your bed last night?" Speaking of things people—he, personally—wanted to be told...

Caught off guard, she had the grace to blush and look guiltily away. "I wanted to know what it felt like to sleep next to you all night."

His grin was almost smug, torn out of him in spite of his best efforts to contain it. "We could sleep together every night, if we were married."

She wanted to smack him. She settled instead for pointing out the norm. "We sleep together a good part of almost every night even though we're not."

His grin slipped. "You mean it's okay to sleep with me, but not marry me? You used to be a nun."

"Used to be, Hank," she said flatly. "Important distinction. And even when I was, it didn't mean I was asexual. If I had any impulses, I ignored them because they weren't part of what I was. And to be perfectly frank, if you didn't ring my chimes I'd be fine, but you do and just because I *want* to sleep with you, because I want...to be with you any time I can doesn't mean I think it's right, it just means I make the choice every time. I'm a grown-up, I can do that."

She held up a hand to stop him when he would have interrupted. "If I wasn't pregnant the answer might be different, but also if I wasn't I don't think the question would be on the table right now. But the fact of the matter is that I am and it colors everything. The way I was taught, the first priority in a marriage should be the marriage, darn it, meaning we have to kind of be able to separate the two. I mean, marriage is a lot of work and so are kids. To go into both at once..." She hunched her shoulders, looked pleadingly at him. "Wouldn't it be best if we were sure what's between us first? Not to mention that in this day and age, a woman does *not* have to be married simply because she's with child."

"True enough," Hank agreed softly. "But wasn't that the point of Noah's Ark? Two by two? Two to make them, two to bring them up?"

"Ah, geez, don't get going on the two-by-two routine, Hank. In the nonhuman animal kingdom the father rarely does any of the child-rearing. Primates, maybe some, but mostly it's the mother there, too."

The truth stung. "You don't believe in Hillary Clinton's axiom that it takes a village to raise a child? That they become better people the more care and love they have around them? The more people share in their growing?''

"Sure, but..." She hugged the slight thickening that her tummy had become and turned away. He wanted what he wanted, she knew. He wanted her and the baby and all of them. And he would care for them all, she knew that, too. But marriage was not a windfall, an accident of circumstance, a commitment to take lightly. She couldn't give him what he asked, not like this. Not without time.

She shook her head, certain of her own arguments. Certain she loved him, but not certain if she loved him enough—or even, quite that way. Not certain that he loved her as well as he liked her—if at all.

"We're not talking about a village here, Hank. It's more and less than that. You don't marry a village. You marry one other human being and you do it on the premise that it'll last for life. And the fact is, you don't have to marry me to be part of our child both legally and emotionally. Bottom line, I may never have borne a child before, but I've filled out a lot of birth certificates and I can give this baby any last name I choose, whether it's yours, mine or the man in the moon's. But I'll give it yours, and you'll sign the papers as the baby's father with all the legal rights that implies and we'll go on from there. Simple.''

"In your dreams," Hank said flatly, and stalked out.

Troubled, Kate watched him go. For the first time in the almost eight weeks of her pregnancy, she felt queasy.

Chapter 15

The day did not get shorter from that point.

After he left Kate, Hank avoided Anden stares and speculation and went looking for Megan. His mind was on damage control, his heart was troubled. Along the fringes of conscious thought ran a faint desire to chuck it all and let whatever would be run away with him if he couldn't run away with it.

When he found his daughter, Megan took one look at him and ran. He didn't want to let her go, but she was too old to chase down, toss over his shoulder and tickle until she was ready to listen. She'd been too old for that for a long time.

So, with communication with Megan stifled by years of re-straining the truth and communication with Kate at an impasse, Hank set his back teeth and stubbornly did what he was best at: gathered up all the pieces of the puzzle around him and tucked them away for later perusal, moved forward as best he could.

He didn't want to win Megan's confidence by destroying her image of Gen; as he'd told Kate, it would be almost the same thing as taking Gen away from her a second time. Not to mention it was probably too late for that anyway. Even if Meg decided to believe him, who was to say that she wouldn't simply hate him all the more for being the bearer of bad tidings, however true?

No, life, as he'd spent most of his learning, was not as simple as "telling" anybody anything. You had to bring a lot more evidence to any revelation than mere words—the justice system that employed him was ample illustration of that. And even when you had it in spades, evidence often lied or could be doctored, witnesses could be coerced or lose their memories, testimony—like statistics—could be manipulated and shaded to reflect what the defense, the prosecution or the coached witness chose it to reflect.

Or appear to reflect.

In a world where Kodak commercials sang about pictures being worth a thousand words, where video-camera enthusiasts intruded everywhere, running rampant in order to capture and "show" everything, and where the axioms "actions speak louder than words" and "show, don't tell" were preached to children by parents and English teachers, but where most people preferred—and thrived on and lusted after—the "tell all," Hank was a man who lived the axioms. Words were items that too often got in his way—the way they had with Kate this morning. Words were not the things that had kept his parents together for what would be forty-three years come November. Words alone had not seen his grandparents through almost seventy years, were only a very little of what bound him to Gen.

Words could be harsh or loving, argumentative, destructive or empty. The things he'd witnessed with his parents, grandparents, his life with Gen were the emotions on the other side of the words: the loving touch, the unworded apology, the welcome in the eyes, the light left burning all night for the absent, after everyone had gone to bed.

So, since he couldn't give Kate the words she seemed to want, couldn't find Megan to tell her what she apparently didn't want to hear, he did what he could: went on with the work at hand, the work he'd grown to appreciate and even love. The trees, the llamas, the kids...while he watched Kate. He knew gut deep and without words that a life with Kate, their baby, her children and Megan was what *he* wanted; knew it was the first and only thing he'd wanted for himself in years. Both because of and despite Kate's too-blunt opinions and self-righteous, goody-two-shoes exterior. He was, after all, hardly perfect himself, what right had he to expect her to be? Not to mention that the woman underneath the sometimes imperfect exterior was warm and genuine and had a heart as big as the universe and an ability to love that was like bedrock. All he needed to view for evidence was her children, her farm, Megan...and himself. Without his willing it to happen, she'd become part of his blood, his peace...

His heart.

He didn't know how to tell her that, the same way he wasn't yet sure how to tell Megan everything she needed to hear, but in his soul he knew these things. And all he could do while his mouth sought the means to form the words his heart wanted to release was go on as he'd begun.

And try to woo Kate without words by leaving wildflowers on her desk, fresh-picked wild berries in the fridge and keeping pints of the hard-to-come-by chocolate-raspberry truffle ice cream she'd lately begun to crave in the freezer.

He also allowed himself the painful luxury of hope.

With the exception of a few questions—like where would the baby sleep, who would have to change its diapers and could they dress it up and stick it on a backboard and sling it from a llama for authenticity in next summer's parades the way some of the South American Indians used to do—the younger boys were much as they usually were.

The older boys, particularly Jamal, had questions they couldn't quite frame about her and Hank, about living arrangements and the chores Kate normally did. But for the most part, they, too, got over the news quickly and went about being who they normally were.

Aside from going overboard about not letting her do anything she normally did, especially if it was heavy, Hank maintained a thoughtful distance.

Li's expression went back and forth between concern and romantic ideals, wistfulness and curiosity. She wanted to know everything from what sex felt like to what love felt like—and she assumed Kate and Hank must be "in love" or the pregnancy would never have happened—to how excited her mother must be about the prospect of the infant Li could hardly wait to hold. Not knowing quite how to voice her questions tactfully, she asked nothing, merely watched Kate from a strict distance and behaved awkwardly when they were near.

Late in the day when she'd had time to work herself up to it, while they were alone together husking corn for supper, she did let one opinion fly. And it was the one Kate least expected and would far rather she'd kept to herself.

"You know, Mom, it's hard enough living with a mother who's such a saint that everybody expects me to be one, too, and who everybody else's mother says—" Her voice went high and unflatteringly mimicky and Kate winced. *"'If Li's mother says it's okay for Li, then go ahead, you can do it, too.'"* Her tone returned to normal—if a tad self-righteous. And painfully truthful. "But now I'm gonna have to live with a mother nobody's gonna want to leave their kids around because she's fallen from grace so far as to get pregnant by a guy she never used to like and won't even marry to make things right."

Carefully Kate put down the ear of corn she'd stripped and looked at Li. Li flinched but didn't look away, letting her mother know this was important to her. Kate worked her jaw, straining for composure.

"Look, Li," she said quietly, evenly, "I'm not going to tell you that the way I got pregnant is right, but what's past is done and it's how we go on with it that counts. Second, you don't marry someone just to 'make things right' because a make-things-right marriage rarely works. *If* I ever marry it will be—I hope— for the right reasons, not just because I'm pregnant or because you think I should. And if you or anyone else can't deal with that, tough. Third, I like Hank Mathison more than I'm going to tell you, but he and I each have more on our plates than we can easily manage right now and neither of us needs to add a hasty wedding to the pot. Whether he knows it or not, he needs time and I never planned on bearing a child or getting married ever in my life and that means I need time, too. Now." She collected the big pot of corn and rose. "I'm going inside to start supper. If you want to talk about the baby, fine, let's. But back off marriage, Li, because much as I love you, it's not your opinion that's going to make me decide."

Then, heart striking painfully inside her chest, she turned and headed smartly for the mud-room door.

Usually almost as forthright as his mother, Tai avoided Kate as long as he could, which was most of the day, since he was out inventorying their salable trees while she was busy ordering wreath rings, wire, tree tags, flagging ribbon and advertising. Determined to get rid of the awkwardness between them, Kate shooed the other kids out the back and joined her oldest son on the front porch after supper.

"C'mon, Tai," she prodded. "I know you've got some judgment to pass, so dump it and let's move on."

He looked at her, pursed his lips over a comment, then let them relax and shook his head regretfully. "I can't. Sorry, Ma, but I really don't know what to say. You've never been pregnant before."

Kate nodded, deciding frankness was the best policy. "I never had sex before, either, Tai."

"Is that what it was?" Disillusion colored Tai's voice. "Sex, curiosity, not love? After all the things you told me?"

Kate sighed. "Tai, when I started talking to you about sex, I was parroting the things I was supposed to say, the things I believed, not speaking from experience. I still believe most of the things I told you, but...I wouldn't say this to the younger kids, but even brief experience offers insight. There were things I didn't understand when I talked to you."

"Like what?" He was both vulnerable and curious.

"Like..." Kate shrugged. She'd gone this far, she might as well go all the way. "Like—and I'm sure you've already found this out with Carly—how difficult it is to stop when the right person touches you."

Tai made a sound of wry disgust, avoiding the backhanded invite to reveal the extent of the relationship she suspected and he knew he had with his lady. "Geez, Ma. You used to be a nun. I think of *me* that way, not you."

"Yeah, I know." Kate puffed a breath of laughter. "And I prefer not to think of you that way, either. Guess that's the growing-up part for both of us."

"Yeah, but for pity's sake, Ma, a baby? Now?" Tai canted a quick glance her way, grinned wickedly when his mother raised her brows in question. "I mean, you're old enough to be its grandmother."

Startled laughter worked its way out of Kate's throat. "Oh,

well, thank you very much, Mr. Smarty-pants. I'm barely what, sixteen years older than you? And my body tells me I'm plenty young enough.''

There was a crunch of gravel as Carly's car came down the drive and parked beside the house. Grinning, Tai moved toward the steps to welcome her.

''Yeah, but,'' he said over his shoulder to Kate, ''you've got to think about chasing a toddler around when you're forty.''

''Go suck an egg,'' Kate advised him tartly. ''If I'm too old to chase a toddler when I'm forty, I'll let you know, and you and Carly can come do it for me.''

''Do what for you?'' Carly asked, coming up the steps.

''Chase toddlers for me when I'm forty,'' Kate said—uncomfortably.

Carly eyed her curiously. ''What, did you find another kid to adopt? Hi, love.'' She leaned into Tai for a kiss, then murmured, ''Did you tell 'em?''

''Oh, yeah.'' Tai nodded, sounding aggrieved. ''Now wait'll you hear what they've got to tell you.''

''Who's got to tell me?''

''Ma and Hank.''

''They're getting married, too?'' Carly guessed, teasing. ''They've only been dating a couple of weeks.''

''Yeah, but they've known *of* each other for eleven years,'' Tai pointed out, thunking his mother with an elbow to her ribs.

''It's not the same thing,'' Carly said flatly.

''My point exactly,'' Kate agreed, poking Tai in the chest.

''Yeah, well.'' Tai crossed his arms and stared at her. ''Now tell her why the question came up at all.''

''The question came up? Really?''

''Well, I suppose it would,'' Kate said, forestalling any comment Tai might make. She settled a hand on her stomach, already a habit, she was surprised to note. ''I'm pregnant.''

''And the baby's due less than a month after our wedding,'' Tai added.

Speechless, Carly blinked at him, then turned to Kate. For maybe half a heartbeat she viewed her prospective mother-in-law with amazement then she started to chortle, then to laugh so hard the tears ran. Tai watched her with concern, fearing hysteria when she kept trying to say something her mirth kept choking off. But all she said when she could finally pull herself together enough to wipe her eyes and say anything was, "And I was afraid the wedding would just be pomp and dull."

Kate rolled her eyes. She should have known this was how Carly would react. Even as a teen, the young woman had been the cheeriest, least flappable person Kate had ever met.

"You don't think your parents are gonna freak?" Tai asked. "They're having a pretty hard time with this, as it is."

"They freak over everything," Carly reminded him, still chuckling. "So tough Tootsie Rolls. It's not their wedding, it's mine." She toasted Kate with a glass of iced tea. "Congratulations, Ma. How's Hank feel about it?"

Kate shrugged. "He's not talking to me because I won't marry him."

Carly laughed again. "Sounds committed to me."

"Or like he should be," Kate muttered and, to the sound of their chuckles, left her son and almost daughter-in-law to spark alone on the front porch swing.

Megan kept her distance by simply staying out of sight, keeping solely to herself, ignoring everyone and basically not showing up until her ten-thirty curfew. And then she came in obviously wired and obnoxiously loud. At that point Kate, up to her eyeballs with worrying about Hank's daughter, pulled Megan into the main-floor den, shut the door in Hank's face and reamed the teen up one side and down the other about the example she was setting for the younger kids and about living by the house rules if she wanted to continue to be welcome at Stone House. Megan blinked at her in some astonishment over the choiceness and quality of a lecture she'd never before gotten from Kate, but aside from one or two surly comments about hypocritical adults presuming to tell her what to do, she kept her mouth shut.

Affronted and royally peeved by Kate's chutzpah in taking on his child without a by-your-leave or at least inviting him to be present, Hank set his back teeth and crashed the reaming out.

"Back off my daughter, Kate. If she needs to be cussed out, I'll do it."

Kate swung on him as though ready for the confrontation. "This is what it'd be like if we got married, Hank. Equal partners in the kids and their discipline. And she's high in *my* home right now, she's sleeping under my roof, she's interfering with my kids, I'm going to say what I've got to say and if you don't like it, think hard about what you asked me this morning.''

Well and truly flummoxed by a truth he'd spent nearly three months accepting—that Kate had tiptoed pretty carefully but had nevertheless called Megan out whenever necessary, the same way he'd chided her kids, if less often—but had ignored this morning, Hank shut up long enough for Kate to return her attention to Megan.

Intent on each other, neither of them saw Megan pale and clutch for something to hold herself erect when Kate mentioned the word "married."

What Hank *did* see, however, was that the same parts of Kate's chidings that struck home with him also bull's-eyed with his daughter. Kate yelled at a child because she cared about the child, and somehow that concern and affection came across. Not because of anything she said, although she said plenty, but in the tone of her voice, in her refusal to lay guilt, in her request for Megan to take responsibility for her actions and choices, in the way she reached for Megan when she talked. Touching Megan's shoulder, earnestly taking her hands, speaking not only to her but *with* her both physically and emotionally on several levels at the same time. Showing disappointment but accepting responsibility for the fact that Megan might also have reason to be disappointed in her.

Chewing Megan out the way a mother chewed out an almost grown-up daughter.

The vision gave him pause. But it was the fear and accusation staring at him when Megan briefly caught his eye that made the iron band form around his heart and start to squeeze.

Life moved forward.

In spite of the children's best efforts to drag summer on forever, August twenty-sixth arrived and with it, a new school year.

The repairs to the guest cottage were finished, and with a mother's blessing and misgiving, Kate watched Tai and Carly move into it together. It was, she knew, probably the best solution all around, allowing Tai to remain on the farm while giving him the distance and privacy he and Carly wanted and needed at this stage of their relationship. But she couldn't help but wish they'd kept the "living together" part of things for after their wedding.

Funny how upbringing always seemed to meddle in your druthers, no matter how liberal you thought you'd become.

Hank did not move himself and Megan back to their house in town with the start of the school year as planned, but instead coerced, then charmed Kate into letting them stay with the simple promise—or was that threat?—that he'd move into Tai's vacated room on the third floor, but he intended to live in her pocket until their baby was twenty-seven, so she'd damn well better just get used to it. He *did* return to work with the DEA, but he went back unwillingly and against his better judgment.

Against the wishes of both his heart and body, he did not set foot in Kate's bedroom. He stole a kiss from time to time, but went no further. Giving her room. Giving them room was often the better part of valor, especially when he didn't want to make things worse. Still, not touching her was one of the hardest things he'd ever asked of himself—pregnancy gave her a glow and a scent he could neither ignore nor resist—but he knew that the more often he was with her, the more difficult it would be to leave her. Until she understood her own heart for the long term, he wasn't willing to settle for the short.

Kate missed his physical presence badly, but discovered it was the simple sharing, the emotional closeness that had begun to grow out of their physical intimacy that she craved most.

With her father back to the regimen eight-, ten- or twelve-hour days away from home, Megan once again began to dress in unrelieved mourning, stopped communicating with anyone at Stone House and though no one knew it spent much of her time in a furtive search for chemical and herbal relief for the ache in her heart. When she was around, she watched Kate relentlessly. More often than not, however, she made up school-related excuses to be gone.

Kate and Hank suspected, but only Li knew for sure that Megan was lying.

The thing that Kate came to realize with a heavy heart was that it was impossible to know your teenager by living with her.

Chapter 16

September 18—11:53 p.m.

Fifth anniversary of Gen's death

Sweating in the late-night heat, Megan leaned against the still-warm brick on the south side of Stephen Gorley's house at the back of her old neighborhood, shivering. She was dizzy, weak and her heart felt funny, pinging, then pounding in irregular cadence, and she couldn't seem to breathe properly.

Beside her Zevo rolled his cheek along the bricks seeking a cool spot to chill the fever in his brain.

"Man," he whispered, "I don't feel so good. Can't get the right stuff since the cops closed down Danny's. Maybe we shouldn'ta messed with a different brand of ecstasy. Never know how it's mixed."

"Ya think?" Meg muttered.

Through the open windows and doors of the Gorleys' house the illicit parents-out-of-town-back-to-school party raged. A little louder and the neighbors across the road and six acres away would call the police. There weren't enough trees to block the sound.

"How many'd we take anyway?" Zevo asked.

"Nine," Meg said. "Salesgirl said the best buzz came with twelve."

"Nuts," Zevo whispered. Hand reaching toward Meg, he slid laxly against the wall. "I think I took more'n you."

She looked at him. By the light from the garage he looked pale and gray, his eyes too bright and wide. *Bad.*

She hadn't seen him much since the day outside the Hallmark store. Funny thing, she'd always assumed she'd only ever gone out with him to annoy Hank, but when Zevo wasn't around, she missed him. Even after he'd banged her into the wall. Stupid and sick, she knew, but she'd read somewhere that even soldiers on leave occasionally missed the abuses and uncertainties of war. It was all in what you got used to; anything new was scary.

Kind of like her and adrenaline rushes and better the devil you understood instead of the angel you were afraid—for reasons you couldn't quite define—to trust.

Like Kate staying healthy and happy while she was pregnant, and Hank not leaving Megan to fend for herself because he had a new and easier child to raise. God knew, she was having a hard enough time holding onto herself.

"Meg?"

Next to her, Zevo slid along the wall, his hand fumbling at her breast. She slapped it lethargically away. She might have missed him, but she hadn't missed him that much.

"Meg."

His voice was a breath exhaled and lost on a syllable. His fingers groped for her once more. In something like slow motion, she turned her head a half a degree at a time, watched without comprehension while Zevo sagged unseeing toward her, skidded roughly down the brick and collapsed against her legs.

Unable to sleep, Kate flopped from one side of her bed to the other, restless in the heat. Flat as it still was, her abdomen felt tight and swollen—even her forgiving cotton underwear seemed confining tonight—and her breasts ached.

For and because of Hank.

A board creaked somewhere in the house and she jacked up on an elbow wondering if he was up. Everything made her think of him lately. Of course, everything had made her think of him fairly constantly for the past three months, so that was nothing new. It was the *way* she thought about him, of him, of late that was different.

She rested her chin on her folded hands and stared at the lightly billowing lace that lent an aura of privacy to her room. Moonlight spilled through the filigree with the scent of mown grass. She'd been taught from birth that people were to be loved, that love was the thing you gave with an open heart to anyone who crossed your path—and everyone who didn't—irrespective of how they treated you. She'd been taught, and learned to believe, that love could move mountains, change attitudes, devour hatred. That you didn't have to *like* a person in order to love them. That love was a simple willingness to accept people as they were, to treat them as you hoped to be treated. And in that way, she'd loved Hank easily from the beginning, even while she didn't like him and was hard put to accept the person she'd been told he was.

In spite of how she'd seen her parents together, her brother Mike and his wife, the thing she'd never really been taught was that love had degrees, could confuse and be tangled with emotions previously foreign to her.

She'd long understood, of course, how the fierce quality of protective love she felt toward her children, toward the infant growing inside her, differed from the unexpectant "love" she kept open for other people. But the way she felt about Hank...lost, insecure, anxious, greedy, aching, lusting, found, full—as if a bubble was expanding inside her chest, buoyant and tight to bursting all at once.

As if she needed to hear how he felt about her before she could spill her heart to him.

As if she shouldn't need to hear how he felt in words, should be able to read and accept it in the illustrations he left for her every day.

She pouched her lips into a self-derisive knot and rolled onto her back. He'd stunned her when he sat her and Tai down earlier this evening and asked if they couldn't use him full time around the farm. He'd been thinking about it for a while, he'd said, especially the past few weeks back at work, returning only to watch

Megan getting further away not only from him but from all of them.

He needed, he'd said, to be around to keep better track of Megan until she didn't need him anymore. Told them that by returning to the bureaucracy at his level of law enforcement he'd rediscovered how much he hated it. Told them that he needed to make a change in his life, wanted to try another direction and that *here* was the direction he wanted to go.

He'd pointed out what he could do and where—between the llamas, the Christmas trees and the workshop—they could use him most effectively, reminded them how useful they'd found having him around over the summer. Offered to buy into the farm as a partner, take some of the weight off Tai. A new baby, he'd told them—mostly told Kate—would take up more time than any of the kids she'd raised so far, including Mike who hadn't been quite two when his parents died.

Life was risk, he'd told them, but there were some risks he'd lately learned were worth more than others. Stone House was one of them.

Tai, of course, had been willing to shake hands and make a deal then and there. He'd never made a secret of how much he liked Hank, but Kate hadn't realized before how heavily the weight of the farm sat on her son's shoulders, nor how much the burden had eased for him with Hank around.

It was difficult to accept—heck, it was nearly impossible to even *contemplate*—that after the many years she'd spent almost believing she knew it all, that she truly knew next to nothing. Knew nothing about Tai, nothing about Li and less than nothing about Megan.

Knew nothing about Hank, or even about herself.

He'd come to her to learn how to deal with his daughter, but Kate was the one who'd received the education.

That Hank would so willingly humble himself to come to her— and not only her, but Tai—in search of a job, a new life...she couldn't think. He floored her, flabbergasted and crushed. She'd decided he was one kind of man—terrific and sexy and great with the boys and all that rot—and here he showed her he was somebody else, too. What kind of a man was strong enough to come to a pigheaded woman and a kid half his age with his hat in hand and, in the same breath he asked for help, arrogantly describe why they needed him around, anyway? To change the direction of his life on a moment and a prayer.

A wry half smile tilted her mouth, chased the answer out of the cobwebs where it had hidden for more than a month and made her admit it. A man on whom it might be worthwhile risking the unexplored areas of her heart, that was who. A man who should be told how she felt about him, confusion or no, no matter what he did or didn't say to her aloud in return.

Whether they married or not. And in the past couple of weeks she'd come to find she wasn't nearly as opposed to the idea as she'd once been. Or else she was beginning to at least get used to the thought.

The desire for it.

She rolled onto her side and shut her eyes, pursuing rest if not actual sleep. In the morning she would talk with Tai about accepting Hank's offer, then she would find the man in his room or at his office and make him one of her own.

"Kate?"

Her name and the light tap on the door brought her quickly around, heart pounding with anticipation. "Hank?" Speak of the devil.

Or was that speak of the would-be guardian of her angels?

"Yeah." He eased through the partially open doorway, careful not to nudge it to the creak.

She sat up and the sleeveless cotton shirt she wore to bed gapped open. "What's up?"

Hank let himself look once, then shut his eyes. The vision played inside his lids, disruptive and enticing: the disarray of her hair straggling out of the unruly bun atop her head; the soft glow of her skin and eyes in the peekaboo moonlight; the invitation in the hand she splayed open to indicate the bed beside her. God, what kind of woman mothered seven kids, got pregnant, turned down marriage but willingly, lovingly invited the father of her unborn child into her bed without conditions whenever he wanted to come?

Only Kate Anden, the keeper of his heart.

Not now, he cautioned himself. *Not yet. Someday...*

"You seen Meg?" he asked, hauling himself forcibly away from the brink of forgetting why he was here in favor of remembering how it felt to love Kate. To be with Kate.

"She's not in bed? I thought she had a past-curfew date she cleared with you, but I thought I heard her come in already."

"No. The note she left me made me assume she was spending the evening with Carly and Tai." The shortest route to hell, he'd learned long ago, was through assumptions. He'd allowed himself the shortcut, anyway. "She's not there, either."

Kate compressed her lips against the discouraged slump in his voice, then twisted to find her clock. "What time is it?"

"Little after midnight. She should have been in an hour and a half ago."

She swung her feet out of bed. "Did you check with Li?"

Hank nodded. "Li thought Lynn came by to pick her up and she went into Brighton to pick up some stuff from the house. I called both Lynn and the neighbor who has a key to the back door. Whoever picked Meg up, it wasn't Lynn. She's not at the house, doesn't appear to have been there and nobody's seen her."

"Zevo?"

Shaking both with apprehension and her own weakness and unsteady heartbeat, Megan slid carefully down the wall to jiggle Zevo's shoulder.

"Hey, Zevo. You okay? You all right?"

The youth lay atop her legs, a dead, unmoving weight. She wasn't sure she could feel his breath.

"Oh, *sh*—Zevo!"

Feebly she tried pushing him off her, away, but the weakness was almost a kind of numbness now, affecting her hands. They seemed separate somehow, not part of her and she could hardly use them. In some part of her brain, it didn't seem to matter anyway. She almost wasn't part of her body anymore and, somehow, that didn't seem too bad a thing. If she couldn't feel, she couldn't get hurt again, the ache would be gone.

Off to one side the light was suddenly brilliant, blinding. A dark figure in what looked like a dress stood inside it. Megan relaxed.

"Mom?" she whispered, lifting leaden fingers toward the figure. "Mom?"

* * *

Restive and uncertain, Hank paced the kitchen while Kate puttered about for something calming to do, finally settling on folding laundry at the kitchen table.

The silence went long until at last Hank slammed the flat of his hand into the wall in frustration.

"I hate this," he exploded. "Where the hell is she? Why the hell can't I do something?"

"What could you do?" Kate asked quietly.

"I don't know. Look for her. Find her. Wake people up until I know where she is and if she's all right."

"Run around like a chicken with your head cut off," Kate supplied seriously. "Tie up the phone so she can't get through if she's in trouble and remembers to call—"

The phone rang. Arrested by coincidence on the far side of the kitchen, Hank swallowed and looked at the instrument. Automatically noting the name Frank Gillespie on the caller ID display, Kate picked it up.

"Megan?"

"Mom?" a teenage male voice said.

Kate shook her head at Hank, who closed his eyes on displaced hope and did not relax.

"Who is this?" she asked, instinct causing her to mentally count heads upstairs despite the fact that she didn't recognize the voice and could come up with a full in-house complement to boot.

The voice on the phone said something in gibberish.

"Who?" Kate asked again. Something in the youth's cranked-up tone put her on reflexive parental alert. She pointed at Hank, at the caller ID display, jerked a finger to tell him to come check it out. He came immediately and without question.

"Brandon," the voice managed.

She yanked the phone book out of the phone-table drawer and handed it forcibly to Hank, once again indicating the ID display, then the phone book. "Brandon who?"

More gibberish cluttered by party noises in the background, then *"Mom, I've smoked too much crack and I don't think I can do this life anymore."*

A wrong-number suicide call? Damn, damn, damn! *Keep him on the phone,* she told herself. *Keep him talking.*

"Brandon, where are you?"

More gibberish followed by a sobbing giggle, then the click of a broken connection. Breathing hard and swearing in a manner she normally didn't employ, Kate replaced the receiver and whirled on Hank.

"Did you get it?"

He nodded. "It's an address in Brighton. What's up?"

"Suicide call from a party," Kate said and grabbed the phone as it rang again. The same caller name crossed the display. "Brandon?"

There was the sound of the party, an instant of babble and another click. Replacing the receiver once more, Kate shoved a hand through her hair and covered her mouth.

"Think," she muttered to herself, "What do I do? Call the police."

She reached for the phone. Hank stopped her.

"Tell me first," he suggested calmly. He hated being at loose ends, but a crisis he could handle.

Kate looked at him, took a deep, tranquilizing breath and repeated the call verbatim.

"Okay." Hank considered the situation for half an instant. "Call the number back. If you can get through ask for Brandon. If not, call the police." He pulled his car keys out of his pants pocket. "I don't know the people, but the address is in the neighborhood adjacent to mine and I can get from here to there as fast as the police or paramedics can."

"What about Meg?"

Hank blew out his cheeks on a breath. "I dunno, Kate, but this is something I can do. I can see about somebody else's kid and after that, since it's a party not far from the house, chances are it's got friends of Meg's at it. Maybe they can help me find her. Hell, maybe she's there. I've got the cell phone in the car, you can call me if anything comes up here."

"Hank—"

He shushed her with a quick brush of his lips across hers. "I'm sorry, Kate, I can't just sit, I have to act. I'll be back."

Then he was gone.

Eyes narrowed, Kate stared at the seemingly almost vibrating space he'd vacated and wondered if this was the reason history had titled some women as ladies-in-waiting.

Kate called back the Gillespie phone number. The line was busy or the phone was off the hook, so she called the police, explained the phone call she'd received, her concerns, told them Hank was on his way and gave them the address. Then she waited.

She sat. She stood. She finished folding clothes and scrounged together a load of dark clothes for the washer—not difficult in a household their size.

She tried to read, but it was a ridiculous waste of effort because she couldn't concentrate.

She pinched her chin and tapped ragged fingernails against her teeth, squinted down her nose at them and went to get a file and Li's creams and gave herself a manicure. It wasn't a very good one, given she wasn't used to paying that kind of attention to herself, but the effort was both frustrating and mildly distracting.

She dusted the living room and moved the load of laundry from the washer to the dryer.

She got out the heavy rosary her mother had given her the day she'd taken her vows and entered the convent, and she prayed. She'd gotten as far as the fourth Sorrowful Mystery when the phone rang. Hank.

"I'm at McPherson emergency," he said hoarsely and without preamble, naming the local hospital. "Come."

Her jaw tightened, but she kept the fear and the questions out of her voice. "On my way," she told him.

Then she called the guest cottage and woke Tai, got Li up to come downstairs nearer the phone until Tai could get to the house, crumpled the unfinished rosary in her hand to finish in the car and went.

It didn't even occur to her to realize that he trusted her enough to call her to him with a single word, without wondering if she would.

* * *

He sat in a waiting-room chair looking tense and haggard, older than his years, defeated. He didn't even look up when Kate approached and perched on the edge of the chair beside him, slid warm fingers into the crook of his near hand.

"Is it Megan?" she asked.

He nodded, eyes blind on some spot in the near distance only he could pinpoint. "She was at a different party a couple streets behind ours with that kid she dates sometimes—Zevo. Call came in right after the police broke up the party at the Gillespies'. Brandon was in the owner's study fiddling with a gun. He's okay, wired to beat the band, but alive. They called his parents and took him upstairs to psych for observation. Zevo's dead. Meg was collapsed next to him. They don't know what she took, but they found a bag of pot and a couple vials of crack on her, no used equipment. Her heart's not working right. They're getting ready to transfer her up to cardiac intensive care. They think she'll be okay, but it's still iffy. If she pulls through, she's looking at charges of possession and drinking under the teen zero-tolerance law."

His mouth trembled; he stiffened his jaw and canted his head to Kate. "I saw her, Kate. They've got her on oxygen and she's hardly with it, but she opened her eyes and took one look at me and said, 'You're not Mom. God, I'm still alive, aren't I?'" His mouth twisted and stretched tight, his eyes filled, shiny with tears he refused to shed; his fingers closed painfully around Kate's. "I don't want to lose her, Kate, but I don't know how to keep her alive if she doesn't want to be."

There was nothing she could say to make it better, to make it go away, so she said nothing, simply touched his chest to let him know she was there to hold onto if he needed an anchor in the storm and sat with him and waited through a parent's worst nightmare.

September 19—4:22 a.m.
CICU waiting room

"Mr. and Mrs. Mathison?"

Hank turned at the sound of the male nurse's voice without

noticing the assumption of Kate's identity. She opened her mouth to correct the mistake, then closed it again. In the face of other things, who she was or wasn't hardly seemed important.

"How is she?" Hank asked.

"Stable." The nurse shrugged. "Comfortable. She's sedated right now, but you can sit with her for a while if you want." He turned at the squeak of rubber-soled shoes behind him, nodded toward the tiny Malaysian woman in pink scrubs who approached. "Doctor Yanga would like a word with you first. Dr. Yanga." He motioned at Hank and Kate. "These are Megan's parents."

The intern on night call acknowledged them with a look, indicated with a question-mark face and a flick of her eyes that she'd like to collect a cup of coffee before joining them. Eyes glued to her, Hank swallowed and shrugged. Couldn't be too bad if the physician thought there was time for coffee before speaking to him, could it?

Either that or else this was going to take some time and Dr. Yanga was fortifying herself for the ordeal.

Kate touched his shoulder, her voice low, "Do you want me to go?"

He folded a hand tightly around hers, moved his head a fraction of an inch to the negative. "No. Stay, please. I need you here."

Dr. Yanga finished filling a disposable cup, then crossed to perch on the edge of the coffee table in front of them. "I think your daughter will be okay." Her voice was thin and heavily accented, difficult to understand. "We'll keep her for observation two or three days to be sure." She paused, consulted the chart in her hand. "She has some alcohol in her system, but the main problem is the *ma huang*. You know it?"

Hank eyed Kate askance, shook his head. It wasn't a substance on his drug-war lists—at least not by that name.

The doctor nodded as though the answer was to be expected. "We see it sometimes lately, not so much, but more often than before. It is a Chinese herb also called ephedra, used to make the ephedrine that goes into asthma inhalers. It's not illegal, but very dangerous for many people if it is not carefully used. It made your daughter's heart go like so—" She fluttered her fingers to illustrate an irregular pattern. "Too fast, then too slow, no rhythm.

Also the blood pressure goes too high. That is what happened to your daughter. The other boy died from it, but he took more. She took too much, she almost died, but help came in time. Very fortunate. You have questions?''

"Where did she get the *ma huang?*" Kate asked.

Dr. Yanga shrugged. "Hard to say. Could be..." She struggled for the word. "New Age head shop, I think it is called. Come in packages like so..." She formed her thumbs and forefingers into a triangle. "...maybe ten to twelve pills in a box. There's no regulation, so it's hard to say if all pills are made exactly the same. Shops can claim they're all natural, give energy, but nobody knows how much *ma huang* is in each pill."

"But she'll be all right?" Hank pressed. In his experience "stable" could mean anything and intensive care units of any sort were not kind to the emotions.

"Maybe so," the intern agreed. She waved a hand toward the door. "You can see."

Without letting go of Kate, Hank rose, pulled her up, and followed the doctor to Megan's bed.

Chapter 17

By the second day, Megan was pretty much her old self once more: surly, uncommunicative, full of At-Ti-Tude...and self-satisfied.

Although initially frightened by her experience, she seemed to view both her father's and Kate's concern for her with smugness and indifference—a combination of "gee, look how fast I made you jump" and "boy, I can do anything and you'll pick me up and I won't have to pay for it." The latter attitude was particularly prevalent when the local law extended Hank the professional courtesy of not arresting Megan on the spot, accepted his guarantee that she would turn herself in as soon as she was released from the hospital.

Her demeanor did not sit well with Hank.

Even when he told her about Zevo, tried to impress on her how lucky she'd been, her only visible emotion was in the muscle that jumped along her jaw and a bored, stony stare.

As a DEA agent, his entire adult life had been spent attempting to correct a balance between the terrible choices people made and controlling the availability of illicit substances that too often turned choice and experimentation into addiction. He'd long believed in imposing certain restrictions and responsibilities on choice, in safeguarding those stipulations with his life if need be. He was having a difficult enough time accepting that for the most part there was likely nothing he could have done to prevent Megan from choosing to be where she was right now. It was devastating that she chose to defy him by flaunting his work and beliefs the way she'd done. That she needed and wanted to escape her life—or enhance it or a hundred other words and justifications he couldn't understand—so badly she'd been willing to risk her life to do it.

That despite the fact she'd been caught "holding" and had any alcohol at all in her underage system, the thing that had almost killed her was a herb he'd never heard of and whose sale to minors or anybody else he couldn't regulate.

When he'd looked at her attached to heart monitors and tubes, saw Zevo's body, all he wanted to do was pick Megan up and hold her tight, bring her home, yell at her and lock her in her room until she was thirty. Mostly he wanted her to tell him, to make him understand, what the *hell* she could possibly have been thinking when she swallowed the *ma huang* with its liquor wash-me-down?

Kate, too, was disturbed by what she saw in Hank's daughter, but instead of bewildering her, all Megan's attitude did was grind—and cause her to narrow her eyes, pull Hank aside and suggest he say thanks, but no thanks to the local law's offered professional courtesy. She also suggested he talk to the would-be arresting officers, cop parent to cop, about posting a showy guard outside her hospital door—Megan had, in the past, posed some light risk after all—and letting them cuff her and take her into custody on her release.

A night or two in jail or juvenile detention might, she pointed out, stopping Hank before he could protest, prove to be just what the doctor ordered. Because, while this might be the worst time—so far—that Megan had figured Hank would rescue her from the consequences of her irresponsibility, it wasn't the first. And if he continued to rescue and protect his daughter, it undoubtedly wouldn't be the last time.

"I mean, for pity's sake, Hank," she said, pounding the point home, "think about it. Meg nearly died this time. The guy standing next to her did. Maybe it's time you draw the line, toss out a little tough love and find out if she's really as tough and as far gone as she acts. Worst case, you find out you really got your work cut out for you. Best case..." She offered him a one-shoulder shrug. "Maybe you find she's really just a scared kid looking for some kind of attention she doesn't know how to ask for and you don't know she needs."

"Butt out, Kate," he told her tersely, angrily, not for the first time. She might be right, but now was not the moment he could bring himself to step back, take a breath and separate his love for his daughter from his need to hover and protect her by lashing back at Kate. "Back off. You've interfered enough. What the hell do you know about tough love? If you hadn't always let Meg run to you and stay, instead of sending her back to me when she was younger, maybe we could have sorted out what's ailing us a long time ago and this wouldn't've happened."

He stooped, nose to nose with her, fighting himself and her, warring with his heart. "You're so damned certain you know it all where kids are concerned, but, lady, maybe all you've been is lucky. And whatever you know, it sure as hell didn't do you any good with Risto and it hasn't made much difference with Megan lately."

Kate stepped back, stung by the verbal slap. He'd asked for her help, all she'd done was try to give it to him. Saint Kate, at your service. Right?

Oh, yeah, sure. She blew herself a mental raspberry. *Get off your high horse, martyr.*

On the other hand, he was also right. She never had done much to discourage Megan from running away to Stone House, the same way she'd never done much to discourage the other teens who straggled into and out of her life over the years. She was, as her mother had often tried to tell her, a big-time buttinsky. Maybe, as that woman had frequently attempted to suggest, the better part of valor in some situations was to back off, not bulldoze forward, to step aside so someone else could pass.

To not assume she was the only one who could right a problem simply because she was good at it.

There was no real way to do it gracefully, to say it without appearing piqued, but she had to say it, "I'm sorry, Hank. You're right. I do overstep. She's your daughter. You have to deal with this from the inside, and all I have to do is peek in your window and think I know it all, tell you this is what I see. I don't have to live with the decision like you will.''

He eyed her incredulously. For reasons he knew exactly how to define, her apology incensed him more than any self-righteous preaching she'd ever done. "Stuff it, Kate," he told her flatly and stalked out.

The hospital hallway seemed too bright and artificial, too confined for the collection of emotions spreading roots and trailing vines through his chest. He pushed his hands through his hair, tried to suck air too deeply into constricting lungs. Had to pinch the bridge of his nose, shut his eyes and concentrate before the sentient overflow got away from him. It was too much all at once, that was it. Megan, a baby, a family, a woman he wanted, needed, almost more than he needed his soul...and Megan wanted to do without him, and the baby and the family had Kate who'd proven over and over through the years that she was capable of doing whatever she set her mind to, whether it was raising children or maintaining her flourishing farm and businesses, without a man to help her.

Without him.

And he needed them all, loved them all—the children equally with each other and Kate...Oh, God, and Kate! He loved Kate more than anything. More than anyone.

More, period.

Everyday, all the parts of her, the impossible and the saintly, the opinionated and the imperfect. Her luscious body and lavish mind and generous heart. Kate. Damn her, she *would* have to live with whatever he decided to do about Megan. The child they shared between them was part of Megan, too, a flesh-and-blood sibling. No way they could change that, no way he wanted to. And that meant Kate would share Megan's life, share *his,* damn it, whether she put her name beside his on a marriage license or not.

His name on the baby's birth certificate wasn't what would make him its father, only his presence in its life would do that. Same way only Kate's presence could make her its mother.

Rationally he knew that her not being around for Megan after Gen died probably wouldn't have made things better but worse. He knew her kids weren't perfect, that she'd made her mistakes with them, but their...learning experiences...had simply, thankfully, taken place on the right side of the law, and had been less dangerous than Megan's blunders and explorations. But rationalization had nothing to do with how he felt at the moment. Passion, fierce and undeniable, was the word most aptly suited to the here and now, encompassed all the other emotions: anger, futility, desire, love. But passion like this was not the way to approach either Megan or Kate.

Or was it?

He stopped short in the hall, staring blindly ahead, causing an EKG tech to swerve abruptly to avoid running her cart into his heel. Losing his head to passion could mean death both literally and figuratively on the DEA playing fields, but he was not working either undercover or behind a desk for the DEA here. Could attaining the future he sought truly be as simple as a word he could illustrate with toughness or a lifetime of care after he said it?

Maybe not always, but in this one instance...he'd tried everything else, entrusting Kate and Megan with not only his silent heart but the word *love* as well...

If it backfired on him, he was pretty certain he was the only one who could be hurt.

With Kate beside him, Hank called the police from the pay phone in the waiting room. When they arrived he did the hardest thing he'd ever done in his life: walked into Megan's room and told her he loved her, that she owned his heart, but that he had no idea how to impress upon her the things she needed to know to survive the course she'd set for herself. Then he stepped back out of the way and stood by while the police read Megan her rights and officially took her into custody.

He could have requested privilege, to stay with her, but when the officers told him to go since Megan was now out of danger, he went.

Megan's eyes shot daggers in his direction, and were looks deadly, he'd have been on the floor, no question. He felt as if he was down there, dying anyway, but though comfort was elusive, he hoped one day to be able to find it in today's act. She had to find her own way through this experience; he couldn't shield her from the repercussions of every choice she made for the rest of her life, had to let her go—a thing much easier to do in theory than in practice. Had to let her separate herself from him if she must, but expect her to take adult responsibility for her adult mistakes.

Had to let her go through the system unless and until, he'd decided, she agreed to go into a halfway house for runaways and make a real effort to help herself by accepting and participating in counseling and therapy both on her own and with him.

And Kate.

Because married or not, Hank told his daughter, Kate was in their lives, a part of them—a part of *him*—with or without Megan's approval.

Heart in her throat, Kate studied him while he said it, when he turned to hold her gaze and wordlessly hand himself into her keeping. Her throat burned and stung with emotion it was the wrong time to voice. But she held onto him, his hand, his arm, tucked herself under his shoulder and hugged his waist one armed when he led her out of Megan's room.

Outraged, Megan screamed defiant epithets after them, demanding Hank's return—then, when he didn't, shouting that he was just like Gen, that he hated her the way he must have hated her mother because he was always leaving them, that he was deserting her the same as always.

That he was killing her the same way he'd killed Gen, by not being around when he was needed.

He stiffened at that but didn't stop, shutting Megan's hospital door behind him.

Staring wide-eyed at the solid wood panel, Megan felt her first flicker of fear. He really wasn't going to make what she'd done okay, wasn't going to stop. She'd gone too far this time and he didn't care, wouldn't let her punch his buttons anymore.

She was on her own.

"You all right?" Kate asked, a short time later when he put her in the van and told her to go home. He planned to stay at the hospital until Megan was released, then follow her through booking. She might not see it as much—certainly not what she thought she wanted from him—but it was what he could do.

For what that was worth.

"No." He shook his head. "But I'll survive."

"Hank..." She hesitated, lifted gentle fingers to his face, smoothed them over the stubble along his jaw. "I didn't mean—"

"No." He shushed her with his mouth on hers in a heartfelt but undemanding kiss that accepted as it gave. "Not now. If it's important, you can tell me later. I've got things to tell you, too."

She cupped his chin, brushed her lips along his jaw. Not to stimulate, but to love. "I could stay with you."

He shook his head and eased her hands away, then stepped back. "No. We've got more kids than Megan who need some attention and I have to do this one by myself."

"Okay." She reached up to kiss him once more. "But if you want me—"

"I'll call," he assured her.

Kate believed him.

It didn't occur to her until she was pulling into the driveway at home that Hank had used the *we*, claiming her kids at the same time that he accepted her suggestion on how to handle Megan.

A slow, wry smile curved her mouth. On the other side of darkness and indecision lay light.

It was easily one of the longest nights of his life.

He prowled the hospital corridors never far from Megan's door, exchanging nods with the cop on guard there as if she was some big-time criminal posing a flight risk. But then, that was what he'd asked for, all the show they could give him.

Give her.

She looked scared—still mouthy and defiant, but with fear setting in—when she was released in the morning, wheeled out of the hospital, handcuffed and put in the back of the squad car for transport. Dry mouthed, Hank watched her with his hands fisted tight at the bottom of his pockets to prevent himself from trying to take her away from the police. This was for her own good, he reminded himself, a drastic response to Megan's drastic behavior.

No justification made the vision of his daughter in handcuffs easier to bear.

He followed the squad car to the station, requested courtesy and walked through Megan's booking with her—fingerprints, photos, questioning, the works. She lifted her chin and kept her eyes on him the entire time, accusing and somehow amused, as though she'd decided that the show was boring, she knew he'd never leave her to spend any kind of time locked up. And the truth was he'd hoped he wouldn't have to. But he was wrong.

So was she.

She spent the long weekend waiting for her Monday-morning arraignment in juvie. He spent the weekend in hell.

He asked to see her Saturday morning. She refused to see him. By Saturday evening she agreed to the visit, then cursed him roundly when he wouldn't agree to spring her. Cursing didn't work, so she tried tears. The tears nearly undid him, but he swallowed the ache in his chest and stood firm. After the tears her mercurial emotions went from sly, to derisive, to abusively hateful, to one of her unnerving rages. He steeled himself, moved table and chairs in the interview room out of her way so she couldn't hurt herself, requested a counselor but flashed his badge and refused to let any of the detention staff into the room or to remove the hysterical Megan from his company.

When she'd played herself out enough to be coherent, she accused Hank of a multitude of things, including attempting to kill Kate by getting her pregnant the same way he'd killed Gen.

It was at that point he lost it.

In front of the youth psychologist who'd sat through the end of her rage with him, Hank hauled Megan bodily into a chair and made her stay there while he told her he'd had more than enough, that it was about damn time she got what had really happened to Gen through her head.

Then while Megan tried hard not to listen, he told her.

Then he left.

He didn't see her at all on Sunday.

On Monday morning, a much quieter and more reasonable Megan asked to see him with the psychologist before her court appearance.

Although moderately repentant, she offered no apologies for what had gone before and Hank expected none—offered none of his own. Locked up with no place to escape herself or her thoughts, she'd been forced to confront five years' worth of feelings she'd been avoiding. About her mother, her father, herself. Found herself recognizing the misinterpretations she'd long put on some of the things Gen had once said to her, understood the justifications she'd made for her mother to live with some of Gen's more bizarre behaviors—behaviors Hank had rarely if ever witnessed.

With no one but herself to verbally abuse, she'd remained in the interview room with the psychologist long after Hank had gone, cycling through the stages of grief, crying and disbelieving at first, then denying, then angry again. She'd gone from anger to a bargaining of the if-you'll-just-let-me-go-I'll-be-good-from-now-on type. Acceptance was harder to come by. She was sixteen years old and acceptance wasn't yet part of her make-up—was, in fact, genetically lacking in her personality. Gen had never accepted less than what she wanted out of life and Hank himself was not good at accepting what he didn't like. Megan did, however, accept and recognize her own need to do things differently, to change her negative point of view—to undergo not only counseling but therapy to help make herself whole.

There were no guarantees, but Hank sat and listened to her, watched the psychologist nod and felt the roots of hope wedge open a closed place inside him.

Megan also asked for alternatives to juvenile detention—no matter how tough.

So, instead of winding up in the courtroom, they wound up in judge's chambers. The judge, a father with teenage daughters of his own, reviewed the case and Megan's history, the psychologist's suggestions, spoke briefly with Hank alone, talked individually with Megan, then called everybody back in and suggested a stiffer solution than he was inclined toward: one month in a halfway house for troubled teens, two years of court-monitored probation, the loss of Megan's driver's license until she was eighteen and individual, family and group therapy.

Face pale and knuckles white with the strain of physically holding onto her nerves, Megan gulped, glanced once at Hank beside her and nodded agreement. The attorneys accepted the bargain and the sentence was set to begin immediately. Megan was released to her father's temporary custody and admonished to report to the halfway house by the end of the school day with a small bag and all the schoolwork she'd missed over the past week.

Kate and company—from Tai and Carly to Bele, Mike and the dog—met Megan and Hank outside in the courthouse gardens. Megan reddened, embarrassed, when she saw them, ready to flee but for Hank's arm about her shoulder. Still, when Mike, Bele and Taz launched themselves at her, she hesitated only a moment before stooping to hug them tightly.

"We were worried about you," Bele said, disengaging himself from her stranglehold.

"Yeah," Mike agreed. "We didn't want you to die from doing something stupid."

"Especially not until we could tell you Harvey got a baby on Annabeth and Mum says if it's built right we can train for a marathon llama like those ones that run in the llamathons, but we have to ask you first cuz you trained Harvey to run with you and know how to do it."

The middle boys were more awkward but nearly as welcoming.

Grisha—bless his tactlessly curious mind—skipped the welcome and went straight to the questions, wanting to know what being arrested in America was like.

Li was standoffish, worried about Megan and afraid to trust her.

Tai uncustomarily held his tongue instead of saying what he thought of what Megan had put his mother and her father through.

Carly gave Megan a quick hug and told her to pay no attention to what Tai was thinking.

Kate smiled a welcome but stood back, letting Megan make the first move. The teen hesitated a moment, glancing at the younger kids then at Li, Carly and Tai. Carly got the message first.

"Come on, guys," she urged. "Meg needs to talk to Ma. Let's go exercise the dog."

When they were gone, Megan moistened her mouth and looked at Kate. "I need to apologize for what I did and the way I behaved," she said tentatively. Looking as if she hoped somehow Kate would disagree.

Kate didn't. In fact, all she did was regard Megan steadily and wait.

Megan licked her lips again, compressed them, gathering courage. "The judge said I have to do a bunch of things like go to a halfway house and lose my license till I'm eighteen and have therapy." She glanced at Hank. Swallowed. "Some of it's family therapy, and I was just wondering—" Another uncomfortable peek at her father. "I don't like the way things—" She shook her head, impatient with the half truth. "I don't like the way *I've* been lately and I know you don't have much reason to want me around anymore but I...I was wondering if you could maybe come to some of the family stuff with me an-and D-dad because you've kind of been part of my family for a long time and now you're having my little brother or sister and maybe...maybe..." Suddenly she pleaded, "I mean it couldn't hurt, could it?"

Stunned by the request, Kate studied Megan for a moment before raising a questioning brow at Hank. He blew out a breath of his own surprise, gave her a barely perceptible nod. In his bed or out, she'd be a part of him and Megan one way or the other.

And more importantly, they'd be part of her and hers.

Reading more in Hank's face than she was prepared to see at the moment, Kate slid her gaze quickly back to Megan. "Sure," she agreed. Breathlessly. Smiling. Not quite comfortable, but more willing than she'd expected to be. "Just let me know when."

She was waiting on the front porch for Hank when he returned from taking Megan to the halfway house.

They hadn't had a chance to say more than a few words to each other in days—and those words had been within range of radar-eared children, so even then they hadn't said much. She came to greet him when he tiredly mounted the steps, slipping her arms around his waist in a full-body hug. Her tummy felt snug and full against his belly, and she had, he could feel, undone the top button of her pants under her T-shirt to accommodate the baby.

He stroked a hand through her loose hair, set her away from him and splayed the other across her abdomen. "Getting big already, is he?"

Kate shrugged. "I've gained five pounds in the past month. She must be."

He bent and kissed her. "He, she, the only thing I care is that it's healthy and has your eyes and hair."

"And your mouth," Kate added, tracing a pinky around his.

"And an easier time getting through adolescence than Meg," Hank said softly. He kissed her little finger. "But you'll be there from the start, so it probably will."

Kate stroked his face. "So will you."

"I'm not sure my presence'll be as necessary as yours."

She pulled back, viewing him with surprise. "Doubts, Hank? That's not like you."

He shook his head and grinned wryly. "Not doubts, self-pity more likely. I just put my only daughter in a halfway home, you know. You've never had to do that with any of yours."

"Strictly prayer and luck," Kate assured him, half laughing. "That and twenty-four hours a day spent in their shadows will get you a lot."

"Like an abbreviated vocabulary and a nervous breakdown?" She grinned. "Exactly."

For a moment they shared silence, then turned as one and moved to sit together on the swing.

"How was the house?" Kate asked.

"Oh, you know." Hank shrugged. "Noisy. Chaotic. Lots of kids, but it seems to be pretty well run. Good house parents, psychiatrist in residence, strict rules—it's not here but what is? I think—I hope—it'll do her some good until they let me bring her home."

Kate nodded, then rested her head in the hollow of Hank's shoulder. She shoved a foot against the porch floor to rock the swing. "Speaking of home..." she said tentatively.

He shifted to rest his head on hers. "Were we?"

"If we weren't, we're about to." She pushed herself up on his chest, close to his face. "Hank, if I said *yes* would you remember the question?"

He stared at her uncomprehending for a moment, then with gradually dawning hope. "Kate...are you saying yes?"

"I think so."

"God, lady, you'd better know, because this isn't going to be easy. Meg's started to come around, but they warn you about backsliding and you and the kids might be better off if you could just walk away, no attachments—"

"Too late," she said softly.

"What's too late?"

"The no-attachments part. I'm already attached to you and so are the kids."

"It'll be rough," he warned, doing his best to talk her out of it, praying he wouldn't succeed.

Kate laughed. "*Rough* was never in question, Hank. Good grief, we've got eight kids between us at the moment and one on the way and by definition that's not easy, but you know, a united front, an us-against-them has a certain appeal. Not to mention..." She looked down at the buttons on his shirt. "I love you and I love Megan. Mostly I love you."

"You do." Not a question.

"Yeah." She nodded. "And I think I said no before because I was half worried about not hearing the words from you—which was stupid, when I thought about it, because everything you do, you do with love and, really, words like *I love you* and *I'm sorry* don't mean anything without the feeling behind them and—"

Hank cupped her head in a hand and bent toward her. "Shut up, Kate," he said thickly and kissed her.

Long and hard and again. Then he said what had been on his mind for quite some time. Hotly. Against her mouth. "I love you, lady, now and for the rest of my life. Tell me again that you'll marry me."

She did.

Postlude

The bathtub drain was clogged again and he was standing in water to his ankles.

Sighing, Hank shut off the shower's sibilant spray, bent and unscrewed the drain, reached into the well and pulled out clumps of long sunset-colored hair. His wife had forgotten to empty the drain again.

"Kate!"

"In here, Hank."

Annoyed, Hank wrapped a towel about his hips and padded, dripping, into the sitting-room-cum-nursery he'd added onto their bedroom just after their daughter was born. October dusk crowded the nursery, carried him back the long hard year it had taken to get them here.

They'd married last All Hallows' Eve while Megan had been in the midst of a major backslide. But it had been that backslide and the psychiatrist who'd been able to observe her at the halfway house that had pinpointed the root of Megan's violent mood swings: a big-time chemical imbalance called manic-depression.

A daily dose of lithium and a lot of family and individual therapy had helped tremendously. All was not perfect, but it was a damn sight closer than Hank had ever expected.

Of the other kids...

Tai and Carly were blissfully, happily married and still living in the guesthouse. Tai in fact had taken out a few trees to make room for the sizable addition they'd need when their triplets were born next February. He and Carly had been more than a little stunned to learn about the multiple babies, but were now taking it in stride—and simply planning in threes. Excited aunts, Li and Megan, had already volunteered for nanny duty, while uncles Mike and Bele had once again reiterated their refusal to mess with poopy diapers or boy babies until they were potty trained.

Always brighter than her peers, Li was graduating from high school a year early and looking at a full ride to Chicago's Northwestern University, courtesy of their music department.

Megan was both envious of and ecstatic for her. Her own high-school career was a bit more up again, down again, but after a session of summer school she was caught up and passing her junior classes.

Grisha had won a scholarship to a private high school that specialized in science and went around with his head in the clouds and his feet catching in every rut and raised up bit of carpeting he passed.

Ilya was happy with life and doing well, which was everything that could be wished and more.

Sadly, Jamal was once more back with them—permanently this time. He was a joy in their lives, but they had all hoped that the last time his mother had gone for help to beat her crack habit she'd had it licked. Unfortunately the crack had other ideas. She lived day to day now in a group home, her mind gone. Jamal visited her often, but it was hard on the fourteen-year-old. Sometimes she knew him, but usually she didn't. He went anyway—and almost always Ilya and some of the other kids went with him.

No matter what you did, there was always something, wasn't there?

Reflecting, Hank pitched the hunk of hair into the basket and looked once more at his wife. Kate stroked a finger down Halla's arm, looked up at him and smiled. The infant's name meant "unexpected gift" and she certainly was. Annoyance fled. Hank touched the baby's cheek where she suckled at her mother's breast. Even after six months he couldn't get over how beautiful she was.

She was also a handful, her personality developing by the day. As though to illustrate precisely how much individuality she'd gained today, she grinned slyly up at her father, letting milk dribble out the corner of her mouth while she pretended to consider being finished with her meal. Hank made a move to take her from Kate and the baby laughed at him, then latched firmly onto her mother's breast once more. The game lasted a couple more rounds until Kate, not Halla, decided she was done playing it and hoisted the silly infant to her shoulder for a burp. Halla noisily obliged, then promptly fell asleep before Kate could get the spit diaper out from under the baby's chin. She sighed and rolled her eyes when some of the baby spit dripped off the diaper before it could be absorbed and onto her nightshirt.

Hank chuckled and felt his hair-in-the-drain irritation fade, suitably avenged by the shortest member of the family. He lifted the plump infant into his arms and cradled her a moment before placing her on her stomach in the crib. He couldn't say marriage with Kate was the most *convenient* thing he'd ever done, but living without her had definitely been *in*convenient. And living with her did have its advantages.

Like the one displayed before him now.

Breast exposed, Kate scrubbed at her shirt. "Remind me to order rubber clothes the next time we have a baby," she said, exasperated.

"*Are* we having another baby?" he asked, mightily interested.

Kate glared at him. "Bite your tongue." She thought about it for a moment. "Although, I don't think I'd mind in, oh, say a year?"

Hank leered at her, eyes lingering on her milk-plush breasts. "I think that could be arranged."

Kate saw where he was looking and huffed at him in mock indignation, covering up. He squatted next to her and drew the shirt away from her breasts.

"Don't hide," he said softly. "I like looking at you."

"I know," she agreed, running her fingers lightly down his chest to find the towel's tuck. She flicked the terry cloth aside. "You like the body very much."

"Oh, and you don't?"

"Well," Kate hedged. "I like your mind, too." She glanced up at him and grinned. "Well, no, I take that back. Actually I love your mind—and everything else—but your mind…is just as devious as mine."

He grinned back at her. "I'll take that as a compliment since that's exactly what I like best about yours, my love." He leaned in toward her, forcing her backward in her chair. "Yes, indeed, no doubt about it. Your mind and what you do with it to make me crazy in the middle of the night is definitely one of my favorite things."

"Flatterer," she whispered. Then he slid a palm up her thigh, took her mouth and stole her breath and she said nothing at all.

And for the foreseeable future, that was exactly what they both wanted.

Because after all, happily ever after was merely a matter of moments and expressions, more than the words at the end of a fairy tale. It was the unconditional love that allowed two people to create a family and to weave the joys and sorrows, the angers and fears into fabric to last a lifetime.

* * * * *

Bestselling author

JOAN JOHNSTON

continues her wildly popular miniseries with an
all-new, longer-length novel

The Virgin Groom

HAWK'S WAY

One minute, Mac Macready was a living legend in
Texas—every kid's idol, every man's envy, every
woman's fantasy. The next, his fiancée dumped him,
his career was hanging in the balance and his future
was looking mighty uncertain. Then there was the
matter of his scandalous secret, which didn't stand a
chance of staying a secret. So would he succumb to
Jewel Whitelaw's shocking proposal—or take cold
showers for the rest of the long, hot summer...?

Available August 1997
wherever Silhouette books are sold.

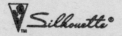

HAWK

Take 4 bestselling love stories FREE

Plus get a FREE surprise gift!

Special Limited-time Offer

Mail to Silhouette Reader Service™

3010 Walden Avenue
P.O. Box 1867
Buffalo, N.Y. 14240-1867

YES! Please send me 4 free Silhouette Intimate Moments® novels and my free surprise gift. Then send me 6 brand-new novels every month, which I will receive months before they appear in bookstores. Bill me at the low price of $3.34 each plus 25¢ delivery and applicable sales tax, if any.* That's the complete price and a savings of over 10% off the cover prices—quite a bargain! I understand that accepting the books and gift places me under no obligation ever to buy any books. I can always return a shipment and cancel at any time. Even if I never buy another book from Silhouette, the 4 free books and the surprise gift are mine to keep forever.

245 BPA A3UW

Name	(PLEASE PRINT)	
Address	Apt. No.	
City	State	Zip

This offer is limited to one order per household and not valid to present Silhouette Intimate Moments® subscribers. *Terms and prices are subject to change without notice.
Sales tax applicable in N.Y.

UMOM-696   ©1990 Harlequin Enterprises Limited

Share in the joy of yuletide romance with brand-new
stories by two of the genre's most beloved writers

DIANA PALMER

and

JOAN JOHNSTON

in

LONE STAR CHRISTMAS

Diana Palmer and Joan Johnston share their favorite
Christmas anecdotes and personal stories in this
special hardbound edition.

Diana Palmer delivers an irresistible spin-off of her
LONG, TALL TEXANS series and Joan Johnston crafts an
unforgettable new chapter to **HAWK'S WAY** in this wonderful
keepsake edition celebrating the holiday season. So
perfect for gift giving, you'll want one for yourself...and
one to give to a special friend!

Available in November at your favorite retail outlet!

Only from

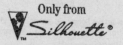

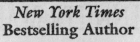

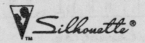

**Special Edition and Intimate Moments
are proud to present**

Janet Dailey Award winner
RUTH WIND

**and three new emotionally gripping
tales of love...**

The Forrest brothers—as wild and untamed as the
rugged mountains they call home—each discover a
woman as special and true as the Colorado skies. But is
love enough to lasso these hearts...?

Lance Forrest—left town
years ago, but returns to Red Creek in
MARRIAGE MATERIAL (SE#1108, 6/97) to a
son he never knew...and finds an unexpected love.

Jake Forrest—lived his whole life by a code of
military honor...until that honor failed him. In
RECKLESS (IM#796, 7/97), he comes home to find
peace...and discovers a woman for his heart.

Tyler Forrest—has raised his son, alone, in the quiet of
the Colorado mountains. But then his solitude is
invaded by the most unlikely woman...who thinks he's
HER IDEAL MAN (IM#801, 8/97).

THE LAST ROUNDUP...
Three brothers travel the rocky road to love
in a small Colorado town.

Available at your favorite retail outlet.

COMING NEXT MONTH

#799 I'M HAVING YOUR BABY?!—Linda Turner
The Lone Star Social Club
Workaholic Joe Taylor was thrilled when his wayward wife returned to him—and pregnant, no less! Then he realized that Annie had no idea how she got that way, at which point joy quickly turned to shock. What a way to find out he was about to become a father—or was he?

#800 NEVER TRUST A LADY—Kathleen Creighton
Small-town single mom Jane Carlysle had been known to complain that nothing exciting ever happened to her. Then Interpol agent Tom Hawkins swept into her life and, amidst a whirlwind of danger, swept her off her feet! But was it just part of his job to seduce the prime suspect?

#801 HER IDEAL MAN—Ruth Wind
The Last Roundup
A one-night *fling* turned into a lifetime *thing* for Anna and Tyler when she wound up pregnant after a night of passion. And now that she was married, this big-city woman was determined to see that Tyler behaved like the perfect Western hubby—but that involved the one emotion he had vowed never to feel again: love.

#802 MARRYING JAKE—Beverly Bird
The Wedding Ring
As a single mother of four, Katya yearned for Jake Wallace's heated touch, for a future spent in his protective embrace. But the jaded cop had come to Amish country with a mission, and falling in love with an innocent woman was not part of the plan.

#803 HEAVEN IN HIS ARMS—Maura Seger
Tad Jenkins was a wealthy, world-famous hell-raiser and heartbreaker, and Lisa Preston wasn't about to let her simple but organized life be uprooted and rocked by his passionate advances. But Tad already had everything mapped out. All Lisa had to do was succumb…and how could she ever resist?

#804 A MARRIAGE TO FIGHT FOR—Raina Lynn
Garrett Hughes' undercover DEA work had torn their marriage apart. But now, after four lonely years, Maggie had Garrett back in her arms. Injured and emotionally empty, he pushed her away, but Maggie was determined. This time she would fight for her marriage—and her husband—with all she had.